THE CONTINUATION
OF LOVE BY
OTHER MEANS

Also by Claudia Casper

The Reconstruction

THE CONTINUATION
OF LOVE BY
OTHER MEANS

CLAUDIA CASPER

PENGUIN
CANADA

PENGUIN CANADA

Penguin Group (Canada), a division of Pearson Penguin Canada Inc.,
10 Alcorn Avenue, Toronto, Ontario M4V 3B2

Penguin Group (U.K.), 80 Strand, London WC2R 0RL, England
Penguin Group (U.S.), 375 Hudson Street, New York, New York 10014, U.S.A.
Penguin Group (Australia) Inc., 250 Camberwell Road, Camberwell, Victoria 3124, Australia
Penguin Group (Ireland), 25 St. Stephen's Green, Dublin 2, Ireland
Penguin Books India (P) Ltd, 11, Community Centre, Panchsheel Park,
    New Delhi – 110 017, India
Penguin Group (New Zealand), cnr Rosedale and Airborne Roads, Albany, Auckland 1310,
    New Zealand
Penguin Books (South Africa) (Pty) Ltd, 24 Sturdee Avenue, Rosebank 2196, South Africa

Penguin Group, Registered Offices: 80 Strand, London WC2R 0RL, England

First published 2003

1 2 3 4 5 6 7 8 9 10   (FR)

A NOTE ON THE COVER IMAGE: The cover of this book is taken from the fresco *El Amor*,
painted by Antonio Berni in 1946 on the domed ceiling of the *Galerías Pacífico*, an
exclusive shopping mall in Buenos Aires, Argentina. In 1987, a secret detention centre
was discovered in a hidden second basement under the mall. This painting makes
several appearances in *The Continuation of Love by Other Means*.

NATIONAL LIBRARY OF CANADA CATALOGUING IN PUBLICATION

Casper, Claudia, 1957–
    The continuation of love by other means / Claudia Casper.

ISBN 0-14-301384-X

    I. Title.

PS8555.A778C65   2003   C813'.54   C2003-903000-8
PR9199.3.C4315C65 2003

Visit the Penguin Group (Canada) website at **www.penguin.ca**

for Henry and George

In the beginning the egg is bigger. Much bigger. It is breakfast, lunch and dinner for the sperm, as well as home. The sperm, like Pandora, is a lifter of lids, an agent of change, transforming with its fierce wriggling two fates of inevitable degradation into a single, slightly less predictable fate.

But an egg is not a woman and a sperm is not a man, though together they can germinate either one.

The human egg is a large moon cell, pitted and stringy like a ball of wool. It pops out of a sac and is ushered by feathery membranes into a tube. From there it floats to a soft-walled triangle shaped like a delta, like Jesus on the cross, head dropped to chest, arms hung unnaturally high, finishing in the arrow of his legs pointing down—the way to life. From above, delivered below.

Everyone in this story starts the same way.

Multitudes of sperm swim in every direction away from where they've landed. Immune to nostalgia, programmed for motion, they're searching for treasure: the fat yolk.

A single sperm that generates a compatible answer to the egg's chromosomal riddle is allowed entry, sacrificing forever its individual "self" for a chance at eternity, a chance to be part of something bigger than itself. The egg's juices pull the sperm apart and recombine it with the egg's own messages. A percentage of the sperm's individual message gets through, yet it is already only a cipher for millions of years of similar encounters, a spark of its former selves. This is true also for the egg. There is no law of big here, no gender war, no power, desire or disappointment.

The rest of the sperm get a quick geography lesson in furrows, ridges, crevices and crypts. Like cars on a planet with no gas stations, their fate is death by petering out. The happy egg cell makes its outer membrane impermeable, and buries its moony meiotic face in a rich carpet of blood, where it begins to spin lifelines.

A plug forms. The uterus becomes a landlocked ocean fed by tributaries of blood. So begins our story, free of the cult of personality, culture, history. Everything in this world is made of blood. And blood is made of earth, wind, fire and water.

SECTION
One

1

GERMANY, 1938

A SEVEN-YEAR-OLD BOY sat on a roof feeling momentarily safe. He was skinny, all knees and elbows, and his short brown hair smelled like woodsmoke, dirt and sweat. His grey-green eyes were like a stream running over limestone—fresh, lively and cool.

A bird flew by in front of him. He pressed his bottom more firmly against the shingles. The roof was quite slanted and his worn shoes afforded only the slightest traction.

Mutti had gone to buy oxtails for the soup she always made when he was sick. His mother was like a nervous animal to him, a skittish horse. Or like a bird—flighty. He knew she loved him, yet when he ran through the house banging doors, or knocked his drink on the floor while turning to see something, her doting changed instantly to an explosive, nervous irritation.

She never let him play in the forest with the other boys or join Karl's hiking club at the church. You might get lost or fall, she said. But young Alfred had boundless energy, so he found ways around her.

Today he really was sick; he felt tired and weak, but he almost never had the house to himself so he'd chosen one from the long list of forbidden activities—stealing biscuits and chocolate from the locked ration cupboard (he'd forged his own key). He had just relocked the cupboard when Karl, in the company of some other boys, had pounded on the front door calling his name.

Karl was tall, stocky, a year older than Alfred, unliked by adults and most of the children, but Alfred found him exciting to play with. Lately however, Karl had been demanding the plum bits of Alfred's lunch and requisitioning his best tin soldiers.

Alfred was going to have to stand up to him and he was going to have to do it alone because, besides Karl, he had no friends. He'd probably take a beating and he was apprehensive—not of the pain so much as not knowing how much damage Karl would be able to inflict. He hoped *he'd* be able to hurt Karl enough to make the older boy choose someone else to pick on.

But not today. When they'd knocked, he'd stuffed the chocolate, biscuits and an empty tin into his rucksack and snuck out his own back door. He'd crept to where the steep street met the edge of his roof, and climbed up. Karl knocked again, muttered something and the boys drifted back down the hill, maybe to the river to throw stones.

Alfred carefully slipped the rucksack off his shoulders and took out its contents. He unwrapped the chocolate, put it in the tin, snapped the lid on and set it in the hot morning sun. The air smelled of warm pine needles.

From here he could see the *Konditorei* and *Apotheke* across the street, then all the roofs of the town sloping down into the valley, three church steeples rising from among them. Across the valley a chain of old mountains followed the river. The bird flew by and he felt momentarily off balance and dizzy.

He opened the tin. The chocolate had melted to the consistency of lava. He dipped a biscuit in and took a bite. The warm chocolate filled him with pleasure; the biscuit crunched pleasantly.

"Alfred!"

She stood, shopping cart at her side, looking up at him. He watched her irritation change to fear.

"Don't move *Liebchen!* Eat your cookie. Stay still. I'll be right back."

She stepped under the eaves. He heard her fumble with the keys, a hint of hysteria in her self-whispering. He dipped the biscuit back in, took another bite, but the pleasure was diminished now that it wasn't stolen and he felt annoyed with his mother for returning so soon.

Mutti came back into view but before she could speak, Alfred stood up to shake the crumbs from his lap and whooshed down the roof onto the flagstones.

Falling through the air felt just like his flying dreams.

Alfred's father, Heinrich, was promoted to general and they moved to Munich. Alfred was nine. The leg that had broken in the fall was mended, but splinters from the shingles left scars that looked like a scattering of short brown pine needles on the back of his thighs. He made new friends, doing adequately in school and poorly in sports but dominating in the outdoor games during lunch and recess.

The promotion enabled his father to purchase a motorcycle with a sidecar. Heinrich shaved his head to disguise a receding hairline and started wearing a monocle, which was the fashion. He had high cheekbones, a trim figure and a roguish smile. In his shiny leather boots and uniform, swastika at his throat, he looked quite the ladies' man.

Only Mutti failed to thrive with the move. She became more querulous and timid, more erratically angry with both Heinrich and Alfred. She fretted about not being able to get the right cuts of meat from the butchers, complained about the spices in the sausages, didn't like the noise or the crowds. Didn't like Heinrich going out in the evenings, coming home drunk. And Hitler's actions did not arouse the same optimism in her that they did in so many fellow citizens, including her husband.

Occasionally Alfred got to accompany his father on trips into the mountains. He loved sitting in the sidecar near the road's surface, his father above him, the wind rushing through their hair as they shot through fields of chamomile and hay.

One night sleeping in a mountain inn Alfred stirred, perhaps because he was in a strange bed, and discovered his father was no longer in the bed beside him. He went back to sleep. The next morning Heinrich smelled of schnapps, cigars and perfume.

"I was just having fun with the boys. No need to tell Mutti."

On the trip home Heinrich stopped for a smoke and Alfred challenged him to a race. He stuck out his small chest and said, "I bet I can run faster than your motorcycle."

His father chuckled, proud of his son's bravado, and said, "I'll give you a head start. And I'll shine my light down the road so you can see."

It was after the next trip that they came home to a dark house. It had never been dark before.

"Mutti must have gone out," his father said after they turned on the lights, and then Heinrich sat down to read the newspaper.

Alfred walked through the house alone. A trap door to the attic had been pulled down. Ever since he was a young boy he'd been in the habit of opening cupboards, peeking under lids, shaking locked boxes, climbing into every nook and cranny in the house to see what was there. Like a scout doing reconnaissance he knew his territory, and he quickly noticed what was missing: a small cosmetic case with silk pouches for underwear and hairbrushes and perfume; his mother's ivory comb and brush set; the book she kept beside her bed.

"Maybe she's visiting her cousin in Leverkusen," his father said.

Alfred went and sat on her bed. Then he laid his cheek on her pillow and started to cry. Somehow he knew he might never see her again. The pillow smelled of her spicy perfume and her skin.

Each time he returned over the next three years, the smell was slightly altered, more stale and faint.

Father and son lived like a couple of tidy bachelors, eating when they were hungry, taking turns doing the washing up, keeping out of each other's way. When Heinrich was away at the front, Alfred stayed with Heinrich's older brother and his wife and their three children: Claus and Jürgen, four and two years older than Alfred, and Petra, Jürgen's twin sister. Petra took a liking to young Alfred, and introduced him to some of the pleasures of sex.

On the eve of Alfred's twelfth birthday, he asked his father yet again where his mother was.

"I told you, she ran off with another man," Heinrich answered. "She deserted us, Alfred. Stop asking all the time. I don't like to remember."

She might've deserted you, Alfred thought, *but she'd have taken me with her.*

Alfred imagined his mother's return. She was wearing a woollen skirt and her favourite moss-green cardigan and he ran to her and buried his face in her bosom. Then he started to feel mad and he yelled at her and made her cry.

On the return leg of their last motorcycle trip together, Alfred reissued his challenge.

"Let's race again."

"Same rules apply," his father answered warily. "I'll give you a head start."

"To the train crossing."

The crossing was just outside the range of the motorcycle's headlight. Alfred started running. His legs were a lot longer than when he was nine. The father watched the son recede, then disappear out of the light. He released the clutch. The motorcycle quickly picked up speed and sped over the train tracks into the night.

He came to a stop on the dark road, did a U-turn and back-tracked slowly, looking anxiously from side to side. At the crossing, Alfred leapt up from a ditch beside the road.

"Ha! Ha!" Bent over laughing, pointing his finger at his father, "I win, I win!"

"I got you," he said, no longer laughing.

A month later the Allied forces bombed Munich. Heinrich gave Alfred a canvas bag to pack his things in and took him to the train station.

"Just stay on the train until Berlin. Here's some money for food. Your great-aunts will meet you."

Goldie and Freda were kind and independent women who had never married. They lived off a small inheritance and the earnings from vegetables they grew on their deceased father's small farm fifty kilometres outside Berlin.

They often came back from the Saturday market with rumours and strange stories about the war.

"Last night when the air-raid siren sounded," Freda told Alfred, "one of the mothers in town turned off the lights and went to get her baby to take it down to the cellar."

"She was feeling her way by the walls," Goldie continued, "because of course the windows are blacked out. When she got to the baby's room, the baby was shining. It was giving off light all by itself. At the all-clear she ran to the doctor and showed him the phenomenon. Now they're calling the priest. Maybe it's the second coming."

He asked his aunts if they knew what happened to his mother.

"Who knows what's happening in a war?" they replied. "We only met her once. She was young and pretty."

There was a loud thumping on the door.

They sent him into the attic. As he pulled the ladder up after him he saw Aunt Goldie take her dentures out and put them on the china cabinet. He closed the trap door and put his eye near a crack between the floor and the trap door.

Soldiers came in, their boots caked with mud. One said something in Russian. The rest laughed. Another swept the dinner settings off the dining-room table with his arm. He lifted Freda by the neck of her shirt and laid her face down on the table.

"For shame!" shouted Goldie.

Alfred lifted his head from the floor and covered his ears. When he listened again he could hear the sound of the floorboards squeaking rhythmically. Then a whimper from his aunt. Then a grunting groan. A man's voice said something short. More laughter erupted.

He opened his eyes. Pinpricks of light came through the floorboards. It was like crouching on the sky, above the stars.

In 1949 Alfred turned eighteen. He was living with his father again, and a new stepmother and her daughter from a previous marriage. His stepmother did not like him. The only place Alfred felt welcome was at the home of his cousins, Jürgen and Claus. Petra had married and lived with her new husband. The boys often did things together. One weekend they went on a caving trip to France.

In the cave, while his cousins ate lunch, Alfred ventured down a long, twisting passage that opened to a small chamber. He went inside, sat down and turned his helmet light off. In the total blackness and silence he could hear his own heartbeat, and joy surged up in him.

He had a vision of his life: he would be self-made, like the explorers and adventurers of old. He didn't start the war. He could be free. A citizen of the world. He would speak English without an accent. He would go out into the world and eat all the different foods it had to offer, and make love to all its women. The world would be his oyster, why not? Experience his pearl.

2

HE WALKED DOWN UNIVERSITY AVENUE toward Toronto
General Hospital, snow squeaking under his feet, the sun
making it sparkle like diamonds. This morning the world was
indeed his oyster. Fresh from the bed of another woman, he
was about to visit his beautiful wife, Beth, and share the joy of
the birth of their first child.

He'd changed his name from Löwen to Lion, which had
connotations in English he liked—masculine, wild, exotic. He
spoke English with no accent other than the faintest residue
of a twang he'd picked up from the American soldier who'd
first taught him. He was on the verge of finishing his studies
in mining engineering at night school and had a job waiting
for him with an international firm.

When he first came to Canada he lived in Sarnia and
worked at an ice rink driving a Zamboni. Then he moved to
Toronto and washed windows on office towers, peering in at
the men in suits. He also joined an amateur spelunking
group and counted some good friends among the less serious,
more jocular cavers.

Now, walking in the bitter cold down University Avenue,
he stopped to look up at the Moore Building where once he
had sat on his window-washing plank, looking out at the
choppy hard grey water of Lake Ontario.

He remembered the day after he'd first kissed Beth, sitting up there feeling his life bursting with opportunity. Her mouth had been sweet and warm. Beth Love. During dinner at a little Hungarian restaurant, she told him she read Bertrand Russell and Rabindranath Tagore, whom he'd never heard of. She was a math teacher in a North Toronto high school, she lived in an apartment with a girlfriend from teachers' college and she was gently rebelling against her family—part of the Toronto establishment. They seemed to her to be square and uncultured. She laughed at his witticisms, listened raptly to his life story, responded immediately and sensually to his embrace.

"Have a cigar," he said to the doctor who stood at the nurses' station, and whacked him on the back. To the nurse behind the desk with milky skin and big blue eyes he said, "I'm terribly sorry, Miss, I don't know what one gives ladies when a baby's born. Would you like a cigar for your boyfriend?"

"No thanks, sir." She smiled. "I don't have a boyfriend."

Beth was in a room with six women. She was sitting up, her thick sandy hair freshly brushed, lipstick on, a white satin bed jacket over her shoulders, waiting.

He kissed her tenderly, then looked in the bassinet beside her. Wrapped in white flannel with two pink stripes along the edge was a tiny red-faced gnome. Her face was like a pressed flower; the delicate thin skin of her cheeks, with a small layer of soft fat, glowed. She was a perfect rosy engine. He laid his finger on her tiny palm and her fingers curled over it like a sea anemone.

He had only imagined being the father of a boy. Now he tried to imagine laughing and playing with a little girl, giving her things, holding her hand, standing beside her. Her scrunched-up face began to charm him and elicit a nascent paternal passion and he decided to call her Carmen because he loved opera and the name made him think of fiery passion and a free spirit. He disliked English names and he certainly wasn't going to give her a German name.

"Little Carmen," he whispered. "She's beautiful, Beth. She's so beautiful."

"Hm-Hmm."

"What do you think of Carmen? Carmen Lion."

"Carmen Elizabeth Lion. It's unusual, strong sounding but still beautiful. She doesn't end up very well in the story though, does she?"

"There've been lots of Carmens since then to break the spell."

Beth looked Carmen up in a book of baby names. "It's originally from the Hebrew, *Carmel*, meaning garden. And perhaps from Latin, meaning song."

He picked up the sleeping bundle. The newborn girl mewled, struggled to open her eyes.

"You smell like perfume."

"The secretaries at the office all gave me hugs and kisses when they heard about Carmen."

"I'm moving out tomorrow. Carmen can visit you on the weekends. Pick her up Fridays after nursery school. I'll get her after Sunday dinner."

He froze. His mind lurched into high gear, frantically searching for arguments, a way out, trying to find his bearings.

"You mope around here like a lost puppy when you're not having an affair. I'm a flesh-and-blood woman, not a jailer. It's been four years since you made love to me with any passion."

He had tried to give up affairs, but life seemed so dull and flat just being a husband and father. All the excitement sucked out. He had started fooling around again, and now that he thought about it, he did recall the perfume of other women wafting around him as he walked through his day, but he'd only been half-conscious of it at the time, never thinking Beth would smell it too, never wondering how she might react. It was an Achilles heel. He could anticipate how a woman would react to seduction, but he couldn't anticipate how a wife would react to anything. He was unarmed in the battle of marriage. And now another man had taken his place, he was sure of it, and that made him feel rejected.

Beth and Carmen moved into a basement apartment near Eglinton Avenue. On the weekends Alfred quizzed his daughter about other men.

"No," she said helpfully, thoughtfully. "Tom Thumb calls sometimes to talk to Mommy, but he's not real."

"Alfred," Beth replied to his accusations, "I am seeing someone I like very much. His name is Oscar and I'd like to introduce you to him next time you pick Carmen up."

He shook constantly, he couldn't stop crying and his heart flopped wildly about inside his chest, as if it were trying to abandon ship. A colleague at work took him to a doctor who diagnosed a nervous breakdown. His employer gave him a week's leave of absence. He was prescribed sedatives. Gradually he reined it all back in.

As he convalesced, he remembered his plan to become a citizen of the world. He was only twenty-nine. His life wasn't over.

One Saturday morning, about six months after Beth had left, he made one of the big German breakfasts Carmen loved with pickles, pumpernickel bread, white rolls, salami, *Fleischsalat* and shrimp in mayonnaise. As she bit into half a fresh roll with shrimp on it, he said, "I'm going to a country with lions, like our name, and leopards, zebras and giraffes. It's hot all the time and there are lots of swimming pools. You can come and visit me there. Would you like that?"

She stopped chewing and looked around as if she didn't know what to do with the food in her mouth any more. She swallowed it unchewed and winced as the big lump went down.

"Are you coming back?"

"You never know what the future will bring, but not for a while. I'm going to live there. I'd take you with me but I'll be working long hours and travelling a lot and that's no life for a child."

❲Divorce set a strange emotional alchemy in motion: his daughter's clear, trusting face no longer filled him with joy, pride and a feeling of belonging, but rather their opposites— pain, shame, loneliness.❳ Witnessing Carmen's love of her mother, for example, which used to confirm he'd married well, now made him smart with a feeling of rejection. Things that had once created unity and harmony now created emptiness.

The kind of child she was—trusting, bubbly, loving, generous-hearted, qualities he'd once taken delight in—now meant that Carmen sat readily on Beth's new man's knee and chatted to *him* about her day. Words like "fickle" and "empty-headed" came to Alfred's mind. Her ability to become absorbed in an activity, like drawing a picture, and stay completely concentrated and focused until she was finished, an ability he'd once watched with admiration, now made him feel ignored, as if she didn't care about being with him.

He was at a loss with her these days; he didn't know what to talk about or what to do. He'd missed a couple of weekends with her to avoid the feeling of disconnection.

"Will we see real lions there?" she asked. "Can I have a baby lion?"

"Hang on there girl, first I have to get a house."

That afternoon, Carmen went from room to room in his apartment, picking up his things and putting them down. At bedtime when he told her to brush her teeth she started to cry. He went over, picked her up and stroked the back of her head, murmuring "There, there." She turned her face into his shoulder and cried until she went to sleep.

He carried her to bed, tucked her in, and paused before leaving. She was curled up like a fairy-tale child in a nutshell, sandy curls on her cheek, peaceful and warm and safe. He found himself thinking of the day his mother disappeared, being a boy looking at an empty bed in an empty room. With a psychological sleight of hand, he felt like his daughter was leaving him and he was all alone and he envied her her happy sleep. She was lucky.

He wept.

3

BEFORE HE MOVED TO SOUTH AFRICA, Alfred treated Carmen and a lady friend to a camping trip on the eastern seaboard.

Carmen played on the beach, pulling up glops of wet sand and flinging it out on the foaming surface. Golden sunshine surrounded her amid fizzing and popping white bubbles. She was so happy playing in the surf, warm salty water flowing over her legs, sand swirling against her skin, the sun warming the top of her head, she felt she could stay forever. And she loved the new bathing suit Alfred had bought her the day before, navy with white sailors holding telescopes. When she peed, because her pee was slightly warmer than the ocean, she could tell how long the waves took to carry it away.

The surf went quiet for a moment. She glanced toward the shore: her father was talking to Birgitte, who laughed. The next instant Carmen was underwater, unable to tell which way was up and she couldn't breathe. Another wave drove the back of her head against the bottom and the sandy frothy water got darker. She felt herself being pulled out to the deeper sea and her lungs were bursting.

Then she was lifted out. She sucked at the air like someone with an enormous thirst drinking water.

Alfred carried her to the tent, wrapped her in a towel and yelled angrily, "You were too far out! You could have drowned! What were you doing?"

She looked up at him and shouted, "You shouldn't yell at me!" and started crying. She wanted her mother. She wanted Birgitte to go away and she wanted her dad to hug her and hold her hand and talk to her the way he used to.

"There, there, little mouse," he relented, "you scared me, that's all." He picked her up and stroked her head and she burrowed into his chest, but she sensed a new impatience and she felt Birgitte watching them. When they went back out, Carmen had to play where the water was so shallow it was paper thin.

The thing Carmen hated the most about after-school daycare was nap time. The teachers made the children stop playing, and whether they were tired or not, they had to get a mat and a blanket and lie down silently for half an hour. She hated being forced to lie there, awake and bored, thinking of all the things she could be doing. She always told the teachers she wasn't tired and they always said the other children needed to rest. "I can play quietly," she'd reason. "No, just lie there if you're not tired. Rest your eyes."

She was always happy when Beth came to get her, dressed for teaching—skirt, nylons, soft sweater; red lipstick and perfume; her short, light brown hair in loose curls around her head. To Carmen, after they'd spent a whole day apart, her mother looked so beautiful and fresh it was as if she'd forgotten exactly who Beth was. As they walked to their nearby apartment, hand in hand, Carmen kept stealing glances to imprint every detail of her mother's face again.

Beth would heat up some soup or fry eggs on toast. The phone might ring and it would be Oscar or Beth's mother or sister and Carmen would float down the hall to play in her room. The early evening sun would slant in through the basement window, sending a thin yellow light over Carmen's bed and toys. Outside, the early spring ground was muddy. This was her favourite time of day, being at home with nothing particular to do.

She'd pull the string on her Casper the Friendly Ghost doll and it would go "Whooooo," and then she'd put her ear against its stomach and listen to it rewind inside. She'd get her pet turtle, Edward, out of his terrarium and build a maze for him with her blocks. At the end of the maze she'd build a home with a roof and put some raw hamburger meat on a saucer from her tea set. She'd lie on the floor and gaze at his tiny turtle mouth as he chewed and swallowed, and marvel at the patterns on his skin and shell.

At six, she was a happy, beatific, fierce soul, content to be alone, making small cities for her pet turtle in the last rays of sunlight, aware of the daffodils and tulips in the flower bed outside, listening to the birds chirping and her mother's voice down the hall, the smell of lentil soup filling their apartment.

However, after her dad moved to Africa occasionally something would happen like a hiccup in the air, and then it was as though everything developed an echo, a shadow, and became its opposite. When that happened, she'd stop playing and search out her mother and ask a question, any question, and try to keep talking until she felt better.

One night Beth kissed her good night, turned out the light and shut the door. Carmen tested what she could see as her eyes adjusted to the dark. She listened to Beth wash the dishes, and began to feel warm and drowsy. Then, at the foot of her bed, a wolf appeared. Every hair of its coat stood out. Its eyes were fixed on hers.

She made herself stay absolutely still, her head flat on the pillow, only moving her eyes. She felt that if she moved even slightly, it might tear her throat open. Her six years had not given her enough experience to know whether something so real-looking could still be just a dream.

Eventually she must've fallen asleep because in the morning she woke up.

One evening at the end of spring, ten months after Alfred had moved to Africa, Beth said to Carmen on the walk home from daycare, "Oscar and I are planning to get married and we want you to be our bridesmaid."

Carmen loved Oscar. She loved sitting on his knee, both of them not talking, looking out the window at the birds and the people on the sidewalk. She wanted to live with him for the rest of their lives. But the formal change of husbands felt like she was losing Alfred even more, like she wouldn't even be able to catch the tail of his coat as he left.

She needed Beth's help to hold onto Alfred, and it felt like Beth was scraping him out of their lives completely.

"Why can't you stay married to Daddy, and Oscar can still be our friend?"

"Carmen, your dad and I want very different things."

"What things?" she asked.

"Well," Beth looked straight ahead down the middle of Yonge Street, "your father wanted to have other girlfriends."

"Like Birgitte," Carmen nodded as if she understood everything. They walked past a bank, a dry cleaner, Carmen's favourite variety store.

"It's going to make Daddy very sad."

"Oh, he's probably already got ten girlfriends over there. I don't think he's suffering too much," Beth replied, her mouth changing to a tight bitter line.

Carmen suddenly felt shy. When they got home she went to her room and took Edward out, but didn't feel like building anything so she put him back. She looked at her crayons, her Casper doll, her stuffed animals, her picture books. She didn't feel like doing anything, but doing nothing felt crummy too. She wished the wolf would come again and she could have a really good look at it in the daylight when she wasn't so scared. She imagined it standing by the door watching her as though it knew her.

The doorbell rang. It was the little boy from the apartment next door. He was a year younger than her. Beth suggested they play outside. Carmen rolled her eyes but agreed out of despair at doing anything else. They went to the patch of lawn at the back of the building. When the boy balked at being "it" for hide-and-seek, she slapped him as hard as she could.

He ran into the building crying for his mother, who shortly afterwards knocked on Beth's door. Carmen was already stunned with guilt, remembering his face looking up at her expectantly, innocently, hopefully.

She wore a new satin dress with a big golden sash that her grandmother had bought her for the wedding. The ceremony took place in an office, Grandma Poppy standing on one side of the couple with Carmen and on the other Edgar, a friend of Oscar's, wearing thick brown corduroy pants, a black turtleneck, and a long beard. He was an English teacher at the school where Beth taught math, and he'd introduced them to each other. After the wedding the small group went to a bar on the roof of a hotel. Edgar poured champagne in Carmen's ginger ale while the bartender wasn't looking and Poppy toasted the new couple.

Beth and Oscar looked happy, and innocent in their happiness. They didn't have much money but they looked creative,

Beth wearing a tight skirt of pearly grey nubbly wool, a white shirt and an ornate Turkish medallion Oscar had given her—a bird whose body was encrusted with three semi-precious stones: jade, carnelion and turquoise. Oscar looked like a heavier-set, bohemian version of Cary Grant. They were the picture of good health from long walks, yoga classes and ambitious garden projects they'd started in their new duplex.

Carmen went home with Poppy so the newlyweds could have a honeymoon at the hotel. Poppy said they were going to make popcorn, her namesake, and watch TV in her apartment, which was bursting with antiques, music boxes and china bowls full of candy. In the elevator going down Poppy confided to Carmen that she liked Oscar well enough, but she'd liked Alfred better. Oscar was too serious.

Carmen was glad someone in the family still liked her dad, but she wanted Poppy to like Oscar too. Serious meant someone who was happy just to have Beth and didn't need other girlfriends, someone who didn't want to move to Africa.

The following summer, the summer of 1963, Beth, Oscar and Carmen drove up north to Poppy's cottage. Carmen had been once when she was three, but her memories were mostly manufactured from photographs in Beth's album. Carmen's cousins Jennifer and Jim were going to be there and Aunt Jeannie and her husband, Randy. Beth said they were thinking of buying a cottage next to Poppy's.

Carmen was glad to be seeing her cousins, and excited too because Alfred was to arrive at the cottage in a week to stay with Carmen while Oscar and Beth went to New York. He was taking her to Quebec and he'd promised they would visit a cave together.

Oscar had to drive around deep potholes in the road from the highway to the lake to spare the underbelly of their

Volkswagen Beetle. When they arrived, everyone was in bathing suits down on the dock. Randy had a fire going in the barbecue and Jeannie had hot dogs and all the fixings in a cooler. A pitcher of bright orange drink sat on a table with plastic cups beside it.

Kid heaven. Beth clipped Carmen, who still didn't know how to swim, into a puffy orange life jacket, while Carmen looked with delight at all the badminton birdies, racquets, croquet mallets and inflatable water toys strewn about. Up on the hill a badminton net was set up and croquet hoops had been stuck around the perimeter in a tortuous course between stumps and over rocks.

The adults drank beer in the sun while the children jumped off the dock and climbed on a big black rock Poppy said was left over from the ice age. Jennifer and Jim showed Carmen how to sprinkle salt on the leeches that occasionally showed up on their legs or between their toes. Then they threw the little bloodsuckers in the barbecue pit and listened to them pop.

Some of Poppy's friends dropped by in a boat, people Beth had known for years, and Carmen noticed that Beth become more animated while Oscar stayed the same. As afternoon turned to evening and the adults got tipsy and boisterous, Oscar excused himself and went to set up their tent on a small mossy promontory as far as possible away from everyone. Carmen followed and afterwards the two of them sat on the moss and looked out over the lake as the sun went behind the trees on the opposite shore. "I wish they'd put a lid on it, just for a minute, so we could hear the quiet," he muttered.

In the morning Poppy gave Carmen white toast with salted butter for breakfast, which she adored. Beth and Oscar used only unsalted butter, whole-wheat bread, unpasteurized honey, and jam that was never sweet enough.

Down at the dock, Beth went to put the damp orange life jacket on Carmen and she balked.

"Okay, it's time to learn how to swim."

Beth waded out to waist-deep water and supported Carmen with a hand under her belly. Carmen practised kicking first, then moving her arms.

"Okay, do both together and I'll slowly take my hand away."

As soon as Beth's hand left, Carmen started to sink and she began to flail about in the water. Her cousins urged her on, but as she became panicky and resistant to instruction they drifted off.

Carmen climbed out of the water, headed straight to the far side of a fallen tree, and sat out of sight of the dock. Everyone else could swim, but she sank.

The lake water was velvety blue with red-brown hues from the rotting leaves at the bottom. A silver minnow flashed among the tree's submerged branches. It was a secret world down there, beautiful and quiet. She didn't want to thrash about on the surface. She wanted to swim like a fish under the water, the way a bird flew in the air. She hated struggling against gravity; she wanted to glide freely.

She compromised with her mother by clipping her cousin Jim's old Styrofoam bubble around her waist. It gave her just enough buoyancy to do the dog-paddle and know she wouldn't sink. She paddled away from the dock to where she couldn't see the bottom and swam around in a circle for Beth.

Alfred arrived the next Sunday. She hadn't seen him in almost a year, since he'd stopped over on a business trip to the United States.

He pulled up in a rental sports car, wearing a blue cravat and an orange cashmere sweater, and sporting a new moustache. Carmen stubbed her toe on a rock as she ran up from the dock, but she leapt into his arms anyway and left beads of blood clustered on his sweater.

He unloaded his bag, changed into swimming trunks and a terry towel robe and settled into a chair on the dock. Randy handed him a beer. Carmen stared at Alfred, trying to make his remembered face familiar again, but then felt worried she was ignoring Oscar, so she went over and sat on Oscar's knee, only to notice Alfred frown and look out over the lake.

She wanted Beth to be nice to Alfred, but then Jeannie, Poppy and Randy started laughing at the stories Alfred was telling about Africa, and she wanted everyone to pay attention to Oscar too. Bedtime came as a relief.

The next morning Beth and Oscar left and Alfred cooked pancakes for everyone. He flipped them high in the air and all the children gathered round to watch. He got a little over-confident and glued one to the ceiling. The next one landed on the floor and he grinned as Poppy scolded him. He took the children waterskiing and played Monopoly with them before dinner. He cooked sauerkraut and sausages and teased her cousins for turning their noses up at the meal.

To Carmen he was like an authoritarian Santa Claus—a source of fun, laughter and gifts, but also unexpectedly strict about her table manners and finishing everything on her plate. He made her sit at the table with her elbows neatly tucked into her sides, while her cousins giggled and threw their napkins at each other and Randy shouted at them and told Jeannie to control the little savages. Carmen looked at every-one around the table. With Alfred there it was like her cousins weren't really hers any more. They were part of his world now and she only got to watch.

He did let her stay up late though. Jennifer was five years older but Alfred let Carmen stay up as late as her. At eleven o'clock when Aunt Jeannie finally folded her hand in cribbage and rose to take her daughter to bed, Alfred signalled bedtime to Carmen. He borrowed a flashlight from Poppy and together they walked to the tent.

Everything was different now that he was here. The shadows were darker, the trees taller, the quiet deeper. The ground under her feet seemed unknown, as though it housed a labyrinth of tunnels and passages and furious activity, where the night before it had felt solid and springy and just like the ground.

The moon was full and the lake sparkled between the trees. Alfred said, "It's good to be here," and took a deep breath in. She squeezed his hand and he squeezed back.

They spread a blanket and a sheet, which Poppy had lent them, over the groundsheet and then unzipped a sleeping bag to make it into a blanket. The smell of his cologne filled the tent as she snuggled up to him and fell asleep with her head against his chest, while he looked out at the moon and the trees.

At the cottage Alfred had noticed that his daughter wore a float to swim with while the other children swam freely and he'd surmised she was timid and cautious, though perhaps also stubborn and independent-minded. So he was pleasantly surprised when they'd emerged from crab-walking down a narrow passage into a large cavern to find Carmen bubbling over with excitement. There was no hint of nervousness about being in the dark, or squeamishness about bugs, the dirt, being underground. She was everywhere, curious, adventurous, full of questions. He didn't know what other seven-year-olds were like, but she seemed unusually articulate and like a complete person to him.

During the drive back to Toronto to drop her off at her mother's, he marvelled that he could be the father of this remarkable girl who talked so much and ran and climbed and who sat beside him now, looking quietly out the window at the world they were passing. She had arrived all by herself it seemed, without him doing anything.

"What about the lions?" she asked out of the blue.

"Lions?" he glanced at her face, then back at the road.

"Have you seen them? Are there any cubs for sale?"

He sighed. It began to rain and he switched on the windshield wipers. He knew what was being asked, more than she did, he was sure. He felt suddenly reduced, taken out of the moment. He thought about Birgitte, what she was up to, and decided to look her up tomorrow before leaving for the U.S.

"No, I haven't seen any," he lied. "I'm saving that for you."

Just before her ninth birthday Alfred sent her a cheque for fifty dollars with a short letter.

February 1, 1965

My dear little daughter Carmen

On the seventh of February you will be nine! Old enough to fly with a stewardess and come to visit me in South Africa. My house is by the sea. We can walk to the beach in two minutes. There are two chickens and a rabbit waiting to meet you, bought in your honour. I have a maid, Constance, who is also looking forward to meeting you, and a room set up for you. I've arranged with your mother for you to come in the summer holidays—maybe we can go on a safari! Also there's somebody special I want you to meet. Her name is Isabel and I'm thinking about marrying her.

love and hugs and kisses

Daddy

Carmen thought all week about what she would buy with the money. She also imagined South Africa, Constance, and most of all going on a safari with her father. She hoped the new woman, Isabel, would not be joining them on that trip.

On the morning of her birthday, a Sunday, she opened her eyes to a rectangular shape hidden under a blanket on her desk. A fish tank from Oscar and Beth. She and Oscar spent the morning setting up the pump and the filter, laying the gravel, planting a water plant, and finally emptying the little bags of guppies and tetras into the water. Oscar went out to shovel a light sprinkling of snow and Carmen lay on her bed and watched the neon red and blue tetras dart among the water plants and the guppies fluttering near the surface.

Beth and Oscar took her for a birthday lunch at a Hungarian café in a little courtyard called the Lothian Mews. They walked from their duplex in North Toronto, past neighbours shovelling snow to the bus stop on Yonge Street, took a bus to the Eglinton station, and took the subway downtown to Yorkville, where the hippies and flower children hung out. Carmen loved walking through the crowds, looking at the colourful clothes, the men with their dangerous-looking long hair and the women with all their beads and no makeup. Oscar's friend Edgar joined them at the café with his wife, Harriet, and their three-year-old son, Ezra.

"We talk about having a child," Beth said quietly to Harriet during lunch. "I'd like to, but Carmen's already nine and it would mean starting all over with diapers and bottles. And we can't quite manage without my salary, and Poppy's too old to look after a baby so we'd have to find a daycare, which would be expensive."

"I'm not so old, Mom," Carmen interjected. "I'd love a baby brother or sister." She thought for a minute. "I'd babysit for free. It wouldn't be so expensive."

"Ears like a hawk," Beth muttered.

Beth sent Carmen over to the fountain with a penny to make a wish. She threw it up high. It splashed in and settled among the many others. A baby sister. That her parents could live forever. A baby lion. All the sponge toffee she could eat. Then she worried she was being too greedy and that the wish fairy would be annoyed.

Carmen had overheard Beth on another occasion, the night after her birthday cheque arrived, while tiptoeing downstairs to get a glass of milk. "At least he remembered this time, I should be grateful for that. He gets all the glory for giving her that money, but never sends a cent for maintenance. I'm sorry Oscar."

"Don't even think about it. I married you and we're a family. I never think about it."

After lunch Oscar and Beth took Carmen to Eaton's to spend her money. She bought a Tressy doll she'd been yearning for for a year. She also got a wedding outfit, a tennis outfit, and tiny high heels, a shiny pink dress and a furry hat. At Beth's suggestion, she saved the money left over.

Back in her bedroom, she opened the packages. There was a key that went in Tressy's back: turn one way and the doll's hair grew, turn the other and it shortened. The cotton-candy texture of the platinum blonde hair was everything she'd imagined: the way it wound gleamingly around her baby finger and held a curl. She angled the tiny pink mules onto the arched plastic feet.

Her pleasure in the doll had a familiar-strange feeling that reminded her of when Poppy taught her how to knit and the next day she made her own first row of sloppy stitches, knitted a second row, and by the third was knitting stitches that were almost as even and neat-looking as her grandmother's. Or at school, drawing a perfect capital *G* or

F with a new pen. The pleasure of repeating something you've just learned.

At Christmas she'd made her mother a scarf and she had enough wool left over to knit a blanket for Tressy. The wool was turquoise mohair, which she'd taken forever to choose at the oddly named Sewing Notions Department in Eaton's. She started the first row of stitches sitting on her bed, the filter of her fish tank burbling away, Tressy propped up against the foot of the bed in her wedding outfit, the vibrant sound of violin music drifting up from the living room where Beth and Oscar were reading the weekend newspapers and having a pre-dinner cocktail.

In March, Beth took Carmen as a special treat to the musical *Oliver!* At a certain point young Oliver sang a soulful song about a woman, as he gazed up with yearning and passion. Carmen felt sure he was singing to her, and when he sang the refrain "Where is she?" she wanted to run down to the stage and say "Here I am!" Later when Beth explained that the "she" in the song was Oliver's missing mother, Carmen was crestfallen.

A boy from England arrived at Carmen's school. He was skinny and knobby and talked really fast as he smiled at her. He drew complicated action pictures that looked skilful but were hard to decipher. One recess Carmen ran up to a cluster of kids. The boy from England was telling a joke. It involved turning his back, crossing his arms over his chest, holding his own shoulders and writhing so it looked like he was necking with someone. The other kids laughed but Carmen didn't get the joke. He offered to demonstrate on her.

She blushed and stood still and her mind both raced and went blank.

She joined in all the conversations with her friends about who was cute and who liked whom, but she never talked about him. He didn't seem cute to her and her feelings about him were not what the word "liked" described. Nonetheless, since his demonstration of the joke she had always known where he was in the class or schoolyard, what he was doing, whether he was looking at her. When he did look at her, she blushed. She continued doing whatever she'd been doing before he looked, but suddenly she was just going through the motions to hide the fact that her mind had gone blank.

4

THE STEWARDESSES PLIED HER WITH POP, which she never got at home, and little packets of peanuts. They also gave her a kit bag with a miniature toothbrush, miniature toothpaste, a nail file, and a hairbrush that folded in half. She found the plane's compact washroom enchanting and checked in all the compartments, used the free mouthwash, the towelettes, the cologne, brushed out her tangled sandy curls with the hairbrush. The stewardess knocked on the door twice to make sure she was all right.

The plane was not flying to Africa. Alfred had been transferred to London, England, to the company's head office, and Carmen was flying to Portugal to be introduced to her new stepmother and her stepmother's relatives.

Beth had told her daughter that Isabel was pregnant, which meant she might not be feeling well so Carmen should not expect too much attention. Carmen was excited by the news, but disappointed to learn that the baby wouldn't be born until after her visit. A stewardess escorted her through the Lisbon airport to the airline's ticket desk. Alfred was leaning against the counter, talking to a woman behind the desk. When Carmen saw him she started running and catapulted into his arms, throwing her arms around his neck. He seemed surprised, as though she'd burst out of a corridor a year and a half long, as though he'd forgotten the physical reality of having a nine-year-old daughter.

He looked more handsome than the last time she'd seen him, less skinny, and he'd grown a beard, but he smelled the same and his voice had the same rich expressiveness, the same unexpected rhythm which, although his pronunciation was almost indistinguishable from any other Torontonian's, made him sound exotic and colourful.

Perhaps she'd absorbed some of this quality, because people often asked where she was from—"I can't quite place your accent," they'd say. "France? Spain?"

As she and Alfred walked to the car park she held his hand and chatted up at him.

When they arrived at the car she asked, "Where's Isabel?"

"We'll see her tomorrow. We'll drive to the southern coast of Portugal in the morning, a beautiful area called the Algarve. We're staying with Isabel's sister and brother-in-law at a very nice villa near the ocean. It has a swimming pool and their son, Fernando, is your age so you'll have a playmate."

They drove to their hotel, a small establishment with a basin in the room and a shared bathroom and toilet down the hall.

"I'm taking you somewhere special for dinner. You should wear the best dress you've brought."

They sat at a table near the stage, Carmen in paisley satin with a gold sash and net underskirt and a black elastic hairband to keep her hair out of her face, Alfred in a dark suit, no tie, with neatly trimmed moustache and beard, hair lightly oiled back. They looked up at the flamenco dancers, resting their chins on one hand, serious and concentrated, a study in family symmetry. He held her hand and stroked it with his thumb, the same circular motion he used to stroke his moustache. She kept her hand very still. She was the only child in the restaurant.

The male dancers wore tight-fitting black suits and flat hats. The women wore brilliantly coloured low-cut dresses with long ruffled trains. They stamped the floor in shoes like tap shoes and clapped and whirled around and flung their heads back with such vigour their hair fell down from where it was pinned by intricately fretted combs. Carmen watched closely to see if they were embarrassed about their hair, but its coming down seemed part of the climax of the performance.

Dinner came during the long intermission and the waiter and Alfred had a short conversation in Portuguese. Carmen asked what they were talking about. "He asked whether the charming young lady sharing my table was my daughter," he said and Carmen smiled happily.

A woman in black took the stage. Alfred told her the woman was a fado singer. She perched on a stool in front of a microphone, while a man with a guitar sat in the shadows.

When she sang, Carmen was mesmerized. She felt the woman was singing to her, trying to tell her something about the promise of being a young girl, hinting at sadness and tragedy down the road. It was frustrating not to be able to understand the Portuguese words.

"What is she singing about?" she whispered.

Alfred signalled for her to wait until the song was over. "It was a sentimental song about a man who loved her and went away and never came back. The nostalgia of lost love."

This answer was very unsatisfactory. Nostalgia? Lost love? Carmen scrunched up her face. She'd never had either of those, yet she was sure the woman had been singing about her. Now she'd never know what the message *really* was.

She fell asleep with her head on the tablecloth. Later, when Alfred lifted her up to carry her to the car she murmured happily. At the hotel, he carried her to bed and all she had to do was snuggle in and fall back asleep.

Isabel was beautiful. She had thick long dark hair, dark eyes, slender eyebrows, high cheekbones, full lips. She'd been a model and she had many talents: she could play the guitar, fly an airplane, ride horses, speak near-perfect English and French. She welcomed Carmen with a hug and kisses on both cheeks. "But she's just darling, Alfred!" she exclaimed. "I'm so glad to meet you at last. Alfred's told me all about you. I've been so impatient."

Carmen liked the way she smelled, of cantaloupe and cinnamon, and she liked her voice, warm and even more musical than Alfred's. Isabel was the kind of woman Carmen had seen but never met—glamorous, fun-loving, fashionable. She approved of Alfred's choice and told him so later that day.

"I'm sure you two are going to get along like a house on fire," he replied.

"A house on fire?" she asked, and he laughed without explaining.

The nephew, Fernando, spoke only Portuguese. He watched TV or played with his friends and completely ignored Carmen.

The swimming pool was unimaginable luxury but there were foreign rules that came with it, such as "No swimming until three hours after eating." With the number of meals these people ate, which she was expected to join, that left only two one-hour periods a day to use the pool.

On the first full day, when the adults retired for their afternoon nap and the Mediterranean sun blazed down, Fernando took off with his friends, glancing blankly at Carmen without even waving goodbye. She sat and stared at the pool with rage and thwarted longing. Her school friends had been envious of her going to Portugal, and she had shared their sense of impending luxury and adventure. When Alfred had uttered the words "villa" and "swimming pool," she'd thought she'd be tasting the rich life and she could almost hear her friends' oohs and aahs.

But this was torture and she knew her friends, if they had to live it, would feel the same way.

"Dad," she whispered when the adults came down for a drink, "at the cottage we go swimming one hour after eating. No one ever drowns. No one throws up. No one even gets stomach aches. Tell them."

"This is a different culture. I know you're right but we have to follow their rules."

It was clear he wasn't going to risk annoying his new in-laws for her sake.

Next she tried Isabel but Isabel, though kind, could not be convinced it wasn't dangerous.

The following afternoon Carmen avoided the pool and wandered to the kitchen. The cook gave her a yellow substance in a small cup with a rooster head. It was delicious. She made it last longer by coating her spoon and licking it as she watched peahens peck near the garbage.

A noise like a fan being opened came from behind her and she turned to see a male peacock, his tail feathers spread in a great glistening arc and vibrating like a woman rapidly batting her eyelashes.

She discovered a path through scrub and airy pine trees. It led to a short tree with big waxy leaves laden with green fruit shaped like teardrops. She picked one of the fruit, broke it open and smelled it. The inside looked like white sperm swimming in a kind of purply red pulp. She knew what sperm looked like from a book her mother had got from the library to answer her question about where babies came from. She nibbled the fruit experimentally.

It tasted like candy and fruit mixed together. She ate twenty. She circled back behind the villa's wall and followed a dirt road that seemed like it might lead to the sea. It took her through a grove of short, gnarled trees on the hillside. She thought they were olive trees at first, like the ones Alfred had pointed out driving here from Lisbon, but there was no fruit and the bark was very thick and knobby. She tried to peel some off and discovered the bark was cork. She broke off a piece and stuck it in the pocket of her shorts to take back to Canada.

Farther on she saw white shells on the road. The ocean was nowhere in sight. She picked a shell up. It was hard and spiralled. She looked up and saw other shells clinging to the branches of tall willowy trees that lined the road. She broke off a branch so she could ask what kind of tree this was that bore shells for fruit. The leaves smelled like Vicks VapoRub.

Past the trees, on the left side of the road, a path led to a grid of shallow pools in sandy red earth whose banks were wide enough to walk on. The sky was brilliant blue and open above her head, the air was hot with a steamy briny smell, the earth went on as far as she could see. She felt like at last she'd found her own personal luxury, one no one could take from her. One she wouldn't be able to explain to her friends. She decided to walkout along the dikes and go as far as she could go.

She passed pools whose water had evaporated, leaving a soupy residue at the bottom and sides encrusted with white crystals. She climbed down and picked up some crystals. They were sticky and hard. She tasted one and discovered that the pools were full of sea salt, but still she couldn't see the ocean.

A couple of hours later she felt thirsty, the sun seemed low in the sky and suddenly she felt anxious about how late she was returning. She hadn't told anyone where she was going. She had no idea how her dad might react, but Beth would have been furious and grounded her for a couple of days.

On the way back, by the aromatic trees, she saw a painted wooden caravan pulled by a horse, accompanied by five people wearing several layers of clothing. In the back of the caravan a boy a little younger than herself sat on the ledge swinging his legs. She glimpsed an unmade bed inside and a sideboard tied shut. Pots and pans hung from hooks. Gypsies, she thought. She stared at them as she passed, feeling awe at their independence, the way they travelled, taking home with them. One of the adults glanced at her without expression or interest.

Everyone was dressed for dinner when she got back. They were sitting by the pool, looking impatient.

"Where were you?" Alfred demanded. "We were just getting ready to call the police."

"I went for a walk and I guess I got lost in the salt pools," she lied.

"Go get cleaned up and changed for dinner. Next time tell somebody where you're going. You can't just wander off whenever the fancy takes you."

"But you were sleeping."

The first course was soup. Carmen prayed the main course would not be a repeat of the yellow salt cod they'd had at lunch, but when the servant lifted the lid off a large silver tureen, she would have been grateful for the cod.

She whispered to Alfred, "I can't eat that."

Alfred frowned and held her plate up. The servant served her potatoes and six baby squid. She looked across the table at her step-aunt, dressed in a tight hot-pink, raw-silk shift and dangling earrings, her hair drawn back against her head in a ponytail and tied with a black velvet bow. Her glossy pink lips moved as she chewed and a tiny tentacled leg escaped from between her lips. It moved up and down as she chewed.

Carmen ate her potatoes, drank her water, asked the servant for more water. Alfred helped himself to seconds. Before starting in, he glanced at her plate.

"Come on now girl. You haven't even tried one. Let's go."

He picked up her fork, stabbed a baby squid and held it to her mouth. She kept her lips tightly compressed. It wasn't a matter of choice. She knew Alfred was getting embarrassed, but that thing was not going into her mouth. She looked pleadingly over at Isabel, but Isabel looked away and whispered something to her sister.

"Eat or leave the table, goddamnit," he ground the words out between his teeth and threw her fork down on her plate in disgust.

First her face flushed. Then she stood and ran from the room, slamming the door as hard as she could. She slammed every door she passed through on her way outside. This was the first time in her life she could remember being so angry.

The garden was tranquil and dark blue. A full moon shone on the swimming pool, which was not turquoise at night but inky black. She stormed over to a wicker loveseat across from the peacock pens and hid behind it. She heard the male's feathers dragging in the dirt.

A few minutes later she heard her father calling her name and, from another direction, the maid, and from the second floor, Isabel, as though they were calling her from the wings of a theatre. She shrank deeper into the shadows. She wanted them to come looking for her, but she didn't want them to find her.

Her eyes adjusted to the dark and she could see the peacocks asleep in the cage. They seemed free—kept and fed for their own sake, for their beauty, not for their obedience.

Everyone went back inside. Carmen waited. Her heart slowed. The moon shone back at her from the surface of the water. She crept out from her hiding place to the ladder, took her shoes off and climbed down into the water. Her clothes pressed against her skin. *I need to cool down*, she thought.

I don't need him anyway.

She duck-dove to the bottom, rolled over and looked up. From underneath, the water's surface looked like a sheet of fluid silver. She returned to the surface for air and was preparing to dive down again when she noticed, from the shadows beside the peacock pens, her stepmother, round-bellied and swathed in shimmering gold lamé, looking silently at her.

Carmen looked back, then took a big breath and dove under again. She hadn't minded having a father she heard from a couple of times a year and saw only once every year or two, a good-time father with unpredictable bursts of strictness, and she'd been happy with Oscar and Beth. But something had changed with the arrival of Isabel that wasn't Isabel's fault. Carmen's place in Alfred's world, tenuous at best, had been reduced.

He no longer needed her for anything.

5

HE LEFT HIS SUITCASE behind a pew. He hadn't been in Germany for sixteen years and everything was both familiar and strange—the smell of the air, for example. After Canada, South Africa and Portugal the air here smelled of different heating fuels, car exhaust, food preparation, history. The solidity of all the buildings was not so different from London perhaps, but everywhere around him was the German language, like a thick blanket, both protective and suffocating. He felt as if he were in a trance, a slightly depressed trance, memories flooding back, trailing emotions with them— sadness, anger, pride and, somewhat unexpectedly, love.

He introduced himself to the Father of the church. As they spoke, two men wheeled in a coffin. Alfred realized his father lay inside and he felt a sharp pang at the thought that he no longer knew what his father looked like. How would his appearance have changed in sixteen years? A second pang struck with the thought that his father would no longer have known what his son looked like either. He'd been twenty the last time his father had seen him—without elegance, experience, success, substance—a skinny kid with hopes in his pocket.

He'd never planned to not see his father again. True, he'd disowned him with melodramatic proclamations of forever, but those had been the words of a twenty-year-old with no real reference to this future. All those years he'd been keeping his father in reserve, to be seen when he, Alfred, was ready. In the same way he intended to find out what happened to his mother, when he was ready, but in the meantime he was busy living.

His stepmother, Gerti, entered the church with the now middle-aged daughter from her first marriage. Both women pursed their lips as they approached.

"I'd like to look at him, before everyone gets here," he whispered to the Father.

"*Now* you want to see him," Gerti snorted. "A son who cuts his father off, never writes, never phones and comes only when he is dead to collect his inheritance. I will not let you see him now that he's defenceless. You broke his heart."

The Father bowed and left the family.

"There's a cardboard box by the front door. It's all you're getting. Old photos and such. You might as well have them, they're no use to me. He was a good man, my husband. He did not deserve what you did to him."

Alfred was wearing his most expensive suit, he had a good job, his investments were doing well; he had a beautiful wife, an adorable son, another child on the way, a large townhouse in central London, a daughter in Canada. He spoke English, Portuguese, German, French and some Zulu. But his step-mother made him feel like a rebuked adolescent.

Broke his heart. If only that were true. He'd probably upset his father, caused him vague discomfort from time to time, but he had never mattered much. What had mattered to his father was his image of himself as a brave and good man, and his son stood in contradiction of that image. An uncomfortable and outspoken reminder of his first wife, a union Alfred was sure his father wished had never happened.

Alfred took a seat at the side of the church. He recognized only a few of the people filing in, his great-aunts, his aunt and uncle, his cousin Petra looking matronly beside her sausage of a husband, two cute kids beside her. He planned to talk to them after the service. Tell them about his life.

A voice spoke in his ear and made him jump. "How are you, you old rascal? You look good, what've you been up to?"

His cousin Claus had snuck up behind him. Claus proceeded to perch on the pew behind Alfred, leaning forward to talk. Not sitting beside him. After they'd exchanged news Alfred asked about Claus's brother, Jürgen.

"Oh him, he's a faggot. Happily he's moved to San Francisco."

The Father stepped up to the pulpit and Claus slipped back to his seat.

Jürgen, Alfred realized, was the only one he'd have liked to see. He'd been looking forward unconsciously to sitting with him, because Jürgen had always mocked everyone, all the uptight, proper, anxious adults, and Alfred needed that now. He'd admired Jürgen for being so un-German, so bohemian and free, and Jürgen had always had a way of making Alfred feel included. They'd often mocked Claus behind his back for being such an ass-licker to his teachers and parents. But homosexuals repelled Alfred.

The service started. Alfred felt more isolated than he'd felt since he was a child, more even than when he'd first arrived in Canada. It was like the loneliness of walking through his house looking for his mother while his father read the newspaper.

Everyone rose to sing a hymn. He thought about how there'd been no funeral for his mother, no acknowledgment that she was even dead. No one to stand for her. All she had left was a son who barely remembered her.

Suddenly he could not bear to be among these people.

He got out of his seat and headed for the door. Heads turned to watch him. He stopped at the back to pick up the box Gerti had left for him. He wedged it awkwardly against the wall as he bent down to pick up his suitcase. He could feel himself blushing. He got his arm over the box, gripped the bottom and pushed the church door open with his hip. It creaked loudly.

He glanced over his shoulder. The aisle was lined with people's faces, frowning or looking disgusted. Gerti smirked and said something to her daughter.

He started to laugh. Then stepped back into the church and turned around. He put his suitcase down, shifted the box into both hands and turned it upside down. The contents spread out on the floor. He picked up a white feminine-looking garment, tucked it under his arm, then crouched down and rifled through a packet of photographs, picking out only those of his father and himself on his father's motorcycle. He stood up again, bowed to the congregation and left, letting the door bang shut behind him. He stepped lightly down the stone stairs and hailed a cab.

In his hotel room, he flipped through TV channels for half an hour. He felt restless. He wanted some life around him. He decided to go down to the bar for a few drinks to get rid of a welling up in his throat.

Three well-dressed blonde women, between twenty-five and thirty he guessed, sat at the bar. A businessman was talking to one of them, laughing too loudly, obviously trying to impress. The other two women talked quietly to each other. Alfred stepped up.

"Can I buy you two charming ladies a drink?" he asked.

6

THERE WAS NO CHRISTMAS PRESENT for Carmen, who'd arrived in Paris on December 23. Alfred had expected Isabel to take care of it, while she had thought, inexplicably (how did women's minds work?), that as the father he would want to do it. He hated shopping, which she knew, and how could she imagine he'd know what to buy a twelve-year-old girl? It seemed to him she must deliberately be trying to sabotage him.

Then his beautiful wife had suggested, in front of Carmen, that they go to the largest shopping mall in Paris and let Carmen choose a dress. He felt himself thrown to the wolves—his wife would have to know that a shopping mall on the day before Christmas, any shopping mall, Paris or not, would be hell for him. She pretended not to know. It was almost funny.

When they got to the mall Isabel promptly announced she was taking the boys for a snack and then to look for another little something for her father and left Alfred to shop with his daughter.

At the first shop Alfred asked what they had in the way of dresses for twelve-, about-to-turn-thirteen-, year-olds. The woman appraised his daughter, who was a bit solid but pretty. She had new breasts, though the rest of her body was still a girl's.

"What about this one?" Alfred asked as they passed a display rack. He held out a pretty yellow dress with a sash and a petticoat.

"*Way* too girly. I was thinking something more grown-up."

"This is grown-up," Alfred said at the next store, pointing to a suit the saleslady was holding up. Carmen was already craning her neck looking at the rest of the store.

"Something I can wear to *school*."

Alfred had a sinking feeling that proved prescient.

"Come on now girl," he spluttered three hours later. "Make a decision. We've been through every store in the biggest mall in Paris. There must be *something* you like. I walk into a store, pick out something nice, if it fits I buy it."

She turned to him. "Dad, maybe you never read those fairy tales—*Cinderella, Beauty and the Beast, Rumpelstiltskin*—but this is like a wish come true for me. This is my chance to be a princess. No one is ever going to offer to buy me any dress I want again in my life. I need to pick the right one."

He went silent. They revisited a few stores. An announcement came on over the speakers.

"The mall is closing," Alfred translated.

Carmen seemed to be on the verge of tears. He'd always thought of her as a decisive, independent-minded child and he was perplexed by this new behaviour. She dragged him back to a store where she'd tried on a beige sweater dress with short sleeves and a collar, which he considered drab. As he got out his wallet and the saleslady wrapped the dress in tissue, Carmen looked forlorn. He despaired of ever being able to make a female happy. Even keeping their dissatisfaction at a tolerable level was very expensive.

That evening Alfred surveyed his family seated around the restaurant table. Isabel had the boys looking adorable, hair brushed, faces clean, cute French outfits on, and she herself looked fabulous. He was gratified by men's heads turning to look at her as they were led to their table. And Carmen didn't look too bad in her new dress. She was angry because he'd told her to put her book away and join the rest of the table. "Get your head out of that goddamned book," is what he'd actually said. She was always reading and he was beginning to suspect it was a way of avoiding him in particular and life in general.

He ordered martinis for the adults and soft drinks for the children. The waiter returned with the drinks and Isabel ordered dinner for herself and the boys.

"What will you have?" Alfred asked Carmen.

"Steak and pommes frites."

"I'll order you something better."

"But I like steak and pommes frites."

"This is Paris. Try something new. Live dangerously."

A second martini arrived. Alfred sipped quietly while Carmen played "I spy" with Daniel. "His little British accent is adorable," she said to Isabel.

Alfred leaned back and looked, not at his family, because he wanted to think about them, but at the restaurant, a good restaurant, an expensive one, not just a showy place for tourists.

Things weren't perfect. After the first week of marriage he'd lost sexual desire for his wife. He wished he hadn't, but what could he do? It wasn't something he had control over. Their passion had moved into arguments. He had a daughter he barely knew, an increasingly sullen child, and he felt no emotional connection with his little sons, thrilled though he was to have boys. "Men enjoy children when they talk in sentences," he said to Isabel when she accused him of never paying the boys any attention.

Nonetheless, he felt happy. The surface of his life was positively glowing. He was doing well financially. He could afford to bring his family to this restaurant in the most sophisticated city of the world and let them order whatever they wanted. He took satisfaction in having paid for the clothes on their backs, their airplane tickets, the bed they'd sleep in tonight.

He tilted his martini glass to get the last drops. From a skinny, motherless fourteen-year-old hiding from the Russians in his great-aunts' attic to the man he was now was a journey that filled him with wonder and pride.

If his father could see him now he'd know that his son had beat him again, in the big race of life. Thoughts of his father, however, led to thinking about his mother. If *she* could see him now? His expansive mood began to shrink. He turned his attention to Carmen and Isabel.

"Where did you get that beautiful shirt?" Carmen was asking Isabel.

"A boutique near St-Germain."

"Was it expensive?"

"Not particularly."

"I think that kind of thing might suit me better than shopping-mall things." Isabel winked at Carmen and put her finger to her lips.

The waiter brought a salad for Isabel, soup for the boys, and two metal dishes with six snail shells nestled in concave dips. Alfred took a piece of French bread, dipped it in the sauce and held it out to Carmen.

"Taste that."

"What is it?"

"Butter and garlic."

She took a bite. "It *is* good," she said, surprised. "What's in the shells?"

"Mushrooms," he said, winking at Isabel.

A bottle of wine arrived with the main course. Alfred held his glass up for a toast.

"Things have not always been perfect for me, God knows, but I can say that at this moment," his eyes misted over and he looked around the table, "at this moment . . . ," he searched for words, "at this moment, Christmas Eve 1968, surrounded by my family, *all* my family," he nodded at Carmen, "I am content. To life!"

The waiter placed a silver tureen on the table and lifted the lid with a flourish. Carmen fell silent. The waiter served her and Alfred, put the lid back on, bowed and left.

She took some bread and dipped it in the sauce on her plate.

"Oh. This sauce is delicious too."

Alfred watched her pick up the seafood fork, twist a mussel out of its shell, make a face like the one she'd made when he held up the yellow dress, and pop the mussel in her mouth, chew once and swallow.

"But I think I like steak and pommes frites better," she said brightly.

"*Moules marinières* is my favourite dish," he asserted. "It is utterly superb."

"I can't eat another thing," Carmen said a few minutes later and put her fork down.

"She's hiding them, Daddy," Daniel burst out, pointing. "Under the shells."

Alfred reached across the table and prodded the dark purple shells with his fork. A couple of orange bodies floated to the top.

"They've got all their organs. And they're gritty. They still have poo in them. I just can't . . . "

"Let her leave them Alfred. She's only thirteen," said Isabel.

The girl wasn't thirteen, she was twelve, and when he was twelve no one had offered him any food, let alone a delicacy like this. No one had cared what he ate, or if he ate.

"She'd still be in diapers if you were her mother. Look at him, still using a dummy at the age of three. You'd turn them into perfect little mama's boys if I let you."

Isabel went tight-lipped and silent. Carmen was tight-lipped too, though for different reasons. No doubt Beth, on the subject of Alfred, also went tight-lipped. It was a conspiracy, a coven, the coven of tight-lipped women.

His daughter stared silently at the little orange bodies afloat in their sauce.

He wanted to tell her—the world is not made up only of good mothers and bad men. You need to experience life, take risks.

"Do they really have poo in them?" Daniel asked with a new seriousness, his young eyes wide open.

Alfred threw down his napkin.

"He's only three," said Isabel.

"He's not three, he's four and she's twelve for God's sake! It would be nice to get support just once from your side of the table."

Isabel looked away and her eyes fixed angrily on some undetermined point above all the happy tables.

"I am never, never taking children to a nice restaurant again," Alfred said, searching for some certainty in this sudden expensive catastrophe of a Christmas Eve dinner. "You can all just sit here while I enjoy these disgusting things in peace."

He chewed each mouthful vigorously and for a long time, took leisurely sips of wine, swallowed noisily and requested more bread.

Carmen watched the mussels leave his plate and enter his mouth. Ivan slept in his stroller. Isabel stroked Ivan's head and sipped her wine.

"Daddy," said Daniel, cheerily trying to fix the situation. "Tell me the story again about you and Mommy seeing the lions in Africa."

"Not now, Daniel."

"Please, Daddy, please."

"You saw a lion?" Carmen asked, sudden hurt showing in her eyes before she clouded it over with disinterest.

She excused herself to go to the washroom. She didn't come back for a long time. Alfred was on the point of telling Isabel to go get her when she reappeared, eyes red and puffy.

I can't win, Alfred thought.

7

IF SOMEONE WERE TO ASK Carmen why the sound of Alfred munching peanuts and coughing as he swallowed too quickly made her so angry, the only answer she'd be able to give would be, "He tried to make me eat *mussels.*" They were on a plane heading for London (Isabel and the boys were staying on in France).

She daydreamed about lions, saw them walking through tall grass toward her, heard the pad of their feet on the hot ground, smelled their carnivorous breath, looked in their beautiful eyes which were the same colour as hers. She was leaving for Toronto tomorrow.

She couldn't wait to see Beth and Oscar again, to give them bear hugs and tell them all about her trip, how cute Ivan and Daniel were, how Daniel fell asleep in her lap once and she stayed still for two hours not to wake him up. She wanted to tell them the gross things Alfred made her eat and how nice Isabel was, and show them the things she and Isabel had bought on their secret trip to the boutique in St-Germain. Isabel had bought Carmen a tunic like hers with her own money as a present and then they'd bought jeans and boots that zipped up the side on Alfred's credit card. They smuggled them back into the hotel underneath a baguette and a bottle of wine.

She wanted to tell them how disappointing the Eiffel Tower was—just a bunch of stairs and a view of the city, and how boring Napolean's Tomb had been—you didn't even get to see the body.

On New Year's Eve, she'd got to stay up with the adults and dance to the Beatles with Alfred. She'd loved how he said, "Young lady, it has been enchanting, but you who are much younger have tired me out and I need refreshment," and bowed to her.

Alfred ordered a double whisky and soda from the stewardess and orange juice for Carmen. She was reading Gerald Durrell's *My Family and Other Animals*, and she wanted to get back to the part describing the author's teenage sister trying to get rid of acne. She sensed, as she started reading, that Alfred was about to interrupt. She willed him silently to leave her alone.

"You can read any time, Carmenita. We won't see each other for another whole year. How about a game of backgammon with your old dad?"

He took out a small, beautifully inlaid wooden box from his briefcase, opened it and set up the pieces inside. He explained the rules and they began to play. He won the first two games, but Carmen won the third.

They started a fourth game. He ordered another double whisky and Carmen ordered herself a Coke. His first roll of the dice meant he had to leave himself open and Carmen proceeded to roll double sixes which meant she could knock him out and advance herself without risk.

"This ceases to be amusing. How can a person have such bad luck? You're not cheating by any chance?"

She laughed. "I've noticed that when *you* lose it's a game of luck but when *I* lose it's suddenly a game of great intelligence and skill."

He laughed. "I assure you I'm playing with great skill to have any success at all with such bad luck. How can a person roll such disgraceful numbers?"

He ordered a third whisky while the second glass was still half full. Carmen won.

"You must have my genes in the brain department to learn so quickly."

"Mom is smart too," Carmen said.

"Of course. She's very smart. She's a math teacher. But women's brains are different. They're not set up for competition."

"What do you mean?"

"It doesn't come out so much till later in life, but you'll see. Female brains are set up to be mothers. That's why the world would probably be a better place if it was run by women."

"Well, I won't be getting married or having babies," she said defiantly.

"Don't be too hasty there. There's plenty of time yet." He looked over his glasses with blurry concern. "You haven't even been in love. Don't rule out babies just yet."

"I'm going to have adventures. Deep-sea diving, and mountain climbing and even my own safari," she said with conviction.

"Hmmm. I'll bet you will," he said, and put his chair back, closed his eyes. "You are a remarkable young lady."

She started reading her book again. She was just getting engrossed in Durrell's explorations of animal life on Corfu when Alfred added, "I'd rather come back as a frog than a woman."

Carmen stared at his face. He looked so happy and cozy and content, snoring faintly and working his lips, as though savouring some aftertaste. Was he talking in his sleep? It sounded like he was putting in an order at the reincarnation desk.

Oscar would never say something like that. She felt sorry for Isabel, being married to a man who thought being a frog was better than being a woman. She did not relate his remark to herself, because she was still a child, and his daughter, and he'd just said she was a remarkable young lady.

He woke up as the plane was landing. He had no recollection of saying anything, or dreaming anything. In fact, when she repeated what he'd said, he laughed out loud. "A frog, eh? Hmm, not a bad life really, swimming around a pond, eating flies, looking for lady frogs."

He gave the airport cab driver an address Carmen did not recognize.

"Where are we going?"

"I just have to pop into the office for a minute."

She groaned. This was her last day with him, her only day without the boys, and she'd hoped he was planning to do something special with her.

He sat her down at his desk with a pen and paper and said, "You never have to be bored as long as you have a brain. Practise equations. Draw a picture. I won't be more than fifteen minutes."

She liked his office—the clean empty space. A picture of Ivan, Daniel and Isabel sat on the desk beside an old one of her in a bathing suit that had sailors holding telescopes on it. A bookcase displayed statues of Buddha, Shiva, Don Quixote, a tall thin African woman with a basket on her head. On the wall opposite hung a plain wooden crucifix with a black Christ and next to it, an inlaid wooden frame holding words written in a strange script.

Carmen multiplied fractions for a while, then doodled geometric flower shapes, then drew a self-portrait. She stared out the window at a small park surrounded by narrow old buildings. Davy Jones, the lead singer of the Monkees, was from England. Maybe he was in London right now . . . walking in that park.

She imagined Davy Jones driving by in a limo, catching a glimpse of her. He tells his driver to pull over, opens the door, leans out and calls to her in his English accent, "Excuse me. I couldn't help noticing you from my window. My name's Davy. What's yours?" Their eyes meet.

"I'm meeting my mates at the hotel, but I saw you and, and," he stutters adorably, "I don't suppose you'd come with me, back to the hotel I mean. We could have a soda or something."

The Monkees all like her. She listens as they talk about their next concert. Then Davy takes her down to his car and leans over as she gets in. "Could I kiss you? I may never see you again, and it's just that, well, I think I'm in love."

He leans over, looking into her eyes, and presses his lips . . .

She felt as if she were sinking into the floor. She had a sensation of needing to pee. She felt thirsty and dazed. She opened the door to her father's office and asked a woman at a desk nearby where a drinking fountain might be and where her father was. The woman told her there was no drinking fountain and pointed to a door down the hall, saying, "I think I saw him go in there, I'm not sure. It's nobody's office, so don't worry, you can go in."

Carmen went up to the door, hesitated, listened for voices. It was quiet. She tapped on the door and opened it.

A woman was on a desk, her skirt up by her hips, legs in the air. A man was standing in front of the woman, rocking back and forth, breathing loudly. His pants were at his ankles. The woman's eyes widened as she saw Carmen.

Carmen watched for a moment. Her face flushed. She couldn't breathe as she closed the door quickly and ran to the elevator, pressed the down button, whispering, "hurry, hurry." It would take time to pull his pants up, buckle his belt.

The elevator door opened; she got in and pounded *L* for Lobby, held the close-door button until the metal door closed. The chamber gave a little shudder before it descended. A mental review of all the thrillers she'd seen did not reveal who arrived first, the person on the elevator or the one racing down the stairs.

The door opened to the lobby. Through a glass wall she saw people lined up at a bus stop with their briefcases, purses, shopping bags and brollies. She stepped out of the elevator and glanced over her shoulder as she walked to the revolving door, entered and was spilled out onto the sidewalk. She walked with her head down to the end of the block, turned right, hurried down another block, turned left and relaxed slightly.

She walked past endless shop windows, looking at things she couldn't buy, glancing in pubs she wasn't old enough to enter. The sun set and she shied away from parks and dark areas. She had ten pounds in her pocket from her mother, but no passport or plane ticket. She wanted to go home. She wanted to phone Beth and tell her what was happening. To hear her mother's voice. To have Beth come and get her. She tried to call her collect from a pay phone, but only got a signal she didn't recognize.

Tears welled up. She wished Davy Jones would show up, smile sweetly at her and take her home.

She wondered if Alfred would phone the police, but what could he say? He'd have to lie. Maybe he'd just kept on with the woman, and expected her to wait for him in his office. Maybe he'd be annoyed with her for not staying in his office.

She wandered for five hours, flipping between rage and self-pity. She stopped once in a tearoom for tea which she loaded with sugar and later at a Wimpy burger place for fries. A weedy long-haired guy with nicotine-stained fingers offered to join her at her table. She could feel him staring at her breasts before she even looked in his face. She saw he'd guessed she was alone and she felt scared. She replied, "No thank you."

"Oh Miss High and Mighty are we? Miss middle-class schoolgirl bitch are we?" He slammed her table with his hip as he left, knocking the ketchup bottle over.

The cashier looked over at her sympathetically. "Never mind him, pet. Are you all right then?" A sob caught in Carmen's throat, but she managed to nod and look away.

At a little after ten o'clock she phoned Alfred and Isabel's number which she got from the operator. "Where are you? I've been worried as hell! I didn't know what to do, call your mother, call the police. I didn't know where you'd gone. Never pull a stunt like this again!"

"Call my mother?" Carmen replied angrily. "And what were you going to tell her?"

"Where are you? I'll come and get you. It's not safe for a girl your age to be out this late."

She loathed him. She needed and loathed him. She laughed sarcastically, fighting off surrender.

"Where are you?"

She wilted a bit.

"I'll take the subway. What stop do I get off?"

"It's not safe this time of night."

"I'll hang up . . ."

She found his stop on the map, got on the right line and sat beside a woman. She sensed the men in the car looking at her, assessing her, sizing her up.

She got off at the right stop and ascended the grimy steps to the street, relieved no one had followed her. Other than a skirt of light emanating from the tube entrance it was dark. No street lights, no moonlight.

A car door opened, the interior light lit up, Alfred got out. He walked toward her, hunched over, hands in his pockets, leaving the car door open. Carmen put her hands up and stepped back.

"I want to walk," she said with a note of hysteria.

"Okay, okay. Follow the car."

His headlights lit up the road ahead of them. She walked toward the moving light, stopping whenever she reached its edge, keeping just outside, in the shadows.

While he parked the car, she waited at the front door. She stared straight ahead as he unlocked it.

"Carmen," he said in a tender voice.

She couldn't give in now. It would be a betrayal of Isabel, Beth, herself.

He saw her face . . .

But she wanted to.

Now he's a believer . . .

She wanted to sob in his arms.

He couldn't leave her if he tried . . .

She wanted to sob in someone's arms.

She took her suitcase from her father, walked up to the guest room without looking at him, closed the door, got in her pyjamas and climbed into bed.

8

SHE WAS FOURTEEN in the summer before high school. An impossibly handsome boy asked her out to a movie. She sat beside him on the subway in uncomfortable silence, racking her brain for something to say. The only subject that came to mind was how good-looking he was. Maybe that was the only subject coming to his mind too because when she did finally think of a question to ask, like, "Do you have any brothers or sisters?" his answers were monosyllabic. He had no questions of his own.

When she got back home she headed straight for her room, closed the door, and collapsed on her bed, overcome with relief that the date was over and despair at being so incompatible with such handsomeness. They hadn't even kissed goodbye.

She did not think of herself as beautiful. Nor did she think of herself as not beautiful. She was tall, with long wild hair, high cheekbones, but an otherwise undefined face, a face in transition from child to woman. Since she'd joined the school swim team the previous year she'd developed the broad back and porpoise shoulders of a swimmer. Her eyes were the most defined part of her, unchanged since she was a baby, their golden streaks shining with exuberance, intelligence and a stubbornness that slid readily to courage.

Carmen got third place for academic achievement in Grade 9 and was presented with an award at assembly at the end of the year. Alfred and Isabel took the boys to Disneyland and Carmen met them there for a couple of weeks in the summer.

In Grade 10 she joined the high school's synchronized swim team and an after-school poetry class for all grades. The poetry teacher, Mr Dalgleish, was young, handsome and counterculture. Male teachers were only allowed to wear their hair touching their collar, but he kept his longer in wild bushy curls. He wore black velvet pants, pink or sky-blue shirts, psychedelic ties and a black corduroy jacket. He looked like Cat Stevens.

Their first poetry was T.S. Eliot's *Four Quartets*. Carmen took Oscar's thin light-blue volume to the ravine near her house on a Sunday morning, found a sunny patch of grass and read all four quartets out loud. The leaves were just starting to turn yellow, the air was crisp and clear and Eliot's words spoken into the autumn wind seemed to convey the universe back to itself.

Independence, excitement, impendingness surged through her body. Her mind already travelled in a world more transcendent and interesting than anything she'd hoped for.

She leaned back on the grass and looked at the clouds shooting past in the wind. She wanted to shoot high like an arrow, free of stupid constraints, conformity, social rules, authority. She imagined herself doing deep-sea research, composing symphonies, trekking across mountains, travelling to remote and unexplored territory. She had no interest in fun and frivolity; she wanted to experience the world, to be one with it, to be where Eliot indicated, "there the dance is."

She phoned a new friend she'd made in the poetry class, April Spinelli, who had moved to Toronto from Montreal the year before and was a year older than Carmen. April lived in a house that was almost a mansion, had three brothers, a fully developed body, and strong opinions about everything, unlike anyone else Carmen knew, besides her father. She was also surprisingly thoughtful for someone so brash on the surface and had given Carmen a homemade card the year before on her birthday, separate from any party.

"You should try reading the *Quartets* outside. They sound amazing."

"I already read them. My dad said Eliot was a jerk in real life."

Carmen wasn't sure how to respond. "I liked them," she said lamely.

"The writing is great, but what do they mean? It's very mystical and all that, but I don't trust him. There's something sneaky about him."

Carmen had missed that, the sneaky quality of Eliot. They talked about April's date the night before with a guy in Grade 13, a friend of her brother's.

"Weeelll," she said and laughed, "the movie was okay, but Doug was pretty boring. He tried to get me to take my clothes off, can you believe it, on a first date? What a creep! Not that I wasn't a teensy bit tempted, but he's not exactly my type."

Carmen had no idea what her own type might be, but she'd seen Doug in the school halls—he was short, he had acne, he looked muscular. She was glad April hadn't done anything with him.

April suggested they hitchhike to Guelph the next weekend to go to an outdoor rock concert with her brother Jim. He was going to university there and they could crash at his place.

"Your parents let you hitchhike?" Carmen asked.

"Of course not. We'll tell them your parents are driving us and you say my parents are driving. We'll meet on Yonge Street. My brother said he would drive us home Sunday."

Carmen was shocked when her mother said no.

"Why not?" Carmen asked.

"A girl your age can't sleep at a young man's place without an adult present."

"It's April's brother. We're not going to do anything. And he *is* an adult."

"You're too young to go out of town by yourself."

"I've been to Paris, London, Portugal by myself."

"With your father."

Carmen rolled her eyes. "Yeah. Like he's a lot of protection."

Carmen had expected Beth, who supported the Vietnam peace movement, did yoga, had read *The Female Eunuch* and had smoked marijuana at least once with Oscar, Edgar and Harriet, to be glad her daughter had a chance to do something cool. Maybe her mother's pregnancy at forty-one was changing her, making her more conservative.

Beth's advice about sex had also surprised Carmen. She'd given Carmen a book about birth control and said, "You know there's nothing wrong with saving it for one person. There's nothing wrong with waiting until you get married."

Carmen dismissed Beth's words out of hand. First of all, she wasn't going to get married and second of all, although she wasn't ready for intercourse yet, she wanted sexual experience and passion in her life.

Carmen did not forgive Beth for saying no. Whenever Beth came into her daughter's room after work to chat about her day and ask about Carmen's, Carmen would look restlessly out the window while her mother talked, or steal a glance at the book she was reading, inwardly rolling her eyes at the way her mother could go on and on about nothing.

At a poetry class after Thanksgiving, Mr Dalgleish introduced Keats's "Ode on a Grecian Urn."

What men or gods are these? What maidens loth?
What mad pursuit? What struggle to escape?
What pipes and timbrels? What wild ecstasy?

He passed around a book with a picture of a Grecian urn and while the students pondered the picture, Mr Dalgleish leaned back, put his feet on the desk, hands behind his head and said, "What wild ecstasy indeed?

"The ecstasy is not that of simple sexual union but arises when the figures of the urn blur into each other, the chaser and the chased become interchangeable.

"I myself had a personal experience of this ecstasy. Last summer when my mistress and I went to Greece . . . "

Mistress! Such a romantic term. It seemed so "man and woman." Carmen felt keenly how confined she was in "boy and girl."

"She is eight years older than I and very womanly. One afternoon we went to a beach that was completely deserted. We had a picnic and some wine and then we made love. Afterwards I was so in love with her, so close to her, she was walking back to me on the beach and she looked so beautiful, I felt myself suddenly transformed. I looked down and I had breasts and wide hips and a triangle of pubic hair. I walked the entire length of the beach like this toward her. And the amazing thing was she saw me like that too."

That was the kind of experience Carmen was looking for. Passionate and transcendent. Teenage sex was completely unappealing to her. She hated words like "horny," she hated the whole notion of letting a guy go so far and no further, first base, second base, that prim control. What Vincent Dalgleish had just described was what she wanted.

"That sounded amazing, didn't it?" she said, walking to April's house to do their homework together.

"I thought it was creepy. Yuck. Can you imagine kissing someone after that?"

Carmen couldn't stop thinking about it. When she imagined the scene, she was Mr Dalgleish walking along the sand, sun glinting off the Mediterranean, and he was waiting for her at the end of the beach, yet gender was diffuse and all around them, and there was no separation.

Beth delivered a baby girl on January 2, and Carmen visited the hospital after school. For two months she had secretly embroidered an off-white, slightly quilted cotton blanket with birds and butterflies and flowers and bulrushes. She had stitched in a bottom corner "love from your big sister Carmen" with peace signs before and after.

It was wrapped in purple tissue paper in the Greek shoulder bag Oscar had given her for her fifteenth birthday. As Carmen approached Beth's bed and caught sight of her mother leaning against the pillows, her hair brushed, lipstick freshly applied, looking toward her expectantly, happily, tears sprung to her eyes. She felt a surge of love and tenderness.

"Her name is Rebecca, did Oscar tell you?" Beth said, as Carmen carefully picked up the little bundle and sat on Beth's bed. She glanced from Rebecca's tiny sleeping face to her mother's hands as Beth gently ripped the tissue around the Scotch Tape of her gift. She unfolded the blanket and read the inscription at the bottom.

"Oh Carmen, it's beautiful, it's absolutely beautiful."

Carmen understood for the first time that her mother had basically been alone in raising her. Oscar had helped, but it had really been Beth who had taken responsibility, Beth who had felt guilty or proud of Carmen's actions, Beth who would have failed or succeeded at parenting.

She left the hospital and walked down Wellesley Avenue in the cold snow, buoyed by love. She felt suddenly adult, free to make her own decisions and embark on her own life. She loved her mother and did not expect another thing from her. She got off at the Eglinton subway stop and decided to walk home instead of taking the bus. On the way home, she went inside a stationery store with a Part-Time Help Wanted sign in the window and filled out a job application. She lied about her age.

She quit synchronized swimming. She had come to detest the above-water part of it, the bright smiles and fey arm movements. Oddly, performing those movements made her feel like she was sinking, losing a struggle against gravity, yet when she was underwater, turning in the turquoise light, thrusting with her arms to lift her legs up above the water, she felt powerful, strong and graceful.

She got the job she applied for and worked Thursday and Friday evenings and all day Saturday, dusting, working the cash register, restocking the shelves. One Friday night she was riding her bicycle home from work at nine-thirty when a limousine pulled up ahead of her and honked lightly. The passenger door opened. She braked a few metres behind the car and stood with one foot on the curb. A man's arm extended out of the door, clothed in a white shirt with cufflinks, and beckoned to her. A voice said, "You're very beautiful. You look like a happy person. Let me give you a ride, there's lots of room in the trunk for your bike. It's not safe for a beautiful young woman like you to be out at night."

This was not Davy Jones.

"Thanks. I like riding."

The hand turned palm up. "I tried." He closed the door. She didn't remount her bicycle until the limo was out of sight, and then she left the main road and weaved through side streets, listening for the sound of a car following her.

9

⌐⊗⊗⊗⌐

THE WHOLE FAMILY was waiting for her at the airport—
Alfred, Isabel, Daniel and Ivan—breezy in their shorts and
sandals, as she struggled with her shoulder bag and suitcase,
perspiring in a long-sleeved shirt and jeans. She'd worn her
favourite pair of jeans, in fact the only pair she ever wore now.
When they needed washing she did it at night so they'd be
ready for the next day. They were covered in patches she'd
sewn on herself with different colours of embroidery thread in
a variety of stitches; they were moulded to her body, but they
were going to be too hot for Mallorca.

"I'm sure she already knows," was what Beth had said when
Carmen asked whether she should tell Isabel about her
father's adultery. "*She* must be able to live with it." So Carmen
had said nothing when she'd seen Isabel last year in
Disneyland among the giant Mickey and Minnie Mice, the
candy floss, hot dogs, screams and lineups, tanning by the
hotel swimming pool, getting chatted up by Goofy. Nor had
she and Alfred ever spoken about it.

They'd been stiff and wary around each other. Friendly on
the surface, and not just on the surface, underneath as well,
but when Carmen returned to Toronto they still hadn't found
a way to bridge the new distance between them.

The first week in Mallorca was spent taking day trips to

different beaches. Carmen built sandcastles with Daniel and Ivan, buried them in the sand, went for long walks on the beach alone, told Isabel and Alfred about school, her report card, her friend April, quitting the synchronized swim team. Alfred was impressed by what a strong swimmer Carmen had become and, she could tell, a little surprised.

One day she struck out for a small island, a little less than a kilometre offshore. She was about fifty metres from shore when it occurred to her she should go back first and tell someone what she was doing, but she didn't feel like turning back. She set out, doing the crawl. As she turned her head to breathe she thought she might have heard someone yelling, but she'd have to stop to find out if it was her they were yelling at, so she kept on.

When she got back Alfred was upset but he refrained from delivering a lecture about being considerate of others. Even Isabel was frowning, and Daniel had been crying. She had ruined their afternoon. "I didn't mean to upset anyone. I had no idea you would worry. I was fine. I'm not even that tired."

Alfred was called unexpectedly back to London to deal with problems in one of the company's major mining projects in Brazil. He apologized to Carmen, but no one seemed particularly bothered by the change in plans.

Isabel and Carmen stopped for espresso at a beachside café on the way back from taking Alfred to the airport. The boys were at the hotel with a babysitting service. Two men who wore love beads and sandals, had long hair and spoke German sat down at a table beside them. They smiled at Carmen and Isabel and eventually one asked Isabel something in faltering Spanish. Isabel answered in English. "Ahhh good, my English is much better than my Spanish," he laughed. His companion smiled at Carmen.

When they left the café, Isabel looked at Carmen. "I think we should have a little fun while we're here, don't you?"

Carmen sat in front of a vanity mirror while Isabel made her up to pass for eighteen so she could get into the nightclub where they'd agreed to meet the Germans. She was wearing Isabel's red high-heeled sandals and a red tie-dye sarong with a matching top that tied under the breasts. She'd never worn makeup. Beth only wore lipstick, so other than trying on Beth's lipstick in Grade 4, Carmen had never really considered it. She was amazed at the transformation makeup could produce.

It was like putting on a Halloween costume, masquerading as another self. So many things about her would have to be different for her to be someone who owned makeup, someone who could apply it with such confidence. She liked the brush of warm evening air on her naked midriff, she liked the way the breeze travelled up her leg in the sarong, she liked the oily lipstick on her lips, the pollen-like weight of mascara on her lashes, the extra height Isabel's shoes gave her, the feeling of being tilted and elongated, her buttocks lifted and ever-so-slightly opened.

She didn't feel glamorous like Isabel, but she felt smooth, gliding, sensual. When one felt this beautiful the pleasure in just sitting, standing or walking made it impossible to think. The pressure of the Germans' eyes looking at her was as exhilarating as jumping into a pool on a hot afternoon.

Her German, Dieter, was the taller one. He had soft brown eyes and a bushy beard, and he was a long way from the boy she'd gone to a movie with in Toronto, a long way from Davy Jones too, or even April's brothers. Not so far away from the poetry teacher.

He talked to her slowly, in thickly accented English, looking in her eyes. Isabel and her German sat opposite, talking and laughing. The four of them got up to dance. During a slow dance Dieter's warm hand rubbed Carmen's back, her bare belly touched his belt buckle. She felt like she was in a trance. He tilted her chin up and kissed her, his tongue warmly filling her mouth.

They sat down while Isabel and the other German danced. Dieter kissed her again. His mouth tasted a bit smoky, like saffron and white wine and corn. His tongue was wide and supple, not snaky like some of the boys she'd kissed. His hand cupped her breast. He leaned over and pressed his thigh against her. The form of doom wasn't specific, but she sensed if she didn't resist, if she didn't stop him, if her sixteen-year-old self didn't manage to say no, there was no one else to intervene. And she wanted to say maybe, yes, to go further, to venture deeper into the cave. She had never experienced anything like this confused mixture of desire and apprehension, a reckless impulse hand in hand with a voice screaming doom, the end of all her plans and hopes, all coming from the pressure of a man's body, a pressure she was turning to like a flower to the sun.

He asked if she'd ever made love before.

"No."

After that, he kissed her gently, kindly. They danced again and he smiled at her with wistful friendliness, not looking at his friend who was still laughing and talking with Isabel.

Over the next week Carmen went walking alone on the beach. She looked for Dieter at the cafés or on the beach, but never saw him again. Besides what could she do if she did see him? Isabel became quite busy and didn't include Carmen in many of her plans.

On the day before their departure she was walking back to the hotel room from the pool when a movement caught her eye. A green lizard charged out of the shrubbery beside the path and ran to a spot about a metre from Carmen's feet. It had red markings behind its ears. Then she saw a beige lizard, slightly bigger than the green one, standing only centimetres away from it, camouflaged against the dry dusty path. She froze.

The green one moved closer, climbed on the beige one's back, bit its neck and struggled to pull it over onto its side. It succeeded after four vigorous yanks. It quickly worked its hind leg over the beige one's leg and inserted a penis. He pumped for about fifteen seconds and then the penis slipped out. The tip was a bright blue-red, round and glistening at the end, like the centre of an orchid.

The female stood back up. The two lizards remained side by side for a couple of minutes, motionless except for their heaving sides. Then the male turned, preparing perhaps to dart back to the shrubbery. A small white gull swooped down, plucked his body up with its beak and flew away. The female turned and ran under the bushes.

SECTION
Two

1

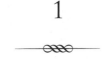

ROMANIA, 1973

ALFRED FELT LIKE PUNCHING THE WALL. Why did He create men and women? It was unbearable. No, really, it was unbearable. *There* was the end of paradise, not biting some apple. The Fall already a done deal when He created them, male and female. Suffering invented—but no one knew. *That* was where the apple came in, a telegram from on high letting them know that God had already done his dirtiest work in making Eve's desires so impossibly different from Adam's.

He'd just hung up from talking with his second ex-wife. He was an unfit father, she said, and she didn't want him setting a bad example for the boys. Her lawyer was going to request twice-monthly visits, no overnights. She didn't trust him not to have some woman fresh off the street lounging around his apartment. And she wanted the house transferred to her name. She felt she'd earned it.

Earned it how? Watching soap operas? Shopping? She equated shopping with work. She thought she was gathering resources by shopping, not spending them. Money was nothing to her. And that she would have the gall to demand anything after hopping into bed with his colleague at work . . . But he would retaliate. He could make accusations of his own. Two could tango.

She'd had the affair publicly, flagrantly; everyone in his office knew except him. What had he done to deserve that? It felt like when he was a boy and school friends had asked him where his mother was. "I don't know."

He already knew what happened with the kids when your marriage broke down. They pined for their mother the whole time they were with you. They wanted more treats and presents and they hugged you, but the hugs didn't feel spontaneous any more. They felt forced and self-conscious. The kids, once your pride and joy, made you feel emptier and lonelier than ever. His favourite time now with the boys was when they were asleep and piled up against him, their cheeks smooth and pale. That was when they felt like his again. And now she wanted to deny him that.

The world could still be his oyster, he blustered to himself, alone in a hotel room in Romania. He was only forty-three, he was getting better-looking with age and, despite Isabel's best efforts, he still had money. Isabel was living with that asshole from work so he didn't have to pay support, only the children's expenses. This could just be a bump. It should just be a bump. You're stuck with who you are after all and life goes on.

Nevertheless, his pain was not abating.

He felt blameless; he was not a bad person, not perfect but not evil or mean. He hoped for sympathy; it felt like his due, though he was unclear as to where it might come from. Sympathy from the universe perhaps, from Mother Nature, female sympathy—though that, he'd discovered, was a brand in particularly short supply. They were not a compassionate gender. At least not for long stretches of time—anything extending past an hour or two.

He finished half a litre of Scotch and went to bed. He should sleep. He was getting up early in the morning to go caving. The idea had come to him in a pub while weeping and drinking with one of his more loyal work colleagues. *You should do something new, something you haven't done for a while, something for yourself.* The next day he'd bought a plane ticket to Romania, whose kilometres of karst landscape contained extensive networks of limestone caves.

He entered the system through a dome pit. He'd hiked in five or six kilometres from the road along a trail. The dome pit was indicated by a sign nailed to a tree. It was surrounded by mossy grass and roots. He changed into his caving clothes, left his other clothes in a bag by the tree, tied a rope around the tree and rappelled down the hole. The smell of underground air, stone, damp earth and faint bat guano restored him instantly to his former self. He was one again with the eighteen-year-old whose whole life had been ahead of him, deciding to strike out on his own and embrace the world. A static tension that had gripped his muscles for months on either side of his spine, a tension he had not been conscious of until now, released as he breathed in the scent of the cave. He almost went limp with relief.

He reached the bottom, unhooked himself from the rope and set off along a passage that according to his map headed west. He progressed for about half an hour, stooping to duck-walk for short intervals, and arrived at a series of interconnected pools that were not marked on his map.

He took off his pack and went over and squatted beside the biggest pool. The light on his helmet illuminated a wide circle and penetrated thirty to forty centimetres down into the water. A white shape floated into this circle of light and startled him. It had long wispy fins and rows of delicate antennae floating out around it. It appeared to bump into something, and changed direction abruptly.

Typhlichthys subterraneus. Angel. He'd read about cave fish but had never seen one. A troglobite—from the Greek *troglos* (cave) and *bios* (life). Confined to caves, unlike the trogloxene (*xenos*, Greek for guest) and troglophile (*phileo*, Greek for love). *I, for example, am a trogloxene.* The fish's vestigial eyes were sightless and its skin appeared to have no pigment whatsoever. It relied on its wispy sensory projections to tell it where things were.

He dug his guidebook out of his knapsack and looked up "Typhlichthys." "The females lay their eggs from an opening in front of their gills and after the eggs have been fertilized, they keep them in their mouths until the guppies are ready to forage for themselves. These fish eat small crayfish, copepods, isopods and amphipods. Occasionally they are cannibalistic."

He smiled and imagined the mother with all the rowdy babies in her mouth. *Oh what the hell, I'll just swallow.*

The book continued. "Cave animals know the difference between night and day and between winter and summer because they're sensitized to the same biurnal changes in gravity that cause ocean tides.

"In fact, one of the ways caves are created is by earth tides. Solids respond to the same changes in gravitational pull from the moon as liquid. This tidal flexing of rock causes displacement at the joints or fault lines, gradually weakening them until water can penetrate and begin the slow process of carving out a cave."

Of course he'd studied this years ago, but he'd forgotten. There were the big changes in rock landscape caused by volcanoes, earthquakes, glaciers and floods and there were the smaller changes caused by earth tides, wind, erosion. Mirroring life, his life, the big changes, divorce, birth, death, disappearances; and the small changes, growing old, creeping alcoholism, slippages of desire.

He watched the fish for about fifteen minutes, then moved on. He wanted to reach a cavern that his map indicated was about two hours away and contained formations of gypsum-rock flowers. He had to follow a passage leading to the left that got tight enough to require a twenty-metre duck-walk before opening into a small chamber. On the opposite side was another dome pit, which should lead to a series of passages that would take him to the cavern.

The opening of the shaft was two metres across. He'd brought his own rope, hammer and stakes but saw that one was already prepared. The metal stake looked new and the rope was even better quality than his. He took hold of it, threaded his rappel rack, locked it and lowered himself over the edge.

He released the rope for drops of roughly thirty centimetres at a time. About a third of the way down the rope's tension suddenly weakened, then gave way entirely. He fell down the rest of the shaft, still gripping his useless rack. His helmet struck a projecting rock on the way down and he lost consciousness.

He came to with his brain screaming *Stupid! Stupid! Stupid!* He'd told no one where he was going. He was supposed to meet Carmen in Paris in ten days, but no one expected to hear from him before that. His only hope was the owner of the *pension* where he was staying. Alfred had asked if the kitchen could prepare sandwiches and a Thermos of hot chocolate for his trip. He'd mentioned to the fellow which cave he was planning to visit and which entrance he was going to use, but whether the man had been paying attention . . .

Excruciating pain seared through one leg. His head throbbed. His mouth was dry. He was shaking with cold. He hadn't even tested the rope, such a basic principle of spelunking, one he'd known for years. *Never use a rope left by someone else.* Micro-organisms in caves caused the fibre to decay invisibly, from the inside out. He turned off his helmet light to conserve the batteries and drifted back into unconsciousness, not caring much if the thread holding him to life snapped, wanting to escape the pain in his leg and the cold.

Death might not be so bad, as long as it was warm and painless. There were no wives in the underworld. No need to worry about being loved.

He regained consciousness more slowly the second time. He remembered what had happened. He felt very cold. Pain seared through his right thigh, and he guessed he'd broken the bone. He tried to summon first-aid instructions from memory. *Do not sit directly on the cave floor. Sit on your pack or some extra clothing to avoid losing body heat.*

He wriggled his pack off, removed a thermal blanket and wrapped it around his shoulders. He turned his helmet light back on, took out a plastic bottle and peed in it, remembering that the body expended heat keeping urine warm in the bladder. Then he tried to look at his leg. He was wearing overalls so he began to roll up the cuff. The pain made him feel like vomiting. Slowly he eased the rough canvas up and was able to see a bulge under the skin where no bulge should be.

He turned his light off again, and wept. He couldn't set that kind of break himself. He couldn't hope to climb back up the shaft, using two arms and only one leg. *Stupid, stupid.* Rescue was his only hope. The bag of clothes he'd left on the surface, visible from the forest trail—which had some litter, suggesting people might use it on weekends. It was Thursday. Maybe someone would notice the bag. Maybe the *pension* owner would look for him. But not until tomorrow at the earliest.

His body relaxed, surprisingly, despite the pain. Now that he was off the stone and mud and sitting on his pack, the baggy overalls and long underwear were keeping him warm.

Time was the problem. It went on for too long. Space, on the other hand, space seemed contained and manageable. For months now he'd mastered time by drinking. He'd counted the hours by the number of drinks. He got out a flask of cognac and took a long swig.

He brought the cave fish to mind, far above him in its dark and coppery liquid home. He let it float through his conscious-ness and calm him down. The fish's feathery gills and projections looked like ruffles, lace fans, frills, rippling as un-uniformly as grass in a spring breeze. And its skin so thin it seemed scarcely a barrier to anything at all, as if the fish were gradually turning itself inside out to avoid touching everything.

This seemed vaguely human. If he could float and not have to touch anything, instead of having to push off from the ground or grip something above to pull himself up, if he didn't have to touch anything he could just float on out of here right now and his problems would be over.

A week after his rescue (he'd been found delirious and badly dehydrated), he set out from the *pension* on crutches to eat at a restaurant in the town's main square. He ordered a big plate of dumplings and chicken paprikash and a bottle of red wine. He felt alive again, really for the first time since Isabel had left him.

The doctors were not recommending he travel yet, which was fine with him. He was content to stay in this small town and recuperate for another week or two. He'd phoned Carmen. She was sleeping overnight at a girlfriend's house so he had had to explain to Beth why he would be unable to meet his daughter in Paris as planned. He'd arrange for a visit at Christmas instead.

The waitress who brought his dinner was a dark-haired beauty with wide eyes, a thin waist, narrow hips. He invited her to join him when she got a chance, saying he could not finish the wine alone.

After closing, she took him to her one-room flat. She offered him plum wine and then they made love. Her orgasm seemed wrenched from her, torn piece by piece. Afterwards she was alternately moody and jocular. He felt like he had just shot a river and gone over a waterfall and he loved everything—the difference in the shape of her nostrils, one from the other, the dust under the sideboard where she kept her kitchenware, the lustre of his own thick but pliable toenail. He sang as he hobbled vigorously back to the *pension* through the dark rain.

His life was not over yet.

2

AFTER HE RETURNED from Romania, Alfred requested a job that required more travelling. He was sent to oversee mining projects in Chile, Canada, India, South Africa and Brazil. He visited Carmen while in Canada. Six months later he was tired of moving around all the time and asked for a less transient position. They posted him in Brazil.

In Brazil, Alfred was mainly lonely. He felt unrooted and floating and unloved by any living thing. The reprieve from depression he'd experienced after his fall was brief. His sons, as was to be expected, had stayed in London with Isabel. Their geographical distance made them seem temporally distant too, as though they were from another lifetime—a good dream he'd had on a good night, but no longer real in the dissociative reality of his waking existence.

He got in the habit of drinking a martini before lunch, wine with lunch, caipirinhas before dinner, wine with dinner, more caipirinhas after dinner, then whisky before bed. He had a girlfriend, not even a girlfriend, a woman he went to dinner with and slept with, called Mariella. She was large-breasted, quiet; she played with her ice cubes and wore cheap tight dresses. When she evanesced, he started skipping dinner altogether, telling himself he needed to keep his waistline down to remain eligible for the beautiful young ladies of Brazil.

Occasionally he'd skip lunch too. He never skipped breakfast, which he considered an essential meal.

The booze masked all his desires, except for an occasional urge for sex. He'd taken to calling a high-class escort agency, a number he got from a co-worker whose wife and children lived in the U.S. Alfred had used call girls before, but only with other guys, after a night on the town, just for the hell of it. This was the first time he'd gone out of his way on his own to call.

At first it had been exciting knowing he was going to get sex without having to go through the usual song and dance, that it was guaranteed, that he could ask for what he wanted and it would not be withheld. He could order room service at a decent hotel and enjoy himself, free of children, accusations, demands for attention, apologies, money, love. It was good value, no question. But afterwards he felt a tinge of sadness as his escort talked about things he had no connection to, and he noticed specific mannerisms in the way she dressed—whether she put her bra on backward around her waist to do it up or asked him to attach the hooks, how she bent over to put her shoes on—with each gesture invariably reminding him of a past girlfriend or wife, or if not, making him think which men in this woman's life these gestures would be familiar to. The absence of love began whispering around the room and he looked forward to his next drink with added fervour.

All his male acquaintances in Brazil were expatriates who seemed content to spend the rest of their lives taking pleasure in what they'd escaped. They revelled in having left the northern hemisphere behind, and with it plodding family life: the suburban materialism of lawns, appliances and cars which they'd traded for a colonial materialism of land and gems, servants, *fazendas*, young women, illegitimate children. Northern suburbs replaced by a roughshod tropical opulence.

When the decadence of his city life finally got unbearable he joined a spelunking club and went caving. The caves in Brazil had the same or a slightly lower temperature than the surface, often staying near 30 degrees Celsius, and one had to be careful not to get dehydrated. Most systems were still unmapped, which he liked. When he couldn't go caving he often went horseback riding in the country, a gun packed in his saddlebag, looking at iguanas and chameleons, birds and snakes along the way.

Six months after his arrival in Brazil his boss called him in and told him the company was offering him a very senior position in Argentina, Director of Field Operations, one of a triumvirate that ran everything there. The salary was not much higher but the job was a significant promotion and came with monthly paid vacations to anywhere in the world.

"You could visit your sons every month if you wanted," he said.

"We need a particular kind of man for our operations in Argentina because of the political unrest there. We need someone without a family to worry about. Someone courageous and good at their work. There have been a number of kidnappings of foreign executives; the danger is quite real, I'm afraid."

When Alfred said he might be interested his boss handed him a box of memos, manifestos and speeches and instructed him to read through them as soon as possible and let him know his decision.

The documents had been drafted by business leaders and various personnel in the military in Argentina. One memo in particular described how Argentina must fight on the side of civilization and democracy, "for the continuance of initiative and inspiration, for creativity, even for nonconformity." For personal freedom. "This is a war between dialectic materialism and idealistic humanism . . . We are fighting against nihilists, against agents of destruction whose only objective is destruction itself, although they disguise this with social crusades." The champions of excellence, creativity, freedom, health, the last bastion against decadence, atheism, an ultimate and terrifying reductionism of the human soul to worker bee in a vast, unthinking hive.

Alfred felt himself coming alive again, shaking off the decadent nihilism he himself had succumbed to; he felt like a hungover warrior recalled to battle. His heart stirred. He'd inherited nothing, really nothing; he'd worked hard for his money and the thought of some over-privileged, self-righteous, commie-loving asshole presuming to kidnap him, to assassinate him, to steal his money and deliver a lecture about right and wrong as melodic accompaniment to murder and theft made him feel eager to accept the challenge. For the first time since his second marriage had ended, he felt the stirring of real passion.

He got in his car and drove to the stable. He would stand for something goddamnit, he thought as he saddled up the horse he usually rode. He'd show the commie bastards they couldn't just walk in and take what they wanted, what other people had worked hard for. How could those people go on, after Stalin, the Gulag, proclaiming their superior goodness, their selflessness and altruism. This was his chance to join a group that would show those bastards that they could be met with force, they could be stopped, they would be crushed, their "goodness" unmasked. He set out in a gallop along a new road through undeveloped hills.

This time he'd face them with a gun, with adult strength, and a whole army, navy and air force behind him.

I have made myself who I am, he thought somewhat later, high in his saddle, alcohol in his blood, humidity and lush growth and butterflies round his head, a red dirt swathe through the green jungle ahead of him. *I have created my life alone from nothing. They will not make me suffer again. This time I'll have a gun.* He spurred the horse faster and faster down the road, past tin shacks along the roadside, an occasional gate to a farmhouse surrounded by barbed wire.

The Russian soldiers laughed as they took turns with his aunts. His father told him to run, run ahead down the road, *I'll give you a head start,* smiling at his superior power. *Your mother was pretty, she didn't think your father was good enough, she liked men. Don't move Liebchen, don't fall, I'll be right back, just stay there.* He felt himself falling and gripped the reins, bringing the horse to a standstill. He was startled to see how the beast sweated and frothed at the mouth.

His apartment in Buenos Aires had good security, an underground parking lot with a remote-controlled door, and was situated in a neighbourhood where streets were lined with leafy trees, balconies had ornate wrought-iron grilles and the facades of buildings were carved in Greco-Roman swirls. A general in the Argentine navy inhabited a whole floor in his apartment building.

In Brazil everything had been falling away, rotting, decaying under his fingertips. Nothing stayed precious there; everything valuable seemed to become garbage overnight. Life was a race with garbage; bodies did not return to dust, but to garbage. The sense of disorder, disintegration, hallucinogenic impermanence had overwhelmed him. Of course his drinking was a contributing factor, but not the only one, not the only one.

He felt better in Buenos Aires. It had an air of order, tranquility, old-world culture predating the world wars. There was old money here, older even than in Spain. People played polo, spoke formally, covered furniture with antique lace. Homes and shops boasted the best selection of European antiques Alfred had ever seen.

No one would dream of walking down a street in a string-bikini top the way they did in Rio. Clothing was elegant and tailored. People were well-coiffed; nails filed, cleaned, painted; suits pressed; stockings unrun; the cologne and perfumes expensive.

During the first week of this new life, Alfred bought books on military history and theory. They were dry going but he delighted in the discovery of the following sequence of quotes, which he felt to be witty and true:

Karl von Clausewitz: "War is the continuation of politics by other means."

Juan Perón: "Politics is the continuation of war by other means."

General Osiris Villegas: "Peace is the continuation of war by other means."

He particularly liked the irony of the last quote, the acknowledgment that all life was struggle, contest, lobbying, argument. He went into an antique shop and arranged to have these quotes done in calligraphy and framed in an antique gold-leaf frame. They would, he felt, give his apartment flair and a personal touch. The woman at the framing shop asked what they meant. He replied, "No one is innocent."

One Sunday he went for a walk in the park near his apartment. A man was flying a kite, his son shouting and running beside him, a puppy gambolled by the child's feet. Alfred was suddenly stricken by a desire for another wife. He didn't want more children particularly, yet he couldn't imagine living with a woman and not starting a family. Too quiet, too dead.

The next week he hinted to the Director of Finance, a chap from Australia, that he'd like to be introduced to a young lady if he knew any. "Sure mate. No worries. You want more of a companion or just some nookie?"

Alfred laughed a little too forcefully. "I'm not even forty-five, man! With these good looks I shouldn't have to pay for female company. In fact, my man, I think they should pay me for the privilege of gazing upon this distinguished visage. I just can't stand spending all day with you blokes, then going home every night to dust the statuary."

The following week he got an invitation to dinner at a South African colleague's house. A petite Argentine with long straight blonde hair was seated across from him. Dora. She was very quiet. She worked as a hostess in the restaurant at an exclusive lawyers' club. She smoked between courses. Her brother worked at one of the company's mines in Patagonia as a liaison between production and head office.

The woman his Australian friend had set him up with sat beside him. She was elegant, engaging, self-possessed and fairly cheerful. She'd known most of the people at the table for twenty years or more. She was forty-one, had been widowed for two years, and had two children—a girl the same age as Carmen, nineteen, and a fifteen-year-old son. Alfred liked her well enough, but felt no sexual attraction.

It wasn't that he disliked women over thirty; he liked them fine, he enjoyed their company, but he was discovering that he felt no sexual attraction to them. Stone cold. He seemed to need something young and lively coming at him in the dark, someone not entirely in control of herself, unformed in some way, malleable and scrappy. He didn't necessarily need a woman he could dominate, but he wanted someone he could try to dominate, someone who would fight back, someone whose resistance he could conquer and reconquer. He didn't want someone with whom such a fight would seem undignified, or worse, be permanently wounding. He didn't want someone he could break.

Break. China hitting a wooden floor. Aunt Freda on the dining-room table, head turned sideways, eyes shut.

He forced himself to listen to the table conversation. They were discussing a car bomb that had exploded outside a general's home, killing his gardener and injuring a postman, but no one else. Everyone agreed what a terrible thing, and how lucky no one in the family was hurt, and how awful about the gardener, and what savages they were, the people who did such things and stupid too since they only succeeded in killing one of the workers they were supposedly championing. Most of the men at the table were possible targets.

After dinner everybody went to the living room for liqueurs. Alfred watched Dora, who was wearing a tight miniskirt and boots that went up past her knees. She looked like a doll in her perfectly proportioned wide-eyed stillness. She wasn't really his type but when he smiled at her, she smiled back.

3

A DEEP-SEA FISH, a gargoyle creature with a cavern jaw and sharp teeth, pulsed dull wattage through the black water to attract a mate. Carmen willed the fish to swim closer as she dozed in the sun in her bikini.

She'd chosen the deep-sea angler for her second-year research project because of its mouth and because it reminded her of her father's rapturous descriptions of the cave fish Typhlichthys, although instead of being strangely balletic, it was strangely awful.

It lived in total darkness, completely isolated from the surface, yet unlike troglobitic species which also lived in eternal darkness, this fish's eyes were not vestigial. At such depths food supply was limited and could only sustain a small population, so individuals had to travel great distances to find a mate. The angler males couldn't afford to miss seeing the faint pulsing light generated by the females.

Carmen checked her tan line by moving the elastic of her bikini bottom. The contrast was satisfying. She refastened the back of her bikini top, put on swim goggles and dove into the small swimming pool of a private club Alfred had the use of. She swam a hundred laps, climbed out, towelled herself dry, got a Diet 7Up and pretzels from the clubhouse and sat down on a lounge chair.

She felt clean, spare, ready for the future. Her face had lost most, though not quite all, of its baby fat and her gold-brown eyes were alert and attentive. Her hair was long and had a wild pre-Raphaelite look, highlighted by red lips and winter paleness. Her chin jutted a little, suggesting both stubbornness and a willingness to take shots squarely on the chin. A slight layer of defeat was revealed in the barely perceptible way her shoulders folded in.

She'd gone through a chunky period in Grades 11, 12 and the first half of 13. After returning from Mallorca she'd retreated to her bedroom, wrapped herself in an old satin eiderdown and read Harlequin romances and the complete works of Jane Austen, Thomas Hardy and D.H. Lawrence while gorging on peanut-butter cookies. She decided she didn't want to be as annoying as Jane Austen's characters, as simpy or bitchy as D.H. Lawrence's, as doomed as Thomas Hardy's, or as spunky as the Harlequin heroines, but she was unsure what she did want to be. It was a painfully self-conscious period.

She started riding a bicycle everywhere because it seemed the most invisible form of transit. She preferred moving through the city quickly—smelling, hearing, seeing—while avoiding being seen. She found a second-hand record store that had turntables with headphones so you could listen before you bought, and this led her to B.B. King, Janis Joplin, Cream, Junior Walker, Simon and Garfunkel. She also liked the English groups Jethro Tull and the Strawbs.

She delighted in her baby sister Rebecca, whom she took to the library, the park, the corner store and to show off over at April's house. She'd urge Beth and Oscar to go out so she could have the house (and the fridge) to herself; she would play with Rebecca and then when the child went to sleep, Carmen snacked and read or watched TV.

In the summer between Grade 12 and Grade 13, a month before visiting Alfred in Brazil to make up for the visit cancelled because of his caving accident, she reached a pitch of pent-up self-loathing. She felt stuporous and numb, insulated from the world by fluffy yellow fat. Her brain spun uselessly around in her skull and reading, like any drug, was becoming less effective as an escape. One day she'd gone out riding, just to get out of the house, and had passed a tattoo and piercing shop on Queen Street.

On an impulse she went in. She had no interest in getting her ears pierced and she thought tattoos were ugly, but she wanted to do something. She'd seen pictures of women from India with studded earrings in one nostril; she visualized herself with one, a small garnet or lapis lazuli or turquoise. She asked the guy in the shop if the hole would ever close and he assured her it would after about a year of non-use.

Mysteriously it was if the needle puncturing her skin acted like a pressure valve releasing the emotions that had been coming to a head inside her. Gradually she stopped eating cookies, started swimming again and felt less excruciatingly exposed.

Beth had been upset by the nose stud, but she was exhausted with trying to work full time, take care of a two-year-old and be supportive of Oscar, who had been laid off work. "I hope they used disinfectant," was all the censure she could muster.

When she'd arrived in Brazil Alfred didn't even notice it he was so preoccupied by his own life. He took her to restaurants, horseback riding, to a beach resort at Ubatuba, empty because it was winter in Brazil and a little rainier than usual. He confided all his troubles to her.

"I seem to have bad luck in my choice of women. Maybe I should get you to pick next time. You seem to have such good insights."

She liked having him to herself, liked being his confidante, hearing things no other eighteen-year-old daughter was likely to hear about their father. She liked her new role as the only woman in his life he could count on (she didn't tell him about the Germans in Mallorca), but when he started ranting about Isabel's nymphomania, her shopping habits, against women in general, she felt uncomfortable and earnestly tried to correct his impressions.

After she'd been there ten days, she ambled into the kitchen of his São Paulo apartment for breakfast, still in her pyjamas, hair unbrushed. He stared at her nose.

"When did you get that? Is it a new style in Canada?" he asked carefully.

"I felt like doing something different. I got it about a month ago. It's from Indian culture. I think it looks beautiful."

"It's very nice. But let's hope you don't look to African culture next time you feel like doing something different. I might have a hard time adjusting to one of those plates in your bottom lip."

She finished her 7Up. Julio Iglesias was playing on the clubhouse radio. She stretched in the lawn chair, enjoying the music's romantic, Latin atmosphere, music she would never in a hundred years have listened to in Canada; Alfred played Julio whenever he was in a good mood.

She returned to the whopping big textbook she'd been reading, propping it up against the waist of her bikini so as not to interfere with tanning her stomach. The Argentine sun was melting away the last traces of Canadian winter. Her blood flowed easily through the expanded capillaries to the surface of her skin; it ran toward contact with the outside world, giving her body's heat away free of charge. Her cheeks glowed and she felt a burst of joy and promise.

The female was the big one in the deep-sea angler species,

often twenty thousand times heavier than the male. As she glided through the dense black water, the tiny male would swim up and sink his teeth into her. The cells of his jaw and tongue gradually fused with her flesh until he became like an external fetus developing in reverse, shrinking and growing more dependent on the female host. His digestive organs withered and disappeared as they became redundant, along with his heart (he gave her his heart); all his food and blood eventually came from her. Only his sex organs grew. When the female was ready to lay eggs, the hormones in her blood induced him into a kind of sperm-releasing labour.

Her textbook didn't indicate whether the male got to keep his brain. It made sense that it would wither too since neither the male nor female would benefit from it any longer, but Carmen imagined it intact. His eyes darted back and forth as his body betrayed him, trapped him, tossed his autonomy over to the female like a scrap, *Here, you have it*, a mere hindrance to the production of more angler babies as Mother Nature turned him into nothing more than a great big pair of testicles controlled by the female's hormones.

The authors did not describe this mating system as monogamy, though Carmen figured one would be hard-pressed to find a more unadulterated example.

She sipped her pop and imagined the female angler in all her terrible glory, the nightmare body with its nightmare appendage, the faint luminescence illuminating only cold liquid darkness. Her fine sharp teeth grazed Carmen's hand and then the cavernous mouth, black on black, receded.

Carmen could hardly wait to tell her father about *this* species. What triumph! A reproductive strategy that was quirky perhaps, but nonetheless really existed. Who was the breadwinner here? Big mama. Who existed merely to propagate the species? Little daddy.

The circumstances of their lives had changed somewhat since their brief airborne conversation about the essential nature of men and women—the one Carmen thought of as their frog reincarnation conversation. Alfred was no longer married or even a complete bachelor any more. His girlfriend Dora lived with him, though she seemed to keep her things somewhere else.

Carmen had stopped wearing nose studs so the hole had already grown over. She'd had a serious boyfriend for the last half of Grade 13, Eric, a friend of one of April's brothers. He wore a beat-up leather jacket he said had been his grandfather's, and owned a motorcycle. His hair was neither short nor long, and he wore faded jeans and a white shirt. He was studying economics with April's brother at the University of Guelph.

They'd gone to a few movies, riding his motorcycle afterwards around Toronto or out into the countryside late at night. In the beginning Beth waited up and tried to punish Carmen's lateness but Carmen felt herself to be beyond curfews. Delicately she'd explained to Beth that she was on the pill, she'd be fine. Beth said she worried that the pill was not meant for someone so young, whose body might still be developing, but Carmen, who'd expected her mother to be pleased by how responsible she was, interpreted Beth's concern as a last-ditch effort to control her.

Carmen didn't actually lose her virginity until the week before grad. Eric was a gentle person and his pressure on her had been uninsistent. She wasn't sure how much it would hurt, so although she became very aroused fooling around, she didn't necessarily expect sex to be all that pleasurable in the beginning.

She'd moved to Vancouver to go to university near the sea. She had broken up with Eric, shipped her few belongings out to the West Coast and followed by train with her bicycle, backpack, bathing suit and sleeping bag. For a month she got off at whatever stop she felt like, strapped her backpack and sleeping bag to her rack, and rode to a lake, a town, a park, or the next train stop. She could ride one hundred kilometres on a good day, without wind. She usually slept in a youth hostel, bed-and-breakfast place, cheap motel or occasionally in campgrounds near a family.

Her only unpleasant experience had been when a heavy-set man in his mid-forties followed her in a car. Whenever he tried to get out of the car to grab her she pedalled away; when he got back in his car to catch up to her, she stopped her bike and waited. Finally he swore at her and left. The feeling of freedom she'd had was diminished by this incident and she always felt watchful afterwards.

In Vancouver she'd rented a room on the top floor of a rooming house near Commercial Drive that had a view of the mountains from the small attic window. She'd set up her turntable, her desk and chair, and bought colourful pillows to make her bed seem more couch-like during the day. She was listening to the Clash these days, the Sex Pistols, Devo, Talking Heads, the Pretenders, and a few folk singers—Bruce Cockburn, Joni Mitchell, Buffy Sainte-Marie. She had a part-time job waitressing Thursday, Friday and Saturday nights at a restaurant downtown and attended Simon Fraser University during the week.

She was studying first-year biology with the intention of specializing in marine biology. The textbook she was reading was for a third-year course, "Reproductive Strategies in Isolated or Sparse Ecosystems." She had begged the department head to make an exception for her and sworn she'd be able to handle the assignments. He relented with an exasperated wave, warning her that her marks would be lower than if she waited for third year when she'd have the necessary academic framework for the course. Carmen didn't care. She needed a taste of where she was heading, something more stimulating and challenging than the bland assembly-line diet of first-year prerequisite courses. Besides, she thought she could handle it.

The course was fascinating. They were studying animal life at high altitudes, extreme temperatures, extreme depths, in caves and underwater vents, in deserts. The only thing she didn't like was the way all extraordinary behaviours and adaptations were eventually explained away as being for the survival of the species.

She found the premise that everything in the universe existed merely to propagate itself depressing. Even the survival of the individual was reduced to a mere necessary precondition for the propagation of the species. It was like her father's theories about women expanded to the whole universe, all of life determined by gender and sex, personal obliteration irrelevant as long as you had babies that survived to have more babies.

In an idle moment in class, Carmen mused that none of her professors had big families. One had no children; another, two teenagers; another, one baby. Didn't they measure themselves by the theories they taught? Were they resigned to being biological failures, or did they think, because they were studying life, they were above it in some way? Was it possible they just hadn't bothered to translate what they taught to their own personal lives?

The only people she knew who might succeed in becoming grandparents to a horde were April's parents and her own father, who intended to marry again and had admitted he couldn't imagine a marriage without children.

She marked her page, closed the book and heaved it into her bag. She stared for a moment at the black lines marking lanes painted on the bottom of the pool. The premise that the purpose of all life was survival of the species, in other words reproduction, seemed tautological. Without reproduction, obviously, people wouldn't exist . . . but did it necessarily follow that that was the purpose of their existence?

She changed into her clothes and went into the clubhouse for a coffee. Someone had left an Argentine newspaper on the table. She'd chosen Spanish as her elective course and she was able to surmise from the photograph and the few words she knew that the Bee Gees were in Buenos Aires to give a concert and women were following them everywhere.

She felt a bit blue. For all the angler fish might be a triumph in her arguments with her father, she didn't want to spend her life swimming around the darkness with some minnow attached to her butt.

She'd been dating a guy in medical school whom she'd been drawn to because he spoke with great passion about justice and politics. He'd read Marx, Lenin, Mao, Franz Fanon, and belonged to the Communist Party of Canada—Marxist-Leninist. He volunteered at a clinic in an underprivileged part of town. They hadn't had sex because he intended to remain a virgin until marriage. Carmen was drifting, listening to his ideas, going out to dinner with him, asking him questions, gradually forming her own opinions about what he thought.

His utopian map of the future had begun to make her feel claustrophobic and restless and when she imagined having sex with him, there was something unpleasantly domestic and confining about it.

A week before her visit to her father, they'd gone out for dinner at a Chinese restaurant downtown and had missed the start time of the movie they were planning to see. On the street corner Carmen suggested checking out a new disco she'd heard about. He'd looked away and said, "No." She'd asked gingerly if he didn't like dancing and he'd taken off his glasses and explained angrily, his voice rising, "Discos are an opiate for the masses. They are a way for capitalist pigs to get rich while keeping workers distracted from reality, from the inequities of the system. They are about indiscriminate fucking, about losing your self, your sense of social responsibility. I don't want to go somewhere I have to park my brain at the door." The anger in his voice drew looks from passersby and he'd caught himself and said more quietly, "How about a folk club?"

"But you can't dance to folk music."

"Square dancing's fun."

"*Square* dancing?" She'd stared at him incredulously. Snowflakes had begun to fall, the street lights illuminating the soft descent around their heads.

"But parking your brain is the whole point. Losing yourself in the music, merging with the crowd. It's a relief not to think all the time. Dancing is Dionysian, primal, it's as old as our species."

"Primal? Read reactionary." Neither of them had called since that night.

She paid the bartender for her coffee and stood in front of the clubhouse waiting for Alfred to pick her up. Alfred was always late and while she waited she observed that Buenos Aires had a disproportionate number of very handsome men. She also observed that they looked right through her.

Dora was in the front passenger seat so Carmen climbed in the back.

"How did you like the club?" Alfred asked.

"Great. It's luxury to get a suntan while I study. The pool's too small for serious swimming, but I'm not complaining. How was your day?"

"Disaster. Inflation went over 300 percent today and they're adding another zero to the currency. All our costs have suddenly gone sky high. We have to recalculate all our employees' wages. This country is a disaster. Let's hope Monsieur Galtieri can instill some order and discipline. That will help."

"I guess that means you'll be working long hours."

"That's likely, yes. We'll still do the yacht trip to Uruguay with the boys, but until then you ladies will have to amuse yourselves."

Carmen looked at the back of Dora's head. Her blonde hair reminded Carmen of Tressy, and Carmen imagined a key in Dora's back to shorten or lengthen her hair.

"I'm planning to explore on my own some of the neighbourhoods where Jorge Luis Borges set his stories. He's my favourite writer."

Dora didn't speak English so Carmen didn't have to worry about hurting her feelings.

"I wouldn't mind doing some shopping though. I need white pants and a pair of sandals. Maybe we could do that in the afternoon."

"Wait a day. I'll get your money changed on the black market tomorrow. It's good we didn't change any yet. After today your Canadian dollars will get almost double the rate."

"That building on the left," Alfred said, "behind the wall, the long orangey-pink one, is known as the Casa Rosada, the pink palace. At the moment the former president of the nation, Isabel Perón, is under house arrest there. Her lover and right-hand man, Lopez Rega, rumoured to be a practitioner of black magic, has disappeared with a huge chunk of the nation's wealth and has yet to be found. That is the quality of people democracy brings to Argentina," he concluded.

"This place needs a dictatorship. It's not ready for democracy yet. It's still too young."

Carmen, still thinking vaguely of Tressy, wondered what Isabel Perón looked like. Was she in a pink room? Were there handsome Argentine men guarding her?

She drifted into a sexual fantasy in which she was Isabel, and the guards were indeed handsome Argentines, and what could she do, her hands were tied?

4

ALFRED, DORA AND CARMEN were invited to a barbecue at the home of one of Alfred's colleagues. Carmen looked forward to the evening because the hosts had a son and daughter in their early twenties who had invited Carmen to go out dancing afterwards with a group of their friends.

"Do you have anything to wear?" Dora asked tactfully.

It had occurred to Carmen that her clothes might be one of the reasons Argentine men didn't notice her. They were too baggy and sexless. Argentine women wore either tight jeans and high heels or tailored skirts, dresses and suits.

Dora took Carmen to a neighbourhood with lots of boutiques and exclusive shops. She was not an ebullient shopping partner, but she was patient and firm in her appraisals of what looked good on Carmen and what didn't. By the end of the morning Dora had nixed anything dowdy and successfully steered Carmen toward tighter, more revealing clothes.

Carmen's Canadian money was like gold on the Argentine black market. It was like finding a money tree. She could buy three pairs of expensive shoes for the price of an ordinary pair in Canada. Suddenly she could afford leather and silk, snakeskin belts, gold jewellery.

She put the clothes she'd been wearing in the shopping bags and donned her new clothes—tight white pants, black high-heeled sandals, a yellow silk shirt, sunglasses. She was transformed into a Latin woman, a *Porteña*, except that she was still taller than most, had broader shoulders and wore her hair in a wild mane.

After lunch Dora had to rush off to a hair appointment and Carmen insisted she could find her own way around the city on the public train. Alfred had told her which stop to get off at for the Jewish garment district.

From Borges's stories she'd imagined narrow streets on sunny gentle slopes with one-storey buildings and hidden gardens and courtyards. Instead the buildings were tall and the streets wide. Everything seemed shadowy and dim even though it was mid-afternoon. Many of the buildings had signs on the first, second and third storeys advertising wholesale fabric, tailor shops, clothing manufacturers, and leather goods.

This did not seem like the kabbalistic world of labyrinths where infinity lurked around every corner and dream and reality intertwined, where mysterious alphabets and texts embodied the universe. She did, however, sense something displaced, not quite at home, different from the rest of the city.

She turned onto smaller side streets, hoping to find there the Borgesian quality she sought. She passed an old synagogue made of beige stone blocks. She hesitated, then went back to look more closely. She walked up wide front steps to a large wooden door, tried the handle. It was locked. Blood was painted on the masonry beside the door. Real blood. There was nothing on the ground. She looked around, but there was no one to ask what it meant, what had happened.

A car screeched by, and she jumped and turned. As it careened around the corner she thought she saw a foot come up in the back window. She felt uneasy in the dream-like atmosphere of the empty street and retraced her steps to the train.

As she walked she became self-conscious of her tight white pants and high-heeled sandals. The women in this neighbourhood wore longer skirts, looser pants, more modest dress, and she felt as though she was exposing something that shouldn't be exposed, uncovering something that wasn't meant to be uncovered.

She'd drunk a double screwdriver at Alfred's apartment and three glasses of wine at the barbecue; by the time she arrived at the club with the other young people and ordered a whisky, she was quite tipsy. She wore a black jersey wraparound dress without a bra and with her suntan and newly shaved legs she felt beautiful.

The club was dark and smoky. She danced with Eduardo, a young man from the barbecue, and with his crazy friend, Salvador. Samba music came on and everyone in the club, friends and strangers alike, started dancing in a chain, each person holding the hips of the person in front. The chain snaked around the room, weaving through tables and chairs.

It was like being in a fiery underworld, or in a dragon's mouth, dancing, exulting in its sharp teeth and steamy breath, her voice hoarse, her skin salty and wet, her energy boundless.

Eduardo was trying to convince her she wouldn't get pregnant. He could withdraw before ejaculating. It was a point of pride.

"I do it every time," he claimed.

"Not very romantic, are you?" She laughed at the tactlessness of his comment.

He turned his head away in frustration, sighing with annoyance. She felt momentarily inadequate, sexually domestic rather than exotic or extreme. The girl next door. Always the peahen, never the peacock.

Eduardo was the ideal Argentine man, just above medium height, a muscular hairless body, a head of thick wavy dark hair, a subtly patrician profile, strong chin, dark brown eyes, large Adam's apple. A polo player, from a family of saddle makers, or rather a family of bosses of saddle makers. He was smooth.

But birth control was a subject, perhaps the only subject, on which Carmen was completely inflexible. She was not going to get pregnant unless she planned to.

They had conversed, in her limited Spanish and his limited English, over the music at the club. When the place closed at four in the morning Eduardo had offered to drive Carmen back to her father's apartment. They started kissing in the car and quickly got aroused. He said he desired her, that she was very intelligent and beautiful, and she replied she desired him too. He'd apologized that he couldn't take her back to his house because he lived with his mother, but he knew a motel where people went that was discreet and inexpensive.

Over the bed hung a framed print of two black bulls twisting round a torero in skin-tight black pants and a short jacket embroidered with jewels and sequins. In North American terms the outfit would have been feminine: the short pants, the tightness of the clothes, the slimness of the man's physique, the flamboyance of the colours. Yet the silhouette was unmistakably male—strutting, proud.

It looked as though the torero had just waved his red cape in front of the bull and swept it to the side where he held it pinned to his right hip. The bull was charging. The red in the painting suggested the bull's rage and the man's courage.

This was a dance between two living beings, each threatening to penetrate the other's skin, each threatening to paint the dirt red with the other's blood. The torero knew the lethal sharpness of life.

Eduardo, having determined that sulking was not going to make her give in, looked at her over his shoulder, cocked his head, and smiled. "Okay, okay. I'll go see. But I'm sad you have no confidence in me."

She lay back in the bed, which enfolded her. It had been a soft bed to start with and the springs had long ago lost their resilience. Here she was, in a motel room somewhere on the outskirts of the labyrinthine city of Buenos Aires, with a handsome stranger, no parents or teachers or school—and it felt like the adventure she'd always wanted and that her father had told her she couldn't have because she was a girl.

Eduardo returned with two condoms.

She lay beneath him, thinking that his muscles were more like the bull's than the torero's, and was both aroused and stunned.

It wasn't reproduction she was engaged in, she'd made sure of that, and it wasn't love. Nor was it lust exactly because how could she know what it would be like with him? It was like the wolf dream she used to have, but instead of lying silent and paralyzed in her bed, she was inviting the wolf into bed with her, seeing what it was like to kiss a mouth with big sharp teeth and a ravenous appetite, what it was like to let him inside her.

He opened her legs with his knees. Her hands touched his buttocks, she felt his penis poking the side of her thigh. The instinct to reproduce was trumping everything else. Eduardo's penis penetrated; the commitment was made: orgasm and risk, sex and death.

"I should get you back home," he said later. "I don't want your father angry with me."

Carmen laughed and there was a bitterness in her laugh. "I've got a long way to go before I get near his record. Besides he doesn't care about that." Which was true. He'd never questioned her about sex. Never cautioned her. Perhaps he didn't feel he had the right. It made her feel unclaimed though, available to whoever might want her, with only her own voice to say yes or no.

Eduardo dropped her off at home.

She wanted to see him again but he never returned any of her calls. She even went by his family's saddle shop, but it was always closed. She'd never been rejected before and the pain was so intense she could hardly breathe. Perhaps he had a girlfriend he'd been cheating on, or he was conquest-driven and she'd been conquered and was therefore of no more interest. Or perhaps he didn't like her. Or perhaps in Argentine culture any girl whose reputation her father didn't care about wasn't worth seeing twice.

5

Daniel and Ivan arrived from Britain. Alfred had arranged to use the financial director's yacht for a five-day cruise on the Rio de la Plata and the Uruguay River before Carmen had to return to Vancouver.

"It's so good to have all my family together at last," he proclaimed as they all sat on the deck, watching the suburbs of Buenos Aires pass by. He expressed his joy by trying to grab Dora's ass every chance he got. She, however, perhaps sensing the affection was displaced somehow and not meant precisely for her, was not receptive, which made him even more persistent.

Daniel had a sulky preteen look. His hair was shaggy and his brown eyes were moody and he looked like he was gathering mass in preparation for a big growth spurt. Ivan was still a child. His sandy hair was shaggy too (Alfred proclaimed an intention to march them both down to the barber as soon as possible) but his hazel eyes were lively and full of laughter.

The first day Alfred hovered over the three of them, anxious that Carmen and the boys should feel a family connection. He listened intently when they spoke to each other about lunch or school. They were politely curious about one another, not jealous of their father's attention, wary but friendly, nothing more.

Dinner was served by the dour Argentine captain whom Alfred both respected and liked to tease. "When we get back we are invited for another *chorasco* at the home of the Director of Communications this time. His wife is American so the boys will have someone to talk to."

"She's a Jew," Dora said to the boys. Dora imagined she had a special rapport with Daniel, since they liked the same heavy-metal rock music. "Loud and pushy. She might as well be an Indian she's so uncultured."

Dora, queen of slumber, fan of Aerosmith, painter of toenails and batter of eyelashes, cuddly Dora who might not be too smart but treated him well enough, had revealed over the months a certain contempt for Jewish, Black and Indian people that Alfred did not share.

"I heard that Argentina was anti-Semitic," Carmen said to Dora in her rapidly improving Spanish, "but I thought they were referring to old Nazis hiding here."

Dora turned to Carmen with a glitter to her eyes, ready for a fight, glancing at Alfred for backup.

Alfred tried to smooth the waters. "Argentina's Jewish population is the third-largest in the world. It's probably less anti-Semitic than good old Canada, where only twenty years ago Jews were not allowed to join country clubs or golf clubs. Guillermo's wife is a bit loud, that's all Dora meant."

"I heard Jews can't join the army here," Carmen retorted. "And what about that synagogue I saw with the blood? And the one that got bombed."

"There's nowhere in this bloody country that hasn't been bombed. And I asked our lawyer—who happens to be Jewish—about your synagogue. It's a Sephardic Passover thing, putting sheep's blood on the doorposts.

"And believe me, no one complains about not being able to do military service in this country. It's not a privilege.

Everyone's trying to get out of it."

Carmen fell silent. The boys started poking each other. Alfred was mildly depressed. At most he had one week a year when he could hope to be with all his children. Why couldn't that girl stop thinking and enjoy herself? Here she was on a beautiful river in the middle of a country she'd never visited before, with her father and her half-brothers and all she could do was hold him accountable for the nation's possible shortcomings. Couldn't she loosen up and live a little? Immerse herself in the experience at hand?

After dinner Alfred took a bottle of wine and sat by himself on the boat's prow, looking down at the passing water.

For the first time he was thinking of himself as a failed father, a father who was never there to raise his sons. He hadn't been there for Carmen either, but she was already twenty and she seemed so capable and confident and strong. Besides, a girl didn't need a father the way boys did. He loved Ivan's impishness, his ringing laughter, and Daniel's serious, methodical manner, and he was depressed at his inability to protect them.

His own father had been another failed patriarch. Sitting in the kitchen in his undershirt, listening to his son berate him. Vacillating between despair and anger.

Alfred had won. How he wished he hadn't, how he wished his father had been able to stop him, convince him, make him submit. Alfred winced, remembering how he'd shouted at his father, "Mutti didn't have an affair with anyone! She didn't run off, did she? You let them take her. You didn't want her any more anyway, did you?" His father had erupted in rage. "How dare you? How dare you accuse me of such things? You have no idea what you're talking about. You have no idea what it was like."

"Where is she then? Why didn't you find her? Why didn't you try to find her?"

"I thought she left me. If anyone took her, I didn't know," he'd whined. His anger had disappeared as quickly as it had risen and he'd looked around for Gerti. "I'd like some tea. Where's Gerti? Tell her I'd like some tea."

"I have no father," Alfred had said.

The father he'd disowned had been strong in some ways. He'd always provided for Alfred, he'd fought in a terrible war and survived, he'd distinguished himself in battle. In the world of men he had been a man, but in the world of men and women he had been a child.

The only concrete trace Alfred had of his father was what he'd taken from that pathetic box at the funeral. The photographs and the billowy dressing-gown thing that tied with a belt. He kept it underneath his pillow. The only form of filial loyalty left for him to give.

All he had left of his mother was nothing. A rumour, a possible secret. He intended to tell his children about his mother, he almost had with Carmen, but then he'd have to tell them about his father and besides it wasn't the right time, not with Dora here. It was irrelevant anyway; he himself had never bothered to find out what had happened to her. She was gone and life had moved on from that time, he had moved on. To them it would just seem a vague, shadowy, distant reality.

He stood up, steadied himself on the rail, and walked back to his family. He rubbed his hands together, determined to get in a good mood, and said to Daniel, "Get the chess board. I'm going to whip your British ass."

The next day Carmen asked if she could swim beside the yacht for a while when they next stopped. The captain had nodded, "Certainly señorita, no problem."

He set down anchor and lowered the ladder off the back

of the boat. Carmen stuck her leg in the opaque red water. It was warm.

"Are there any piranhas?" she asked suddenly.

The sullen captain cracked his first smile of the journey. "No piranhas in this river. Just snakes."

"Is it safe to swim?"

"Sure, all the children swim. Snakes are very rare."

Carmen shrugged and lowered herself in. She'd never swum in a river before and the force of the current took her by surprise. She had to swim continually upstream just to stay near the anchored boat. She climbed back on and asked for a rope. She tied one end around her waist and the other to the boat, then re-immersed herself. Once the boat got going, it was exhilarating to swim downstream. Like going downhill on a bicycle forever, like flying, like dreams of infinite power and energy where you never get tired or cold, hungry or bored.

She swam for an hour, just ahead of the boat so it seemed as if she had the river to herself. Then it was time for lunch and the captain anchored the boat near shore where the current was slower; Carmen took the rope off her waist and tied it to Ivan's, and the boys came in for a swim.

Alfred and Dora enjoyed a quiet moment sipping vodka and orange juice and sunning themselves, watching the swimmers.

Daniel swam to shore and clambered up the slippery mudbank. Everyone was watching him when his head turned toward a clump of reeds and grass on his right. A strange grinding grunt or moan came from between his clenched teeth. Alfred leapt out of his chair and ran to the railing of the yacht. "Are you okay, son? Is it a snake?"

Daniel failed to answer. Alfred yelled at the captain to lower the rowboat, and ran to get his gun from the cabin; Carmen struck out for shore while Ivan climbed back on the yacht. Daniel managed to call out, "I'm okay," but didn't move.

Carmen reached the bank at the same time as Alfred. The mud was slippery but they scrambled ashore by grabbing grass tufts. The body of a very young man—judging from his smooth skin, scant facial hair and barely developed muscles— lay akimbo, as though he'd been thrown from a height. His arms and legs bent the wrong way, as though they were broken at the joints. His lips were drawn back and his milky white teeth showed. Two were missing and the gum was red and bloody. One arm rested on grass, while the other rested on a patch of mud, palm up. They saw a bloody stump where a finger had been cut off. A bloom of blood flowered on his pants over his groin.

6

THE PHONE RANG. Alfred answered.

"Yes, she is my girlfriend."

"No, she is not a terrorist. She's a hostess at a club. Yes, I'll come and get her."

The problem wasn't that Dora was unstable. The problem was that she didn't need him. That her screwed-upness made him irrelevant. She was too independent in her screwed-upness.

She seemed to be up for sex any time, but she was always a million miles away. Half the time he felt invisible inside her. The only pleasure she brought him really was her beauty. Walking into a restaurant with his friends and Dora, it felt like having a perfect china doll beside him, a living sex toy. Same blank gaze.

He guessed she had a drug problem. Downers most likely because she never got excited, except on the occasions she was craving something. He had no idea what her plans for the future were, but he could not imagine her changing much. Either she'd be worse or exactly the same in ten years, accepting her fate with the same indifference.

He drove to the address he'd been given in a distant suburb. A house at the end of the street, abutting a garbage dump. He got out of the car and knocked at the door. A man answered, a man in shirtsleeves, unkempt light brown hair, a cigarette hanging from his mouth. "Get the one with the long hair," he called to someone, and presently Dora appeared at the end of the hall. Another man, short, neatly dressed with pressed suit pants, a jacket, tie, pink shirt, unlocked her handcuffs and pushed her forward. He invited Alfred into an adjacent room, leaving Dora standing in the hall, and closed the door behind him.

"As a man I must tell you, sir, I don't think you would have been pleased with the situation in which we found her. She did not have many clothes on. None to be precise. And she was not alone."

"Thank you."

They returned to the hall. Alfred took Dora by the elbow, turned to leave, then stopped. He lifted his head and met the man's eyes. Saw the question. An angry sense of unfairness— of everything the world had taken from him with its rapes, disappearances, abandonments, two divorces, and now this— converged on him.

Still meeting the man's eyes he said, "On second thought, why don't you keep her for a few days. Let her sober up. How about I pick her up Tuesday?"

The man smiled. Dora, who was still drunk, did not humiliate herself by begging Alfred to take her home with him. The man took her elbow. As they went down the hall Alfred heard her ask the man in her dull voice, "Can I call my parents?"

Alfred didn't even see the middle-aged woman who walked by his car as he sat parked at the side of the road. She was pulling her grocery cart. She glanced inside and saw, to her surprise, a man, a middle-aged man, staring ahead of him, tears streaming from under his glasses into his beard.

He could not bear the emptiness of it all. The picture of himself, standing in front of that man, defending his manhood, his macho, to prove he wasn't a coward and a cuckold but the punishing master of his own life. The picture of Dora asking a man with no mercy, "Can I call my parents?"

She hadn't seen her parents since she was fifteen.

But Alfred did not want to be merciful either. He was weeping for that too.

He returned in two nights to pick her up.

The guy in the suit told him she was no longer at this place. He was sorry but he'd have to come back the next day. Alfred asked if she was okay. The man shrugged.

On Wednesday Alfred picked her up, took her back to the apartment and made coffee. Her hand shook as she brought her cigarette to her mouth. She rummaged through her purse and found a bottle of pills, took two. Settled down. This was the first time she'd taken anything in front of him.

"They threw me in with Indians. Indians! Me! They stank. They threw *me* in with Indians. Can you believe it? What is this country coming to? There's no order any more. No decency."

She looked around the kitchen nervously. "What did they tell you?"

"They told me you were at a party the police had under surveillance for subversives. When they took everyone for interrogation you told them to phone me, that you were just at a party to have fun. They said you were drunk. In fact the good man suggested I find myself another girlfriend. You were not dressed, he said. And you were not alone. He concluded that you were not smart enough to be a socialist."

She packed her bags without a scene. He offered to pay the taxi, to loan her some money. She asked for five hundred U.S. dollars. She didn't bother denying anything.

The address she gave the taxi company was one he recognized. One of the young fellows Carmen went out with. Not the polo player, the other one, the slob. The one who espoused anarchy, though Alfred doubted he had the guts to act on it. Though you never could tell with those guys, they could be unpredictable. Like this for example—having a perfectly coiffed blonde china doll in his pocket.

Alfred wished not to think any more. About betrayal, punishment or pride. He drank a couple of straight vodkas in a chilled shot glass and fully appreciated the warmth as it flowed through his veins.

It wasn't until he stumbled into bed that he became aware of the renewed emptiness of his apartment, the sudden absence of female presence.

7

THE WALLS were not where they were supposed to be. Light came from the wrong direction. The smell was not of home and her own linen, but the institutional odour of freshly vacuumed carpet.

Out of her disorientation she pieced together that she'd fallen asleep while studying in a carrel in the university's main library. She'd been in such a deep sleep she'd drooled on her notebook. Saliva still pooled in the corner of her mouth and she wiped it on her shirt sleeve.

She looked round to see if anyone had been watching. Another student looked at her, but when she returned his gaze, he looked away neutrally.

Several volumes of different encyclopedias and reference books lay open on the desk. One was open at a glossy photograph of a brilliant Indian peacock. Beside it lay a periodical article that described genetic research tying symmetry in human facial features to an ability to resist intestinal parasites. The author referenced another study that suggested symmetry was the only cross-cultural feature that all humans found beautiful. The conclusion—symmetry equals beauty equals intestinal fortitude—Carmen found funny. A beautiful face advertised, "I can get rid of intestinal parasites."

The book with the photograph was about sexual reproduction. The peacock was its prime example of an animal that used elaborate visual displays to attract a mate.

The peacock's tail feathers, intended to make a female choose him above all other suitors, came very close to utterly compromising his individual survival. It wasn't a dignified scenario—the male peacock confronted with a predator having to quickly shut up his flamboyant tail and drag it behind him as he fled into the bushes. Impressing the opposite sex was a risky game.

She couldn't imagine calling so much attention to herself. Generally her strategy was to add a subtle touch—vintage earrings, a Guatemalan belt, a Turkish carpet bag, lipstick—but otherwise look inconspicuous. She preferred to rely on eye contact and small adjustments in the way she carried herself for sexual advertising, thus allowing herself to be selective about when she drew attention to herself and from whom.

Occasionally, at formal events, she'd been inadvertently conspicuous because she'd been underdressed. She knew how to do *Porteña*, but that was too overtly sexy in Vancouver, and she knew how to do conservative with pumps, skirts and blouses like Beth's teaching outfits, but she found it hard to strike a note in between.

She tried to set her mind to the work at hand, but it kept rippling out to thoughts of clothes and romance, so she went to the cafeteria for lunch and began reading about the male Malaysian Argus pheasant, whose fanned tail was a dizzying geometrical pattern of taupes, black and white.

This bird's strategy for attracting a mate went one step further than the peacock's. The male would hold a morsel of food in his beak and approach a female, twittering to get her attention. When she reached up to take the food, he'd lift his tail, fan it out and bend way over, so that only his tail was visible to her and then he'd vibrate it before her eyes.

She had five peacock feathers in a vase on her dresser from her childhood visit to Portugal. There had been six but Rebecca had got hold of one when she was little and scrunched it up and bent its spine. Even eleven years later, the quills still shimmered when she blew the dust off.

She could still summon the sound of the feathers dragging in the dirt, and the stirring of dogs sleeping in an adjacent cage. The moon on the surface of the pool, which wasn't turquoise at night but navy-charcoal. All the shades of blue and black.

How mysterious the peacocks had been to her even then. Unlike other animals—dogs, cats, chickens, sheep, cows, rabbits—that were expected to obey, perform tasks, produce things, the peacocks were kept just because they were beautiful. She'd looked at them in silence; voices calling her name; shrinking deeper into shadow.

The words the text used to describe peacocks—"outlandish" and "flamboyant"—were apt; the birds embodied those words, their very existence a rebellion against camouflage and caution, a magnificent, eccentric bravado evident in the fact they had even evolved.

The next morning she woke at ten, tired from waitressing until 1:30 A.M. She changed from her pyjamas into yesterday's clothes and stopped at the shared bathroom of her rooming house to brush her teeth, her hair, and put on lipstick; then she clomped down to the front hallway in her suede clogs. She put her backpack on and wheeled her bicycle out of the garage into the potholed back lane. She rolled up her right pants leg and started riding west.

It was a Saturday and she planned to ride out to the University of British Columbia at one of the many ends of a city hemmed in by mountains and intersected ubiquitously by water, because the library there had a book she wanted for a research project. It was such a beautiful clear autumn day she decided to take a detour and ride around Stanley Park. She emerged from the park and stopped at a red light on the corner of Denman and Davie. A small crowd had gathered near the beach at English Bay to watch a muscular man of average height with shoulder-length light brown hair, in a pink tutu, tights and ballet shoes, dance on a small wooden stage. At the moment he was frozen, mid-pirouette.

The light changed to green and he finished the pirouette. Carmen pedalled across the intersection, stopped, lifted her bike onto the sidewalk and glided over toward the stage. She stopped, leaned her arms on the handlebars and watched him.

The performer began a ballet curtsey that evolved into a martial-arts kick. It took tremendous strength to control this motion and perform it slowly. Sweat bloomed on his tutu. His left bicep was tattooed with a green dragon.

The visual impact of this hairy man in pink tulle was startling. She'd never heard of performance art, which is what a bystander she asked said it was. It seemed risky, pioneering, serious, free-spirited.

She dropped a green dollar bill into a black cowboy hat at the foot of the stage and glanced up. The performer looked down at her, batted his eyelashes, began to smile, then froze as the light turned red. She smiled back, a flutter of excitement in her stomach.

As she rode along Beach Avenue, the crowded waterfront on her right, she remembered Mr Dalgleish and his vision of becoming female on a beach in Greece. Perhaps this man in the tutu was pushing gender to a state of mind like that, somewhere poetical, mystical. Perhaps he, like she, was unwilling to settle for a reality segregated by gender.

He wasn't there on Sunday when she went back to check.

He fluttered his eyelashes at her over two plates of goulash, and she laughed. She was charmed by his employment of feminine wiles to seduce her. They'd emerged from his cockroach-ridden walk-up off Main Street, newly rented on a Canada Council grant, to eat at this Hungarian restaurant— a dark, small, smoky place with cheap good food.

"Carmen's such an unusual name, it's Italian isn't it, no, no, it's Spanish isn't it, that fiery gypsy factory girl who stomps around in red and gets into fisticuffs with other factory girls and steals somebody's boyfriend, only to treat him like shit when he falls in love with her. She wasn't very well behaved. What were your parents thinking? You seem so nice, not pugnacious at all. By the way, you've got the most beautiful shoulders and neck I've ever seen in my life, not to mention those long legs and," he grasped his throat as if he were going to die, "I better not go on . . . "

She laughed again. "But your charms don't stop there. You've got serious brains, and you like the Sex Pistols," he tailed off reflectively.

"And look at me. What am I? Just some penniless guy from Marathon, Ontario, with a tattoo and a dress you happen to find so alluring I have to put it on to get you into bed. Some guy who can't even finish one year of art college for fuck's sake, still married to a broad he knew in high school. A guy who hankers occasionally for another guy—what does a beautiful, smart, nice girl like you *see* in a guy like me?"

"Maybe I don't *want* to be in Kansas any more, Dorothy," Carmen laughed. She didn't like being categorized as a nice girl.

She was flattered that someone like him, with such bona fide rebel credentials, found her attractive and interesting and smart, though she was uncertain whether her brand of smartness was the type he admired. He seemed to have a prejudice against universities and ivory-tower academics. Nothing in his list of failings daunted her. She was only curious about his professed bisexuality, time in juvenile detention, drug use.

The candle flickered on the table, on all the tables around her. It was like being in another city, not Vancouver where she went to work and school, but in an unknown, dangerous and thrilling place, the kind of place she'd always wanted to explore but hadn't known how to get to. The hidden world of men and sex. The father's undomesticated den. The place he returned to without his wife or mother. A place women were excluded from, where they could only enter as servants or if they were young and nubile like Persephone, when they could make old kings yearn once more for innocence.

After the waitress had taken their plates away and left two coffees, he pulled out a mickey of rye he'd got her to buy on their way to the restaurant, pleading lack of cash and the imminent closure of the liquor store on a Saturday night, and poured a big splash into both of their cups. Booze or drugs were the rites of passage into this world.

Suddenly she felt his foot in her lap. "Do you think you could have an orgasm here?"

The suggestion had some appeal; she liked the daringness, the flaunting of convention, yet the appeal was twinned with a slight feeling of invasion, of being put on the spot, of subtle coercion.

She was sitting at her desk in the living room, working on a paper, when Ron came home. By the heavy-footed way he walked up the stairs to their apartment, and his multiple attempts to insert the key, she knew he was drunk again.

They were arguing a lot lately. The tutu was in storage.

Her father had sent Carmen a plane ticket to visit him over the Christmas holidays. It was the last one his company would pay for because Carmen was turning twenty-one soon. She wasn't sure how often she'd be able to see her father after that.

In her effort to show Ron that she was not Pollyanna, that she'd had some real experiences, she'd told him about her father's girlfriends, about walking in on him screwing his secretary, about her solo bicycle rides across Canada, about her affair with Eduardo, about Argentina's anti-Semitism and about the dead boy on the riverbank.

She heard him walk into the living room.

"Look at the middle-class girl scurry to get her studies finished so she can go on a *vacation* to a right-wing military dictatorship where people are being tortured and murdered under her pretty little upturned nose. You wouldn't want to miss an opportunity for a suntan."

He went to the kitchen, poured himself a drink, and came back. She didn't turn around.

"Why would you want to visit a father who's screwed you around so many times? Why do you go when he snaps his fingers, like a good little daughter? The bastard screwed around on your mother, on your stepmother, on everyone it seems. Because you can't wait to swan around the nice restaurants and bars and beaches with him, rubbing shoulders with fascist pigs, hopping into bed with over-privileged polo players. What is it with you? To quote a folksinger of some renown, 'You're an idiot babe, it's a wonder that you still know how to breathe.'"

At first Carmen had been glad to find an ally in her indignation against her father, but Ron's anger quickly surpassed her own and made her feel a little protective of Alfred, and guilty— guilty about telling Ron about him, and guilty about wanting to shield him. She was shocked by Ron's revelations of what was happening in Argentina, shocked to learn people had been disappearing already during her last visit, that they were being tortured, raped and killed by their own military. Yet she wanted to explain to Ron that her father wasn't a bad person, he wasn't torturing anyone and the situation might not be quite as black and white as Ron was portraying it, although of course it might. But whenever she started to speak it seemed to only fuel his rage.

So she stayed silent. He went back into the kitchen, opened the fridge, swore, slammed it shut, returned to the living room. She felt guilty about being middle class and privileged, guilty about not being one of the leftists who were being tortured, guilty about going to Argentina and inevitably being in the company of fascists. Yet she sensed Ron was trying to control her and she did not want to submit.

"There's nothing in the fucking fridge again. You couldn't make enough dinner for me too?"

"I didn't eat dinner. I had yogurt."

"I can't eat *yogurt* for fuck's sake. I need bacon, eggs, toast, something. We've been *over* this."

He enunciated his words through grinding teeth, his tongue thick from booze.

"I'm *writing a paper.*" His drunkenness filled her with contempt.

He smacked her so hard that she and the chair went over together. He stepped in and kicked her. She curled up in a fetal position and gasped for air until she got her breath back.

"Oh Jesus I'm sorry, Carmen, I'm so sorry."

What had just happened? Had she gone too far in some way she didn't comprehend and could never have predicted?

"Say something sugar. I love you so much, I'm so sorry, please say something."

"I'm okay," she said and got up. Her legs started to tremble.

8

AT THE AIRPORT Alfred seemed tense and on edge when Carmen stepped forward to hug him. Underneath a liberal application of French cologne he smelled strongly of booze. He gave her a quick bear hug, then rubbed the top of her head. She flinched. Her jaw was sore, and her ribs, and her scalp. She couldn't remember what had happened to make her scalp sore but she guessed her hair had been pulled. All her memories of the attack were snapshots: falling backward on the chair, apprehension about hitting the floor, curling up. She knew she'd been kicked, but couldn't remember whether once or twice, where Ron had stood; she didn't know what kind of blow had made her fall.

Alfred had a bodyguard now, a short man with light brown hair, a large moustache, white short-sleeved shirt unbuttoned at the top. He took Carmen's suitcase from her and she experienced a small pleasure at being taken care of. They walked swiftly through the airport's sliding doors to a car waiting outside—a sky-blue sedan with a dint on one fender and rust on the outside and a pristine interior with tan leather upholstery, front and back speakers, tortoiseshell ashtrays, a built-in ice bucket.

The chauffeur was a large man with short dark hair, dark eyes, wide chin. He was clean-shaven and smelled heavily of spicy cologne.

The bodyguard and her father slammed the doors quickly and the car pulled away. The chauffeur checked his mirrors, and changed lanes frequently. About five minutes later the three men relaxed at the same time.

The bodyguard put his arm around the back of the front seat and smiled at her. "This character here is known as Pepe, El Pistolero," Alfred told her by way of introduction, "and the other fellow driving like a maniac is Corrado. It's their job to keep me alive."

The first night she and her father got drunk together. Marta, her father's new girlfriend, went to bed around midnight, bored by all the discussion in English. She was six years older than Carmen, and although she dyed her hair, wore makeup and had manicured fingernails, there was something of the tomboy about her. She wore jeans and had soulful brown eyes.

"What do you think of Marta?" Alfred asked when she was gone.

"She seems nice. Why?"

"Well, I'm pretty serious about this one. I'm thinking of proposing."

"You're staying in Argentina for a while then?"

"It looks like another couple of years anyway. There aren't many volunteers for my position. She's going to learn English. She already speaks Italian and Portuguese. The boys get along well with her."

"That's good." She took a deep breath.

"Dad? Remember that boy's body last year by the river? I think I know who killed him. Soldiers. They're torturing and killing thousands of people here."

Alfred leaned back against the sofa, sighed. "This is a country with a violent history and these are violent times. You met my bodyguards. This government is dealing with terrorists. Not nice little students, but people who don't play by the rules. There's only one way to deal with them. Like the Israelis. No messing around."

She'd expected him to be shocked, outraged, perhaps even weep a few tears. "Amnesty International, a very reputable organization, has proof of torture, rape and murder. And not just of terrorists. Social workers, lawyers, journalists, union organizers. Students. Anyone who has even a relative or friend who is leftist."

"And quite rightly so, young lady. They should just shoot the bastards. Shoot them like dogs. Baff! Baff! End of problem thank you very much. The rest of us can get on with our lives in peace. If you let those assholes alone, not only will they continue killing innocent people, they'll destroy the whole country to boot. And the poor people they profess to care so much about will die of starvation, not torture or murder."

He harrumphed, sat forward in his chair, no longer relaxed, and took a big gulp of whisky.

Her legs started to shake. It felt as if the boy was being murdered all over again, and she knew about it and she was sitting on the sofa. She didn't know what to say.

After last year's transformation from hippie girl to sexy *Porteña*, Carmen had backslid to a unisex student look. She wanted to buy some leather things, shoes, belts, maybe a jacket. She asked Marta to take her back to the district where she and Dora had gone shopping.

Marta proved to be a much less discriminating shopping companion than Dora, and after visiting a few matronly type stores Marta suggested going to a nearby mall to get out of the heat.

Ever since the experience of shopping with her father in the mall in Paris when she was twelve, Carmen had shunned malls. But Marta insisted this one, Galérias Pacífico, was worth visiting if only for the frescoes inside its dome.

It was a beautiful neo-baroque three-storey building, about a hundred years old Carmen guessed, and it occupied an entire city block. Most of the shops inside were closed or out of business. Muzak played in the background. An unexciting exhibition of local Argentine artists was mounted in one section of a wide corridor that traversed the building. A shoe store was open across from the paintings and Carmen found a pair of high-heeled sandals she liked; then Marta took her to see the frescoes.

Two stood out for Carmen. In one, naked men with ropy muscles like the roots of trees struggled among cubist elements of wind and earth. In the other, a young man and woman sat under a tree, leaning against one another and staring into the distance ahead. Beside them a naked woman reached for the heavens with one hand and held a blade of tall grass with the other. Beside the naked woman a naked man reached down to a stream. The figures in both frescoes reminded her of Steinbeck characters; they seemed like poor farmers, peasants, factory workers.

Lots of people walked along the main corridor—ballet students with their toe shoes dangling over their shoulders, businessmen, office workers—coming or going to the offices above, but the mall itself, despite its beautiful architecture, was depressing and empty.

At the exit a guard checked their bags. He wasn't a security guard, but a young soldier. He smiled and asked where they were going and Carmen couldn't tell if he wanted a date or if he was interrogating them. She let Marta do the talking.

On the sidewalk outside Marta asked, "Why would he worry about anyone carrying a bomb *out* of the mall?"

They were driving home from the Sheraton lounge, where the women had met Alfred after shopping. Alfred had sent Pepe and Corrado home early because he wanted to relax and drink without having to think about them. Besides, the most dangerous trips were routine ones like to and from the office.

They'd only had lounge peanuts for dinner, along with mixed drinks and much whisky, so they were all a bit drunk. Alfred was playing "Gimme Shelter" on the car stereo for Marta, who was bopping in her seat. Carmen was in the back, feeling like the celibate witness to yet another of her father's mating dances. It was after two in the morning.

Alfred held the wheel firmly and conducted himself in the slow, elaborately deliberate manner of the inebriated. They turned onto a roundabout with a grassy square at the centre. The exit Alfred headed for was lined with young trees. Beneath these trees, three dark-blue Ford Falcons with no licence plates were parked on the sidewalk. Loafing beside them were a dozen men in civilian dress holding machine guns or Lugers.

"Shit," Alfred said and turned off the tape player.

One of the guys stepped out onto the road and waved Alfred to the curb.

"Carmen, don't move. Don't reach for anything. Don't blow your nose." Alfred's voice, usually authoritative, vibrated with fear.

Two men pointed machine guns at the car. The one who'd waved them over ambled laconically to Alfred's window and asked, "Where you going?"

"I'm going home with my daughter and my lady friend."

"Okay. You better get out of the car. The women too. Keep your hands in full view. No sudden moves, ladies."

While men searched the car, the one who'd waved them over asked to see everyone's papers. The papers were taken over to the men by the Falcons and they radioed the identity and passport numbers in, then waited, lit cigarettes and joked. No observer would have guessed that Alfred and the men holding submachine guns were on the same side.

Their questioner, who seemed to be in charge, looked Alfred up and down, noting perhaps his expensive suit and shoes, his beard, the signet ring on his finger, his conservatively cut hair streaked with grey. He seemed contemptuous as well as mildly curious, as though he'd never take seriously any man without a gun. He asked casually, "Where did that ring come from?"

Alfred answered with all the earnestness of a law-abiding citizen who found himself suddenly needing to convince society's enforcers of his honesty and unflagging loyalty. "It was my great-grandfather's on my father's side, a general in the Polish army, as it happens. I got it from my father who was also a soldier."

Alfred and his questioner both knew Alfred made more money than any soldier would ever get his hands on legitimately, yet Alfred, by suggesting they shared the same roots, was trying to communicate submissiveness.

The man handed Alfred back his papers. "It's late to be out driving in these dangerous times. You should think about going home, directly. Otherwise one might get suspicious."

Alfred felt like a young boy dismissed by a teacher as he got back in his car and drove away.

"Boy, *those* guys sure make you feel like law and order's in good hands," Carmen said a few minutes later. "The Argentine economy should be booming any minute now."

Alfred looked sharply at Carmen in the rear-view mirror. He started to speak, then stopped. Women did not understand the nuances between men; they didn't seem to know what was at stake. They had no premonition how serious the consequences could be. They lived their lives as if everywhere was a beauty salon or grocery store. They didn't appreciate the burden of being a man, of being the sex expected to fight. They were content to think only of their own interests, what they could get out of a man. They were the more selfish gender.

As he drove carefully toward home, he was revisited by memories of the last time he'd been unarmed and in the company of women when soldiers with guns had appeared. And now he was a man and did not have the excuse of being a boy. He had to remind himself that these men were protecting him and people like him, they were preserving his right to exist without being attacked. They were sacrificing themselves, risking their lives, so he could live his. In fact, they were serving him. Yet manhood was a dicey thing, and he couldn't quite rid himself of the impression that his had been reduced in the encounter.

9

———— ❦ ————

"Chop them lengthwise, not in chunks. Have you never chopped a pickle in your life? What do they teach you at stewardess school?" Alfred was hovering affectionately over Marta, in an excellent mood.

"Carmen, you're like an ostrich with those damn books. There's a world around you girl. Yoo-hoo. I'm out here. Set these up on that table," he opened a cupboard and pointed at the glasses inside. "A napkin underneath. Move the liquor out there so people can serve themselves. And some ice."

Alfred was throwing a cocktail party this New Year's Eve because he felt happy, because he wanted to introduce his daughter to his friends, and—most importantly—because he intended to announce his wedding plans.

"Olives in the middle. Sandwiches thus, around in a circle."

The phone rang and Alfred answered. A gravelly voice asked for Carmen.

She seemed surprised as she picked up the receiver. She listened, then said, "I love you too."

She hadn't told Alfred about any boyfriend, and she hadn't said "I love you too" with much enthusiasm or passion.

More gravel, a pause, a bit more gravel.

"Well, I'm listening to lots of Julio Iglesias," she sounded falsely bright. "And my dad has a new fiancée, Marta, who's a lot of fun and likes the Rolling Stones," she nodded at Marta across the room, who was going through Alfred's records at that moment in search of something she could stand to listen to. Marta smiled back. "And did I mention beautiful?"

Interrogative gravel.

"Maybe I'll tell you about it when I get home. We went shopping today," Carmen continued with brittle brightness.

Now Alfred could hear that the guy was yelling.

Carmen looked across the room at him and interrupted the yelling with a sarcastic, "Yeah, I love you too Ron," and hung up.

Alfred asked carefully, "Your boyfriend?" She closed her eyes and nodded. "Sounds like he has a pleasant disposition."

"He can't afford to travel," Carmen said.

"Well why doesn't the fellow get a job?" Alfred asked. "Surely they aren't that hard to come by in dear old Canada."

"He's an artist and a musician. He needs time to write songs, do performances, be available for gigs."

"Well that's a choice surely. Not a reason to yell at my daughter across three thousand miles."

She walked over and hugged him. "Thanks, Dad."

The intercom buzzer sounded and the first guests arrived. Carmen and Marta passed food around, Alfred poured drinks. When everyone was on their second drink he relaxed and sat down with his own drink and a couple of hors d'oeuvres.

He'd invited his neighbour the general; a lawyer friend; his chauffeur and bodyguard; Marta's mother, whom he liked well enough; Marta's brother Guillermo, also an affable sort; her second cousin Alejandro; and four colleagues and their wives and some of their children and their children's friends from last year's barbecue for Carmen. Included in this latter group was that fellow Eduardo, whom Carmen seemed to have taken a shine to, a bit of a lazy arrogant sort. This year she seemed less taken with him and talked more to his friend, the slovenly drunken lout whose house Dora had gone to when he kicked her out.

Harry Belafonte's warm honey voice crooned Caribbean songs from the stereo. Alfred surveyed the throng in his living room and went over to the general and whacked him heartily on the back.

"Viejo, how were things? You put any of those bastards away lately?"

The general smiled. "I think it's safe to say we're winning the war for now. We penetrated another one of their "cells" last week and got over twenty. Grenades, ammunition, plans of a government building. One has already spilled the beans about another cell we're going to visit tonight."

"Good work man, good work! Before you know it Pepe and Corrado will be out of a job."

Marta came over, leaned against Alfred and patted his somewhat round (though shrinking, surely shrinking) belly. He was content. She was great in bed, passionate, beautiful, funny. She was still a bit unstable from the premature death of her father, whom it appeared she loved very much, but maybe that was where he came in, maybe that was why his being older didn't bother her.

"My dear fellow, let me introduce you to my future bride!" A colleague overheard them and asked, "Alfred, my good man, did I hear correctly? Are there wedding plans?" Alfred confirmed there were and his colleague called out, "Everyone, everyone, listen to this. Our good host has been accepted by the lovely Marta as a future husband. Let's toast these brave and crazy people!" Everyone held up their glasses, smiling at Alfred and Marta in the glow of the lamps and the room was filled with warmth and happiness as they clinked glasses with whomever was near and drank to the future couple's health.

The party ended at about three in the morning and after seeing the last guest out, Alfred poured himself a double whisky. Marta subsided to the bedroom, but Carmen was still in the living room and Alfred joined her, sinking into the couch and sighing, tired but satisfied.

"You didn't seem to hit it off with that Eduardo fellow this time? He's not a bad sort. Sort of handsome I would think?"

"About as good-looking as a guy can get. But he's just a pretty boy. He plays polo and loafs around looking good. He told me his mother got him out of military service by talking to a friend of the family."

"I'd think with your political sympathies, avoiding the military would be a famous recommendation."

"He's exactly the type of person they're fighting to protect. It would never occur to him that his privilege might not be worth the deaths of so many other people."

"He does seem a bit on the lazy side, I'll give you that. And a bit free with my best Scotch. But I might have to take exception to the notion that subversives are being killed so he can loaf around."

He was in an expansive mood. The party had gone well; the booze was still hitting him nicely; Marta waited for him in the bedroom; his daughter was here for the holidays; he was alive, making money, working hard. Nothing should be taken for granted. He missed his boys and he was pissed off with Isabel for taking them to Portugal for the Christmas break, but he'd get to see them for longer in their summer holidays.

"When I arrived in this country, whose economy should be better than Canada's but whose rate of inflation is so high they have to add zeros to the currency every time they print more money, which is frequently I might add, when I arrived to help develop a gold mine, to employ people, to give your so-called working-class people decent jobs, a viable export, in short to improve this country, some of this country's inhabitants, who don't give a damn about anybody but themselves by the way, well these people decided they knew better than everyone else what was right and they were so sure about it they gave themselves permission to try and kill, among a whole bunch of other innocent people, me. *Me.*" His voice trembled.

"Why, you might ask? Number one," he held his hand up in front of her face and pulled one finger down with the forefinger and thumb of his other hand, "money. Number two," he pulled another finger down, "to destabilize the economy by scaring away foreign investment. What's the logic there, you might ask? Tell me what the hell good is stopping the gold mine going to do for the poor? Kidnap and kill me, that's going to help the poor sons-of-bitches of this nation.

"All their revolution will accomplish is to set up a new group of assholes to skim off the cream instead of the ones that are doing it now. That's their progressive thinking—it's greed and murder and bloody lack of good manners."

He noticed Carmen shrinking back into the chair. Her face was looking angry again and withdrawn.

"Profit skimming varies from one group to the next, it's true, and some are worse than others. But let me tell you no group is free of it, no group is not going to take what they can get. That's politics."

Carmen spoke in a small voice, "What if they really do want to improve things for other people? What if they really are less selfish? And they're being tortured and murdered for it?"

"My darling daughter, more people die for someone else's idea of utopia than anything else in the world. If they got into power they might be decent for a month or two, they might hand a few farms over, issue a few government cheques to the poor, take away a lot of money from people like me who've worked hard their whole lives, and then it'd be the same old shit but worse because there'd be no freedom.

"Let me tell you, daughter dearest, what kind of lovely self-less people they are, these ones you think so highly of." Carmen started to interrupt. "No, you listen for a minute.

"I'll tell you a story. One of those lovely, selfless people befriended the daughter of one of the generals, a friend of my neighbour in fact. A girl of thirteen. For two or three *years* this girl visited the house as a school friend. Every day. Talked to the maid, the mother, the brother, the sister. And then one day she goes in after school and plants a bomb. Everyone is killed including the maid (who would have to be a worker, no?), except the father who happens to be away. She didn't even warn her friend. What kind of a person does that?"

Carmen started to say something but he silenced her again. "This is the kind of people you like so much. Another story. The military raided one of their terrorist cells one day and one of them, a woman, a mother with a young child, grabbed her child and held it in front of her as a shield so the soldiers wouldn't shoot her. What kind of woman does a thing like that? An animal, that's who, someone who is no better than an animal. Worse than an animal even because animals treat their young better."

"No they don't," Carmen muttered. "Fish eat their babies. So do mice. Male gorillas kill the babies of other males."

Her voice got louder. "But Dad, what kind of man tortured that boy? Come on. How dangerous can a fourteen-year-old boy be that he has to be mutilated like that? Surely you don't think it's necessary to murder children?"

He felt a secondary conflict going on behind her words. He sensed it, but couldn't quite put his finger on it. Something more personal.

He took another gulp of his drink and felt the booze taking over.

After Alfred went to bed, she stayed in the living room and stared out the window. Her face felt like stone. The "disappeareds" were not happening in her head. There was blood in the streets, on people's hands, all around her. She wasn't imagining it, she just couldn't see it. Was this what it had been like during Hitler? In Russia during Stalin? Blood in the air, but you couldn't see it?

You knew people you met must be killing people, but they weren't doing it in front of you. You didn't know where, you didn't know when. And it wasn't simple to ask. Like the cocktail party, what were you supposed to do, demand the general tell you, fess up right there in the living room, and then what, throw a drink in his face? Get the carving knife from the kitchen and stab him? What if you were wrong? How could you know? And it wasn't as though they were coming at *you* with a cattle prod, a syringe, a gun, an erect penis and you were defending yourself. And could you be sure their enemies were really innocent? That they didn't need in some way to defend themselves?

So you kept your head down, listened, spied, waited for a chance to help secretly. Typical female strategy. And it wasn't as if an opportunity to help was handed on a platter. You waited, a silent spy in the bosom of the enemy.

She'd always been capable of complicity. She'd kept quiet around Isabel about the secretary in London and kept quiet around Alfred about the Germans in Mallorca. She hadn't told Alfred about Ron and she wouldn't tell Ron about the general and she hadn't told the general, or anyone at the party, what she really thought. She was complicit in her silence and knowledge. Now that she was almost twenty-one, it had become a quality she despised in herself.

But what would Ron have done in her position? Got a machine gun and started shooting? "I Shot the Law and the Law Won." A favourite song of his, an anthem. Mr Integrity. Mr Integrity Outlaw. He would have created an ugly scene, at the very least. The party would have ended in ruins. He would have had to get out of the country fast.

She thought about his phone call. "I'm such an asshole," he'd said. "I miss you so much. You can't believe how much I miss you. I just wanted to tell you."

She'd been both alarmed and relieved to hear his voice. A voice outside of her father's living room.

She hadn't considered leaving him; she didn't understand yet what had really happened or why. She was still learning from him: his analysis of rock music was impeccable; his perspective on Argentina was proving dead-on; and he seemed to be right about her middle-class background, that there were certain things about privilege that blinkered you. She didn't want to live a blinkered existence, and he still seemed like her only ticket out of it.

Nonetheless she'd felt safer being in Buenos Aires, away from their apartment with the empty booze bottles, the loud music and looming violence. His voice on the phone had been like the menacing voice in a dream, interrupting a pleasurable, albeit unstable, narrative, a wake-up call, danger lies just below the surface.

I love you too, she'd answered.

I wanted to tell you I missed you, he'd continued. And then he'd said something like, I just wanted to make sure you're having a good vacation.

And there it was. The flicker of menace in the word "vacation." She'd bridled. Maybe because she was far away she decided consciously, defiantly to prattle on about how much fun she was having.

That's nice, he'd answered. His tongue'd clicked as it lingered too long on the roof of his mouth. You guys going out dancing? Going to fancy restaurants. Are you being nice to the fascist pigs?

She hadn't been able to resist throwing in the shopping and it had had the expected effect. Shopping! A moment's silence. What the fuck! That's perfect. That's gutsy. I think I'll go back to my bacon and eggs and admire the cockroaches. You know what? I like my life better. I don't even know why I called you.

She drank two more whiskies and passed out on her father's couch.

10

"A BARBECUE IN THIS COUNTRY harkens back to the days of animal sacrifice," Carmen said to Alejandro, seated on her left. He was Marta's second cousin and a commander of some kind of military unit. "It feels so primitive—half a cow on a spit, all the organ meats cooking on the grill." He'd been at her father's cocktail party, but they hadn't spoken.

"It's called *chorasco*, and the grill is called a *parilla*," he replied helpfully. Amnesty International had reported that *parilla* was the Argentine nickname for the steel tables used for torture.

The party was in honour of her twenty-first birthday. A man in chef's whites cut pieces of beef for everyone while it was still on the spit; another served salad, fried potatoes, tomatoes, baguette. The guest list comprised the same people who had been at the cocktail party, with the addition of two young engineers just returned from caving in Patagonia and Eduardo's and Salvador's girlfriends.

Were there any leftists among them, Carmen wondered. Any liberals, anyone even concerned about the disappearances? Salvador, Eduardo's friend, might be a leftist, but he might also just be a debauched party animal. The guests seemed completely at ease in the officers' compound an hour's drive from Buenos Aires.

Except for the barbed-wire fence surrounding it and the machine-gun tower manned with armed soldiers, it was an inspired choice of locale for a young woman's twenty-first birthday celebration. It had a large swimming pool, a patio, a huge barbecue pit and bar, a staffed kitchen and uniformed waiters. It was like an intimate version of the Sheraton Hotel. Carmen presumed Alfred had obtained its use through his connection to the general.

He'd even hired a singer, who perched on a stool and accompanied himself on guitar. His eyes were pure blue and a bit buggy, his face youthfully round and smooth and he had a beautiful, pure voice. He stared at Carmen as he sang his ballads, which made her feel uncomfortable. She was touched by the effort her father had put into the party, but it was odd being surrounded by so many virtual strangers, and the extravagance of a private singer, half a cow, a chef and waiter made her feel a bit unreal.

Nonetheless, she also felt wonderful. She'd gone swimming before dinner and felt satisfied for once with how she looked in her bikini, enjoying the male gazes as she'd slipped in and out of the water. Eduardo's girlfriend was more curvy and feminine, but Carmen looked stronger, lithe, less predictable.

For dinner she'd changed into the black jersey wraparound dress she'd bought the year before. She was the only unattached female present.

It seemed ironic that back in Canada, the land of the free, she felt so drab and unsexy, while here, where repression and machismo ruled, she loosened up, came into her body, became more beautiful. Perhaps it was just getting away from classrooms, libraries, textbooks and Ron.

Feeling beautiful could be a complex, unpredictable phenomenon. You couldn't buy it in the biggest mall in Paris, get it at a gym or plastic surgeon's office, create it with your brain. It came capriciously and, at least for Carmen, with an uneasy undercurrent; though its aesthetic was one of balance and symmetry, its power felt off-balance, volatile, unstable. She started downing her drinks quickly.

Alejandro was looking at her. He had jet-black hair, black eyes, a large aquiline nose. He looked part-Indian. Smart, alert. A formidable opponent and a good ally.

A cake was brought out and the bug-eyed singer strummed the opening chords of "Happy Birthday to You" and everyone sang the Spanish version—"Feliz Cumpleaños." Her father presented her with a dozen red roses and a bottle of French perfume.

"I still remember the day you were born. It was in the other hemisphere you see, so it was well below freezing. There was fresh snow on the ground and it sparkled like diamonds in the sun and squeaked when I walked on it. I went to the hospital and there was this little red-faced girl, peeping out from her flannel blanket. I was so happy I wanted to sing a whole opera, which is where the name Carmen (after we considered Norma and Lucia) came from."

Cognac was served with the cake and the celebrants moved to the poolside, where Chinese lanterns had been strung and a bonfire started. The singer took a break and had his dinner alone at one end of a table. Alejandro joined Carmen at a table facing the moon. Looking at the moon over the pool, she half expected the sound of peacocks moving in their cage. *The same moon*, she thought.

She wanted to ask him if he'd tortured anyone, but worried it would appear impolite, abrupt, unfriendly, voyeuristic. Instead she asked if his work was dangerous. She imagined Ron rolling his eyes.

"Yes. A civil war is always dangerous, but it must be fought if my country is going to have peace. I want to get a good job when this is over, have a family, settle down, but first the situation has to be dealt with. You can't have people blowing things up in your country without opposing them."

It sounded so reasonable. She took a deep breath. "You know about the disappearances."

He studied her face for a long time. He smiled at her, tenderly, gently. Nodded almost imperceptibly.

Eduardo looked up as Salvador yelled, "Your balls are the size of peas. Your tool is a tiny little bunny rabbit, soft and furry." He was taunting one of the engineers, with whom he'd been arguing. The level of boisterousness had increased with the amount of booze drunk and gradually the women had moved closer to their men.

The engineer let out a hearty roar of protest—"We'll see whose tool is smallest"—then whispered to his friend. They jumped out of their chairs, rushed Salvador, lifted him up, one under each arm, and while he was still blinking in astonishment, dragged him over to the swimming pool and threw him in.

When Salvador rose spluttering to the surface they retorted, "Now yours is like a little worm waving around looking for a tiny hole!" Eduardo and one of his friends erupted out of their chairs and bunted the engineers into the pool.

They were pushed in turn by Eduardo's girlfriend and one of their friends. A free-for-all ensued, with only the women spared. Alejandro was chased, but easily escaped around some shrubbery.

At a certain moment a group of wet people found themselves by the pool, huffing and puffing, dripping and chuckling. Salvador glanced over at the singer, who was quietly putting away the last of his dinner. Salvador nudged Eduardo, who nodded to a still-dry Alejandro.

Eduardo ambled over to the singer and said he had an unusually pure voice, had he recorded any of his music? Alejandro, Salvador and one of the engineers meanwhile snuck up behind him. Eduardo gave the nod and simultaneously they grabbed him and lifted him out of his chair.

The singer remained motionless for one moment, then metamorphosed into a twisting, thrashing fury, stabbing Eduardo's arm with his fork and kicking Alejandro in the jaw. Eduardo let go in surprised pain and the singer struck the engineer in the mouth with a flailing fist. He got loose and started running, but Alejandro dove for his legs. The other two came over and they carried the still-thrashing singer firmly, grimly, to the pool and threw him way out in the water like so much garbage, turning their backs on him before he landed.

Carmen was uncertain what had just gone on. The singer, whose resistance had been so disproportionate to the circumstance, had forced his own humiliation. She wondered if maybe he didn't know how to swim, but when he surfaced he swam to the edge easily enough. He'd fought like someone who thought he was about to disappear. Was he a terrorist? A socialist? Was he at risk of disappearing? But he was a soldier. He was in uniform.

The general was on the grass talking to Alfred and appeared not to have noticed anything, but Alejandro had gone.

A call went up for the birthday girl to go in. The hair on the back of her neck stood up and she kicked off her shoes and started running for the bushes, feeling like the maiden bounding away on Keats's Grecian urn. Salvador and Marta's brother intercepted her and carried her by the arms and legs over to the pool. Her dress gaped open just short of exposing her nipples and then she was in the pool. She climbed out holding her dress together and laughing. She tightened the sash and enlisted Alejandro, who had returned, to go after her father. They caught Alfred by surprise. He surfaced good-naturedly roaring for revenge, but Carmen sprinted off and hid behind some bushes. She spied her father wrapping a towel around his shoulders and ordering another drink.

She was the only woman who'd been in and Alejandro was the only man who had not, besides the general. He was talking to the engineer and watching Alfred warily out of the corner of his eye.

She ran up behind him, silent in her bare feet, but just as she was about to push him in he turned, wrapped his arms around her waist and took her in with him.

The warmth of his body in the cool water, the feel of her clothes clinging to her, bubbles tickling her skin as they escaped—suddenly they were alone together, away from everyone. He held her round the waist and kissed her. She stayed still in his arms. Then they floated up.

Alfred, Carmen and Marta drove home from the officer's compound after sunrise. No one talked. Marta was passed out in the back seat and Alfred was tired and still a little drunk. Besides, Alfred had noticed Carmen disappearing with his friend Alejandro and didn't know what to say.

Carmen was happy and dishevelled. Her legs were tired but springy. She worried vaguely that Alfred might be too drunk to drive safely and she wondered if anything was happening to the singer, but mostly she was exalted by her tryst beyond the shrubbery with Alejandro. For the first time she had not felt absent in any way, she had surrendered completely to the experience and been shaken by several intense orgasms.

She realized she didn't want to return to her apartment with Ron. In fact, she never wanted to set foot there again. She'd try to find a place in residence until she could rent another room. She could already hear what Ron would say,

"Oh, the middle-class girl goes to visit Daddy in his fancy apartment, hobnobs with fascists, goes to parties with the indolent rich and drops her broke boyfriend when she returns. How *unpredictable*."

She wasn't able to think her part of the conversation through yet.

Alfred pulled up in front of the automatic garage door of his building. He pressed the remote control. Nothing happened. He tried again. Same result.

"Stupid bloody thing."

Suddenly he was alert and sober. He peered all around them—at the bushes, the walls, the sidewalk behind them.

"Where are those guys when I need them?" he said, almost sadly. He sighed, paused, then opened his car door and got out. His shoulders were stooped. Carmen got out too and moved away from the car and her father. She looked around, ready to run, duck, dive for cover. As Alfred walked slowly toward the unopened garage door and wrestled with the handle, fear ran through her.

The door slid open.

There was no spray of bullets. No one put a bag over Alfred's head and threw him in the trunk of their car. No bomb exploded. He walked slowly back. Told Carmen to get back in the car. He drove into the garage, stopped, got out, pulled the garage door shut. Then parked the car.

They pulled Marta out of the back seat, each holding her under an arm, and guided her to the elevator. They did not breathe easily until they were inside the apartment with the door locked and Alfred had gone through every room and closet. Alfred went into his bedroom, where they'd laid Marta on the covers, called goodnight to Carmen, Happy Birthday, and closed the door.

11

THE NEXT DAY they all woke up with hangovers. They drank coffee, ate a little; Marta and Alfred smoked. They wandered from room to room, watching TV or reading magazines. Alfred had a game of backgammon with Carmen.

The police buzzed the intercom. Alfred changed into jeans and a T-shirt, but kept his slippers on and went down to talk with them.

"Hmmph," he said when he returned and plopped himself down on the living-room sofa with a cold beer. "Somebody monkeyed around with that door all right—they cut a whole variety of wires. And the police showed me where someone camped out in the greenery beside the driveway. There would have been others waiting in a car so the police are asking the neighbours what they saw. They would have had to abandon their stakeout at sunrise. It's lucky we stayed out all night, otherwise we'd be dead. Thank you Carmenita for having such a roaring good twenty-first birthday party." He raised his beer in a toast to her.

During this report he stroked his beard gravely, not without a certain sense of drama, even melodrama.

Carmen didn't say anything. She couldn't suppress a certain skepticism, both because of her father's obvious pleasure in the drama, his lack of real fear, and because she suspected the

Argentine police probably reported evidence of terrorism in every petty theft or crime. She thought of secret hideouts she'd found as a child in the shrubbery of Toronto, places where hoboes went, teenage lovers, kids who belonged to secret clubs.

Nonetheless, she remembered the hair standing up on the back of her neck when they'd stopped at the garage door and she'd edged away from Alfred and Marta. She'd had no thought of protecting them, just distancing herself, saving herself. Now that the danger was past, she felt a need to compensate for her behaviour, which she hoped had gone unnoticed.

That evening she was uncharacteristically helpful and solicitous with Alfred and Marta, which she disguised as gratitude for her birthday party.

She was lying on a deck chair in her bikini, trying to read a page of her zoology textbook for the sixth time, when Alejandro walked into the small athletic club, freshly showered and shaved, with a big, unguarded smile on his face.

He sat sideways on the deck chair beside her, elbows on his knees, hands dangling, head bent forward. He seemed like a careworn man on leave from his worries.

"What are you reading?"

"I'm reading, although I'm having trouble concentrating for some reason," she grinned at him, "about worms."

"Ah, worms."

She slipped her dress on over her head, buckled her sandals, untied her bikini top and slipped it off under her dress. As they walked to his car he explained that he, like everyone else in Argentina, lived with his family. It was unheard of for a single person under forty to have his own apartment. Lovers used motels for privacy but he didn't want to go to one of those with her.

They drove for more than an hour, leaving town and then turning off the highway onto a dirt road, and off that onto a farmer's road. He parked, got a big brown blanket and a cooler from the back seat and walked to a spot under a tree overlooking a pasture where cattle grazed.

"This is not true pampas, but it gives you a flavour."

He laid the blanket out under the tree and brought out a bottle of red wine and two tin cups. He uncorked the bottle, poured, presented her with a cup.

"*Al amor*," he said.

"To love," she echoed hesitantly.

"For a minute, an hour, a year, a lifetime—love is love."

He leaned against the tree and patted the ground between his legs. She moved there and leaned back against him and they gazed out at the range. She felt as though on her left there should be a naked woman reaching for the sky with one hand, touching a cornstalk with the other.

Did he know that fresco in Galérias Pacífico, she asked? He thought for a moment.

"Yes, perhaps. I was there with my aunt and my cousin when I was a boy. They left me to sit under the dome while they shopped and gave me an ice cream to keep me happy. I think I remember one with two lovers sitting as we are now. "El Amor," it's called if I'm not mistaken. They're very well known, those artists. Great Argentine artists."

She sank into the earth, the warm brown blanket underneath, surrounded by the smell of dry grass, a canopy of flickering green leaves above, blue sky beyond, his arms all the way around her so she was in a cocoon. She felt the heat of his penis inside her, and her lungs sent oxygen into her blood for more strength to hold him.

One of her hands held the back of his head—she loved the thickness of his straight black hair. Her other hand gripped his shoulder, pulling him to her. His eyes looked down at her intently and her heart broke open.

As she climaxed, the boy by the river with the bloom of blood on his pants rose to mind and she began to cry. Alejandro ejaculated and the image transmuted into a woman lying on her back, legs open, tied to a table, metal under her, not blanket and earth, cement above her not sky, and the object entering her not flesh, the face looking down at her not Alejandro's but a face whose humanity departed with a speed that caused pain by its sheer velocity. Not a universe of love, but one of hunger. ❚

12

ON HIS DAUGHTER'S LAST NIGHT in Argentina, Alfred took Carmen out for *chorasco* at one of the huge restaurants that seated big crowds outdoors. He chose a table right in the middle and ordered a litre of wine.

Carmen went to the ladies' room and he looked around out of habit to see if there were any good-looking women. There were a lot of families, a few men, but nothing else. His eye settled on an older woman at a table across from them, wearing a wool skirt, thick stockings and old-fashioned lace-up shoes. She was bending over the table to help a grandchild out of a high chair and Alfred got an unexpected view of the tops of her stockings and her naked thighs. Soft dimpled skin bulged over the tight elastic.

It was exactly how his aunts' skin looked when they reached to the back of the potato bin, or pulled up radishes from the vegetable garden.

He heard the soldiers laughing and cheering again and saw a large, dirty hand with grey hair on the knuckles, pressing down on the small of Aunt Goldie's back, allowing the soldier to penetrate deeper. He heard his aunt's whimper, perhaps from the sharp pain caused by deeper penetration.

What was strange was this: he felt like going over to that woman helping her grandchild into the high chair and

152

shouting at her, telling her to have some decency and cover herself. He was angry at *her*. He fantasized knocking her down, seeing fear in her face, shock, embarrassment.

How could he think like this? He imagined the men in the restaurant swarming him and administering a beating. He imagined being beaten so hard he'd be helpless, unable to move, too stunned to feel pain and, at last, with every flicker of will extinguished and action no longer possible, being able to relax.

He signalled a passing waiter and ordered two double martinis. He offered one to Carmen when they arrived, but she declined, so he magnanimously took the drink himself. *Thank God for alcohol.*

His daughter knew so little of the world. She'd grown up in Canada, a country without a war except those fought on other people's land, a prosperous country, with rosy-cheeked farmers and complacent old chaps who thought the world owed them a soft seat for their bottoms whenever they took a crap. And kind women who kept clean houses and cooked plain food. These people were not prepared for the real world. His daughter wasn't prepared for the real world. He must try and drill into her that the world was not Canada. Not Sunday dinner, university studies, part-time jobs, pleasant though those may be.

He suggested they order the mixed grill for two. Carmen eyed him suspiciously, then laughed.

"You never give up. I'm twenty-one. I still like plain steak. I don't like brain and tripe and sweetmeats and all that stuff. I'm *glad* you do, believe me, I'm *glad* the whole cow gets eaten by someone. Just not me."

The sun was setting and someone turned on the strings of coloured Chinese lanterns. Carmen looked radiant in the orange glow of sunset. He realized she'd come through the awkward stage. Her gold-flecked brown eyes looked directly at him, the whites whiter with her suntan, her even teeth flashing when she smiled. Her smile, he realized, defined her even more than her anger. It was joyful; it expressed openness, friendliness, curiosity, an engaging liveliness and warmth.

Everything looked beautiful to him suddenly. The coloured lights strung around them, the shadowed trees in twilight, the dark purple sky. As the martini warmed his throat and stomach, he regretted that half their time together was spent saying hello or preparing to say goodbye.

He ordered sweetbreads and a platter of grilled organ meats. She ordered steak and salad. He ordered a carafe of wine.

How to explain to her what it was like to have no freedom to choose your own life. Maybe it didn't sound like much. Watching strangers take your house, your family silver, your grandfather's suit, anything they wanted, when they ordered you from land that had been in the family for hundreds of years. Just possessions, she'd say, just things. But so much was attached to things. When strangers took what they wanted, you felt it in your body, that they could do anything they wanted to you. That they'd pissed on all the laws protecting you; that your police, your army, your adult males, your soldiers were all impotent.

He wanted her to understand how unbearable that was. How you would never willingly let yourself be in that position again. You'd kill first. A life was such a pitiable amount of time —you wanted every scrap that was coming to you. You didn't want anyone else stealing even a moment away from you.

A starving man sits down to a meal and some other guy comes along and says sorry, that food's mine, and what's more, it is morally better for me to have it. Who would take that sitting down? Whether the other chap says "good of the

people this" and "good of the people that" or he's just a greedy
shit who wants your dinner, it makes no difference.

This was not something you could learn about in university
or books; it was life and it knocked on your door any time of
day or night.

But . . . he could already predict her response. All the idealistic claptrap. Freedom wasn't freedom if it was at the cost of
other people's freedom. He could hear it all coming, the
words, just words, theories, ideas, nothing from experience.
He began to feel tired and irritable without having spoken
a word.

Carmen smiled and took a bite of bread and butter.

"Dad, I wanted to ask you about your religion. I know
you're Catholic, but I don't know what you believe. Do you go
to church? Do you believe in life after death? Do you believe
in Jesus?"

"I've been once or twice. Isabel and I had your brothers
christened, and I *adore* singing hymns." He poured himself
more wine. "But I don't believe in a God who worries about
each individual life. We have free choice, and if God
controlled every aspect of our lives, there could be no free
choice. You can't have it both ways."

Perhaps this would be a way to explain himself to her. He
refilled her glass.

"I'm definitely not an atheist. I agree with the Pope, who I
think is a magnificent man. Life is sacred."

She answered, "That's not entirely at odds with a biological
perspective, where more life seems to be the 'aim.' Free
choice probably doesn't come into it much though." His
daughter seemed to be trying to find common ground.

The waiter laid a plate with an enormous steak, French
fries and salad in front of Carmen, and a wooden board with
various meats still sizzling from the *parilla* in front of Alfred.

He also received a side plate of French fries, asparagus, and tomato salad. The smell of grilled meat, tomatoes and vinegar, and hot oil on the potatoes rose from the table. Alfred lifted his glass and toasted Carmen, "To a long and healthy life for us both."

They took a few bites, and then Carmen said, "There's something I've never understood about Catholics. Like the Crusades for example. How can a Catholic ever kill anyone? For any reason."

Ah. So it wasn't curiosity after all. There went a pleasant dinner. Excess acid began to leak into his stomach. Young people truly were a punishment for the middle-aged's sins of youth. Vengeance served. He missed his father.

She had an ultra-earnest expression on her face that he recognized and loathed—humanity bloated with the thrill of its own goodness.

"I'll tell you how this Catholic can do it, Carmen, and you can decide for yourself how hypocritical it is." He looked her straight in the eye, the extra blood of intense emotion heightening the green of his irises. "I happen to think *my* life is most sacred of all. An opinion you obviously are very far from sharing."

A variety of responses appeared to cross her mind, but she said finally, "I don't want you to get hurt." She looked back at him and he thought again how truly unusual her eyes were, the golden flecks giving the brown an unsettling sunburst effect. He saw love there for him, but other emotions were even more powerful. "I'm just not happy about anyone else getting hurt either. It's not a pecking order for me."

She seemed to hear a harshness in her last sentence that wasn't quite what she'd intended. She touched his hand. "The truth is, Dad, I never really think of you getting hurt.

If I were to imagine *you* lying naked on a metal table . . . " She shuddered.

He looked at her and made a decision.

"I'm going to tell you about the two times I've been most hurt in my life. One was the day my great-aunts, who cared for me during the war, were raped by Russian soldiers and I had to stand by, helpless to stop it from happening. The other—and this is the most painful—was the night I came home with my father . . ." He began to cry and had to stop. He took his glasses off and pinched the bridge of his nose to force the tears back. He took a deep breath, exhaled slowly, put his glasses back on. "I was twelve. My mother was not there.

"I looked through the whole house. There wasn't even a note, only a little suitcase gone along with her hairbrush and comb. I went to her bed and lay on it and smelled her perfume on the pillow. I knew somehow that I was never going to see her again. I don't know how I knew. For years I'd go into her room to smell her pillow every night before bed. Whenever I told myself she was dead, a voice would say, she's not dead, she just left you behind, and whenever I allowed myself to think she was alive, a voice would say, she's nowhere on this earth any more.

"When the war ended I went back to my father and asked him. I told him I thought she might have been taken to the camps. He became furious and refused to talk about it. That was when I wondered if he might have had something to do with it."

Tears gathered again in his eyes.

"After the war he married a woman who hated me and never once did he stand up for me against her. When I moved to Canada I started my own life. Then he died."

He stopped trying to hold his tears back.

"It's your last night and I want to be happy, but your dear old dad has had some hard moments . . . " He wiped his tears with the back of his hand.

"I read they kept lots of records, Dad. Have you checked?" she asked tenderly.

"Yes," he said, regaining his composure, sounding suddenly less emotional. "Sure. The German government traced her name, both her married name and her maiden name, which was Fogel, and there was nothing. If she's alive, she doesn't want to be found, and if she's dead, there's no record. Maybe she left me. Mothers do desert their children. And in wartime anything can happen. I suppose I could do more to find out . . ."

On the way home they stopped at a club with a dance floor. The DJ played early Beatles, the Bee Gees, early American rock songs. Carmen asked Alfred to dance.

A mirrored globe turned slowly, sending lozenges of soft light rippling over everything. A song about the time of the season came on, with a moody organ and a hypnotic male voice. His daughter looked like she was floating with her long soft hair and her luminescent white pants. He felt weightless too, as though he and she were on their own separate platform of night sky, stars twinkling around them, this young woman who was part of him spinning out to the edge of the dance floor, and spinning back.

The song asked about a father, a rich father, showing his daughter how to love. Carmen danced well but oddly. Her movements were loose, joyful, faintly masculine. He imagined his own dancing looked neater, more delicate, even though he was a bear of a man. His feet in their soft leather loafers touched the floor more lightly than hers, feet that knew how to waltz more than stomp, feet that responded more to a violin than a bass guitar.

13

---∞∞∞---

THE ROOM SHE'D RENTED in September had a fire escape and its own entrance up steep wrought-iron stairs. She'd bought an orange kitten when she moved in that she called Angel. Angel had already grown into a cat and now ascended and descended by the fire escape, entering and exiting the room via a cat door she'd covertly installed.

When she'd returned from Argentina, she'd slipped back into her relationship with Ron. He'd promised never to hit her again, to cut back on his drinking, and he told her he loved her, and inspired her with talk of his future artistic plans.

Carmen felt less vulnerable, armed with memories of Alejandro, whom she did not tell Ron about.

For her Alejandro had been outside of politics. He was a soldier, like most soldiers on any side, concerned with protecting those who were weaker—women and children and the old—and guarding a stable society free of violence, the only kind of society, Carmen guessed, that ensured any freedom for women. He embodied the altruistic, self-sacrificing side of males, the warrior willing to risk his life to protect others. And he was working class in a way that Ron, with his artistic ambitions, counterculture mentality and unemployability, no longer really was. Maybe Alejandro was fighting on the wrong side, but that was an accident of birth, not a

159

personality deficiency. He was the sort of man who would protect someone like her from someone like Ron.

And yet she knew she could never have a serious relationship with someone like Alejandro. He was too pure in some way, too straightforward. She needed a muddier soul, a cloudier person, more like herself.

Alejandro was her amulet, allowing her to re-enter the battlefield from a stronger position, but he was not her way out. She still felt too uncertain about herself to leave Ron, too uncertain about the morality of having visited Argentina, rubbing shoulders with generals and foreign executives, while knowing what was being done to political prisoners there. She also felt uncertain about who she was when she visited her father: what being his daughter meant, how she might be like Alfred and how she wasn't, and which part of not being like him was simply because she was female.

Ron made her feel free of her father, as if she were in a world beyond him, more licentious and unconventional than anywhere he'd ever go. She couldn't imagine the two men even in the same room. They'd gravitate to opposite corners, oil and water. And in the world of sex, Carmen wanted to outdo her father, to leave him in her dust. She wanted to make it so he could have a million affairs, trysts and flings and they would have no more power to shock, hurt or touch her.

She and Ron decided to try an open relationship. It would free Ron to pursue a flirtation with a transsexual singer in another band and it appealed to Carmen as a way of ensuring she would never end up in the same position as her father's women—cheated upon. She could be independent, have adventures, her own sexual life, and still have someone she could call her own.

For a while Ron was less a boyfriend than a partner-in-arms. He told her about his romance, ultimately unrequited,

with the transsexual singer and she told him about her experience, requited, with a married friend of one of her professors.

That affair had been enough for her to decide that sex
without love, or at least the promise of love, was basically
uninteresting. Clay humping clay.

And it had been enough to make Ron jealous again.
Bisexuality notwithstanding, he reverted to a man driven by
singularly unprogressive impulses. Dominate the female, try
to isolate her, make her yours without becoming hers. He
belittled Carmen's studies in an attempt to get her to quit
university, he belittled her family though he'd never met
them, he belittled her friends, her job, her plans. He began
drinking heavily again and not long after that, he hit her.

One day at the library, rubbing a bruise on her head, staring
down the rows of bookshelves at a window, she was visited by
the dreamlike image of a male chimpanzee. He was sneaking
through the forest, followed in single file by five others, all
listening to another unsuspecting male from a neighbouring
band, blissfully eating fruit. They were studying territorial
behaviour in mammals in a third-year animal behaviour class.

The image came from one of Jane Goodall's books.
Goodall was not in vogue on campus, and was not on her
professor's reading list, but Carmen liked the unpretentious
personal quality of her writing, her hopeful pragmatism.

It was the chimpanzee's silence as he moved forward that
got her. The silent chimp was not Ron. It was her. She
planned to survive. She'd always planned to survive. It was
her, moving stealthily through the forest, listening, waiting.
She had nothing in common with the carefree chimp eating
to his heart's content in the fruiting tree. The one oblivious to
danger. The one about to die.

She moved out that weekend and stayed with a friend for
the remaining weeks of the term. She got a summer job doing

field research with a couple of other undergrads for a marine biology professor. They camped all summer by a rich intertidal zone on the Queen Charlotte Islands. She learned how to scuba dive, and learned also that she hated it, thus eliminating marine biology, except in tidal zones, as a possible field of study. She forgot about Ron.

She did not forget about Argentina, however. She continually monitored the newspapers—looking for lists of *desaparecidos*, Amnesty International news releases, the regime's counter-releases. She read that a torture room was decorated with the words *"Arbeit macht frei."* She read more about the *parilla* and the *picana*, the grill and the prod used for torture. The mothers of the disappeared marched in the Plaza de Mayo with placards bearing the names of their lost children. There were reports that unconscious prisoners were being taken up in airplanes and dropped into the sea, bodies thrown away like garbage. More than twenty thousand citizens had disappeared.

She happened on an announcement that Johnny Rotten had left the Sex Pistols, and two other band members, Cook and Jones, had flown to Rio de Janeiro to record with Ronnie Biggs, the Great Train Robber. She thought briefly of calling Ron to tell him. For some reason, this piece of celebrity trivia electrified her. It was as though the unexpected collaboration of punk rockers with a middle-aged train robber living the expatriate high life in Brazil pointed somehow to the possibility of a new collaboration within herself: the Latin side of her life, her father's world, collaborating with the North American side, her mother and Oscar's world, to form a new creative universe.

Hidden in the midst of fabulously coloured birds in birdcages, among giant foliage and bougainvillea, the bank robber ate mangoes and recorded with the great punk rebels, their green and pink hair still bent from sleep, dream remnants floating in their eyes of jungle stretching forever, drums and poison darts and the great figure of Christ on Corcovado Mountain, arms raised to embrace all the world from this virgin point.

She slept on a mattress on a boxspring that became a couch in the day when draped with an Indian embroidered cover. At night she frequently woke to the sound of the cat door swinging back and forth. The sound always roused her because Angel often brought in a live bird or mouse to playfully torture and Carmen wanted to be ready to intervene.

This month she'd already rescued two birds and wrapped two mortally wounded mice lightly in tissue, gently tucking them under brambles either to die in peace or survive, if that was their destiny. She knew the notion of destiny was indistinguishable from superstition, but it was the only way she could understand her limitations as a saviour.

She would fall back asleep, picturing the cat ascending the fire escape in the dark, in rain or moonlight or snow, or imagining its sleek body descending with long easy steps until it reached the ground. Every night she slept like this, with a background awareness of ascent and descent, of herself on high, yet only relatively high, still essentially underneath something—sky, space, God.

It was Sunday morning. She didn't have to steel herself to go out in the world, to go to classes, labs, or hand in late assignments. She went down to the kitchen, made coffee, carried it back to her room in a Thermos on a tray with cream, sugar, a large pottery mug, an orange and a dish of almonds and raisins. A short paper comparing reproductive behaviour among hermaphroditic species such as snails, flatworms, slugs, barnacles and sea cucumbers—all parasitic, slow-moving or stationary animals—was due on Monday and she was only half done. She was finding it difficult to concentrate. Her mind kept dodging off to freewheeling thoughts, resisting her efforts to lasso it back to academic essay-writing. By the time she finally started to focus, she was tired of sitting still and wolfing down raisins and almonds.

She got out of her chair and opened the fire-escape door. Cool autumn air drifted in. A robin flew by so close she could hear its wings flapping. The doorway was across from a chestnut tree where starlings often congregated and chattered shrilly. The tree was quiet now. She peered inside its branches of yellow leaves and felt a little ripple of dizziness, a slight floating sensation, perhaps from following the robin with her eyes at such close range.

She went back into her room, poured another coffee from the Thermos, and reread her last paragraphs.

> Both flatworms and snails are described as having violent, painful copulation, their penises, which are proportionately long and dartlike, are said to "stab, thrust, be hypodermically inserted, penis-fence," and the reactions of the recipients described as "rearing or twitching in pain."
>
> Mating descriptions read like two males copulating, movements are interpreted as fighting or war-like, anthropomorphized, and therefore almost certainly distorted. Nowhere in the article do authors outline their methodologies, how they determine "pain," as opposed to—pleasure, excitement, surprise, reflex, a simple reaction of the autonomous nervous system.

The telephone rang. She answered it.

"Is this my long-lost daughter? The one who neglected to send her poor old father a new address or phone number? The one who hasn't called in months and months? Your mother, who was nice enough eventually to give me your new number, told me first that you'd gone to join the revolutionaries in Cuba. She's still got her sense of humour, I see."

His voice caught her completely off guard. She was so involved in her own adult life that her father had disappeared from her present. She thought of him often enough, but in a kind of indeterminate past tense, more history or story. Even talking to Beth or Oscar these days was like calling down a long dark tube.

"I thought I sent it to you," she lied. "I'm sorry. I'm studying hard. Plus I've got a part-time job TA-ing. I'm very busy." She hoped she sounded busy but happy.

"Your brothers are coming to visit for Christmas. Also there's another little Lion on the way and, if my divorce comes through, Marta and I are planning to get married when you're all here. I realize my invitation can't compete with working in sugar-cane fields, but I thought I'd make it anyway."

"Dad, I don't have any money left after paying rent and books and tuition."

"Consider it my Christmas present."

She didn't want to play the daughter any more in his world. She couldn't face struggling to find an emotional connection with two pubescent brothers who were virtual strangers, let alone relate to a newborn baby to please Alfred. Nor did she want the job of welcoming yet another new wife, even though she liked Marta. She had her own place, her studies, her own life; she paid her own bills. Most importantly, *she paid her own bills*. She didn't want to fly into his territory and have to rely on him again for everything. Nor did she want to be silent any more, to endure complicity in any way about what was going on in Argentina.

Yet she wouldn't mind a suntan. And she missed that smell, that mildewy, woody, mango smell of a semi-tropical climate. And she'd like to exist in a Latin language again for a while. She'd like to dry out and smooth the white, bumpy, oily winter skin, stride down an *avenida* in high-heeled shoes and tight jeans and sunglasses without feeling like a hooker. She'd like to go to a nice restaurant with her father and have wine and steak and salad and look at all the other people under Chinese lanterns. She'd like to walk the streets of Buenos Aires thinking of Borges and labyrinthine mystical infinities.

"How's Alejandro?" she asked. "Are you still in touch?"

"Yes, sure. He's got himself a very nice girlfriend. Marta likes her a lot. He's going to be my best man."

"It's very tempting, Dad. And thanks for the offer of a ticket. But I don't think I can leave my studies for that long. I want to get into graduate school and my marks are really important."

"Listen, Carmen. I haven't seen you for a year. Now you're an adult, who knows when the next opportunity will come. You haven't seen your brothers in two years. Bring your books with you."

"I can't." She steeled herself. "There's a chance," she said, searching for a softening argument, some reason over which she had no control, something he couldn't dispute, "there's a chance I'm on file as a left-wing sympathizer. I've signed petitions here. I might be in danger."

After she hung up, a rowdy flock of starlings landed in the chestnut tree. She didn't remember any animal sounds in Buenos Aires. Birds must have chirped and dogs must have barked but she remembered only the sounds of cars, and people. Buses. She tried not to think of her dad hanging the phone up on his end in his apartment.

Well, she was free for Christmas. Boundlessly free. Maybe she'd go back to Toronto for a week and see Beth and Oscar and Rebecca. She went back to her desk and stared down at her essay. She flipped through one of her textbooks, looking for a photograph of slugs on a lawn on a midsummer's eve. She found it. Fifty-two pairings, ranging from almost black brown to yellow-green with black spots. A close-up of two dark brown slugs showed them curled head to foot in a circle, in the centre a large raspberry-sized clot of a creamy gelatinous substance.

At night the slugs buried the fertilized eggs under moss. She wrote:

> Slugs on the other hand, are described as reproducing in a softer, more feminized manner. Words like "balletic" and "sensual" appear. The creatures circle each other, touching each other with their antennae for hours before mating. There is no mention of the thrusting and parrying that occurs between males competing for females, but rather an acknowledgment that each individual slug has both male and female within. No competition is mentioned at all between individuals for mating rights. What's described is a sensual and slow-moving dance that ends in about 200 fertilized eggs.
>
> The peacefulness of their mating is further enhanced by the fact that slugs have almost no natural predators, hence a whole lawnful can mate all night without apprehension of attack.

She began to cry. What she'd been writing about, she realized, was a kind of nirvana she was never likely to experience herself.

In fact she was beginning to realize more fully what being a sexually mature female really entailed. You had a treasure, something men wanted. It was an impersonal kind of treasure that wasn't really yours but because it was buried deep inside you, you had to protect it, though you'd been given very little in the way of armour or weapons. Your only real protection lay in social alliances or hiding.

A certain unstable power came with the fact that men desired what you had, power that you could trade for things you might want: comfort, security, status, wealth. But she didn't want any of those things and the treasure was more an obstacle to what she did want: adventure, freedom, love, independence. She hated the feeling of having something someone else wanted. Oocytes. Feathery fallopian tubes. Womb. Having to guard a treasure you'd never asked for.

There was a big difference between having a treasure and being a treasure.

Two weeks later a letter arrived from Argentina. One thin piece of onion paper. "I have no daughter."

No hand reached into the briny tumult to pull her up into air. She was grown up now.

She went back to her desk and continued studying. The phrase came to her, "Work shall make you free."

SECTION
Three

1

BRAZIL, MARCH 1995

ALFRED DRANK A VODKA MARTINI, straight up, chilled glass, black peppercorns gambolling at the bottom. It was the first of the night—the only one he still completely enjoyed. He drank it alone, sitting at his empty banquet-sized dining-room table.

He could see Dalva in the living room watching TV. The blue light flickered across her face in the dark. She was pissed off at him again. The end of her cigarette flared bright orange as she sucked hard, then slowly released the smoke into the air. Like a fish breathing.

It reminded him of when he first saw a truly troglobitic cave fish, Typhlichthys—the way the fish's mouth had slowly sucked in water. He'd been alone, and the light from his helmet had penetrated the black water to reveal this creature that was un-public and rare, even sacred somehow.

He loved her youth. Her skin. Elastic, supple and smooth. Her unusual blue eyes like rock crystal, sharp, refracting light at straight angles. Unusual because of her dark complexion. The first night he'd made love to her, two years ago now, he had not been able to believe his luck. He still marvelled at it, although he'd had to add a grain of salt, a few grains, coarse grains, in fact the dish was so salty now he grimaced before he ate.

Four years earlier his third wife, Marta, had taken their two daughters, then eleven and nine, back to Argentina to live with her mother. They'd held it together as a family in Chile, the United States and Malaysia with the help of nannies, country clubs, private schools, alcohol and tranquilizers, but the marriage had broken down when he decided to take early retirement and move back to Brazil.

He chose Brazil because: he owned land there; it was a country with beautiful and challenging caves; he had mining contacts and could augment his income with consulting work; his pension's American dollars would go a long way there; it was a society in which it was easy for an older man to attract beautiful young women. He failed to consult Marta about this move because, he reasoned, he was the only one who knew the economic realities.

Their last few months in Malaysia, Marta had come to hate him so much she could no longer be trusted around knives. It had been years since they touched each other even out of basic affection, let alone desire. Worst of all, she'd become obsessed with not just spending his money, but *wasting* it, buying things she didn't even want, had no intention of using, buying only to throw away. This last form of revenge had been intolerable and he had called a lawyer.

To reward himself for enduring the last years of that marriage, he'd spent many nights out on the town. He'd gussy himself up, spray on fresh cologne, and go out, not hunting exactly, that was too harsh a word, but looking with a keen eye. One evening, Dalva had been sitting at the bar with one of her girlfriends. She'd smiled at him. He offered to buy her and her friend a drink. She accepted without hesitation. It had crossed his mind later that she might have decided right then and there she was going to move in with him.

He knew money was a necessary part of the equation, but he didn't think it was the only reason she was with him. Perhaps not even the main one. She said he looked like a movie star from spaghetti westerns, only more handsome. And he was tickled pink to be able to call a woman like Dalva, a sexy twenty-four-year-old with a good heart (though somewhat moody and changeable in disposition), his own, no matter what the motives. Her presence kept a lot of things at bay for him: memories, thoughts about his life, aging, the shrinking opportunities for a clean slate.

Like all women she was a subversive. She'd recently stopped taking birth-control pills, thinking he wouldn't notice. He wasn't surprised. He could rage and storm, but in the end, they all just went around him with an expression of scorn. Slim reeds to his mighty oak. The old king.

He didn't particularly want another child, but he didn't really mind either, although he had no intention of letting her know that. If having children was what it took to keep a young woman interested, he'd go along.

Most of his friends, many of whom he'd met when he'd lived here twenty years ago, ostracized him after he brought Dalva to a Christmas party at the golf club. Even he had to concede Dalva had behaved badly. She'd gotten quite drunk, to the point of falling down, which in fact she had, several times. Before the evening ended she had told the wife of one of the most popular men, who'd suggested in the ladies' room she'd had enough to drink, that she was a dried-up old cow.

The woman in question had replied that Dalva was a person of no education or culture who should only be allowed in the clubhouse bathroom to clean the toilets. Dalva forbade Alfred to speak to that woman ever again. So, even if he hadn't been excommunicated, he would not have been able to attend any function attended by that woman, which was almost every one.

He didn't give a damn what they thought anyway. In fact, he didn't give a damn what anybody thought any more. No one these days admitted to caring what other people thought—the claim had become ubiquitous—but in his case, at the moment anyway, it happened to be true. The opinions of other people only had one effect on him: to make him irritable. After he'd retired, they'd ceased to have even that effect.

Who would fret about being excommunicated by such a group of hypocrites anyway? Only one was still happily married to his first wife. The rest had young Brazilian mistresses, their first or second wives stashed back in the U.S. or Europe and faithfully visited once every few months; large tax advantages were an ancillary benefit to the arrangements. They never married the young Brazilian women, never made them family; though they had children with them, they never introduced them into the expatriate society as equals.

He guessed jealousy might be a factor. They wished they had the courage to give themselves to a young woman. To risk something, the bastards. He couldn't imagine why any man would say no to a young woman offering her heart and soul. Even knowing there might be big bills to pay down the road.

The age difference made it lonely at times, but life was lonely, as was marriage.

In any case Alfred didn't have a choice when it came to women. He still couldn't get an erection with a woman over forty.

Alfred looked at Dalva with melancholy and lust—what a sublime combination! Her bare legs were folded under her like a deer. She had long, slender legs, painted toenails. One of his friends' wives had said in his hearing, "She has farmer's feet. She'd do better not to call attention to them by using such colourful nail polish." But he loved that her feet were big and bony and callused while her legs were wonderfully smooth and slender. The juxtaposition excited him.

She stubbed her cigarette out on one of his antique Chinese ceramics, knowing this drove him crazy. She knew he was in the dining room sitting in the dark, looking at her. She ignored him. She unfolded her legs and changed the channel.

Then got another cigarette out of her purse. She kept her purse beside her at all times, as though it were a refugee's suitcase, the last thing in the world that was hers.

He never gave her money for cigarettes; he disapproved of her smoking. Somehow she scrounged it herself. It was a tactical error on his part—making her scrounge—he knew, but he couldn't help himself. In fact, just when she was behaving pleasantly, running her hands through his hair, or giving him a nice massage as she had earlier this evening, he'd say something like, "Dalva, woman, could you breathe in the other direction. Your breath smells like a stale fireplace. And your fingers too." He seemed to be unable to resist stirring up trouble.

She clicked the channel changer impatiently, dissatisfied with what was being offered. She stubbed out her half-smoked cigarette, turned the TV off and stalked past him to the bedroom, closing the door behind her. The anger was so familiar it felt like air. Female anger, as inevitable as death and taxes; female tenderness, a grace note in a symphony of anger.

Young females seemed to have an extra dose, at least in his experience. Angry young women. With his sexual disposition, he was going to be stuck with them forever.

He mixed himself another martini. His latest routine was to delay the first drink until nine o'clock, not because he cared about the amount of alcohol he drank, though his liver did feel tender, but because he still worried about getting fat. He'd read that alcohol was the most concentrated form of caloric energy and his belly already extended alarmingly over the waist of his pants. Any more and people would think it was him having the baby; they'd look like twins in profile walking down the street.

Nooo-no-no-no-no, he'd be damned if he was going to let that happen. He'd eat a diet of ice cubes if necessary.

He took his martini to his office and sat down in the wing-backed chair overlooking the little courtyard he'd designed where goldfish swam lazily in a sea-green mosaic pool. He wrote a quick letter to Ivan, whose twenty-eighth birthday it was today, included a cheque for one hundred U.S. dollars in the envelope and put on a stamp for overseas. Then he picked up a book he was reading about bats, in preparation for a spelunking expedition to the American northwest with Max, an old friend from South Africa. They planned to explore a cave system renowned for its bats.

When he was ready to go to bed, he went around the house checking that all the doors were locked, bolted and double-bolted. He went into each room and switched off the lights which Dalva had left blazing in flagrant disregard for his electricity bill. In the bedroom he took his clothes off, folding each item, even his underwear, before laying it on the Louis Quinze chair he'd bought in the early days with Marta. He placed his shoes side by side under the chair. He lifted his pyjamas out from under his pillow, put them on.

He padded into the bathroom in his bare feet, checked himself out in the mirror and was not unhappy with what was reflected. He rubbed hair tonic into his scalp, took eleven different types of vitamins, brushed his teeth, squeezed four drops of a naturopathic remedy for indigestion under his tongue. He felt headachy so he took a couple of acetamino-phen with codeine.

He returned to the bedroom, folded back the sheet and sat down carefully, trying not to disturb Dalva. He propped his pillow up against the headboard, leaned back and slid his feet under the sheet. He slid his left leg stealthily over until his foot touched a wisp of her silk nightie. He felt like a little boy, trying not to disturb his mother. Sneaking warmth. The smell of onions and lemon-scented soap. Wanting to be near her without arousing anger, knowing, without asking, that his presence if noticed would not be welcome.

He guessed Dalva was awake, but wasn't going to admit it and give him an opening. She lay still while he leaned over to turn out the light. He felt a sharp pain in his head and lost consciousness.

2

⁕

CARMEN SWINGS WAY HIGH UP in the air, waiting for her best friend, April, to come walking down the country lane. She holds herself steady on the gymnastic rings, arms straight, preparing for a somersault.

From this lofty vantage point she can see into the backyard next door where a father and his young daughter sit without speaking or playing. She is strong and flexible and happy. *I could stay up here forever and be perfectly happy.* The rings are not attached to anything.

A man with long brown hair and an acne-scarred face takes her clothes off. They are in the Northwest Territories. He tells her to lie back on the cold snowy ground. He's a sensualist and says it will feel good to make love with her back on snow. Yeah, *my* back on the snow, she thinks sarcastically—but then they are both on their sides and he is staring at her nipple, letting erotic tension build before he touches her.

He is going to lead her on a sexual journey, but she also knows that he is thrilled just to have her naked in his tent, so though she may not be the leader, she is the one in control. All she has to do is leave and his magnificent sensual journey will be over.

The frilled ripple of nausea, like an oyster's black edges, pulled at the top of her stomach. She was waking up.

Immediately she tried to return to the man in the tent, but the narrative was broken and now her mind hopped around, commenting on the man's unsavoury appearance, on the interior of the tent, wondering what was outside.

The alarm buzzed and Robert reached over and turned it off. He got up, shuffled into the kitchen, made weak tea with milk and sugar, and brought it to her. She saw his hand put the cup down on her bedside table—the hand of a man in his midforties, with big veins on the back, some black hair on the knuckles and some grey; callused, not the broad flat hand of a farmer, or the muscular sausage-fingered one of a construction worker, but the lean hand of an athlete. She felt a flicker of desire looking at Robert's hand, but was too sick to utter a word.

It was a strange nausea that left her appetite intact, though unbendingly specific. Each morning she drank weak tea, ate some crackers and thin slices of cheddar cheese and then, if she could, went back to sleep. She wanted only to stay near familiar smells, her room, her bed, her sheets.

The smell of other people made her lips curl. The sound of her aged cat Angel licking himself was like a fork scratching on a plate. Damp carpets, perfume, cleaning agents, sour milk, coffee, all made her nostrils flare and her teeth grind in revulsion. The oil in Robert's skin. Not Oliver's, thank God. Sunshine was revolting. She no longer liked fresh air: her nose was sensitive enough to parse the smell of car exhaust and dog feces. She craved warm, clean, neutral solitude. This, she imagined, was how she would feel on her deathbed.

As often as he could, Robert took Oliver to preschool so Carmen could stay in bed until she had to pick Oliver up at noon.

Recently her dream life had been a luxurious counterpoint to waking reality. Asleep, she enjoyed a life of physical liberty and erotic abandon; awake, she was sick as a dog.

She'd read somewhere that inmates of Nazi concentration camps used to dream of elaborate and sensual meals. The dreams had been explained as the psyche's way of fulfilling frustrated desire. But what if dreams were reminders of a person's identity, telling you that you were not, by definition, a prisoner or a starving person or a piece of furniture— you were also a person who, in other circumstances, ate banquets and feasts. The inherent balance of this was appealing—the Taoist correctness of it. That humans might have a built-in subconscious system to remind them of who *else* they were.

Oliver's husky little voice asked Robert, "Is Mommy getting up? I want to give her a kiss. She won't mind. I won't wake her up. I'll do it very quietly." The light rustle of socks on carpet as Oliver tiptoed to the side of the bed and stared at her. She opened one eye, smiled, kissed him, closed her eyes again.

The next time she woke, Robert was gently shaking her shoulder and calling in a musical voice, "Carmen, Carmen. You've got to get up. It's the amnio today. We have to be there in one hour. Remember not to pee."

In the waiting room in her white knee socks, shoes and two light-blue hospital gowns, one front-to-back to cover her rear, she read the newspaper to distract herself from her nausea and the urgent need to pee. A full bladder was necessary for the uterus to be properly visible during the ultrasound. Robert had gone down to the lobby to get himself a coffee.

Carmen's approach to newspapers was to scan the headlines for subjects of interest: science, archeology, astronomy, movie stars, murder, torture, genocide, Argentina, Patty Hearst, guerrilla warfare, avalanches, shark attacks, cougar attacks, grizzly bear attacks, child rearing, breast-feeding, fashion, shoes, the Dalai Lama . . .

Today a headline in the international news section caught her attention. "Torture Chambers Uncovered during Renovation of Exclusive Mall." While renovating a shopping mall in Buenos Aires, construction workers had uncovered a hidden second basement with fifteen small unventilated rooms and two larger ones.

At first they'd assumed it was a bomb shelter of some kind, but then they noticed graffiti on the cement walls—names, dates—splattered blood, words in German over the doorway, "Arbeit Macht Frei."

The mall, the article reported, Galérias Pacífico, was best known for five frescoes commissioned from Argentine artists famous in the forties. The renovations were part of a plan to revitalize the building for such upscale tenants as Armani, Issey Miyake, Gucci, Versace and Chanel.

A former prisoner had visited the site and recognized the room he'd been held in seventeen years ago. With eyes shut, he could retrace the steps from his cell to the room with the German words where the torture took place—the number of steps, the turns, everything—because he'd always been blind-folded. He'd known he was underneath a shopping mall because one of the doctors whose job was to make sure he didn't die had joked that his wife was shopping for shoes upstairs while his daughter took ballet lessons on the top floor. The whole family at work in one building.

Life could take your breath away sometimes. The world truly seemed a Borgesian place, a labyrinth of infinity and meaning, of barrenness and fecundity, of paradise and night-mare, sex, death and life tumbling all around you. Here she was in the waiting room of the Women's Hospital in Vancouver, three months pregnant with her second child, her husband coming up the elevator with hot coffee, needing to pee so badly she doubted she could walk, and she was the same person who had gone shopping with her father's soon-to-be third wife on the opposite hemisphere of the planet. She had walked on marble floors, the heels of her new sandals clacking, while this man who had talked to a reporter yesterday had lain naked and defenceless beneath her. He had screamed in pain perhaps at the exact moment when she had looked at a painting of lovers—the personification of the goddess of fertility, she realized now, in the tangential figure of a naked woman holding a cornstalk and the personification of the god of the underworld in the man who held his hands in the cold downward-flowing stream. Ten days later she would speak of that painting to a lover, who might have already known then what she was learning only today. She had gone home from that mall to a father she no longer knew, who would tell her two weeks later about his mother disappearing when he was a child and that he guessed she might have died in a concentration camp. Earlier this day she'd been thinking about the dreams of a prisoner in such a camp.

So, all that contained in one moment of consciousness. The mind reeled. Would the baby growing inside her ever even suspect the layers of reality it was connected to, the reach its tiny life had?

Carmen showed Robert the article when he came back with his coffee.

"I shopped there, I shopped right in that mall with my father's girlfriend. Someone was being tortured beneath us while we fretted about which shoes to buy. Talk about a metaphor for capitalism. Can you believe it? There was a soldier at the entrance and I remember we thought it was strange that he checked our bags when we left, not when we went in, as though he was looking for shoplifters not terrorists with bombs."

She intended to amplify the moment for him, but someone called her name, "Ms Hillier." Anyway, he hadn't finished the article yet, and, although she thought he would understand the subtleties, the subject of her father always seemed to irritate him. He had to make sure as a man he wasn't somehow lumped in. Besides, why explain this moment and not the next equally layered one? It was a Sisyphean endeavour at the best of times.

The technician squirted cold gel onto her belly and pressed a device that looked like a blow-dryer with a metal roller against her abdomen. On a TV-sized screen an image appeared of her uterus. It looked like a beam of light dissected longitudinally or the dress of a primitively drawn angel, a cone of light moving in turbulent waters. At different moments a tiny hand was decipherable, a beating heart, a rounded curve the technician said was the bum, not the head. The baby had grown substantially from the bean-shaped creature she'd seen in the ultrasound two months earlier.

An assistant stood by her head and told her to relax, breathe slowly, visualize the most beautiful place she'd ever been. The assistant suggested a Caribbean island with white sand, turquoise water, and a soft wind blowing. She told Carmen to expect a sharp jab as the needle went in, but that the procedure would be short and to concentrate on being on that island.

Instead Carmen pictured a night from the early days of her relationship with Robert, walking from their tent in a huge bowl-shaped meadow on top of a mountain, the air icy cold after sunset, toward the sound of Gordon Lightfoot's clear voice wafting up from the stage of the Stein Valley Festival, a benefit to stop logging in the virgin watershed. Grass and moss and lichen-covered stones passed under the beam of their flashlight. She loved that Robert was a mountain climber and so at home in this magical place on top of the world.

The needle was a foot long and quite thick, and she looked away immediately. It didn't hurt as much as she expected going in. In the ultrasound it looked like a straight white line. She closed her eyes and communed telepathically with the fetus, *don't move, stay on the right, stay still.* She'd been told the chance of the syringe injuring the fetus was minuscule, but it was so counter-instinctual to let a sharp foreign object near the baby it was all she could do not to bolt.

She ignored the assistant, who was still talking to her about white sand and warm water, and focused on the fetus until the needle came out. Then she lay back and returned to the memory of her and Robert, a blanket wrapped around their shoulders, in awe of the small gathering of people under the stars singing to save, it seemed at the time, not just one valley of trees, but everything that was good in the world.

That night had been a turning point for her. Under the starry sky on top of the world she decided to jump into a life with Robert with both feet. The period when work was the only driving force in her life had come to an end; she was ready to start something new.

She'd become a long-distance swimmer in the intervening years and the decision felt like a colourful, multi-faceted version of starting a swim: in this case, however, barring obstacles she failed to navigate, the other shore would be death.

It wasn't a blind decision. She'd known Robert could be obsessive, critical, a bit disconnected at times, judgmental, aloof, but he was also passionate, drawn to nature, idealistic, perceptive, physically and sexually charged. She'd felt strong, happy, full of life, confident; she could have children without being like her father's wives, including her mother, and without being like her father. All her images of their life together were pleasant: a warm and busy home, everybody rushing in and out to do their activities, coming together for meals to talk and laugh and lie around, and taking time out to go after Robert in hotel rooms or cars or fields wearing something sexy.

On the drive home from the hospital she retreated again to a world of mental magic where love, intensely protective maternal love, could alter anything that was an obstacle to the baby's well-being. She thought of the prisoner's mother going now to his cell under the shopping mall, knowing the extent to which her telepathic efforts to protect her child had failed. When they got home she curled up on the couch and willed the contractions of her uterus to calm, to ebb, to disappear. She told the fetus she would never let anything like this happen again. It could grow in peace and warmth and safety now.

Robert left to pick Oliver up from a neighbour's house and Carmen drifted down through grass and moss, moving in the beam of a flashlight surrounded by starlit darkness. She walked over rubble as men with headlamps looked down a staircase into unexpected rooms. As she slipped below consciousness, a deep-sea angler floated by, surrounded by cold black ocean. The fish passed through the headlight of a submersible and receded into black, a faint baby-blue light dangling in front of its mouth, advertising food without specifying for whom.

3

No shred of light. No reflected light. Black. Temperature just above freezing.

On the ceiling thousands of dark warm-blooded bodies breathe slowly, hearts beating ten, at most fifteen, times per minute. A male crawls carefully over other hibernating bodies and rouses one female from hibernation. He nuzzles her small furry face, her furry belly, and strokes her for a long time with his cold velvety wings.

How could he see them when there was no light? He also perhaps was a bat.

He moves onto her back, spreading his wings over her. His penis is curved and works independently from the rest of his body, moving up and down like a lever. It feels vulnerable in the cold air. It prods until it finds the opening, then quickly pushes in. The tip immediately swells up and wave after wave of ejaculation begins. He can't pull it out until the tip detumesces, which won't be for a couple of hours.

The female's body begins pulsating rhythmically, seizing his penis and prolonging his ejaculation, carrying the sperm high into her uterus. He begins to fall back asleep, still clasped to her, the slowing pulsation of her sleeping body rocking him in pleasure.

He could feel the form of her tucked inside his arms, her soft fur under his nose, the billows of her lungs filling, emptying, filling and emptying. He was warm. His pleasure in this warmth was absolute. *Absolut!* his mind muttered raucously. The cool heat of vodka travelling down his throat. All he cared about was staying *this warm*. He luxuriated in the heat, and sank into a deeper sleep.

The next time he became wakeful he shivered. There were blankets on him; he could feel their weight, but they just seemed to trap the cold in, near his bones. She must have gone back into hibernation because her body no longer radiated warmth; it was just another cool object next to his bosom.

He was at the bottom of a dome-pit cave. Except for the bats hibernating on the ceiling of an adjacent passageway, he was alone. More than a hundred metres below the earth's surface. Alone and hurt. He didn't know how yet. He had never been so cold in his life.

The earth's centre was molten so why could he not feel even a trace of the heat? In the Middle Ages they located hell underground and defined it as unending fire. Fire—the gods' unstable gift: without boundaries it could destroy life, yet a body that did not burn oxygen, a body without heat, was dead. Life and fire were mutually essential. Hell must be life without boundaries, life run rampant; eternal life and heaven must be cold death.

Sold! Make way! I'm coming down! He really wanted that heat and he could live without death.

His confusion was so pervasive he didn't know he was confused. It occurred to him he was dying and perhaps hell did exist and he was about to go there and those medieval chaps had got it wrong and hell was going to be very cold. Now that was frightening. He wondered about the bats, where they were now, why they'd disappeared. His arms felt empty. He must've fallen asleep reading again, continued reading a dream book, advancing twenty or thirty dream pages. Making love to bats.

A sharp smell wafted into his nostrils, making him want to cough. He tried to stifle the urge but was only partly success-ful and a sputter erupted from his lips. Two voices floated across the dark, back and forth—a singsong. Something warm touched his wrist. Fingertips. He wasn't alone!

"You see, I cured him! I knew my cigarettes would pull him back. He hates them so much."

Another waft of smoke drifted up his nostrils.

A male voice angrily remonstrated above him, after which the cigarette seemed to be extinguished.

He needed to tell them how cold he was.

The fingers, which were so warm, lifted his wrist, held it, then touched the side of his neck. *Please*. It was a man's hand. A male voice spoke in serious tones under a soothing veneer. He could decipher the tone of the male voice, but not the words, whereas he could understand every word the female uttered.

"I think I should light another cigarette, don't you? I'm telling you. It will bring him back faster than anything. He's an old woman. You watch. He'll be yelling, 'Put that thing out!'"

The man's voice—Alfred believed it was the voice of an angel and that was why he couldn't parse the sounds—responded tersely.

Just before he drifted back to sleep he wondered what these familiar intonations had been. Words on the one hand, words he understood, and then some kind of tonal male music. What strange performance was he attending? What were other people doing in his netherworld?

The questions were infinitely fatiguing.

Gute Nacht alles.

4

A CROW CAWED among the pink blossoms of the sour cherry outside the kitchen. She poured coffee. Through the open window she could hear its wings brush the air as it flew straight up; then she saw it dive-bomb an eagle.

The morning sickness had lifted and once again she was engaged in everyday life. She fed Oliver, washed his clothes, folded them and put them away, set him up doing playdough or finger painting, played hide-and-seek with him. She walked him to preschool, holding his little hand, and bent her ear down to listen to him chat about angels and clouds and bees and other kids and neighbours and which animals ate which animals. Then she dashed home to enter field observations of the Stellar's jays on her computer and begin a preliminary analysis of the results.

Yesterday on the way to preschool he'd asked out of the blue, "Mom. Who would win, a Minotaur or a grizzly bear?"

"I think the grizzly bear would win," she'd answered, after reflecting. "They're so strong they can peel the roof off a car."

This was not the answer he'd wanted so he thought for a moment, then asked, "What if four Minotaurs were sitting in a car and their horns were sticking through the roof and the grizzly bear got on top to peel off the roof and one of the horns stuck him in the penis? Who would win then?"

"Well," she laughed, "then I'd have to say the Minotaurs would win."

Lately she cried reading the newspaper or called cheerful hellos to her neighbours. Leaves blowing in the wind filled her with calm. Robert came into the kitchen and wrapped his arms around and under her belly.

"I dreamed last night we were in the birdhouse again."

The house of their early courtship, a small cedar-shake cottage in North Vancouver with tiny rooms, unfinished wooden floors, and wood-frame windows that looked out into the forest. She'd lived there two years free of rent in exchange for guiding information walks through the bird sanctuary.

"We were in bed and I was looking at you. Your face was pale and your golden brown eyes looked at me from that tangle of sandy hair with such love I couldn't believe I was with someone like you."

"This doesn't sound like a dream," she laughed. She remembered afternoons with Robert in that house, lying in the bedroom half-dressed, bare feet resting on the wall, looking out the window at the leaves and talking all day, getting up only to make coffee and toast and bring it back to bed to talk some more, and eventually make love again. At last she'd found the nirvana of mating slugs, only a more mammalian, warm-blooded version.

"I was so impressed by how strong you were, your physical strength," he murmured, brushing aside her hair and kissing the back of her neck, "and by an unusual combination of bold-ness and shyness. And how curious you were; I loved the way we could hold any subject up like a golden ball and look at it from every angle."

Carmen smiled. "You were the first person who never told me I thought too much."

"I remember the first time I saw you watching birds. How immersed you got in the experience, your mind taking you so close to them. Most people can't do that."

She turned around and kissed him. The last time, sex had been like a Sunday walk in the park: pleasant but not particularly lustful. Very family and slippers. But this morning, she *wanted* him.

She wanted to take him right now and pin him beneath her, so all he could do was move, slowly, against her huge weight. She felt lustful and magnificent, like a queen, as though the cosmos existed to feed and groom her; fear and destruction were her handmaidens. The power of a storm, a tidal wave, thunder—all hers. Life was brewing: it smelled like death and it was coming through her.

A mother raccoon trotted across the lawn followed by five large kits. The raccoon was heading for the cat door where in the past weeks she'd entered, washed her paws in the cat's water, eaten the cat food and left a feral smell and dirty paw prints all over the mudroom.

"I'll deal with you later," she said to the raccoon and went and closed the door leading from the mudroom into the house.

Oliver was riveted to Saturday-morning cartoons in the living room. They tiptoed quietly past him and closed the bedroom door behind them. Robert had been reading the newspaper in bed and had left it spread out over the covers. She swept it onto the floor and pushed him onto the bed.

She felt triumphant. Her body was geographical, topographical, magnificent. She climbed on top of him and hoisted up her nightie. She put her hands on his shoulders and looked him in the face.

"You're feeling spunky," he said.

"Yeah, well, I'm in the thick of it now aren't I?" She leaned over and kissed him, felt his penis begin to harden.

"You're like ten different kinds of fruit," he murmured.

"Shh," she whispered. She didn't need flattery this morning.

It was true, though, that Robert got many different bodies with her, while she only got his one, fairly stable, masculine body of imperceptibly eroding muscle. The female body in contrast was so revolutionary, a locus of radical, tectonic change, change in form *and* function. It was like riding a whale bareback. How did Robert reorient himself so quickly? It must help being a mountain climber, she thought and smiled.

He grabbed her haunches and adjusted her motion slightly, and she had an orgasm feeling him close in on her.

The phone rang. She could hear Oliver run for it. "Who is it?" he demanded by way of greeting.

"Who is it, Oliver?" she echoed.

"I can't understand very well," he called.

She climbed off quickly and pulled her nightie down just before Oliver brought the phone in.

"Thanks dear," she said and rubbed Oliver's head. "Hello?"

"Your daddy is very sick," a woman said in an uncertain, defensive tone. The accent was very thick, familiar, but not the voice.

"Who is this?"

"Dalva. Your daddy's *esposa*." She sounded like a Lilliputian her voice was so tiny and distant.

"Is he alive?"

"Djes. He can no speak."

"What happened?"

"Achh, *não e possible!*"

Next a man's voice enunciated in clear English, "Hello? Is this Alfred Lion's daughter?" It sounded like he was speaking way down in a deep valley.

"Yes."

"This is Dr Valenciega. Your father has suffered a stroke. He is paralyzed on the left side and hasn't regained consciousness yet, but he is responding to pain stimulus."

"I can hardly hear you. Where are you calling from?"

"Rio de Janeiro. Hospital São Vincente. Mrs Lion instructs me to say she wanted you to know about your father so you could have a chance to see him. His condition is stable, but he could have another stroke any time. However, we do expect him to regain consciousness; his CT scan is showing signs of increasing wakeful activity. In fact, we're not sure he isn't already conscious."

"Will he be able to talk?"

"He'll be able to hear. He may not be able to answer."

"Can you call back? This line is terrible."

"There isn't much more to tell."

"Look. I haven't seen my father in seventeen years or so. I'm seven months pregnant. I don't even know if I can travel on a plane."

All those years of hoping he'd call, and now, when she really couldn't need him less, he called. More precisely, *his wife* called.

"If you're healthy and the pregnancy is going well, you should be able to travel safely for another two or three weeks. You may need a doctor's letter for the airline."

"I don't have my father's phone number."

"I'll give you my number here at the hospital and put Mrs Lion back on."

Yet another Mrs Lion.

They finished making love that night after Oliver went to sleep. Carmen no longer felt triumphant and queenly; she felt large, confused, teary, the first twinges of a dormant anger and pain reawakening, as though a spell had been broken. She succumbed to vulnerability and her orgasm, when it came, was a wave of emotional surrender, erotically tinged with emotional pain. She clung to Robert with her eyes tightly closed.

Afterwards, Robert kissed the back of her head. "That was wonderful," he said.

"It wasn't foxes and hedgehogs, that's for sure."

He laughed, "Excuse me?"

"It's in a Woody Allen movie. While her husband is making passionate love to her, the wife runs through all the people they know and decides who is a hedgehog and who is a fox."

He rolled over and turned out the light. "It wasn't foxes and hedgehogs for me either."

One of the things she loved about their relationship was how different making love was every time. From the very beginning they'd enjoyed a highly attuned, rapid-feedback sexuality that built on nuance, responding to the degree of pressure in a grip, an adjustment of position, a look in the eye, a hunger of the mouth—animal, tender or transcendent. She had felt Czechoslovakian, Indian, Tibetan, Quebec voyaguer, Masai maiden, prairie cowboy, Yukon hermit, French tart, Chinese gymnast, Dallas cheerleader, Victorian chamber-maid, tango dancer, Mick Jagger, Janis Joplin, Bruce Springsteen, Colette and Brunnhilde, and Robert was always right there with her. Their palette was both unpredictable and inexhaustible.

She loved sleeping together, the baby growing as they slept. Kicking Robert's back through her skin. A couple of hours later Oliver trundled in and climbed over Carmen to insert himself between his parents. Carmen kissed the top of his ear and whispered, "I love you."

5

His mother is speaking to him. He knows it's not right for him to be hearing her voice, but he's so happy he doesn't worry. He's back home at last! In bed. The sun is shining through curtains with a flower pattern on them. The pattern is so familiar. His boyhood worries come and go like birds in the sky; he feels a happy blend of upcoming adventure and present safety.

His mother says, "Don't worry *Liebchen*, I'm waiting. I'll always love you. I'm here in the North Pole." This last piece of information seems natural enough. His mother with her thick hose, her dirndl for dress-up and frilly white blouse, her khaki shirtdress for everyday and her good walking shoes, her light-brown hair in a French knot, her confident bone structure and anxious blue eyes. She wouldn't be anxious in the North Pole. It would be home to her now.

But he's so warm here in his bed and not really in the mood to visit snow and ice. His mother is more adventurous than he ever would have guessed.

The smell isn't quite right though.

She must be using a different cleaning powder. Suddenly he is irritated. He thinks how could she be so stupid as to use powder that doesn't smell right? It smells like a bloody hospital. Why would she change her powder? Why change it to something worse? He is going to speak to her.

"Warum hast du verändert sich der Seifepuder?"

She replies, but in a wilfully incomprehensible gibberish that is neither German nor English. A string of sounds that resemble, but are not, language. He thinks she is teasing him, not taking his anger seriously. So he says in a more threatening tone, *"Warum sprichts du diese Verrücktheit? Ich frage dich etwa seriös!"*

She leaves in a flutter and it occurs to him he should open his eyes.

He popped them open. A hospital room, empty except for him.

I'm sorry, Mutti. My fault again.

He closed his eyes. His leg ached in two places where the bone had knit back together. He remembered falling. Or rather, remembered sitting on the roof, remembered knowing he was going to fall, and remembered gravity pulling him down. Thinking he was flying.

He remembered looking out over the city, being above it, away from mother and father, friends, tormentors and cousins, alone, with seemingly endless free time.

That moment might have been a few hours ago, not fifty-four years ago. He remembered his mother's voice calling to him. Afraid. Afraid for him, but also afraid for herself, for the pain she'd suffer if he died. Pleading. He had not wanted to be drawn close to her fear, to be held near it. Yet he should have been the one pleading. *Don't fall Mutti, don't fall into darkness.*

Footsteps sounded on the stone floor. He closed his eyes and a teardrop ran down his temple into the pillow. He wasn't ready yet.

6

SHE WAS WASTING TIME. Oliver, the apple of her eye, was zoned out watching "Arthur" and "The Magic School Bus," while she played the oxymoronically named FreeCell, a variation of computer solitaire that did not depend on luck and could always be completed. She should be entering the week's data on her observations of the jays or at least starting dinner or cleaning up Oliver's playdough, but her mind was snagged in an Escher world.

The pleasure was decadent, yet somehow also puritanical: creating order without meaning; repetition creating an illusion of infinity. Nothing random, nothing combined, nothing sexual. The clock ticking. Time leaking away as she feverishly built edifices of playing cards, red on black, black on red, King, Queen, male, female, stylized representations of generations and authority. A gift to no one. Chicken, egg, chicken, anything that alternated.

Playing FreeCell reined in the unstable flow of her days, days unharnessed from economic necessity by Robert's paycheque and her own decision to quit teaching at the university for a year.

She'd decided to have another baby, spend more time with Oliver and keep her hand in by continuing her research on the mating habits of Stellar's jays. A government program to enhance science and technology education paid her to do occasional outreach lectures in high schools and colleges in remote areas across the province. She intended to submit a paper on the jays for publication, but she also wanted to try writing something in a less academic style.

After twenty years of university life, interrupted only by a year working for the Western Canada Wilderness Committee and a two-year sabbatical as parks guide at the Seymour Flats Bird Sanctuary—the birdhouse of her courtship with Robert—she felt she'd earned the right to let her mind travel more adventurously.

Exploring connections between animal mating behaviour and human behaviour had always been her true interest and, if she was honest, an embarrassingly unacademic one. Although she loved the detail of scientific study and the precise revelations that kind of study afforded, and she had complete faith in academic discipline and rigour, she occasionally felt impatient. What she was really looking for were imaginative leaps, revelations of meaning and connection, mystical truths, assembling a larger picture through intuitive accretion of observation. Which was not to say she was interested in any ideas that were contradicted by scientific fact.

If she wanted to pursue her interest further in an academic context, at the very least she'd have to complete a doctorate in anthropology. During her year off she planned to decide if she wanted to spend that many more years studying or if she should continue teaching at the university and go for tenure or if she should do something completely different—start a business, study art, or get more involved in environmental activism.

But instead here she was, indulging in FreeCell. People suffered torture, died of starvation while she played FreeCell in warmth and comfort.

"Eat your peas. Children are starving in China." Instead of her mother's rationale (appreciate having peas since other children have nothing to eat), Carmen gave Oliver the selfish reasoning, "You need them to grow strong and healthy." Oliver still said no but eventually ate them anyway. As she had. She dragged a red eight over to a black nine, released the button. It popped into place.

She despised herself for wasting time.

And yet, what did it matter? Why not enjoy the luxury of the last trimester where she could be productive without doing anything. Let her body run things. How often did that happen?

At six o'clock, she pulled herself away from the computer and pulled Oliver off the TV. She took some trouble with her appearance. Brushed her hair. Changed into an ironed white shirt, put lipstick on, chose the stretch pants without the baggy knees.

It was dark out. The last of the leaves had been pulled from the trees by the day's wind and rain and the sidewalks were covered with yellow and brown drifts. Halloween was past but it was too early for Christmas lights. The street lights, the lights inside houses, and the smell of woodsmoke from homes with fireplaces made Carmen feel cozy.

She indulged in maternal pride pushing Oliver down the street in the stroller. For once all the pieces had been assembled, nothing was missing or awry, no noses unwiped, rashes untended, food stains on chins, hair unwashed, buttons popped. Oliver looked cute and a little old-fashioned in the forest-green sweater-jacket Beth had knitted for him. His sandy curls stuck out from under a mustard-coloured toque, his feet dangled in their light-brown Italian boots with embroidered hikers climbing up the ankles.

She said "Hello" to the little girl who lived two houses over, playing hopscotch with her friend under the street light. The moment was a small taste of heaven, of the sweetness of life: walking with her son to meet her husband on an autumn evening calling hello to the neighbours.

A spiderweb, still wet from the rain, hung in a tree and glistened in the street light. She crouched down and with her face next to Oliver's cool rosy cheek, pointed the web out to him. She felt like a good mother. This was one of the best feelings she ever had, second only to the ever-expanding love she sometimes got after making love with Robert.

Six buses came and went. Robert did not arrive. Carmen checked her watch. In the morning he'd said he'd be home at six, and it was quarter to seven.

Why couldn't he at least phone if he was going to be late again? He just assumed she'd be waiting, happy to see him. He'd made the transition overnight when she quit her job. And now it was as if her time had no value because she earned only a token salary.

Last night he'd forgotten to tell her he was going out for dinner with a friend. He'd come home at eleven, tipsy, playful, in a good mood, shocked that she wasn't happy to see him. He'd tried to cajole her, kiss her, touch her breast.

Early in her studies she'd learned the first impulse of all life forms was to avoid touch. The first instinctual responses to touch were flight or attack. The main exception being, in some species, the physical bond between mother and child. Courtship evolved to overcome that first impulse to avoid touch, so that conception could occur.

Even at the best of times his boyish side evoked a complicated response in her. There was a sweetness to it, an innocence, and she was happy he could let off steam, be carefree. But she always felt like a voyeur around it, because she wasn't invited to be boyish too, she was invited to watch from the sidelines, to be amused, to indulge. This was a role she disliked intensely. It made her feel asexual and matronly, a big female authority, the mother—not the lover—whose power the boy wanted to subvert while making her laugh as he did so. Charm as subverted aggression. Carmen did not mistake Robert's behaviour for courtship.

She hated the role of angry wife too. She felt so cornered sometimes she wanted to run away or scream or punch or laugh hysterically.

Robert liked the company of men. He was a geographer so his work involved doing surveys in the north, flying in by seaplane, camping in the wilderness for weeks. He was comfortable with men, he liked their smell, their big guffaws, the way they could be quiet; he thrived in the good-natured rivalry and held his own well enough when the rivalry wasn't good-natured. He'd told Carmen it connected somehow to his father, his exaltation at his father's big body, the joy of leaping all over a big strong man who loved him.

Carmen liked hearing about this physical love between father and son. She felt gratified she'd chosen a father in Robert who would be able to give that to her children. Already Oliver loved to wrestle with his father and pit his four-year-old strength against him.

But there was a little tug. Although she had leapt into Oscar's arms when she was little, it was never with such sweet abandon, never with the feeling that he was completely hers. And she'd never felt she could climb all over her own father. They were always in the process of getting to know each other again and he was always distracted by whichever woman he was with.

As she watched bus after bus leave and scanned the people getting off, she became certain Robert was not going to be among them. Her sense of warmth and happiness faded and was replaced by a feeling of being discarded, set aside. She was being made to understand how little she mattered. She felt like crying.

"What an asshole," she muttered. She avoided meeting the gaze of other people at the bus stop, not wanting to reveal that she'd been stood up. She wanted to hide. She walked back home.

"Who's an asshole?" Oliver asked.

"Daddy," she answered.

Oliver took on a look of deep concentration, as if he was absorbing something.

"Oliver, don't pay attention to me. Daddy's not an asshole. I'm just mad right now."

She parked the stroller in the garage, helped Oliver out, held his hand as they walked through the dark to the back door, then got her keys out, unlocked the door and went inside the empty dark house.

An image, both menacing and ridiculous, flashed through her mind—a white peacock, twittering, offering a grub in its beak, its crest a bobbing bouquet of starry flowers. Just as she reached for the grub, flap! The head disappeared and a geometric fan vibrated in front of her eyes, leaving her dazzled, hungry, cheated and confused.

It was as though she could see love was on offer, but when she went to actually take it, it was replaced by something else. There seemed a meanness to the process, like someone was trying to fool her into giving something for nothing.

She tried to hide her sudden sense of desolation from her son. She went through the first floor, turned on lights in every room, quickly made a couple of poached eggs and toast and sat down to dinner in the kitchen with Oliver across from her.

Robert came home at a quarter after seven. Her anger was like a bivalve's foot: it had exuded too far out of the shell to be pulled back quickly and he knew it the second he saw her face.

His own face took on a trace of discomfort and guilt, the recognition that evasive action and damage control were going to be necessary and a hint of irritation that any action was necessary, a suspicion that it wasn't fair that he couldn't just come home and relax after work.

"We waited three-quarters of an hour at the bus stop."

"Honey, I'm sorry. I had no idea you were going to walk to the bus stop."

"We wanted to surprise you."

"I would've phoned. I had no idea."

"Well, what did you think? We'd just be waiting here? What if I had dinner ready?"

"No offence dear, but you never have dinner waiting."

"That's because I never know when you're going to choose to come home."

"I don't *choose* to come home. I have deadlines. Your time is more flexible these days."

"More flexible? *I* can't disappear for an hour without telling anyone. *I* can't go out for dinner with a friend and forget to tell you. *I* don't get two hours to work out—who are you building that body for anyway? . . . . what the hell! We're talking about a phone call."

"You chose to stay home. You could have kept working and then everything would be *equal*. Everything would be the *same*. I'm already bending over backward to accommodate your need for everything to be equal and the same, when it just isn't right now. It's not that I love my work that much, you know. I'd love to take a year off. I do it for you and for Oliver and then I have to come home and take abuse for it."

"Without Oliver and I you wouldn't work, is that it? You'd be on welfare? Come off it. It was my earnings that bought this house. You'd climb a few more mountains. Watch some more sports."

Oliver came in. "What's an asshole?" he asked.

Carmen blushed. She suddenly felt like a little girl caught doing something bad. Maybe Robert was right, maybe she should just give up, stop being mad, get on with it.

A second child had not been his idea. It was her thing. He wanted to climb specific mountains, Mount Rainier, Mount McKinley, Mount Silverthrone, and he wanted to do it before he got too old. He wanted to be a good father; he didn't like being away from Oliver for the long periods of time it took to do a climb. A second child would delay everything further. She had swept his concerns aside, certain that they should have two children, needing to create a specific feeling of family, warmth, home. What was wrong with that? Nothing. But she wasn't thinking of him, was she?

She looked at his face. She wanted him to climb his mountains, to walk along a snow-covered ridge, ice in his eyelashes and eyebrows, scarf around his face, the tops of his cheeks scarlet from windburn. She liked imagining him on top of the world, looking out over miles of mountain peaks and valleys— all uninhabitable and wild—standing in the sky, clouds swirling past, the last remnants of energy burning in his thighs. It had never been her intention to take that away from him.

His curly brown hair was streaked with grey; his eyebrows were bushy, the kind described as "knitted"; his warm brown eyes set deep in his skull, sullen now, resentful, but pleading too. He was a big presence in their kitchen, a mountain man, with powerful legs and a hairy chest with a dip in the middle, a pigeon chest where water collected in the bath and Oliver could sail a miniature sailboat he'd got in a Kinder egg.

She relented. "Phone next time. It's inconsiderate." She rubbed the top of Oliver's head. Later in bed Robert mimicked in a falsetto, "What's an asshole?" and she burst out laughing.

Family life: heaven to hell and back again in one hour.

7

SOMETHING ALWAYS RUINED the pure darkness when he tried to picture it. There was always a small tear in the fabric. A spot in the distance, below him, which he squinted at, trying to decide if it really was a spot of light or if his brain was making the spot inside his eyes.

The light seemed not to be really there. He stared and the blackness was absolute, but as he turned away, he saw it again. Something on the edge of his mind. Eventually he determined that it was something very distant swimming in and out of a beam of light.

He smelled beans, beans and rice and not very fresh fish. A clatter of wheels on hard linoleum tiles. A plate, or a cup or some kind of dishware smashed. On the floor. Something sailed past his head on the right. Smashed on the wall behind him. Not exactly a Ming vase, but a plate from the Middle East painted with real gold, another plate he'd packed and unpacked for thirty years. Shattered. He turned his head to the left just in time to catch a glimpse of another plate going by, worth several hundred dollars. Hit the wall, smash, slide to the floor in a shard waterfall.

Adrenalin hit his stomach. Alertness. Joy even. He felt engaged, alive, ready for the next thing. Which was a crystal ashtray, lamentably full of ashes and butts, flying straight at his face. He blinked.

She was a violent woman. But then she'd had a violent life. She'd had a son whom she'd left for an afternoon with the husband, not the boy's father, and then come home to red swirling lights, an ambulance pulling away, the bastard explaining to the police how the boy had hit his head on the corner of the coffee table, smashed his face on the stone floor. Two years old.

Then she got pregnant with the husband's child and they had a fight and he kicked her in the belly. The baby was born dead. A baby girl.

Two dead children. Poor kid. No wonder she picked a man whose children were at least alive, had made it to adulthood. But she was a violent one. He had scratches to prove it, deep ones; the scars hung around for a year or two. What did the nurses make of them?

He ducked. Then the crockery stopped flying. Her mouth was on his. Warm and dark. The cave fish floated back into view, more beautiful than any he'd seen before. It was light blue and it had long feathery fins that ruffled in some invisible current. It was lit like a ballet dancer on a dark stage. *Swan Lake.* Swan Song.

He had his pyjamas on. She was taking them off. Her hair brushed his face, like a feather, or a curtain, and he felt innocent and wide-eyed. She rubbed herself against him slowly until he got an erection, then she rolled around, playing hard to get, making him come after her, until he got her under him, and got inside her, and felt like a boy again.

Sometimes this worked out, sometimes it didn't. If she managed to continue coaxing him, teasing him, indulging him, if she could find his orgasm and take it out of him, he was able to surrender fully. He experienced a climax that was earth-shattering and all-encompassing and left him spent, in a daze, affectionate and submissive for hours afterwards, even days.

But other times as soon as he felt like a boy, she seemed suddenly too hungry, too ravenous, insatiable; her mouth suddenly seemed too full of saliva and alarmingly red inside, her teeth too hard, her jaw too strong, her eyes too bright and greedy and his erection would go soft. He would just roll over and go to sleep.

This did not bring out the best in his bride. Nor did her resulting attacks bring out the best in him. The downward spiral could go on for weeks. Eventually the day would come when they would not be able to pull back up from the nosedive.

Some clown banged a tray down right in front of him and over the sound of loose wheels yelled, "Time to eat, you sack of bones. One more pleasure before you die. Beans, beans, what else?"

He went back to the cave fish. The beam of light illuminating it slowly faded and he wondered if he was having another stroke, if this was what it looked like. He couldn't remember the last one.

8

SHE TOLD OLIVER it was time to brush his teeth.

"I'm not brushing my teeth. I hate brushing my teeth. I'll do it tomorrow."

She launched into the speech about why we have to brush our teeth, but he squirmed away from her. "You can't make me. It's my life," he said. Her belly tightened with a Braxton Hicks contraction and she sighed, maternal patience edging toward maternal rage.

"I'm going into the bathroom and I'm waiting until you're ready to brush your teeth. You come when you're ready." She got her book and went and sat on the toilet. In half a minute he came in scowling, "All right, I'll brush my stupid teeth. I hate you."

The strategy worked because he knew she was only too happy to read for hours and it hadn't occurred to him yet to tear the house apart while she sat in the bathroom.

He squirted toothpaste all over the front of his pyjamas and looked at her accusingly. She sighed, heaved herself up and thought, *So this is where it leads.* The flushed excitement in Grade 2 when John from England hugged her; all the fuss about dates and beautifying oneself and appearing intelligent or cool or sexy; the blushing, the anticipation, the arousal and the requitement of desire; the serious relationships that followed; the marriage, the hope and love and idealism. It all led to fighting about brushing teeth with a boy who was almost the same age as she'd been when she had her first crush.

It led to spending your time trying to convince someone to do something they didn't want to do: to eat, to go somewhere, to leave somewhere, to put things away, to get dressed, get undressed, get in the bath, get out of the bath. Threat, bribe, promise, explain. Explain, explain, explain. Until finally she couldn't bear the patient drone of her own voice and she'd shout, "Just do it!"

She didn't get to that point this time. She took off his pyjama top, laid a dab of toothpaste on his dinosaur toothbrush, handed it to him and kissed his cheek.

The pleasure she took in his small boy's body was intense. She loved his wiry muscles, the way his limbs stuck out and his rib cage showed, the heat of his skin and the warm dirt smell. She rubbed his hair and kissed him again.

Oliver jumped off the counter, had a pee, and they went to pick out a story. A wave of tenderness overtook Carmen and she stopped to hug and squeeze him. He wriggled away, instinctively she figured, because he was so adorable she just wanted to eat him up, a desire not without its alarming aspects.

That expression "to want to eat someone up" had always intrigued her, because it so accurately described the feeling of overwhelming love, a desire to bite without hurting, to consume without eating the love object. A primal, unworkable solution to a desire for union.

She remembered playing with Rebecca when her sister was an unbearably cute baby, and wanting to eat her up. She bit Robert sometimes when her desire got so intense nothing seemed able to satisfy it.

She propped up pillows against the wall, sat up straight to avoid heartburn, and waited as Oliver went through all his books. He chose *Sir Gawain and the Green Knight*, a story about a stranger who dares a group of knights to cut off his head. When the story reached the part about love, Oliver's little body went slack. His head sank more heavily against her shoulder. She closed the book, pulled the covers over his shoulders, turned the light off and lay back to doze and enjoy Oliver's presence curled under her arm.

Maybe she had it. If a kiss were a displacement of a bite, intended to override the fight-or-flight response for mating or nurturing purposes, then if that survival response became too compromised and an organism was in danger of losing itself completely, the brain generated an urge to bite to remind everyone who was who again.

She heard Robert let himself in. She eased herself out of Oliver's bed and went to greet him. He made himself a couple of poached eggs and some toast, got a beer out of the fridge, and they sat down at the kitchen table.

"I checked out the airfares to Brazil. I can fly out on Monday and be back ten days later for about fifteen hundred dollars return. My mom said she could fly out next week and help with Ollie. The doctor said it would be fine. I'm healthy and the baby's doing well."

Robert went quiet. He stopped eating.

"Have you forgotten I'm going to Alaska the day after tomorrow?"

"I thought maybe you could postpone it for a couple of weeks."

He paused, and spoke while looking at his plate. "Carmen, I've paid for the plane ticket, the Helijet; I'm going with four other guys who've also all paid and those tickets are all non-refundable. I've planned this trip for months. It's probably the last climb I'll be able to do for a while because of the baby. It's not something I can just postpone. I'd have to cancel."

"I don't know if Oliver can handle two weeks without either of us. It's a long time."

"Look, your father hasn't spoken to you for seventeen years. Come on! Why should I just drop everything because you get this call out of the blue?"

"I haven't been away since I had Ollie."

"What about the Bahamas? The swim around Long Island?"

"Okay, once then."

"You could have gone away more."

"It's my father. If he dies I'll never see him again."

"Yeah, well that's usually the case when someone dies. I can't believe you. You're ready to drop everything and go running to a father who disowned you. After I've listened to you go on and on about how much pain he caused you, what an asshole he was. *I've* been there for *my* family. There are only small windows in the season when you can climb a mountain like this because of the weather, as you well know. I'll be damned if I'm going to say, 'Oh. Okay. You want to see your daughter now, all of a sudden, nothing for seventeen years, I'll drop everything, stay home and babysit.' I don't think so."

Robert ripped a bite off his toast. "Besides, *he* didn't call you. It was his new wife."

"*I have* to go. And I never went *on and on*. What a jerk-off thing to say."

How had she ended up having to beg for the right to visit her dying father, having to justify that to anyone? Where had her independence gone? Was this what happened when you became a mother?

In the past, before birth control and feminism, a woman risked dying from childbirth; she was exhausted all the time, but still she had value as a mother, as someone who could give birth. Now, particularly for urban, middle-class couples like herself and Robert, the economic argument for having children had vanished. Reversed. Children were an economic impediment. And the survival of the species relied more on *not* having children than on having them.

The only reasons for having them now were whimsical or narcissistic: you wanted to populate the future with more like-thinking individuals—more Christians, more Muslims, more Chinese, more proponents of materialist democracy, more Jews, Tibetans, more concert pianists, more blondes . . . or you just wanted them.

"How long is the trip?"

"I told you. Three weeks, with the boat ride, acclimatization, the hike, and the return time."

"I'll wait till my mom gets here. Oliver will have to manage." She refused to stoop to asking him for permission.

"Why don't you go when I get back?"

"I'll be too pregnant. And he might be dead."

She sat in the dark living room, looking out at the park across the street. She could make out the shape of a bird's body, lying on its back, its legs sticking stiffly out in the air.

That afternoon, as she'd picked up Oliver's dinosaurs from the living-room floor, she'd stopped and watched a flock of sparrows, finches and juncos eating seed scattered near a bench, juggling their time between pecking the seeds and pecking each other.

The dead bird, a dark-eyed junco, had careened over from some bushes, and landed with a wobbly run on the grass. It had tried to pick up a seed at the edge of the group, but a sparrow had rushed over and pecked at its head. It retreated and pecked half-heartedly at the ground for a while, then tried again. Again the sparrow rushed over aggressively, and this time another came from the other side and pecked too. On its third attempt, the junco ignored the pecking and grabbed a seed anyway, attempting to hop away and eat in peace. The two birds pursued it, till it dropped the seed and retreated to taller grass at the base of a lamppost, its feathers sticking out at odd angles.

Now, alone in the dark, Oliver asleep in her bed and Robert deplaning in Alert Bay on Cormorant Island with his Sierra Club group, the junco made her feel like crying, its thin legs sticking straight out in the air, beak to the night sky.

Robert had been cold, distant and aloof right till the end. As he was leaving with his pack and bag, she had swallowed her anger and asked, "Are you seriously going to leave without even talking to me?" She couldn't believe her determination to see her father could cause that much distance.

"I've talked to you."

"You know what I mean."

"What do you want? Do you want me to fake it? This is how I feel. I *am* angry. I don't agree with you ditching Oliver for two weeks, even if it is with your mother, so you can see your father. I think you're doing it to prove a point. I'll get over it, but I can't just snap my fingers."

He gave her a grudging, sterile kiss on the cheek and left. She wondered cynically how long his bad mood would persist once he joined the guys. When would it shift into carefree, back-slapping, beer-drinking mode, glad to be free of women and their demands? Free of her. When was he faking it and when was he being real? She felt like throwing something at him. She wanted to hear something smash on the sidewalk or against the back of his head.

Something wasn't adding up. She couldn't put her finger on it, but as she looked out the window adrenalin started to pump through her blood and she got up out of the chair. What was it? That he would risk leaving his wife feeling so alienated? How could he feel so sure she'd be here when he came back? True, she was hugely pregnant; she was physically, economically and emotionally dependent on him at the moment. Nonetheless. Maybe he didn't really care if she left. Maybe he had less on the line than she. What might she have overlooked, failed to notice?

She went to the hall closet and checked his coat pockets. Read any business cards she found, flipped them over for handwritten messages. She went upstairs to his desk in the corner of their bedroom. Opened the drawers, flicked through the junk, the envelopes, bills, papers, old faxes, surveys.

All the while fantasizing about living alone, being free again. *I don't need him*, she thought, *I'm fine alone. I'm tired of having to beg for everything. I'll get a bungalow in the country. Oliver and the baby can be country children. I'll study grouse. I'll teach part time at a community college.*

The fetus did a seismic turn, then gave her a sharp jab in the pelvis. *Am I nuts*, she thought. *This is marriage. This is life. He's just being an asshole right now. I married him. Would I marry a complete asshole?* She laughed to herself. *Sure, why not? No lack to choose from.*

She noticed his briefcase under the desk, shoved to the back near the wall. She took it out. It was locked, but she knew he hadn't changed the settings from when he bought it—three zeros. It popped open.

Her heart was racing. She felt the risk; this was an invasion of privacy, this was theft. But it also felt like a matter of life and death, of survival, as though the well-being of her baby were on the line, and the flourishing of dear, young, openhearted Oliver. She needed to know what Robert's intentions were. Who he really was. She needed the information.

Inside, after a few minutes' searching, she found what she was looking for. She knew it the minute she saw it. An envelope with a handwritten address, a return address she didn't recognize.

9

‒‒‒‒‒‒‒∞∞∞‒‒‒‒‒‒‒

SHE SAT AT A SMALL TABLE set with a white linen cloth and modern flatware. April was always at least half an hour late, so Carmen took out the blanket she was embroidering for the baby and worked slowly, distractedly, filling in a black lamb.

She paused and took a bite of bread. This week she'd fed Oliver toad-in-the-hole, Kraft dinner and pancakes, but had herself barely eaten anything. She chewed and swallowed the bread only out of duty for the baby.

She considered a nest she'd embroidered in a stand of bulrushes with three eggs inside. They looked like stones. No matter how tiny the stitches, embroidery could not approximate the smoothness of a real egg, an object from which nothing stuck out—no leg, tail, fin, wing, feather or hair. The party was all on the inside, a walled garden, hors d'oeuvres built in. A stone was stone all the way through, but an egg had life inside which made you want to open it up and take a peek.

She'd had an odd impulse while trying to conceive this baby—an impulse to go out on the town and find another man to conceive with. It had not arisen from sexual boredom or dissatisfaction with Robert; it was simply a dispassionate, biological urge not to put all her reproductive eggs in one basket. She knew, of course, that even though the urge felt normal—as if heading downtown with such a purpose would be the most natural thing in the world—it would be completely anomalous with every other part of her life. There was no question of acting on it, but not because it would be immoral: because it would not be sensible, rational, mathematical.

It was always a struggle for human beings to integrate the behaviour required for conceiving children with the behaviour required for raising them. She'd thought she was up to it though. She thought she could juggle sexual passion, commitment to her work and a need for freedom, with a happy submission to domestic routine and its ensuing stability. She took pleasure in changing a diaper, planting a flower, sweeping a floor, rearranging furniture.

And she'd thought Robert was, if anything, more suited than she to moving fluidly between the different realities. He seemed less anxious about his identity, less prey to sudden irrational (or rational) fears that he wasn't amounting to much, less likely to develop an addiction or have an affair.

Fantasy and delusion. She so desperately did not want to be the stable one, the one waiting at home while the other sowed wild oats, the domestic party to the party animal. The pain of finding herself almost certainly in that exact role was blinding. And it was made worse, much worse, by the fact that any action to alleviate her pain—getting drunk, having an affair herself, leaving Robert, assaulting the woman who'd written the letter, taking off unannounced on a trip—would hurt Oliver.

So she embroidered. She threaded her needle, made a knot, created a blanket that would make her new child feel welcome in the world, enveloped in love, cherished and anticipated. She embroidered, while writhing inside on the head of a pin.

She felt desperately like going for a long swim. Putting on her wetsuit and setting out for the fishing villages of Japan; setting up sponsors and a spotter and striking out across the

Pacific, surrendering to the hypnotic rhythm of crawl, breast-stroke, backstroke, the erasure of everything but the sea and her own motion through water, immersing herself in time in a pure and egoless way.

It would have to wait a year, until she'd finished nursing the baby, but just knowing that, if all else failed, she could go on that swim made it possible to go on now. She consoled herself further with the thought that each pregnancy enlarged her heart, increasing her endurance and fitness for long-distance exertions.

She thought of the sea cucumber's response to external threat. Auto-evisceration. A poor man's metamorphosis. The sea cucumber expelled all its organs—its heart, digestive and reproductive systems—in a sacrificial diversion so the organism could get away and later grow new organs. Long-distance swims were like that, emptying you of everything but the basic platform of life. You re-emerged from the water ready to form whatever new self was needed for the next episode.

A sea cucumber, however, was hermaphroditic and could reproduce alone. And it didn't have to raise little sea cucumbers to be responsible members of society who were loved and supported by their parents until adulthood.

"With a father like mine, what did I expect? It was inevitable that, despite my best efforts to be the kind of woman no one would cheat on, I would become the wife, the hugely pregnant wife, of an unfaithful dickhead.

"I hate, I hate, I hate being the deceived one, the idiot whose happiness is based on illusion, the one with the frozen smile on her face. I feel like Sandy Dennis in *Who's Afraid of Virginia Woolf?* That's it, isn't it? The only choice, Sandy Dennis or Elizabeth Taylor. Simp or bitch. How did this happen? I had an education. I was smart, independent, strong.

This is all because I wanted kids."

"Okay, okay, calm down girl," April said tenderly. "I think hearing from your dad has put you in a tailspin. It's just a letter from an old girlfriend checking out the turf. It's not impossible, Carmen, that you would get a letter like that from an old boyfriend and carry it around as an ego boost."

"It was an answer to a letter he wrote," she said, and had to stop to choke back tears. "Who knows what was in his letter? Maybe she's single and testing the waters, but what the hell is he doing? To get that kind of answer, he must have written something fairly steamy. He just left on a three-week expedition without even saying goodbye to me."

"Why would he suddenly, after ten years of a great marriage with you, get obsessed with an old girlfriend? C'mon. You're having a baby together, that's one of the most meaningful things you can do. And he's nuts about you. Besides, if you were fooling around and you wanted to hide it, wouldn't you go out of your way to be nice, to say goodbye, keep things smooth?"

"Not if I was looking for emotional justification. Not if I wanted to prove that my wife deserved it in some way. He had mixed feelings about another child, you know. Maybe he's rebelling. Decided he deserves more fun, he's worked hard, what harm will it do if I don't know? People are pigs, April."

The image of her father standing at that desk in London, thrusting into the woman, her pearly white thighs shining across the room, her legs sticking out in the air, her father grasping one behind the knee. The image had become double-edged over the years; despite her contempt for her father's frivolous disloyalty to his family, she also understood the excitement, illicit thrill and erotic pleasure of the situation. She identified with both sides, the cheaters and the cheated on, with her father and the other woman on the one hand and with Isabel, Beth and his children on the other. If she was honest, she probably identified more with her father, since he was the one in control, the one driving the action, though all her loyalty was with the wives.

She'd always seen herself as a potential adultress who chose not to indulge out of intelligence and commitment to family. If Robert was being unfaithful behind her back, it changed who she was. She was no longer a woman making an intelligent, noble choice—she was a victim and a dupe.

"I take exception to that remark. I for one am not a pig, well not usually anyway," April laughed. Carmen smiled wanly. "And you're not a pig either. Can you really assume that we are that much better than everyone else?"

"Yeah sure, why not? My mom, Rebecca, probably Oscar, and you are good people, people who actually love other people. Everyone else is a question mark."

She sipped her water. Then kept thinking out loud. "I need to know if I've been fooling myself. If I really am Sandy Dennis."

No, she thought, *I may feel like the simp at the moment but I'm going to act like the bitch.* "Oh man, I really wanted Robert and I to transcend all this crap. I wanted to be past this juvenile stuff."

She took another sip of water. "Well, in the big world this is really a nothing. It's only the kids that are a problem. I told you about that mall in Argentina? Shopping and torture hand in hand. You couldn't get a more apt metaphor."

April nodded, but chose this moment to go the washroom.

"I can't wait to wear a belt again," she said when she returned. She was pregnant too, at the end of her first trimester, so she could still wear pants with a loose waist and big T-shirts or sweaters. "Not to change the subject. But jeans. Maternity jeans aren't jeans. They're just pants made out of denim. Denim *material*. After this one comes out I'm only wearing real jeans for the rest of my life."

"And cowboy boots," Carmen added. "And sleeveless black T-shirts," she smiled. "I'm going butch after the baby is born."

The waiter came and Carmen and April ordered two glasses of cranberry juice and soda.

"How are *you* feeling?" Carmen asked. "How's the morning sickness?"

"I'd take three labours to be free of it. I feel healthy-sick. Like a vegetable garden with lots of compost, rich in minerals, but the very smell of myself makes me want to puke. What a way for life to start."

Carmen glanced up as a handsome man entered the restaurant. He wore a dark suit, white shirt, pink tie and had chin-length curly dark hair, streaked with grey. He sat at a table with two men and a woman, also in business clothes. She recognized him.

Here lies one whose name was writ in water. Keats's gravestone inscription. Written before he died of TB. Babies in water. Nameless.

Carmen recited:

"No, no, go not to Lethe, neither twist
Wolf's-bane, tight-rooted, for its poisonous wine;
Nor suffer thy pale forehead to be kiss'd
By nightshade, ruby grape of Proserpine."

"How does that relate?" April asked.

"See that man across the room? Look familiar? Remember, romantic poetry after school? Vincent Dalgleish. Remember? He had longer hair then.

"Or if thy mistress some rich anger shows,
Emprison her soft hand, and let her rave,
And feed deep, deep upon her peerless eyes."

April rolled her eyes. "I hate when people recite things. You have to look all serious while they go on and on trying to impress you. Yeah, I remember. Didn't you have a crush on him?"

"I certainly did.

"Though seen of none save him whose strenuous tongue
could burst Joy's grape *against his palate fine."*

She emphasized "strenuous tongue" and "burst Joy's grape" like a teenager trying to make a friend laugh, as if Joy were a classmate they both disliked.

"Well, what are you waiting for? Reintroduce yourself. Too bad you had to go and get yourself knocked up."

They laughed. "At least my face hasn't done that ballooning thing yet. Remember we had one class at his apartment—their apartment—and we got to meet the mistress? She was dark blonde and very English. I sort of hated her, because he was so in love with her. I was shocked when she moved out before end of term. How could you be dissatisfied with someone so handsome and poetic?"

"He's not that handsome."

"Yeah, well, she was in her mid-thirties I guess. She probably wanted kids and a man with a steady job. Remember that amazing story he told us, about walking on the beach and turning into a woman?"

"I always suspected he was high on more than love," April said.

"You know, I never even thought of that. I was so inspired by the mystical aspect of the story."

She walked toward his table: rebellious, defiant, keen to break free of her role as jilted wife. Crossing the room, she felt she was returning to the open-endedness of youth, where anything could happen. She felt impetuous, like flexing her sexual muscles; she felt a little predatory and reckless.

"Hello," she said. "Remember me?" She smiled.

Mr Dalgleish was agreeably flirtatious, interested in her, very un-teacherlike. It was quite different speaking to him as a woman with her own money, a son, a house. She could look him straight in the eye. Her pregnancy didn't make her feel unattractive; on the contrary, it made her feel powerful, vital, a potent sexual force. Anyway, he would not be the kind of man to be put off by evidence of womanliness.

She returned to April. "He's quit teaching and become a stockbroker. Can you believe we're all here in Vancouver twenty years later, and we're all in the same restaurant? Who would have ever predicted?"

"He looks a bit creepy. Handsome but slick and boyish. He always smiled too much. He's looking at you with raised eyebrows," April smirked. "There's something too feminine about him."

Carmen laughed. "No kidding. That's what's so attractive."

"I beg to disagree." April looked at Carmen across the table. She was getting ready to *say* something. When they were younger April's habit of speaking with absolute authority made Carmen feel diminished. Now she delighted in it. So many people spoke carefully, strategically, protectively. April just laid it out. It wasn't that she was any more right than anyone else, but at least she spoke in declarative sentences. Besides, they both knew how absurd it was to speak with absolute certainty about anything, so it made them laugh.

"Carmen, you're not thinking clearly right now. Don't do anything stupid. You've got to talk to Robert. You should see a marriage counsellor. Even if that letter turns out to be nothing, the effect it's had on you isn't nothing. You're not happy."

"Happy. I'm happy," she sighed. "Yeah, you're probably right. I'm keeping Dalgleish's card, though, just in case."

The waiter removed their plates and returned with a dessert menu. Carmen checked her watch because she had to pick Oliver up at three from preschool. She was feeling better. Unstable, tired, but better. Maybe her life wasn't a nightmare after all, maybe everything would work out.

"I have time. Do you want to order dessert?"

"Sure."

Carmen looked at the menu. "Ah, the ubiquitous tiramisu . . . Do you want to share an apple crumble?"

10

THE PLANE VIBRATED to a quick acceleration and took off and part of her wanted to yell, "Stop the plane, I'm getting off!" It didn't feel right to leave Oliver with Beth and Oscar, while she, his mother, went up in the air in a great hulking piece of metal and his father picked his way up an icy mountain.

The fetus seemed to feel the plane's vibration because it began doing somersaults. Suddenly she worried about its ears. Had anyone tested the effects of airplane travel on unborn children's ears? Presumably if there'd been a rash of newborns with burst eardrums, there'd have been an investigation. But for a moment she entered a nightmare in which she was ignorantly risking her fetus's eardrums and submitting to a blind faith that who—airline authorities, the government, medical research facilities—would have protected it.

Don't think about it. You're here now. How often in a lifetime does one try to relieve unbearable anxiety by resigning to the *fait accompli?*

Marriage, for example. *Don't think about it. You're here now.*

She had tried several times to reach Robert on the radiophone but it either wasn't working or was turned off. He had left one crackling message on the answering machine explaining that they were fine, they were turning into bed and beginning their ascent the next day. He ended saying, "I love you very deeply, Carmen. I miss you. I'll try to reach you again if I get a moment alone."

Carmen had been unable to suppress a slight leap of heart at those words: maybe everything would be fine, there was no other woman stealing from her and Oliver, no husband with split loyalties and secret desires, tricking her into laying everything on the line while keeping his own options open.

Since Alfred had cut her off seventeen years ago she hadn't thought about him often. On birthdays she felt a fleeting stab of pain, at her graduation and on her wedding day. Sometimes a song played on the radio or in a restaurant that she'd first heard in his company—Julio Iglesias, Roberto Carlos, Rodrigo's symphony for classical guitar. She'd find herself transported back to a Latin country: watching the sun set; dressing leisurely for dinner in semi-tropical air; feeling excited, uncertain, freewheeling, tipsy. Alfred's adventurousness, carelessness and exuberance, his passionate yearning and equally passionate annoyance with the world, would suffuse her and linger even after the song ended. She'd feel like calling him, but the actual prospect of a conversation was daunting and she didn't have a number for him. And the feeling would pass.

There'd been only one occasion when it hadn't passed—the day Oliver was born. Her labour had been difficult. The umbilical cord was wrapped around Oliver's neck and after twelve hours in transition, he went into distress. They'd done an emergency C-section. After she was sewn back up, the nurse handed him to her. He was so beautiful, so perfectly whole, with his glowing skin and his beating heart and his little fingers opening and closing, tiny puffs of warm air coming out of the nostrils in his tiny nose.

She'd thought of her father then and the joy he'd described on the occasion of her birth. Oliver's arrival made the rift between them seem utterly stupid and irrelevant, so after Beth and Oscar left to go back to their hotel, she decided to call him. She got his number from the mining company's head office.

As soon as she'd identified herself on the phone, Alfred went silent. She continued talking. A racking intake of breath made her think he might be weeping, but when she asked, he still said nothing. She spoke for a minute or two and never heard another sound until there was a click, followed by a dial tone.

Two weeks later a package arrived. She understood from the enclosed letter that Alfred had been successful in not thinking of her in the intervening twelve years. He wrote that she had two new half-sisters, who were now teenagers, and that his marriage to Marta had recently come to an end. Given Carmen's new family responsibilities, the geographical distance, the expense of such long-distance travel, he calculated that they could expect to see each other at best once every five years. He was now close to sixty. If he lived to eighty, that might mean three or four visits. He wrote that he loved her but doubted she'd like him any better now than she had when she was twenty-one.

In the package was a stuffed pink dolphin for his grandson. She was annoyed with herself for being suckered by nostalgia and letting her relationship with him interfere with even a moment of her joy at Oliver's birth. One month later she wondered why she'd ever even considered bridging such a painful void. The pink dolphin remained however, floating puffily from room to room as Oliver got old enough to carry it around.

She unbuckled her seat belt and stood to get past the passengers beside her. She had to sidle out with her back against the seat backs in front, belly facing in. She made it past the elderly woman beside her, but it was immediately apparent she would not be able to get past the large man sitting on the aisle without her belly brushing up against his face. She laughed and said perhaps this wasn't the trip for the window seat. The man replied humourlessly that he needed the aisle seat to stretch his legs.

The tiny washroom was impossible to negotiate. She couldn't stand up straight without her belly hitting something, so she had to lean against the walls and angle herself into position.

Back in her seat she ordered orange juice from the cabin attendant and considered the novel she'd brought to read on the plane. She picked up the *People* magazine she'd taken from the attendant instead.

When she was young everyone in this type of magazine had looked desirable and unattainable. Now they looked mostly dull: inelegant, overdone, phony. The bodies were predictably toned and shaped, groomed and manicured, given the best of every service money could buy, yet despite that almost no one on the glossy pages looked truly beautiful. They didn't even look interesting.

Perhaps after all, real deceit was not possible. People revealed themselves in aesthetic nuances: tiny betrayals of shade and proportion, what they combined with what from an infinite choice of size and colour, texture and shape, makeup, jewellery, hair, expression, posture; all these choices signified different things depending on the specific context of the occasion the star was photographed in. You could guess how conscious or unconscious they were of the meaning of each aesthetic choice: the connotations of class, education and culture.

Carmen loved how the meaning of fashion was always shifting, going from one thing to its opposite within weeks—bell-bottoms for example—ultra-cool and sexy one day, ridiculous the next. She was in awe at how attuned to nuance human brains were, how able to place a person's appearance in a complete sociobiological context in a nanosecond, and even to make the appropriate adjustments when first impressions proved mistaken.

Oh Fluff. Oh Ephemera. Oh Girl Stuff. What a relief it provided from academia, from worry and trouble. Jumping into the passing parade. The simple pleasures of looking good, of playing dress-up, the light distractions of surface. The power of a pair of cheap sunglasses and some lipstick.

The cabin attendants began their backward progress down the rows delivering dinner. It smelled good. The only thing Carmen disliked about airplane dinners was how awkward it was to continue reading while eating. Without a book she felt pressure to talk to the person beside her.

The cabin attendant politely asked if she'd like anything to drink with dinner and didn't flinch when she ordered a glass of wine. The man on the aisle looked at her in disgust and the woman beside her shifted slightly away. Carmen did not believe a glass of wine at almost eight months was going to harm the baby. She resented the new puritanism and seriously doubted men would ever accept such exaggerated sanctions. "Make that two," she called after the attendant.

She propped her magazine up between the tray and the seat in front of her, but didn't bother to read it.

Instead she remembered a pair of red corduroy bell-bottoms she'd worn in Grade 6 that laced up at the front like sailors' pants. They were hand-me-downs from her cousin Jennifer who was five years older but tiny so most of the clothes fit right away.

They had a clean, fresh, lemony suburban smell that repre-sented to the young Carmen ping-pong tables, rec rooms, Rice Krispie squares, neighbourhood barbecues, packaged sugary breakfast cereals, French's mustard, waterskiing in the summer, downhill skiing in the winter. Wearing her cousin's clothes had been like having a foot inside that life, and Carmen soaked it up.

Every time she wore those pants she'd felt beautiful. They had the kind of transformative power she'd been searching for at the mall in Paris when she'd had to settle on the horrible puke-coloured thing that had so unfailingly made her look dumpy and plain.

Her cousin lived in Ottawa now, had kids of her own. Carmen guessed Jennifer was the same kind of freewheeling parent her aunt had been, just as Carmen, like Beth, was not. Oliver wasn't allowed sugary cereals, for example, except at Christmas and on birthdays. Carmen took him for walks to the park, or the art gallery or Science World, structured adult-involved leisure, nothing where he could just run free and wild while the adults got slowly potted on martinis, or beer, or screwdrivers.

Robert was not the drink-your-highball, let-the-kids-run-wild type of guy either. Although he was quite capable of forgetting about Oliver, he expected Oliver to be contained by someone, whom he left unspecified since he realized it wasn't fair to always expect Carmen to do it.

Everyone's dinner trays were cleared away and the over-head lights turned off. The movie started. The wine was going to her head more than she'd expected, probably because of the altitude and not having had anything to drink for seven months. She decided to call Robert and detached the airplane phone from the back of the seat in front of her, ran her credit card through, entered the sequence of numbers for the expedition's radio phone.

"Hello?" a man's voice answered with the sound of howling wind and static in the background, then smoothness.

"Hello. Is Robert there?" she shouted. Heads whipped around toward her.

"Just a minute," said the voice, then cut out.

"Hello. This is Robert."

"I'm phoning from the plane," she said more quietly.

"What? Speak up. We're in the middle of a blizzard. In our tents halfway up the mountain."

"I found a letter in your briefcase," she said loudly. Let them hear.

He pressed the button on the radio phone to speak, but didn't. In the background she heard, "Oooh, you're in deep shit."

"I'm in a tent here with two other guys who can hear everything. I can't send them out in this blizzard. It's nothing to worry about, I promise you."

"I guess I'll decide that," she answered. There was a crackle of static and the phone went dead. She redialled, but a recording told her to hang up and try again.

She felt tired suddenly and pushed her seat back as far as it would go. She turned on one side, then the other, but it was absurd to try to get comfortable in an economy-class seat while pregnant. At least the heartburn was eased by being semi-upright.

Since she'd discovered the letter, Carmen had comforted herself by imagining living alone, reclaiming her life, making a home for her children free of compromise and conflict, being happy without Robert. A fantasy predicated, of course, on Robert being unhappy without her. Or she'd considered what her life would have been like if she'd married one of the other men she'd been involved with.

What if she'd married John, for instance, the grad student she'd dated after Ron? He'd made professor at the University of Florida and asked her to follow him. He was a brilliant, interesting man but not someone she'd wanted to raise a family with. She could not imagine herself living in Florida or the claustrophobia of two obsessive scientists in the same family.

She'd considered marrying Carlo, whom she'd lived with after getting her M.Sc. when she took a year off university to work with the Western Canada Wilderness Committee. She'd sold calendars door to door, written copy for their newsletter, organized data about endangered species, helped lobby the government for more wilderness reserves. Carlo was a conservative, family-values corporate lawyer, a slippers-and-dressing-gown kind of guy, a second-generation Italian who planned to go into politics later in life.

She'd gone back to university to do a Ph.D. in ornithology, having lost patience with consensus building and committees and meetings. She'd loved returning to the discipline and focus of academic inquiry and it had been wonderful to come home to pigeon and polenta, or spaghetti *carbonera* after a long day in the library, to get into her pyjamas and slippers, make a fire, drink wine and listen to music on Carlo's amazing sound system.

But when she'd left in May to do fieldwork up near the Yukon border, Carlo had protested. When she'd returned in August they'd had a romantic reunion, passionate lovemaking, the whole thing, but before the month was out he was suggesting she think about converting to Catholicism and explaining to her that it would not be possible to continue disappearing from his life for four months at a time.

Then she'd met Robert, a nonconformist compared to Carlo, easygoing, in his body. Because he was a geologist employed by the government who worked in the bush for a month or two at a time, her fieldwork was anything but an obstacle for him. Everything had been easily negotiated between them; she made less money than him, but he lived at her place in the bird sanctuary for two years rent-free, so it was balanced. It wasn't until they had Oliver that the relationship had started to shift.

Trying to imagine the letter he must have written to engender the response she'd read from his former girlfriend was a masochistic exercise. Now of all times, when neither fight nor flight were possible, when she couldn't walk around the block at a normal pace let alone tell him to stuff it and leave him until he got his head straight.

She began to cry, and was glad of the relative privacy of the window seat. A tipsy pregnant woman crying about love— how pathetic. The hope she'd felt earlier that she might be able to avoid the pain that letter promised no longer seemed realistic. Being a mother was the loneliest thing in the world.

It turned you into a supplicant or a hermit, unless you were the kind of woman who could successfully issue marching orders, trade sex for power, or just tough it out.

She was no longer the happy expectant mother of a sought-after second child, nor was she bringing this baby into the warm stable family environment she'd so much wanted for it. Poor Oliver. Poor baby. Poor her.

Nature should have programmed humans to mate like winter ptarmigan and Stellar's jays and swans and wolves. Maybe the intelligent ones did. She had hoped in Robert to have chosen someone capable of love as fierce and loyal as that of a wolf. She'd even said that to him in the early days.

She knew as well as anyone that reproduction was moved by impersonal forces, seismic and uncontrollable, like the weather and the plenitude of crops, the number of berries on the bush and fish in the stream; or politics, whether neighbouring nations were hostile or friendly, weak or powerful, how many soldiers one's own nation had or needed. Whether a woman conceived could be affected by education or wealth; by the nearness of wild animals—lions and tigers and bears; by the relaxing scent of honeysuckle; by water; by the number of espressos consumed before lunch; by the mistral, the chinook, the Gulf Stream; by the swiftness of one's camel or the thickness of the soles of one's feet; by the crow on the dead log, the colour of the heather, the way the tide settled separate pebbles at Dieppe; by how many mouse droppings there were in one's cupboards; by how often one looked up at the sky.

All these factors influenced whether a woman conceived. But when you were that woman, sitting on a plane, going to visit a father who'd disowned you, leaving behind a husband who was straying, such connections were difficult to fully appreciate.

She felt like biting someone's head off, Robert being the obvious choice; her father, a close second. Whether one could speak in terms of fault or guilt for wandering males she didn't know and didn't care. Nature, God, family of origin, capitalism, Western alienation: it wasn't her fault, she'd delivered her end of the bargain. The men in her life seemed programmed for stupidity and waste. Didn't they understand what they were throwing away: the abundance of beauty, love, sexual pleasure; the flourishing of their offspring? Did they believe the universe would provide an endless supply? Did they believe in the big tit? A Mother Nature who loved her boys, when she wasn't killing them off in wars.

11

THE IN-FLIGHT VENTILATION SYSTEM was switched off and the cabin's static air was instantly replaced with a redolent humidity. The surface tension on her skin dissipated. The door opened and a wave of heat entered, carrying the smell of fruit, earth and rot. It loosened her pores, made her skin smooth again. Even her belly felt more buoyant in this thick, warm air.

She followed the other passengers to the baggage carousel, carrying her winter coat over one arm. Her feet felt like swollen fists of meat balancing on two tiny unstable points that clicked down the hallways, past large empty rooms. She felt like a teenager again, walking through this airport for the first time. North American, pale, big-boned, thick-fleshed, slow and blunt and plodding, wearing patched jeans and one of her mother's old paisley-patterned blouses, her father waiting somewhere at the end of these corridors, smelling like no other man she knew, spicy and warm, his cologne permeating his skin and his clothes.

He'd been the only man she knew who wore jewellery. Two gold rings, one with a pale green stone and the other a large lapis lazuli, and a gold chain with a crucifix bearing a tiny figure of Jesus buried among the dark hairs of his broad chest. She had run into his arms, but then had not quite been able to surrender to his hug, though she'd wanted to.

What would he look like now? She claimed her baggage, walked through customs and out to the waiting crowd, searching for a face that recognized her. Dalva knew Carmen was seven and a half months pregnant, but Carmen had no idea what Dalva looked like. A young woman rounded the back of the crowd to the exit and held out her arms. "Carmen? Carmen! Ah Carmen. Hello!"

Carmen remembered the expectations of adventure and romance she'd always arrived with, and the letdown discovering instead there was a new girlfriend or wife to contend with, a new half-sibling. Even before leaving the airport she'd have to modify herself, to be gracious and effusively friendly, to communicate that she was not a threat, that she had not come to interfere, or compete. Might as well have been a bastard child.

Suddenly she felt exhausted. *"No hablo portugues. Entiendes español?"* she asked.

Dalva was average height, slim though very curvy. Her hair was long and straight, dyed blonde with streaks of brown; she had clear dark brown eyes and an angular face. A waft of strong perfume enveloped Carmen and made her a touch nauseous.

"Não fallo, desculpe. Seu pai esta melhor. Vem."

Carmen smiled.

"Cansado?" Dalva put her hands together and mimed laying her head on a pillow. "Yes. Very sleepy." Carmen patted her belly as justification for extraordinary fatigue.

Dalva pointed to Carmen's belly and gave a thumbs-up sign. *"Bonita, muito bonita. Seu pai vai ser avô."*

"De nuevo," Carmen replied, noting that Alfred didn't seem to have told his young wife about Oliver. Not wanting to admit being a grandfather if he didn't have to.

They smiled back and forth at each other until they reached the car. It was a small burnt-sienna four-door with cracked beige vinyl upholstery. Dalva hoisted Carmen's suitcase into the trunk and Carmen climbed in. No seat belts.

"*Vamos ao hospital.* See daddy. Hokay?"

"Okey-dokey," Carmen said, still smiling, then mimed laying her head on a pillow. She reclined the seat as far back as it would go and closed her eyes. As Dalva pulled out of the parking lot, the tiny car felt about five centimetres from the road.

She slowed her breathing to give the appearance of sleep, and tried to relax her flickering eyelids. Would he be conscious? Would he know who she was? Would he be angry to see her? Would she be angry when she saw him? Politics seemed a separate issue now, but the emotions underneath their political disagreements still had power. Would she still be enraged and have to choke down despair if he persisted in thinking it was fine to torture and kill people who politically opposed the government? The ancillary message: she might be expendible. Had been.

Carmen mimed sleep long enough that it became reality. She slipped into a dream about baby bats in a cave and communal nursing and fear of the babies falling.

The fetus kicked her pelvic floor hard on the right side. She shifted onto her left hip and just as she was drifting off again, Dalva geared down. Carmen opened her eyes and saw that they were turning into a hospital parking lot. She closed her eyes again. Her father had been right about one thing.

Now that she was a mother it was no longer conceivable, as it had been when she was twenty, that a mother would hold her child in front of her, use the child's body strategically under any circumstances unless it was in some way for the child's sake, no matter what the odds. That notwithstanding, she thought the story of the terrorist mother using her child as a shield was probably apocryphal.

She and Dalva got on the elevator to the fourth-floor heart disease ward. The doors opened. Some basic Portuguese had reactivated in Carmen's brain and she understood most of the directions to her father's room.

The walls were painted a light blue-grey, the floor was granite tile and blinds were pulled halfway down all the windows, so it was dim and cool. Dalva led her to his door, which was ajar. The foot of a bed was visible and a shape under a sheet. She hung back. She was about to lose seventeen years of disconnection, years of freedom from disappointment and expectation. She was worried what he would look like.

She turned to Dalva and asked in Spanish, "Why did you call me?"

Carmen understood from Dalva's reply that the mother of Alfred's daughters in Argentina would not let them visit and his sons could not afford the airfare. Other than his friend Sam, she couldn't think of anyone else who loved him. Carmen refrained from asking why Dalva was so sure she loved him.

Dalva reassured her that Alfred was barely conscious. He hadn't spoken yet. There was nothing to worry about. She nudged Carmen in, then left to talk to the nurses.

He was on his side, facing the window, his back to the door. She walked to the foot of the bed. His eyes were closed. She had the impression he might've just shut them. His face was not so different. Some weathering of the skin, new lines, some added texture but not much. His hair was streaked with grey, and had receded marginally. His beard was grey, streaked with black.

Most of the changes seemed to arise more from the stroke than from aging. The stroke had probably sunk the flesh around his eyes and ten days' immobility would have been enough to cause his big muscles to slacken somewhat against the bone. It looked, through the fine thread of the sheets, as if there had been thick muscle not long ago. His skull showed through his face.

"Hi Dad," her voice croaked.

She pulled up a chair beside his bed, on the door side, facing his back. She felt shy about staring at his face while he had his eyes closed—it seemed too great a liberty to take while he was so defenceless—so she stared at his back and thought about the stuffed pink dolphin in Oliver's room, its friendly, knowing expression, and about how much she missed Alfred's smell, which had seemingly been replaced by one that was institutional and sickly.

Eventually she reached over and touched his shoulder, still round with muscle, and felt how this fading body both did and did not belong to her. She remembered this back, shoulders hunched, pausing, squaring itself, as he walked toward the automatic garage door of his apartment building in Argentina. She remembered how he walked, slowly, flinching, alone, and she flushed with unexpected shame.

He'd accepted his solitude. No mother, no mate, no daughter. And she, blood of his blood, had backed away from him. The sneakiness of her action. The lack of loyalty.

Now it seemed unusual to have imagined herself friend and ally to people she'd never met, in a country whose history she did not know, while backing away from her own father without a second thought. The alacrity with which she'd discarded what was hers in favour of what was somebody else's. How much better a fit it had been.

Here he lay, enclosed in a mute fortress of sudden frailty, and she felt more connected to him than ever before.

Probably only because he can't talk, she thought to herself, and smiled.

12

ALFRED WOKE TO VOICES he recognized. Female voices heard as though through water, as though through added membrane, as though he were in his own space capsule. What was it he recognized in such muffled and indistinct sounds? The timbre. Yet if he asked himself who these women were he became confused.

Drifting, he understood everything about the universe. It was when he tried to pinpoint his thoughts that he grew uncertain and anxious about his ability to understand even the simplest thing. With relief he re-embraced the floating omnipotence that came with vagueness, the unexamined sense of oneness with the universe. He dozed again. Then, like a fish hooked in the mouth, he was pulled back up to the surface of wakefulness.

He kept his eyes closed. Pretended to be asleep so the nurses would leave him alone, and that woman who smoked, and now this one. Kept them closed so he'd be safe from all their demands and desires.

Then a disturbing thought occurred to him. What if they didn't want him to regain consciousness? What if they were happy to have him out of the way so they could dip their hands in his bank account? He detected a carefree quality in the voice of the woman who smoked, an alarming cheerfulness.

She'd come in wearing a leather dress the other day, one he was sure he'd never seen before.

But limbo was more pleasant than suspicion, like floating in a small boat on a slow river. He managed to get the hook out of his mouth and float back down, surrendering to the river, feeling it carry him, like driving without steering.

He recalled driving home after seeing his friend Sam, listening to some kind of science program on the radio. They were interviewing someone about luminescence in animals.

Even before he heard it Alfred knew he was at last going to get an explanation of the glowing baby his great-aunts had told him about in Germany. As he drove through the suburbs of Rio (even the memory of driving seemed so free, like flying, to his paralyzed body), he was carried back to his twelve-year-old self, scabby knees, short pants, loose knee socks, skinny, dirty, curious and diffident.

"One of the bacteria that help the immune system fight infection is mildly phosphorescent," the voice said enthusiastically. "If a great many of these bacteria congregate in one place, for example when fighting a serious infection, they can generate enough light to be visible to the human eye. There have been reports of glowing wounds . . ."

The baby's body would have been small. A baby boy. The child must have been fighting a generalized infection and his body was so small that the whole baby glowed. It seemed no less miraculous an occurrence with the explanation than without. It still seemed to Alfred an amazing state of affairs that animals could create energy through digestion. Why shouldn't a baby emit light? Weren't we all walking generators anyway?

He was driving the narrow stretch of road between the Sheraton Hotel and a sheer rock face, above which was a *favela*. The road was barely wide enough for two cars, yet a man about his age was walking toward him carrying a string bag with an unplucked, freshly killed chicken in it. The man didn't even bother to press himself against the rock face as Alfred sped past, edging nearer the centre line to avoid striking him. The man just kept walking, looking straight ahead, seemingly determined to live life on his own terms in whatever space was available.

How big the world had seemed when he was twelve, how endless a lifetime, even with his mother missing, while now the world and life . . . you got to go out for dinner a few times and then the restaurant closed, permanently. The Earth had seven continents—he'd visited them all. There was nowhere on the planet he couldn't conceivably reach in sixteen hours, and there was nothing undiscovered outside of parts of the ocean floor, the tops of a few mountains, and his beloved caves. In his life only rediscovery awaited. The stroke was the first completely new experience he'd had in twenty years. He couldn't even be bothered shopping any more. His antiques, hand-tailored suits, cashmere overcoat, Persian carpets, topaz cufflinks and Cartier watch all irritated the hell out of him.

He'd succeeded in becoming a citizen of the world, but the world seemed to have shrunk. The only activity that still gave him a sense the world was bigger than a restaurant at least was spelunking.

The baby glowed quietly in the room, while Alfred watched—the skinny Alfred with bruised knees and holey socks, and shoes with the soles tied on—feeling like a shepherd boy beside the manger looking at baby Jesus, humble and poor and unluminescent, but glad that somebody in the joint was glowing. Someone said, "Hi Dad," and he suddenly felt like crying.

When next he woke and opened his eyes everyone was gone and there was only the little red circle of the emergency call button, the white line under his closed door, and the glow of city lights through his blinds.

13

LITTLE SPOTS OF LIGHT, like stars too weak to shine, or little rips in the floor of the sky. Up north, camping with Beth by a pond, just before mosquitoes drove them inside; sitting and watching the sun set. She was sitting beside him, the baby, their baby, lying on the blanket between them staring up at the sky. He stared and stared at the fireflies. There, and then invisible but still there.

Don't die Alfredo, don't die. A hand brushed his brow like wind, a warm wind lifting the hair from his forehead and he wept and pressed his head against the trunk of a tree. He was sweating and his muscles were going into spasm from the tension of trying to decide whether to propel himself over the edge of the cliff and extinguish his miserable, puny existence.

Don't die, muffled into his mother's pillow before going to bed, a boy alone in a house, his father God-knows-where. *Don't disappear.* The wind was almost hot as it crossed his brow.

Die, Alfredo, die. He'd left believing that, because he took no possessions, he had taken nothing from his father's house. And now the mistaken belief of a young man had become actuality. He had no memories worth calling memories; they had become too indistinct without objects or people to keep them sharp. The only concrete thing he had was the garment with no memory attached, which he planned to be buried in (maybe he should put it on now?).

Something hot slid down the ridge of his cheek into his ear. It left a cool track. Something soft rubbed the track and dried it and another hot thing slivered down his face. *Don't cry my darling, it's all right. I'm here. I won't leave you.* He smelled her perfume and was comforted and fell back asleep as though waking from a good dream.

Two female voices, speaking to one another, approached his bed and it was like getting an injection of heat. He relaxed, anticipating their touch, their greeting, their gaze. Like a baby, unable to move, unable to speak, trying for a smile. Anticipating being embraced. Warm milk.

What the hell?

His emotions had gone nuts, flooding through him, leaving him defenceless—he was no longer even trying to resist. Reason seemed to have abandoned him altogether.

One woman sat on his bed and kissed his forehead. Stroked the side of his head, a touch that electrified him. He opened his eyes. The other woman was sitting on a chair. Very pregnant. He still thought of her as a teenager, running into his arms off the plane.

There were snapshot memories with nothing much beneath. Pleasant but vague. An ocean of memory might lie somewhere, but he couldn't access it.

What he remembered about her, and strangely the memory filled him with affection, was anger. Youthful anger. Sitting across a table from her, while she judged him, raged against him, argued with him. Tenaciously, unrelentingly. Never giving up and never losing interest.

She sided with my enemies. He had cut that thorn from his side. *Silly,* he thought now, *very silly, since even I side with my enemies from time to time.*

"*Ich fühle mich wie einer Säugling.*"

He merely surmised it was he who spoke, since the voice, though his, felt like it originated somewhere else. The pregnant woman leaned forward and spoke to him.

A statement followed by a question.

He closed his eyes. Too taxing.

He can taste fluffy white bread and see big fluffy clouds. He's on top of the world, sitting on something solid, solid but precarious, as though someone were tipping a plate to scrape him off. He's sliding . . .

When he opened his eyes again she was looking down at him. Her mouth moving. Saying his name. Calling his name from below, near an upturned milk box. Her face like his, like his father's; about the same age as his mother. Love pouring out of her.

"*Gruss Gott Mutti.*"

He meant daughter but there was no path to that word at the moment. This time he knew it was his voice that had spoken because of the physical vibration within his chest. It was so unused, so weak and damaged it frightened him.

He heard a woman give a little cry. The call button beside his bed was pressed. Nurses came running. A doctor stepped in.

14

THE WOMAN WHO GAVE A CRY was Dalva. She started laughing. *"O que que ele falou?"*

"It's German," Carmen answered in Spanish. "'Hello Mother.' And, 'I feel like a newborn baby.'"

Carmen felt a shadowy kick inside. Then a stronger one. At that moment she felt more like a place than a person. Person, place or thing—all of the above—but mostly home for the baby, a place things moved through. The person and the thing aspects—great, big, lumbering thing—seemed like fluff. Her father closed his eyes again, maddeningly, and fell back to sleep.

Dalva talked excitedly to the doctor and the nurses. The baby kicked harder. *If a chicken is an egg's way of getting to another egg, a woman is an embryo's way of getting to another embryo.*

The feeling of being a conduit was not unpleasant. It was peaceful. Regal even. Decisions and choices made not just for oneself—a single stable entity—but contributing to the creation of someone else. A small whiff of divine being, being that is not for itself but for things to pass through. A dwelling place. The cave dweller sitting at the mouth of the cave watching for the sunrise.

She was glad Alfred had uttered words. She wished to speak with him before she went back to Canada.

She pulled up a chair, raised the head of his bed and tucked a napkin into his hospital gown. She checked that the fork was clean.

"Dad, are you hungry?" He was still unable to will speech. He had spoken several times since his first outburst in German, but no one could predict when or in which language, as he'd spoken in Portuguese, English and German. He nodded. She brought a forkful of fish to his mouth and he shook his head.

"The beans?"

He nodded. Carmen remembered—he who had travelled to every continent in the world and eaten almost every cuisine and relished all of it, liked Brazilian black beans and rice the best.

She touched the beans to her lips to feel how hot they were. The last time she'd done this was when Oliver was a baby. Feeding a person with adult consciousness, a lifetime behind their eyes and an awareness of needing to be fed, was a very different experience.

When Oliver was a baby sleeping in his carriage people had said things like, "Ah, the life of Riley. I wish I could sleep like that. They don't know how lucky they are." Carmen had taken such comments as more like curses than blessings, preludes to an evil fairy's revenge rather than wishes for bounty and joy. She found it hard to believe anyone would actually choose such helplessness and dependency. Perhaps people were just expressing their disappointment in life.

Alfred's face was still somewhat slack, but his eyes appeared focused and alert and the flexing of muscles around his lips and jaw suggested he was enjoying his food. When he'd last spoken, in English, he'd said something about going caving again.

The doctor had told Carmen and Dalva that he would consider it a great success if Alfred walked again with the help of canes. It would be excellent even if he could sit up in a wheelchair. "Even so, it's too soon to rule anything out." The neurologist's report showed brain damage, but in a spot that other areas were known to be able to compensate for. A near-complete recovery, though improbable, was not out of the question.

She held a cup of milk to his lips and he drank. Then he turned his head toward the window and stared at the smoggy blue sky. She felt his mind working, considering something, maybe deciding whether it was worth trying to come back.

He'd always been built like a bull and though weakened, he still looked substantial. With enough determination, Carmen believed, he could still do anything.

"They're going to start physio today. They said you'll have to relearn many things, like how to walk. You'll be teaching a new part of your brain to do these things so even though you're sixty-four you'll be like a baby learning to walk."

He turned his head toward her and looked at her with a mixture of fatigue, affection and a spark of energy. He nodded, lifted a finger. Then dozed.

The fetus propelled itself against the side of her abdomen, causing a sharp jab of discomfort. She reached under her shirt and tried to touch its foot. A small round bump bulged through her skin, the bum she guessed, and again the fetus propelled its head against her abdomen. She laid her hand flat, waiting for another bulge.

Dalva's arrival was preceded infinitesimally by a waft of concentrated perfume that covered the whole spectrum of floral. The air in the room bristled and vibrated in anticipation of her entrance, making way for the belligerence that rippled all around her. Every time Carmen saw Dalva she wanted her to go away.

"Goodje morning Carmen. *Bonito*. Good daughter," she said in English. Then in Portuguese, "How is the *Velho*? How you sleep? Good? Ahhhhh. Good." She sat down. Lit a cigarette.

Alfred opened his eyes and glowered. She raised her cigarette to him, as though clinking glasses, and smiled, not maliciously, pleased to engage in familiar banter. "Ah Mr Pure of Lungs. And how are you this morning *cariño?* Our bed is cold. Get to work and get yourself out of here. Don't worry, I'm not ready to inherit yet. I still want another ten or fifteen years in which to annoy you. I'll feel cheated if you escape into some lovely institution."

Carmen noticed Dalva frowning at her and realized she'd let her jaw fall open. She closed it. Then she looked over Dalva's right shoulder as she passed on her latest conversation with the doctor.

"Good, good. No more vacation. Back to work. That's what he likes best. I'm telling you. Germans. Work, work, work. The man doesn't know how to relax. I warned him, if he didn't learn to be more Brazilian, it was going to kill him."

Carmen scrutinized Dalva from the side. She was a slim woman and so the swelling of her lower abdomen was quite noticeable. She looked pregnant. Her father's sixth child. Carmen, Daniel and Ivan, the two girls in Argentina she'd never met, Esther and Lola, and now this. How she envied him his biological profligacy, being able to combine his genes with four different women, have six children walk the face of the earth and still be able to lead his own life. And her own baby, his second grandchild, was so clearly coals to Newcastle. Not that she'd had any expectations of grandfatherliness.

Dalva tapped Carmen on the knee. "I want to invite you for lunch today. Your baby needs good food. My aunt's restaurant is not too far and she's a very good cook."

Carmen smiled. No was not an option. "Thank you. Actually, what I'd really like is a good cup of coffee."

Dalva rose to her feet. "How do you like it? Brazilian style? Italian?"

"With hot milk and a teaspoon of sugar. Thanks."

Divorce robbed a girl of the Electra complex. Murdering your mother no longer got you any closer to Dad, it just meant there'd be no one to tuck you in. You'd have to murder your mother's rival, and where was the conflict in that? Now it would mean Carmen had to murder a woman young enough to be her baby sister.

Divorce made a daughter stop competing altogether. You took what scraps you could get. Strangely, now that she was an adult and had her own family, it seemed that scraps were fine. She simply felt glad to see him. What he'd done or not done in the past no longer seemed relevant. Even knowing him well seemed irrelevant.

For example, he now had a whole life with Dalva, who was a complete stranger to her. Anything Carmen knew about him came from when she was a child, and how much could a child understand about a grown man, a child whose knowledge was so framed by her own pressing needs?

What was her bond with this man, this body lying in this bed under hospital sheets, whose sperm had been absorbed and taken apart by her mother's egg so many years ago? How was it different to her connection to any other man, to any other human? The tie of father was not like that of mother. The phrase "spring from the loins of." Wishful thinking. It was the mother's loins children came from, though "spring" was hardly the right word. It was from the mother's blood they grew, and then mother's milk. A father's physical investment was so tiny as to be invisible to the human eye. And hard to prove. Hopped like a sand flea more like.

Was it mainly genetic then? When they'd walked down a road and Alfred's best friend Sam pointed at them and burst out laughing, "You two look hilarious. Like human ducklings," it had made Carmen happy. On the other hand she remembered Alfred ranting about the supremacy of blood ties, "You are flesh of my flesh young lady. Nothing is more important." She, the sullen twelve-year-old, had snapped back, "What about your parents? Where are they? You never even talk about them. Flesh of your flesh, you don't even have a photograph."

The role of father seemed darker, more problematic than that of mother. She noticed it even between Robert and Oliver—an occasional wariness on Oliver's part around Robert, particularly when Robert got angry. Oliver sometimes abandoned it when he knew Robert was in a good mood, but he still always came to Carmen if he wanted something.

She felt bad for Robert sometimes. She could see he sensed Oliver's ambivalence and didn't understand where it came from. He tried to overcome it, which often just made Oliver feel more threatened. And in truth his efforts did seem sometimes to carry an element of aggression—he tickled too hard, teased too insistently, didn't let Oliver retreat. Other than being totally vigilant and never getting angry—an unrealistic expectation—Carmen couldn't see much Robert could do to improve the situation.

And that was with a child he hadn't abandoned. Whose mother, she still hoped, he hadn't betrayed. How much chance had Alfred had to be loved by Carmen?

And yet, he was.

She heard the hard click of heels and a hiss of fabric as her stepmother re-entered, walking slowly, carrying a cup and saucer. Dalva pulled the bedpan out from under the bed with the toe of her shoe and poured the coffee that had spilled in the saucer into it; then she whisked a tissue from the box on his bedside table, wiped the bottom of the cup, wiped the saucer and handed Carmen her drink.

Carmen took a sip. It was hot. It warmed her throat. It was perfect. She watched Dalva go to the other side of the bed and reach past the IV drip to touch her husband's cheek. Carmen stood and offered the chair.

"I'll drink this in the lobby. You visit." Dalva protested, "No, no, stay. You're his daughter. You haven't seen him for so long."

Carmen left before Dalva could protest any further. She went to the waiting room down the hall and sat on a vinyl couch. Dalva's willingness to get Carmen coffee and deliver it hot with the right amount of milk and sugar, a gesture of service, disarmed Carmen.

She thought about the loyalty she'd established with her father's women, how quickly she'd subordinated her own claims on him to theirs. Maybe she'd lost sight of the prize. Probably she'd despaired of having him anyway. And then she'd told herself it wasn't a prize she needed, a father. Window dressing.

She noticed a tiny green leg and foot sticking out from behind the bottom of the other couch, kitty-corner to the one she was sitting on. Perhaps it had just moved and that was why it caught her eye, but now it was so still it could have been painted on the wall. She stared, waiting for it to move again, unable to look at anything else. The toes were delicate as a fern. Like the toes growing inside her. Tiny, little pads of flesh.

Another betrayal came to mind. Dancing with the Germans. She realized now that Isabel would have almost certainly slept with her German, meeting him somewhere after Carmen had gone to bed. Several times probably, why not? She could even vaguely recall being left for hours with her stepbrothers and

Isabel's cousin, and Isabel returning breathless from unspecified errands or visits to the "chiropractor."

At the time Carmen hadn't felt a twinge of guilt toward her father. Why would she? Hadn't she seen him screwing another woman while Isabel was back in France? Not that it was Carmen Alfred had been betraying exactly there, but she'd felt betrayed nonetheless. Underneath it all, she felt interchangeable with the other women in his life. Perhaps he only treated her with more respect because she was part of him, but that left all the other parts of her in the same boat as the wives.

She and Isabel had had fun with the Germans. She remembered Dieter touching her back while they danced, and how her bare skin felt in the warm night air, his dark eyes as he looked at her with a wistful smile. How lovely it would be to see him again. To have a man like him to turn to, with Robert so far away, so mean, so faithless.

The tree frog pulled its leg back behind the couch. Carmen got up and peered between the couch and the wall, wondering how the creature was ever going to escape from this building, back to a place where it could survive.

15

---⊗⊗⊗---

HE DREAMED OF HIS COUSIN "Jay," the one who lived in San Francisco, whom he hadn't seen since he was a teenager. Jay was laughing as he entered a room in stiletto heels, black corset and garter belt, stockings, hard thigh muscles. Jay pirouetted, then cocked a hip to make the round, muscular cheek of his buttock more prominent, and Alfred the dreamer felt both sides of desire: he was aroused by Jay's curves, his nakedness and the overt frankness of his seduction, and he was also aroused by the thought of doing what Jay was doing. The freedom. He wondered what he'd look like. He the dreamer laughed at the wanton abandonment in Jay's maleness. Two men laughing together. When he woke he was filled with sheer joy.

He hoped Jürgen had had a fun life, a life filled with moments of pure happiness and gaiety, of luxury and light-hearted pleasure, free of concern about the minds of people like himself. What a waste of time his own mind had been.

And what an enormous crime wasting other people's time was. More unforgivable than wasting their money, because time was irreplaceable (though eventually even time was a throwaway, a few leaves blowing away in the breeze).

He thought of his daughter who was hugely pregnant, and thought how women could actually grow time, a whole lifetime, though not for themselves. In fact they had to spend a portion of their own precious time to do it.

His mother had done that for him, but with her it was harder to see it that way. What else would she have done with her time? All she'd sacrificed really to have him was going out dancing with her husband; the rest stayed the same.

A worm wriggled at the edge of his mind. Dancing. Not being able to dance. She couldn't dance because she was home with Alfred so Heinrich danced with other women. All she'd sacrificed was her life.

Alfred wept. He couldn't help it. She had been alone, her only ally a small boy, her son, who was busy rejecting her need for love.

What was happening to him? What had the stroke done? Sympathizing with faggots and women. It was as if he could suddenly get into other people's skin.

Hadn't he heard someone whispering to him in Portuguese that they were pregnant? But Carmen didn't speak Portuguese. And then he remembered his suspicion that Dalva was trying to get pregnant. Father to yet another baby. Just what was missing.

He knew he hadn't been the best father, he wasn't attentive, he never spent much time with his offspring, and he doubted he had the energy to change that, even if he did recover. Nonetheless, there were ways in which his lifeblood had gone into them.

Whatever the situation, another baby was growing—child, grandchild, what difference did it make? A little curl of flesh with all its life before it. He felt joy. He wanted to see that baby. To look in its face and give it a blessing. He wanted to make sure it didn't embark on life without his blessing, for what it was worth, not much maybe, but . . . *you should have fun, you should laugh, you should fly sometimes, you should be free at least from time to time, free and happy and not too stupid.* He was going to get back on his feet, he decided.

16

SHE ATE TWO MANGOES in her hotel room and went looking for a coffee at one of the stands along Praia Ipanema. Her hair was long and loose and in the bright sun it looked blonde. She'd put lipstick on and sunglasses and as she walked along the beach sidewalk she got whistles.

At first it was pleasing, then it wasn't, and she sought more camouflage on the city side of the street where pedestrians included restaurant patrons and apartment residents, as well as tourists. She carried her money in a plastic bag. The thieves of Brazil had subverted most visible class distinctions on the street: expensive purses, jewellery, gold watches, expensive clothes had become signals of imbecility rather than wealth.

She heard a bird and looked up. The sound appeared to come from the balcony of an apartment building ahead. She could see part of a large birdcage, but not the bird inside. She only had two more days in Brazil and she wanted to find a convivial place to have her coffee.

She walked along the sidewalk. The music from one restaurant faded out as the music from the next grew. In a lull between restaurants a woman's voice could be heard from one of the apartments above, a voice rich with longing and sadness singing of broken promises, a voice she recognized instantly, but couldn't quite place. It was not the song of a young woman; it was the song of a life lived, with no more new promises to come.

A dark and smoky room; beside her young father, stroking a beard with no grey hairs, she a child in an adult place, mesmerized by a woman singing as though her voice were torn from her chest. This is life, the woman cried, you are left alone with broken promises and memories of a time when you believed happiness waited for you. This is life: love comes but never stays, you lose everything and you look out to sea, loving life even more.

Amalia Rodriguez. Carmen stopped walking and leaned against a wall. A girl in knee socks and sandals and shorts and blouse watching the passion of Amalia Rodriguez. A girl watching a woman, glistening with sweat and singing, eyes closed, everyone riveted on her face. The girl felt the promise of passion, her heart beat in anticipation of a woman's life, of experiences that would make her feel the way this woman sang. It was all to come. The woman was singing the girl's future to her.

She looked out at the ocean across the road. The waves, foaming and new, rolled in with water from deep, black icy places where monster fish lived; with water that had passed through the gills of a great white shark or the body of a delicate sea anemone, that had flowed beneath the huge shelves of ice in the North and South Poles. The water felt like it pounded down on her heart.

She'd forgotten about the kind of love that song was about; somewhere she'd started suspecting that romantic love was a grandiose disguise for self-interest. A good trade on the emotional meat market.

A woman in another apartment above burst into song, accompanying Rodriguez's plaintive lilt in a husky but tuneful voice.

It was strange and wonderful to be here in this heat, leaning against a stone wall beside the Atlantic Ocean, on the opposite side of a different continent from her first child; in the opposite climate from her husband, at sea level while he touched the sky; hearing a voice singing a song she'd heard thirty years ago, while the young father—who'd stroked his beard and held her hand then—struggled now just to take a baby step in a hospital in nearby Gavea, and she was about to give birth to a baby who would soon be nine too and feel whatever promise she or he would feel about their future.

Rodriguez's voice took her back to her pre-married self and another time she'd been alone in a city street in the morning. Walking down the sidewalk back to her rooming house, as the sun rose over the buildings. She'd met someone the night before and spent the night at his place.

It had been spring; the air was full of city blossoms. It had rained during the night and the sun was making the rain rise in steam from the pavement and everything still glistened. No one knew where she'd been, where she was at that moment, what she'd done, except the person she'd done it with. She felt lithe and light, the reins of life gathered in her hands.

What had changed? Was it just getting older? Or was it just that this was real love and real life instead of romantic projection? Was this simply what being a mother entailed? Where had that marvellous sense of self gone, where walking down a street alone in the morning sun was perfect joy?

There were times she saw herself, and females in general, as trapped in the need to manipulate others for their survival as mothers. And there were times men seemed to be able to retain a purity of heart and a transparence to their intentions that women could not. Occasionally she even wondered if there weren't something selfish at the heart of being female, something not comparably selfish in the male.

Several friends, men of forty or fifty, men who had gained some financial security and who had families, had proclaimed that now their families were provided for they didn't mind dying. There was a selflessness in that statement that took Carmen's breath away. Certainly she'd never felt anything like it. She'd fight to be there every minute of her children's lives.

Men could be jerks, but they could also sacrifice their whole lives working at jobs they hated, or go to war and risk dying, for the good of their families.

Maybe a certain amount of selfishness in females was tonic, even essential. Maybe when you were incubating and nursing the helpless babies of your species, you needed a degree of maternal selfishness. Without it the babies might not survive because your self-interest and the baby's were indivisible.

Carmen stood again and started walking toward the next restaurant. The caged bird in the adjacent apartment building sang its heart out; the unknown woman too sang loud and unsubtly over the recording.

Had love delivered all the broken promises, the longing and heartbreak that Amalia Rodriguez's voice promised? Had it delivered the masochistic passion anticipated by a girl in knee socks so long ago? Probably, but she'd never have guessed it would feel like such a one-way street, or so much like defeat.

She entered the next restaurant and ordered coffee and Cocoa Puffs, which sat among the little boxes of cereal displayed beside the cash register. The cereal came with creamy milk.

A fresh fig sitting on a gold-leaf bone china plate. A lone fig on a plate. Her father cutting it into quarters, popping the first quarter into his mouth. Chewing with gusto. She, glancing at his plate, seeing movement.

She sensed he had woken up. "Dad, do you remember in Portugal when they had figs for dessert? And I looked at yours and worms were sticking out and waving around in the air? After I'd eaten fifty right off the tree that afternoon. Everything in my fig looked like a worm after that and I couldn't eat any more. And you got so mad at me. You popped every last bit in your mouth, worms and all, and took another fig too and ate it slowly." She laughed. A noise escaped him that she took to be a laugh.

He looked at her with a twinkle in his eye; the left corner of his mouth rose and the right corner dropped in a smirk.

"To this day I inspect figs for at least five minutes before taking a bite. *Dare I eat a fig?* I think it's a peach in Eliot's poem, but anyway, for me the question is literal."

You were so mad because you expected me to love life. And everything in it. To be grateful. Not to turn away.

He squeezed her hand.

17

ALFRED'S SPEECH CAME BACK to him in waves: first German, then Portuguese, the first and last languages he'd learned; then English. Sometimes he could access words at will, sometimes he couldn't get to them. His ability to speak deteriorated with fatigue, but every day was better in leaps and bounds.

He had feeling in every part of his body now except the left side of his face, where sensation remained intermittent. All his muscles had atrophied and he was extremely unsteady, but slowly he began to regain the use of his legs, holding a walker in front of him. His sense of balance and sequence were improving rapidly.

He tired easily, but his joy was palpable. He was out of the cave and ready to engage whenever he had the energy.

Seeing Carmen made him happy though he hadn't quite pieced together how it was she came to be here. Whatever anger he'd felt toward her had finally disappeared. Since he'd disowned her, other women had come to hate him so much they'd tried to stab him, bankrupt him, smash him over the head with his own crockery, and even murder him. Beyond sympathizing with his enemies, they'd *become* his enemies. Carmen's youthful betrayals now seemed relatively mild.

A small part of him had even begun to ask, with so many women angry at him over the years, might there be something he was doing that was out of kilter? Yes, perhaps yes, but who could figure out what?

He did remember the fig incident she'd been talking about. Isabel, pregnant with his second child, all his new Portuguese in-laws watching, and Carmen behaving like a spoiled brat, refusing to eat anything except potatoes and *batidas*. At last she'd discovered she liked figs too, only to turn her nose up because one had a worm; she'd retreated back to her worm-less, Saran Wrapped, homogenized North American world. He could still feel the rage that had welled up inside him, he who was so wormy, so unhomogenized and volatile.

And yet when she'd spoken about the incident today, he had no trouble seeing it from her point of view. What child wouldn't be repelled by a fruit filled with maggots? Only a starving child, and even then that one might wish for a fig with no worms.

His father had once fed him soup made from maggoty meat. Alfred had protested and his father had struck him across the side of the head. He had pulled himself up off the floor, sat at the table and eaten the soup, silently, hands on the table, elbows in tight by his side. He hadn't thought anything about it, hadn't hated his father or himself. That was just how life was then.

Dalva came in and kissed him absent-mindedly on the head.

"Where's Carmen?" she asked.

"Sleeping at the hotel," he was able to answer.

"When is she coming back?"

"Soon."

He looked at his wife with a mixture of wonder and wry appreciation. He knew he was lucky to have her; he really didn't understand how it came to be that he did have her. She was a gift with a few thorns sticking out here and there, to make sure one didn't take good fortune for granted. He appreciated her loyalty, heretofore untested. That alone caused his libido to stir.

He watched her begin pacing up and down, obviously dying for a cigarette, fretting out loud about logistics, who to phone, who not to phone, what to tell the clerk at the import business they ran together, when the dry cleaning needed picking up, what would need to be arranged before Alfred came home.

He spoke her name. She stopped and looked at him, catching the tone in his voice. She had gone to a little more trouble than usual with her appearance today. Her nails were freshly painted and her hair washed and dried at a salon, making it full and shining and even.

She walked over to the bed. Leaned over and kissed him. Her hair made a curtain around their faces. Her blouse, a thin silky beige fabric, fell open and he saw her burgundy lace brassiere. He was able to lift his arms and pull her against him, his hands able to find her buttocks. She pressed against him and they both laughed when they felt his erection.

"I can still put that thing to use," he whispered through her hair. Someone came in the room.

"Oh Christ," Carmen said. "I'll leave. Take it as a good sign on the recovery front. I'll be in the cafeteria."

18

IT STILL SHOCKED HER to see her father in a sexual context with a woman. Repelled her. She still carried, absurdly enough, a child's egoistic hope that Alfred existed mainly to be her father. Just as Oliver thought she existed to be his mother. The rest of her life was an irritation to him, a possible threat, something he had to accept like broccoli and spinach.

Dalva came to get her half an hour later. Her lipstick fresh. Her shirt tightly tucked in. Looking just like broccoli and spinach.

"You're leaving tomorrow and your daddy's friends have not had a chance to see you. The doctor says he can go out for a couple of hours in the evening. I'm planning a little party at the restaurant across the street. We can take your daddy in the wheelchair."

Carmen dressed for dinner carefully. Her one good maternity summer dress—a navy jersey shift. Clean hair. Lipstick. Eyeliner. The shift hung well, revealing all her curves at the same time as smoothing them and making them flow together. In the mirror she saw not beauty exactly, but vitality, health, an alert and friendly face, a pleasant solidity. To Robert she'd look beautiful.

Dalva picked her up at the hotel an hour late wearing spike-heeled shoes, black stretch jeans, a bejewelled bustier in black and gold, long dangling earrings, perfume, red lipstick. Carmen cursed her fate of always being wholesome-looking in the company of overtly sexual women. Once, just once, she'd like to be the hot-looking babe.

"I don't want Roger, the old bastard, to see me in a wheelchair," Alfred muttered as Dalva wheeled him into the restaurant.

It was an unpretentious place with plastic tables and chairs, yellow-and-white-checked tablecloths, paper napkins, posters of bullfighters on the roughly plastered yellow walls, fake plants. The dinner crowd would not arrive for another two hours, so the restaurant was empty except for the table of Alfred's friends.

"To Alfred, the old fart," they cried, and raised their glasses.

"Old fart?" Alfred roared, raising himself in his wheelchair. "You dare!"

Sam interjected. "Alfred, if I may quote you, there's only one alternative to getting old, and it's even less attractive."

Everyone laughed, with affection and relief, as Dalva wheeled Alfred up to the table. Dalva introduced Carmen, starting with Roger. He shook her hand. "Your dad and I have known each other for twenty years. I'm his oldest friend. How old do you think I am? Guess."

"Sixty-one?" she said, choosing a number that was both charitable and believable.

"Hah!" he smiled in triumph. "Seventy-five!" He struck himself on the lower ribs, as if to demonstrate his hardiness in the face of time.

Carmen thought, and not for the first time, what a strange species we are. How absurd that we are so comforted by favourable comparisons with one another, as if comparisons made any difference to reality. Nonetheless, she too was comforted by the fact that she looked good for thirty-nine, that people were surprised when she told them how old she was.

Dalva introduced Carmen to Roger's wife, Mimi; Alfred's caving buddy, Sam; to a man called Fernando and his American wife, Nancy; and Maria Teresa, a sculptor and former neighbour.

Alfred was wheeled to the head of the table with Roger on one side and Sam on the other. Wine glasses were raised and Alfred's amazing recovery was toasted. "I'm coming back!" he said, and was able to raise his own glass and bring it to his lips.

Carmen saw in Alfred a man on the watershed of convalescence, right at the point where the body's response to extreme illness, that inward-turning to conserve every speck of energy for survival, was turning outward toward purpose and recovery. His face had regained much of its expressiveness, though he was still gaunt and a bit hollow around the eyes.

He wasn't able to speak reliably in full sentences yet, but he was able to respond with three or four words. Carmen noticed that his friends seemed to enjoy taking advantage of his inability to shout them down by teasing him and regaling the table with amusing stories about him. *It must be a guy thing; women would never do this to each other*. Alfred beamed, satisfied perhaps to have so many good anecdotes about himself, glad that his friends remembered them all.

Carmen ordered *casquinha de siri*, sat back and sipped her wine as she listened.

" . . . we measured everyone's widest part to make sure they'd fit through the squeeze. Alfred here was found to have one centimetre too many around the middle, so he was put immediately on a reducing regime. For three days he ate nothing but carrot sticks and mangoes, but what we didn't know is he continued to drink like a fish.

"The day of our departure he measured himself . . . and measured himself again. He could not believe it but he'd actually increased his girth by a half a centimetre. He kept this impossible result to himself and swore up and down to the rest of us he'd lost the weight and off we went.

"Well, you may know the story of *Winnie the Pooh*. Fernando, perhaps you don't, and Dalva also not? It's a charming children's book in which the main character, Winnie the Pooh, is a bear of very little brain but plenty of charm. In one chapter Pooh is visiting his friend Rabbit in his burrow and during the course of the visit eats rather too much honey. When he goes to leave Rabbit's house, he gets stuck in the entrance. Rabbit decides to take advantage of the bear's lower half by incorporating it in his home decorating and hanging tea towels, et cetera, off his legs. His friends push and pull but it takes a week of being very hungry indeed before he pops out.

"Well I probably don't need to illustrate the situation any further, but I will add this. The people ahead of Alfred in the cave, of which I was one, were quite annoyed because they could not get out of the cave either until he was removed from the passage. It was one of the few sobering experiences our friend Alfred has ever had."

Alfred laughed and raised his glass. Bread had arrived on the table. Carmen, who was hungry, leaned over to ask Fernando, who sat next to Roger, to pass the bread, but had to wait until he finished talking to Roger's wife, Mimi.

"I thought Alejandro was coming," he said.

"Yes, yes, he's coming but he's at a sales conference today so he has to sneak out," she answered.

"Excuse me, but where does this Alejandro live?" Carmen asked.

"Córdoba," Mimi answered.

"In Argentina?" Carmen asked.

"Yes. His wife is Uruguayan."

"May I have some bread please?"

Carmen finished her first helping of *casquinha*, which was quite rich and filling. She chatted with Maria Teresa about her sculptures, madonnas made from enormous single pieces of rain-forest wood, when Alfred stopped eating and called out, "Julie! Julie, my dear man." He stopped for a second then continued, "Come, sit, have some wine."

A strong, broad-backed man of medium height walked across the room to Alfred. Hair still jet black. There were fine lines on his face. Crow's feet round the eyes. He was wearing a suit, a light-blue shirt, a tie. He had the round but hard stomach of a man who was middle-aged, had put on a bit of weight, maybe drank too much, but was still strong as an ox. He clasped Alfred's head to his chest and kissed the top of his hair. Then he looked around for a chair and that was when he saw Carmen.

He stopped for a moment, then smiled and nodded at her. Carmen smiled back, looking him in the eyes, where the biggest change in his appearance had taken place. They were softer, sadder, than they'd been before. There was defeat in them.

"How are you, *Viejo?*" Alejandro asked Alfred, searching his friend's face.

"Well. I'm alive. Not as pretty. But coming on, coming on," he paused. "Sit and drink! Bloody pep talks. Fate worse than mine."

Alejandro pulled up a chair beside Alfred and polished off a pan of crab and cheese. He no longer looked like a soldier; he looked like a family man with a job and time to teach his kids how to ride a bicycle and go to the park on Sundays for ice cream. A family man with a good build and excellent posture. He still had a vigilant quality though, as if he were watching everything from the corner of his eye.

Just as well I'm pregnant. And then she thought about the letter from Robert's ex, and how hard she'd had to argue just to be here, and thought, *Or not.* Things were coming back to her from eighteen years ago, the swimming pool, the effervescence all around her, being young and free of responsibility, the future wide open.

After speaking with Alfred a few more minutes, Alejandro pulled up a chair beside Carmen. They asked each other about children, spouses, work—smiling, listening attentively to each other's answers. The attraction between them was strong enough that Carmen worried it was visible. She glanced at Dalva and Dalva nodded at her with a knowing smile. Oh well, she'd never see any of these people again.

"Do you miss the army?" she asked eventually.

"What would I miss? The time to keep in shape maybe," he patted his belly and smiled, but the expression of his eyes was serious. He knew what she was asking. "The rest I not only don't miss, I'm happy to do without for the rest of my life. *Finito.*"

"Did you hear anything about Galérias Pacífico? I read an article in Vancouver recently about construction workers finding a secret basement hidden under the real basement with prison cells, a torture room and separate exit. I'm pretty sure I remember you and I talking about one of the frescoes on the ceiling of the dome. To think I was upstairs shopping while people were being tortured."

He looked at her for a long time.

"We were soldiers not secret police. Several of my men were lost in las Malvinas."

She wanted to know what he thought about the Dirty War, the disappeareds. She wanted to know and she decided she didn't care if it pissed him off. She wasn't about to have all this eye contact and not raise what was on her mind. It wasn't voyeurism: she didn't want details, she didn't want to know exactly what he'd done or seen or known; nor did she want to blame him.

She nodded and looked at her hands. She wondered if his wife knew. He was probably a good husband. A good father. Strong, steady, loyal and hard-working.

"How old did you say your daughter was?" she asked, to fill the silence temporarily.

"Thirteen. She's very saucy. She and her friends march through the neighbourhood terrorizing everyone with their giggles and laughter."

She smiled. Unfortunate choice of word, *terrorizing*.

It took so long for understanding to sift down through time, through one's own stupidity. While she ate bread and spoke with Alejandro, at that exact moment there was someone being tortured. The time was known; it was just a question of place. Why did it seem so different if it was next door or next continent? A deceit of geography, creating the illusion of separation. False separation.

He sighed. "There's nothing to be gained from talking. No matter how big the change in heart, talking can do nothing to heal it." He turned his head to look at the wall and brought his mouth closer to her ear. "I sometimes wish I had killed myself."

"I have dreams," he leaned back but continued to speak quietly. "The naked bodies. And the expressions on their faces. And the look of something stripped away from them. The same thing that got stripped away from me. Some belief in the universe. It's not there any more. The difference is I got to walk out of that room.

"I met one of them once. At a bus stop. She was looking at me and looking at me and then I recognized her. She saw me recognize her. We spoke. It's hard to believe. You don't find that in the newspapers. We spoke to each other at the bus stop.

"She understands more than my wife. She knew everything. She knew I thought I was doing the right thing. That everyone supported me. Applauded the 'action' I was engaged in, my parents, my neighbours, my friends, the priest I confessed to, my old granny. I was serving society. I was there for good. She knew that.

"It was such a relief to talk to her. My wife wants it all to go away. Naturally. She's a mother. The woman at the bus stop knows it never goes away. It fades for a while and then it's back all over again. You have to do service, you have to give it its due, you have to submit. And always you ask how did this happen? Who is to blame? Can it be me, can it really be me?"

He paused and drained his glass of wine. Poured some more.

"You study birds. I dream of birds that can't fly. Birds with no wings. Sleeping birds. Pushed out of the nest. Stripped naked and pushed out into the rushing air; only the sea below, thousands of feet below. They fly down and never wake up. They're not *desaparecidos*. They're dead."

Her eyes filled with tears. Her father laughed and she looked over to the head of the table where he sat, reprieved from death for now, speaking, moving, animated in a slightly blurred way. It was her last night with him. Quite possibly forever.

She looked back at her plate and put her hand over Alejandro's where it lay on the yellow-checked tablecloth.

"Only the clothes were left. On the floor of the plane. No one touched them until we landed. Once, I had to gather them up. They weren't warm any more. I put them in garbage bags and tossed them to somebody on the ground."

Alejandro excused himself and went to the bathroom, and when he came back he sat beside Alfred for the rest of the dinner.

When it was time to leave, however, he came back to where she was sitting, took her face in his hands and kissed her forehead.

"Where are you staying?" he asked quietly.

"Hotel São Cristobal."

"May I see you?"

"I'm leaving tomorrow."

"Tonight then?"

Dalva wheeled Alfred back to the hospital and Carmen and she helped him into bed. He smiled up at them from the pillow. "That was just ducky," he said, and fell asleep immediately, exhausted by the evening.

"I'll drive you back to the hotel," Dalva offered.

"I want to sit with him for a while. I can sleep on the plane tomorrow. I'll walk to the hotel."

"It's not safe at night. I'll wait with you."

Carmen did not want Dalva with her in the room. "I'm a big girl. I'll take a taxi. Go home and get some sleep." Dalva looked at her, thought for a minute, started to say something, then stopped and shrugged, "Okay. But Rio is not safe. Don't walk by yourself at night."

Carmen turned the lights out except for the one directly over Alfred's bed. She sat and looked either at him or out the window at the car park below. A statement replayed. *They're not* desaparecidos. *They're dead.*

Her father had kept his mother "disappeared" his whole life, not dead. He could fantasize that she still might be alive, and indulge in self-pity at being "abandoned"; he could let his father off the hook for betraying her and not feel himself to be the unfortunate product of victim and betrayer.

She thought she understood the fragility of this need, the brittleness of self and identity, the necessity for protection. She was an unfortunate product too.

She smiled at Alfred, who snored for the first time since she'd arrived, a stentorian in-snort, a peaceful exhalation. He must be getting better; his grip on air was improving. She smiled too remembering her adolescent self stating defiantly to her father that she was never going to have children, she was going to have adventures instead. Never guessing that adventures were safe, the scope of their danger limited, compared to having children.

His large belly, his short muscular legs, his black eyes, his sadness, the way he spoke in a considered and deliberate way all made her legs tremble with desire. Their drinks sat on the table in rings of condensation; the lounge singer took a break, the air conditioning was too cold; Alejandro's mouth was warm.

His tongue in her mouth, her ear against his arm, his hand on her side; he called to a self that had been hidden and alone for a long time. She kissed him passionately, wrapped her arms around his neck, pulled him to her ferociously, put her leg over his. Her dress rode up to the top of her thigh; she pressed her leg against his, and met him—tortured memories, family burdens, anxious and ruthless wife, sales conferences, nightmares and bus-stop conversations. His falling birds. He leaned into the corner pocket of the couch and pulled her against him; their bellies met and pushed up against each other as they kissed without calculation, with the force of the past, but completely in the present.

The waiter came over, and with no embarrassment at their entanglement, said the bar was closing. Alejandro gave his credit card, and Carmen started kissing him again, but when the waiter returned and Alejandro sat up to sign the bill, she made a decision. She would spare all four of them the chaotic force of *her* sexuality at least. Alejandro, his wife, Robert, herself. She was a fire, but she didn't want to burn anyone.

"Alejandro, I'm going to go home and have this baby and see what's what with Robert. If we don't sort it out, and you don't sort things out with your wife, well I'll come running."

She had to tell herself, all the way to the elevator, all the way up the elevator, unlocking her room, going inside, closing and locking the door behind her, she had to tell herself she was only delaying passion. She breathed in, went to the window and cried. Trying to find a bit more courage to keep loving one person.

19

He was sitting in a chair beside his hospital bed with a blanket on his legs. He looked up as she came in the room. She dropped her bags on the floor by the wall and sat on his bed.

"Hi."

He smiled. She swung her legs up on the bed, raised the head of the bed as far as it would go and leaned back. Saying goodbye as a middle-aged mother to a father struggling to complete a sentence was both easier and more difficult than when she was a young woman with a lot to prove.

The sun lit up one side of his face and deepened the line running from beside his nose to his chin. He looked more substantial than when she'd arrived; he was already starting to regain muscle mass.

"What were you talking to Alejandro about?" he asked. The timbre of his voice was so familiar, even the slight irritation with which he now spoke gave her pleasure.

"The old days."

"He's a good fellow," he said, as though preparing to defend him.

"Yeah, I like him," Carmen laughed.

"Carmen." She sensed he was getting ready to talk about why he'd disowned her.

"They raped my aunts," he paused. "They don't share. They take."

"It's okay, Dad," she said gently.

He took a deep breath. "I was fourteen." His voice broke. The stroke had made him very emotional and he could not go on.

Carmen said gently, "I know, I know. But Dad, in Argentina you were on the side of the rapists. I had to disagree."

"Assassins! Terrorists!" he said angrily.

"Sure, they weren't all good. But most of the people who were murdered were simply good people trying to help the poor."

She couldn't stand hearing her own voice. Who was she to sound so idealistic and innocent? She recalled a framed piece of calligraphy her father had up on the wall during his bachelor days in Buenos Aires: "Peace is the continuation of war by other means." That certainly described American foreign policy. But who was she to speak? At the time, she'd been thinking mostly about sex. She'd made out with Alejandro, for God's sake, without even batting an eyelash. She'd gone shopping.

"Some. Maybe," he nodded. "But they did not fight cleanly."

Nothing had changed. She'd read everything she could about the Dirty War in an effort to come to terms with Alfred disowning her. Army brass claimed illogically that there were no disappeareds because there were no bodies or that the missing were all living somewhere on the Mediterranean coast. Leftists did not admit any use of violence. The good, the bad and the innocent were not perfectly segregated. Russia and Israel, for example, had supported the right-wing, anti-Semitic regime, while France and the United States, the countries that had first trained the Argentine army in torture and counter-insurgence, had denounced the abuse of human rights.

She looked up at the ceiling and didn't know what to say. Her father had never seemed like a real fascist. A fascist's hand-maiden perhaps, a symbiotic friend. Life was cheap in most of the world; people didn't have the time to be overly concerned about their enemies' fate. Maybe she was the clown.

Suddenly she wanted to know why Alfred seemed to have reclaimed her. Was it only because the stroke had left him with no choice?

Maddeningly he dozed off just then in his chair, perhaps exhausted by the effort of the discussion.

War is the continuation of reproduction by other means.

War was really a subset of reproduction; it was about secur-ing resources for one's offspring, one's family, one's people. It certainly wasn't about the survival of the individual.

Alfred began to snore. She didn't want to argue with him. She just wanted to love him and she was going to have to say goodbye soon.

She thought of all his attributes, his enormous energy, his self-madeness, his humour, his will, his tremendous capacity for life. The courage of identifying himself as a citizen of the world.

She had only recently imagined what it would be like to have no country to call home. Quebec had been close to sepa-rating and becoming its own nation, which would have meant Canada as she knew it would have disappeared. It had been a revelation to her how much of her identity relied on being Canadian. Alfred had had no home since he'd lost his mother, and no country since he'd left Germany. How could she judge him? His life was not her life.

She maintained a fundamental belief that "behaviour," animal and human, simply existed and every behaviour was

natural, by definition. Rape, torture, war, mutilation, infanti-
cide, sexual abuse, Cambodia, the Holocaust, Hiroshima, the
Dirty War—all were a function of millions of years of
Darwinian cause and effect. The label "aberrant" was a function of statistics, not essence.

Nor did she worry any more that might made right. In
biology the days of the "haves" are always numbered. Nothing
dominates forever.

And yet, and yet, and yet. She could not get rid of the idea
that genocide should never happen again. That torture could
somehow be stopped, forever. She had an expectation, hard-
wired she was beginning to think, of arriving at a utopian,
messianic time when murder, torture and rape would be
extinct.

She heard the unmistakable sound of high heels clattering
down the hospital hall. Dalva came into the room and Alfred
stirred, opened his eyes.

"Alfredo, *cariño*. Carmen's leaving."

He harrumphed and struggled to sit up straighter.

"The package."

Dalva handed him a plastic grocery-store bag. Alfred held
it in his lap for a moment, squeezing it and making the plastic
crinkle. Carmen sat up. He gave it to her.

"From my family, Carmen. For you."

20

On the plane Carmen took the strange garment that had been in the plastic bag her father had given her and wrapped it in her sweater to use as a pillow. She had been bumped up to business class because she was so pregnant and she had no trouble sleeping in the roomy seat with her head against the window and her feet tucked up beside her.

She dreamed of a school party. A group of thirteen- and fourteen-year-old girls having fun, laughing raucously, mugging to the music, showing off; a few men lounging in the big room, smiling at their high spirits. The party's happening all over the school and there are boys in other rooms. Suddenly one man—about thirty, strong, handsome, regular-looking—says, "Let's put them in the garbage cans."

Then it's done and he's relaxing at the bottom of a large wastebasket with this thirteen-year-old girl, her skirt up over her face, above him. A couple of other men are doing the same thing in other rooms. The expression on the girls' faces have gone numb. They had no idea this was even a possibility, let alone a danger.

It's so sad. In the dream, Carmen wishes she could have warned them, protected them, got them out of there.

She woke up thinking the words "I've always depended on the kindness of strangers"—Blanche DuBois in *A Streetcar Named Desire*. Who doesn't? Every minute of every day.

Prey depending on the kindness of predators. Stupid. Sandy Dennis. She thought about Robert and felt like crying. She'd know the minute she saw his face. Without a word being spoken, the information would all be there. Suddenly, it seemed inevitable she would discover he loved someone else. That he was a stranger. The world would answer her hopes, her laughter, her naïveté with sadism. Her effort to stick her head up crushed.

She remembered affairs she'd had, when she was younger, with married men. Men with children. She hadn't even thought about it. As far as she'd been concerned the world was full of free agents. Loving your neighbour as yourself meant free love. But the teenage girls were just being girls, just living.

She asked the flight attendant for some water and took her father's gift out of her sweater and unfolded it on her lap. It looked like part of a Greek man's wardrobe.

SECTION
Four

1

BRAZIL, SEPTEMBER 1995

HE HAD, in his forties and even when he was single in his early fifties, enjoyed dancing to rock 'n' roll, but now the thought of the pounding bass and drums made his ears hurt and his eyes sting, elicited no thrill or quickened pulse—only weariness. Maybe after a couple of drinks he'd be able to muster a little enthusiasm. He should be grateful he could still do it. But at his age why do anything you had to "muster enthusiasm" for?

Dalva wanted to go clubbing. The woman was restless again. Contentment, harmony, peace—such words did not enter her vocabulary.

He would certainly be the oldest person there. He no longer had any desire to impress himself, or her, or admiring strangers. Dancing was a single man's activity. And yet this evening she had been particularly insistent, so he'd relented in the interests of domestic peace.

He'd recovered miraculously from his stroke and he consoled himself now with the thought that it might be good physiotherapy to concentrate on moving his right leg, which was still a bit sluggish, to a rhythm. He took a long, hot shower, washed his hair, clipped his nose hairs, trimmed his beard and moustache and splashed on cologne. He donned black dress pants, a sky-blue cotton shirt, a colourful woven Guatemalan belt and tasselled loafers. It was the loafers he was most pleased with—they were handmade, Italian, the colour a rich oxblood brown, with the softest leather inside. He went to the laundry room to get a polishing rag.

He loved shoes. In the war he'd had to wear the same pair of shoes for so long that the soles had had to be tied to the uppers with string. This had meant he could not climb or play. He could not even run, because the soles kept getting bent and then he'd fall.

When she was a teenager, his oldest child had had the temerity to question this story. "Your shoes wouldn't have been that much worse than all the other kids'." He could still feel traces of the rage this had caused in him. How dare she presume to know more about his childhood than he himself? Insinuating he was lying, begrudging him even the slightest sympathy.

It exhausted him now to recall even one source of his former rages. In the laundry room, while buffing his left shoe, the last ember went out. He didn't care any more about any of it. He even felt curious. As a general in the army, his father would have earned as good a salary as anyone, so why had his son's shoes been in such singularly bad shape? Maybe it had only been for a month or two, which was an infinity for a child. It was after his mother disappeared. Maybe no one had time to get him new ones.

Even with his recovery, the stroke continued to change how he saw everything, still made him unpredictably emotional. The shoes tied with string wasn't a story about poverty, or the hardships of wartime, or even about losing a mother; it was the story of a boy no one cared about.

The shoe polish jar was empty and he could not polish his right shoe. He returned to his room and looked through the bathroom cabinet, then his dresser. Where had that woman put his things while he was in hospital?

Sadness passed over him. Why had he been so angry with Carmen? He had still seen her once a year, so he'd never understood that to all intents and purposes she'd lost her father when he'd left Canada. Then she came and visited and he got angry at her for not caring enough about him. Then he cut her off.

It had never been his intention to abandon any of his children. He'd just been trying to live his life, and one thing had led to another. Even if he'd known then what he knew now, it was unlikely he'd have acted differently. This was his life. Just as it was their life to have him as a father. Foresight, in the love department at least, was a lucky guess in hindsight. And he just hadn't been lucky.

He had a sudden impression of the empty space between himself and his children. Between the unit that was him— the unit that carried his personality, memories and soul— and the units that were them. After twenty-five years he had come to understand one small thing about Carmen. And another small thing about himself. That made two small things in half of an entire adult life. How could anyone hope to communicate more than superficially with anyone else?

He found a new jar of polish in the back of his top drawer. *Hallelujah!* He opened it, dabbed polish on the rag and rubbed it into his right shoe. Carefully he placed the newly polished shoe beside its fellow on the floor to dry.

He hunted through his sock drawer for an old pair that had worn thin or had a hole. He found a pair of white sports socks with the elastic worn out and set it aside, then placed all his socks back in order of colour and function. As he did so he had the impression he was forgetting something.

He'd found some old socks, he'd found the polish, he was wearing the dark socks he needed for tonight; what was it? Something wasn't there. He thought about the grandchild that was due to arrive in a week or two, about the grandson he already had, about his own sons—Ivan had visited two weeks earlier—no, it was something else. Dalva was pregnant; he was going to be a father again which, though it wasn't a surprise, was not a cause for celebration either. He was going caving while the going was good.

Something missing. Ah! The garment he'd given Carmen. Yes, definitely. It used to be in his sock drawer. The thing from the box his wicked stepmother and her evil daughter had given him. The garment that'd drifted down from heaven.

The polish on his shoes was dry enough now. He took one of the sports socks and vigorously buffed the shoes until they gleamed. He put them down beside each other on the wooden floor and slipped his feet into them.

Damn fine. On his way to look in the full-length antique mirror in the hall he passed the maid. *"Bello!"* she said and clicked her tongue. He laughed and his step lightened. How many times in his life had he thus transformed himself? From muddy caving clothes, or work clothes from a mining site, to sharp dresser.

He was always pleased with the effect of a little grooming. He examined himself in the mirror, with the new eyes he'd developed since the stroke, looking for signs of internal failure, greyness of skin, slight sagging of the features, darkness in the eye sockets, cloudiness of the irises, guanines. He gazed back at himself with crystal green-grey eyes, his complexion ruddy. Every part of the skin on his face had colour. Blood was reaching all the capillaries easily. The tone had returned to his muscles and if anything he felt even stronger since he'd lost four kilos. He had a new, leaner energy. His libido was up too.

"*C'est pas mal,*" he said to himself. "*Pas mal du tout. Pour un viel grandpère.*" He imagined shapely women eying him with ironic but not unappreciative smiles. Perhaps he could still show them a thing or two.

One thing was sure: he'd have surprise on his side. He laughed again and went looking for Dalva to show her that she wasn't doing too badly after all with her choice of men.

2

HE STARED OUT a plate-glass window while the travel agent looked up airfares to Spain. A pack of young bare-chested men loped by, laughing, slapping each other, baggy shorts and jeans hanging low on their hips, the elastic of their underwear visible, stomach muscles banded and rippling down to their groin. Sunglasses in front of their eyes.

There was a masturbatory aspect to youth. He didn't remember actually masturbating much when he was young; he remembered chasing a lot of women, and catching quite a few. Birth control had been a cruder affair back then; he'd often had to withdraw, or wait until they returned from the bathroom smelling chemically altered. He'd paid for a few abortions in his day. But the sex had been directed at himself. That Yankee expression "getting your rocks off"—that had been him. His desires had been immediate, uncomplicated, eminently satisfiable.

He'd never been one to fall asleep afterwards. He'd be charged, ready to study or work or, if it was nighttime, cook up a late meal—goulash, dumplings, stuffed cabbage leaves, pigeon and polenta, his famous *moules marinières*—something the North American women of that era had never eaten before. He'd taken pleasure in introducing their palates to something wonderful, foreign, new, and he'd taken pleasure in being the first, the man they'd always remember, however faintly, when they ate those dishes afterwards, no matter whose company they were in.

There'd been an element of conquest for him. *And man did I win*, he smiled ruefully, thinking of all the horrible evenings of disintegrating relationships, smashed objects, grating voices.

The travel agent returned to her desk from the fax machine. In hospital he'd fantasized about returning to a cave in Spain. He wanted to go alone, which would be foolhardy at the best of times, but he doubted he'd ever go caving again and he planned to have his last experience uncompromised.

The agent explained a series of possible itineraries, each more indirect and unpleasant than the last: layovers of four hours in the middle of the night, stopovers adding seven hours travelling time, midnight transfers with baggage claims and customs checks, plane changes allowing fifteen minutes to race from one check-in to another.

The world is not so big I need to endure that, he thought. He wanted to get on a plane, fly, eat a decent meal, have a nap, get off the plane, rent a car and go to the cave. Period. Maybe take a tent and bag and sleep near the entrance. Buy food along the way. He rubbed his beard and gazed out the window, then asked about flights to Victoria, British Columbia.

He'd always disliked the change in women after they had babies. He found his own demotion in their line of duties extremely unwelcome. Now that he'd had a stroke, the thought of another child—an infant, diapers, feedings, crying in the night, temper tantrums, injuries, illnesses, a cranky, tired wife—was also extremely unwelcome. Already, now that he'd regained his health, Dalva hardly paid any attention to him. She seemed to expect him to take care of her, which he had no intention of doing since he'd made it clear from the start he had no personal interest in being a father again. If she wanted to have a baby, it was her deal.

The arguments had started again. He couldn't resist taking out the old weapons and sharpening them, making comments he knew would enrage her, statements about intelligence, fitness, who should serve whom—and then watching the steam rise. Nevertheless, he was always surprised at the vehemence they unleashed, the hatred even, and by how long she bore a grudge.

He still half expected her to laugh and say something equally outrageous back to him, the way a man would. His sons, for example, would just shrug, or tease him or punch him on the arm. He could only conclude she liked being angry with him. Liked hating him. He'd had enough of that for a lifetime however, thank you very much. At sixty-four, being unloved was as unbearable as ever.

Thank God there was a universe out there that didn't rely on words or people to exist. *It's a good time to be getting out of here*, he thought.

"I'm going on a trip."

"Where?" she asked, turning, fixing her eyes on him.

"Canada. Vancouver Island."

"For how long?" she said lightly.

"Three weeks. Maybe less."

"And when?"

"Next week."

She appraised him.

"Typical. The first thing you do when you get your strength back is leave. I nurse you back to health and do you think to repay me, to ask me what I'd like after putting myself out for months? A new dress? A vacation? A piece of jewellery? No. Now you're ready to do what *you* want. Go! Do what you want! Who cares?"

He snorted. "You have your whole life ahead of you. What are you, sixteen? I've got maybe a week, a year, who knows, if I'm lucky, ten. I don't have time to play loverboy. I assumed you took care of me because you loved me, not because you hoped to be repaid for your efforts."

He sat alone in his office once again. Dalva had stormed off to bed and he, the grizzled old bull, got tanked on good vodka while watching his fish swim around in the pool. He was excited about caving again.

He remembered in the hospital fading in and out of sleep, memory and dream; his immobile body wishing to walk lightly once more through rock, to slip inside and move through passages using his arms and legs and eyes. To balance and step and lean his weight back on a rope, to move down a rock face. To flow through a cave, through passageways and openings and hidden places and sumps. How he'd yearned to be in a dark place again, to be fully *body in place*, body moving through place. That was freedom.

He poured what he told himself was one last drink and remembered the sun on the hilltop in France the day he decided to leave Germany forever. He had left forever. It hadn't just been a dramatic youthful impulse. He'd found light and heat and that superficial and playful sensuality he'd dreamed of when he was surrounded by heavy Germanic defeat, but he hadn't considered that structurelessness had a weight too, that lightness could induce paralysis, and amorality bring lethargy. It made him irritable to think of it. More irritable the older he got.

He took out his plane ticket and reviewed his itinerary. It seemed so pleasant—a direct flight to San Francisco, layover of one night at a four-star hotel, then a two-hour flight to Victoria. A rental car waiting at the airport.

It was just as well getting to Spain had proven so awkward. It was time to do something new instead of revisiting the past. He felt strong. Clean and healthy like a new leaf. Relaxed.

He might even look his cousin Jürgen up in the San Francisco phone book, see if he was still alive. And if he didn't feel up to a full exploration, he could just go into the caves a small distance. Just be in the cave. That was all he really needed. He could do whatever the hell he wanted.

The goldfish floated past the lights of the mosaic pool.

He performed his bedtime rituals: turned out all the lights, checked that all the doors were bolted and locked, brushed his teeth, didn't floss, urinated, took his vitamins, rubbed hair-preserving lotion into his scalp, dropped a naturopathic remedy for indigestion under his tongue, folded his clothes neatly, put on his pyjamas, slipped under the covers.

He didn't want to lose Dalva. Maybe he should have considered her more. Maybe she did deserve a holiday. In his mind, her whole life was a holiday, but probably she didn't think of it that way. When he got back from this trip he'd take her somewhere nice. He reached across the bed. She grunted crossly and moved away to the far edge of the bed, pulling the covers tighter around her.

He turned his reading light on, opened the drawer of his bedside table and took out bifocals for reading. He put them on, then took up his book, *Memoir from Antproof Case* by Mark Helprin. Roger's wife, Mimi, had recommended it to him. The old man who was the main character, an American/European hybrid, was explaining to the reader that Brazil was not a country for old men.

"You can imagine," Alfred read, "what it was like for me, then, in a country where, if a fly alights successfully upon a mango, ten thousand dancers take to the streets in delirium and euphoria, a country where a man who wins the lottery spends twice what he has won on a party to celebrate his winnings. They're not Scotsmen, these Brazilians."

He chuckled. He shifted to get more comfortable and his leg touched the silk edge of Dalva's nightgown. Blood began to flow into his flaccid penis, filling networks of capillaries, until he wanted friction, the tight grip and release and slide and burial, connected to the smell of her skin and the perfume of her soap and the texture of her hair falling on her shoulder and eyes that looked up at him half-asleep, surprised, then drifting off again, her body responding. He exploded into her, then slumped and drifted.

He roused again momentarily to turn off the light.

3

---◦✸◦---

It was quiet and dark.

Outside there was the usual amount of light and noise, but inside was soft, silent, and deep. Time collected like moisture on a cave wall. Slowly, a drop formed, then fell. Almost all of the self hibernated, storing up energy. Waiting.

She was a root being now—a bulb, a tuber. Not Persephone the maiden, but Persephone the defoliated, after eating the pomegranate seed, the winter Persephone, sitting in the underworld away from her mother.

Conversation was like a long-distance telephone call. People's voices seemed disembodied, which was ironic because she herself was only body. Involuntary movement filled her consciousness: heartbeat, breathing, peristalsis, cramps.

She was in the lull before a violent storm. Like a prophet, but with a package more concrete than words to deliver.

"May I take your order?"

The restaurant was bustling on a Saturday night. She ordered chicken souvlaki and moussaka for Robert, who'd gone to the washroom.

The waiter left and she gazed vacantly at an amateurish mural across the room. A mermaid with strangely triangular, pointy breasts floated beside a man in traditional Greek dress looking through a telescope at the sea.

Robert, of all people, had known what her father's Greek-looking garment was. His father had been the son of an English Communist Jew and an Italian Catholic. In his will he'd written, "Since my mother's infant christening dress won't fit more than my big toe, and besides, my sister has snatched it away for her brood, bury me in my father's kittel. I want something from my parents to go with me."

It had fallen to Robert to find out what a kittel was and identify one among his father's effects. He'd discovered that it was a garment of unbleached cotton worn by Jewish men on their wedding night and then every year at Yom Kippur and Passover. When they died they were buried in it.

"I can't imagine a more effective way to bring home the seriousness of wedding vows," he'd said to Carmen, and kissed her tenderly.

Carmen had phoned her father. "It must have been your mother's. It's a Jewish thing. But it's for men. Do you think she was going to give it to you? Was it her father's? Did she have a brother?" Alfred had no answers.

It seemed so strange that something as impermanent as clothing should remain while the people who owned it and their stories were gone. She'd thought of the plane Alejandro had described, clothes strewn on the floor as it landed, the bodies gone forever.

"I need to walk around," she told Robert when he returned to their table. The pressure on her pelvis made it uncomfortable to sit. She walked to the front door of the restaurant. Waddled actually because she couldn't get the tops of her thighs together. It felt as if there were an orange or a hard-boiled egg between her legs that she couldn't remove.

She sat down again. The band of muscle around her belly went hard with a contraction. It caused an ache in her lower back where the muscles attached to her spine, a tug that developed into a broad pain expanding down through her pelvis, ending at a point inside, like an exaggerated menstrual cramp.

Now she felt like the wolf in "Little Red Riding Hood," with rocks sewn inside his stomach. She stood and leaned on the chair back, waited for the discomfort to pass.

"You know what? This might be it." She grinned. "I can't wait to see this little tyke."

By the time they left the restaurant the contractions were four to five minutes apart. Carmen felt like someone on a beach watching a tidal wave roll in, knowing she doesn't have time to run away—all she can do is wait for the right time to duck under and hope she can make her way back to the surface.

They drove down Arbutus to Cornwall Avenue, past Kits pool, around Point Grey. Carmen kept track of the time between contractions. The lights on the cargo ships in the harbour shone through the rain.

The doctor told them to call again when the contractions were almost two minutes apart. They drove out to the grounds of the University of British Columbia and by the time they were back at Kits pool Carmen was finding it hard to catch her breath between the end of one contraction and the start of the next. The wave had hit and she was drowning.

"I need to go to the hospital," she said as another contraction hit. She was distressed. "Not that way, take Burrard . . . "

They pulled up to emergency. Someone helped her out and she crept to the admitting desk. The nurse asked her address but she couldn't answer. She gripped the counter. They eased her into a wheelchair, placing her feet on the footrests. She wanted to not move.

In a large room two nurses quickly undressed her and put her in a hospital gown. The air on her body seemed to increase the pain.

They helped her to a metal bed. She felt she was arching unnaturally just lying on the mattress. "Relax if you can. Just take little breaths." One of the nurses slipped ice chips into her mouth.

An intern came in, snapped on latex gloves and examined her. "You're fully dilated. If you can wait just another fifteen minutes, your doctor will be here. He's on his way. You're almost there. You're doing great."

The nurse offered her a mask with gas. She could barely breathe; why would she want to put that thing on? She shook her head. When the bulk of the contraction had passed, the nurse told her she really should try the gas. "It helps make you breathe and it'll help get you over the hump." The next contraction came and she turned her head and sucked in the air from the mask. It made her dizzy but she kept sucking and then she shook it away.

Her doctor walked in looking happy and dapper in a new leather jacket. He liked delivering babies. He asked the intern some questions, said hello to everyone, got his gloves on and sat by her feet. "Okay, next contraction start pushing."

It was like trying to flex over a pumpkin. She pushed with all her strength yet nothing seemed to move. She stopped and sucked in more gas as another wave of pain hit.

From deep inside herself she heard someone starting to wail, then scream, "Get it out." It felt like she was breaking open from the inside.

She bore down several times more, keening with a new pain that was not letting up between contractions, thinking *You never have to do this again.*

The nurse said, "Good, good, now breathe." It was like pushing against a trampoline. When she stopped she could feel the head get sucked back in.

Robert said, "I can see the head, the head's right there, you're doing great hon, you're almost there." She sucked some gas.

"Next one don't stop," the doctor said. "Keep going, keep going, keep pushing." She took little gulps of air and kept bearing down until the doctor said, "Stop. Don't push until I tell you."

"Okay now, one more big push." She bore down again and there was a huge slithering feeling. The pain disappeared instantly. A long white slippery body with a purple cord still attached lay in the doctor's hands.

It was a girl. She seemed so big. Not like Oliver at all. The doctor invited Robert to cut the cord, then carried the baby to a well-lit table to clean her and wrap her up. Carmen lay in a pool of painlessness and warmth. And then there she was—a little round cameo of new skin and tiny nostrils breathing in air for the first time. The eyelids opened and her eyes rolled around blearily. Carmen put her nipple to the baby's mouth and she suckled for a short time before falling asleep.

Robert went home to be with Oliver and Carmen continued to lie, warm and comfortable and not sleepy at all though it was four in the morning, happy just to look at Catharine's sleeping face.

4

HE WOKE AND LOOKED OUT the unclean motel window. Clouds. He got up and opened the door to see if it was raining, and was overcome by a sense of déjà vu. He'd lived this moment before. The same light, same cloud density, same speed of wind, same pattern of gusts, same size raindrop, same temperature, season, time of day, even similar smell outside.

He couldn't place the other moment but he knew he'd been younger, it was northern Europe, he'd been heading for a cave. So much had to be aligned for just the weather of one morning to be the same as the weather of another. As far as he knew this was the first time it had happened in his life. Once in twenty-three thousand days and how many billion moments? Life might be repetitious but it had infinite variety.

He got out of bed and shivered in the cold air of the thin-walled, poorly insulated room. Washed his face, brushed his teeth, shaved. He scrutinized himself in the mirror as he had every morning since the stroke, to see if he was all there.

He put on long underwear, a one-piece caving suit, high-topped waterproof hiking boots; tied a yellow cashmere sweater around his waist; picked up his pack; and went out to the rented car. He threw the pack in the trunk and drove to a nearby restaurant for coffee and breakfast.

There he perused a speleological map. He had already visualized the cave. The entrance appeared to be in a forest. The
map indicated flowstone and scalloping, ledges, chimneys. It
showed a steep drop a short distance in and then a gradual
slope down past a couple of bedrock pillars to another
chamber. This chamber was a hub for several others. A large
passage exited from the eastern side and ran a couple of
hundred metres before reaching another chamber that ended
in an unexplored sump. A sandy crawl led out of the northwest
corner, gradually expanding to a walkable passage that ran
1400 metres to a large chamber. A passage on the opposite side
of this chamber ran 50 metres before arriving at a T-junction.
On the right was a 35-metre crawl indicated as very tight,
leading to a chamber with interesting formations noted. On
the left of the T-junction a long passage with no noted obstacles led to another cave system, unmapped to date.

According to the man at the motel desk it was a two-hour
drive from Comox to the logging road and a further half-hour
on that road to the parking lot where the path leading to the
caves started.

He had not phoned anyone since his arrival on the island.
He had not felt like rewarding an undeserving Dalva with
his dulcet tones, his departure having elicited the usual
torrents of tender love and affection thinly disguised as rage
and scorn. He'd considered phoning Carmen last night, but
she tended to go on and on about the baby and he had not
felt up to generating enthusiasm should it be required. He
wanted to indulge himself completely in caving; he wanted
no distractions. He'd call her when he returned tonight.
He'd be able to enjoy the conversation then.

He turned the radio on, listened to country music for a
while, but all the commentary and advertising began to
grate on him, so he switched it off. The road was clear. The

landscape reminded him of Romania. Probably that was the source of his meteorological déjà vu.

The logging road was creviced and rutted and twisting; it took more than an hour to arrive at the parking lot. The wind was everywhere. The trees—fir, hemlock, maple—were in constant motion. The ground was littered with needles and twigs and pine cones and dead leaves. The sky flowed fast; the cloud thinned and briefly he felt the heat of the sun before the sun was covered by heavier cloud and rain began to spit.

Starting out he felt strong; his pack felt light, his feet warm and dry. The area was a karst landscape, with holes, rises, irregularities in evidence everywhere. It made him aware he was on an island: rock, stone, humus, clay, a bit of earth underfoot; surrounded by a cold deep ocean inhabited by seals, fish, mollusks. A rare whale. Of course all land was an island in some way, surrounded by ocean or ice.

The wind began to make him edgy. It masked other sounds. Bears and cougars were abundant on the island; the man at the motel's front desk had told him both had been responsible for human deaths in the past year. He whistled for a while, but the sound of his thin whistling in the middle of the loud wind unnerved him even more, so he fell silent.

The cave's entrance was in a sunken amphitheatre with one large and two smaller openings, ledged and uneven, partly camouflaged by a profusion of boulders. He climbed down. Opposite the caves was a sheer rock face covered with ferns and moss and tree roots. High above, pearly grey light filtered through a wet canopy of leaves.

He stopped to smell before getting any closer to the entrance. Bears and cougars would not venture far into complete darkness so their smell, if they were in a cave, would be quite strong near the opening. The air smelled faintly of earth; clean, still air; rock dust.

He stepped onto the scrabble that sloped inside the cave and climbed to a ledge sheltered by the roof of the cave. He slipped his pack off and poured himself a coffee from the Thermos. As he drank he appreciated the way light filtered down across the plant tapestry on the opposite wall, making complex patterns of green and brown and grey. He was happy. Just five months ago, pinned in his hospital bed, confused and immobile, surrounded by people, he would never have believed he could be here now. Alive, strong, alone. Time on his hands. Time on his shoulders, in his legs and eyes and nose. Time everywhere. The coffee could be a little hotter.

He checked the batteries in his helmet light and the backup cartridge. Put his yellow sweater on under his overalls, buttoned them up, put his helmet on. He really should have told someone where he was going. It was one thing to go alone, which was already quite reckless, but it was stupid not to have told the man at the motel exactly where he was headed and when to expect his return. Still, he was not about to turn back now. He'd just have to be careful.

He put his empty Thermos, which was red, in a visible spot so anyone looking down from the path could see it. Wrote a quick note documenting the date and time at which he was entering the cave, folded it and tucked it under the Thermos. Pathetic. At least there was the rented car in the lot for loggers to see.

He explored around each entrance, following ledges to the floor or ceiling, climbing up chimneys, getting his cave legs back. One entrance had a white marble floor, deeply scalloped by water.

When he felt ready to go farther he put his pack back on, turned on his helmet light and entered the corridor on the left of the main opening, duck-walking around a corner to a slightly higher passage that led shortly to a steep drop. He attached a rope to a piece of jutting rock and lowered himself down to a level area covered by rubble and mud. From there he walked, stooping carefully under rock and stalactites, until he arrived at a large chamber, the hub chamber on his map. The floor was sandy.

He sat on a ledge and turned out his light. He could hear water drip. And silence. He was in the dark once again. He sat for an hour.

He lay down and peered under the lip of a boulder and found a wedge-shaped passage underneath veering to the left. He wormed back out and checked his map and determined this was the only way in. He removed his pack, hooked it to his ankle and began to wriggle in. The squeeze was wide enough for him to spread his arms out, but not high enough for him to hold his head with his helmet up. He had to turn it sideways, cheek to sand, to move forward. He paused, mentally checked if he could reverse out again if necessary, then proceeded.

Crawling through this passage was not casual even for him, even knowing that it opened out to another chamber and that it was passable. Alfred thought of the first person, the one with no map, no knowledge of what lay ahead. Those were the guys who impressed him, the guys who did not turn back until they knew how far they could go.

And the ones who explored sumps, who dragged diving equipment through squeezes into chambers, then put it on and slipped into inky water. If their flippers accidentally touched the bottom, silt plumed up through the water, destroying visibility and thereby completely disorienting them because the only way to tell up from down was by the direction of their bubbles. If they ran into trouble with their equipment, there was no surface to head for. What he was doing was easy by comparison.

The squeeze opened up a bit and he was able to crab forward with his head up. The floor changed from sand to moist dirt. Condensation appeared on the ceiling, glittering in his helmet light. He crabbed out into a chamber that was about thirty metres in diameter. Toward the ceiling on the right were popcorn formations and light coppery green crystals. On the left, the opaque water of a lake absorbed light.

All morning he'd been trying not to think about the other time he'd neglected to tell anyone where he was going. Now he thought about it. He remembered lying at the bottom of the dome pit, his leg broken, thinking he was going to die and beginning to feel peaceful, how the will to survive had faded and been replaced by a surprising acceptance. Then hearing a sound like a huge breath enter the cave, a clatter of equipment, and realizing someone had found him. The rending pain, akin to anguish, as the engines of hope started up again and he realized he'd have to re-enter the world.

This chamber seemed like a good place to stop for lunch, but he felt restless. His muscles were stiff. After a cursory look, he decided to explore more thoroughly on the way back. He continued down a passage that was marked on the map as running fifty metres without any significant obstacles. The map indicated an overall descent of two metres with short intervals of duck-walking and some clambers over rubble. He arrived at what the map described as a T-junction but was really an irregular Y-junction. He had to choose between a muddy crawl on the right leading to interesting formations, or a passage on the left which the map described only as leading to another uncharted cave system.

He'd been in the cave for three hours now. He sat and forced himself to eat and drink. He felt a trace of loneliness, eating alone, with no sunlight, nothing green, nothing animate. He was probably only thirty metres below the surface, forty at most, not far from life. He looked back down the passage he'd arrived by, memorizing its appearance for the return. It was kidney-shaped, while the one leading to the tight muddy crawl was round with the ceiling coming down quickly inside. The passage leading to the other cave system looked quite large.

He felt brittle and stiff in the damp cold. He decided he'd better get moving again and chose the long roomy passage which the map indicated only with an arrow. It was unclear whether anyone had ever done it, but he reasoned he could always turn back if it seemed too difficult.

There was a mark after the words "another cave system" that might have been a letter or a number or a question mark, and might mean the author thought there was a link, but it had yet to be explored. It excited him to think he might be the first to travel between two cave systems. The Alfred Lion connector.

He opened his pack and took out a plastic bag holding notepad, pencil and a soft tape measure and put it in the chest pocket of his overalls. Every two metres he stopped and wrote down the dimensions of the passage, and some notes describing it. He continued like this for a couple of hundred metres and then the passage began to tighten. He felt warm and fairly limber now and the trace of loneliness had vanished.

He removed his pack and carried it slung over one shoulder. The passage soon necessitated going on hands and knees, and here he hooked the pack on his foot so he could drag it through. There was lots of chunky rubble on the floor and he guessed there'd been a breakdown of the ceiling or wall. The sharp rocks were hard on his knees even with knee pads, and harder still on the shins. Air blew on his face from the direction he was headed. It would be nice if he could return to the surface this way and avoid having to pass back through the muddy squeeze.

He marked "209 metres" down on the pad and slipped it into his chest pocket. He put the tape measure in his hip pocket and shone his light ahead. The passage widened somewhat and turned to the left. He snaked forward and entered the turn. The rubble appeared to diminish and his light illuminated another turn about a metre ahead. The air seemed fresher and the breeze even a little stronger. He sensed a large chamber just around the corner.

He wormed his way down the passage and around the corner. Instead of opening into a chamber, the passage tightened.

It was too small for him to crawl through. Perhaps a boy of ten might have passed. He rested for a minute, his body lying in the curve, waist at the turn. Then began inching backward. The back of his helmet clunked against a jutting rock and he had to inch forward again and try tilting his head at several different angles before he found one that allowed him to pass. Also he now had to move his pack backward with his feet, centimetre by centimetre. Thank God he'd already eaten lunch so the pack was that much smaller. Every part of him felt constrained. He hated moving backward, hated not being able to see the direction he was travelling.

To move straight ahead in a squeeze one pushed with the toes and heaved forward at the same time. The toes were not as effective moving backward; pushing down on the fragile bones and thin skin on the top of the toes, against the curl, afforded hardly any pressure. The hands, however, gained more force pushing away rather than pulling and he managed to inch back several centimetres before feeling another snag.

A jutting rock had caught the fabric of his overalls on his right hip and he had to inch forward again to unhook himself, then press himself against the opposite wall of the rock to try and move past without rehooking the fabric. He reached the other bend and began to visualize which way his legs would have to bend to mould to the tunnel.

The bottom of his boots came up against the wall and he adjusted the orientation of his body in the tunnel so he could bend his legs at a somewhat different angle. He inched back and felt a pull on his left shoulder and then a tear of fabric. He moved forward again, unhooked the tear and pressed against the right wall, bruising his flesh but not caring, easing back. It snagged again.

He tried pressing against the left wall as he eased back. Again the tear snagged. He inched forward and thought for a moment. He pressed his back against the ceiling to flatten the fabric, then pressed against the right wall and wiggled back. Again it caught. He rolled as far over as he could on his right side, his left shoulder digging into the passageway ceiling, and eased backward. Still the bloody thing snagged. He rolled over on his left side: same result. Every combination he could think of, every nuance of pressing against the outer edges of the tunnel and still he could not get past whatever was snagging the tear. He crushed his shoulders in painfully, turned on his side, only to find his hips wouldn't fit through the bend at that angle. He inched forward again.

He could feel panic, like a mouse running through his body towards his brain. He tried to think through what would happen if he pushed back as hard as he could against the tear, how far the overalls might rip. Was there nothing to lose? He tried to force his way against the fabric, but the canvas was too thick and would not tear further, and the pressure he could exert lying at such an angle with his hands stretched out in front of him was too feeble.

It quickly became unbearable to think about his situation— he couldn't keep his panic down any longer—so he willed himself to sleep. The only available anesthetic. He calmed his breathing down, slowed his brain, closed his eyes, tried not to think that when he next woke it might be to permanent darkness because the batteries of his light would be dead and he couldn't access the fresh ones. It took some time to push that thought down. Then he dropped off.

5

HE WOKE THINKING he was a baby who was never going to get born, stuck in the birth canal of a mother who was dead and cold and turned to stone.

He woke, forgetting he had already lived a life. Thinking that was a past life, and now the new one would never start.

He even smiled at the irony that in his past life he'd travelled the world as though he were a giant in seven-league boots and in his new life he couldn't move ten centimetres.

His mother was dead and whatever remained of her was cold as stone.

For the first time in his life it seemed strange he'd never tried harder to find out what had happened to her. Burned, maybe? Though not in memory. His memories had all become like dreams.

Might as well be dreams, because they were coming to an end. There was a baby about to be born. A tiny hand, opening and closing, somewhere in the world, connected to him. Something in him relaxed. The dream went on. He could remain still and drift backward . . . his mother and father looking at him. He could see himself.

A nurse held a baby wrapped in flannel up to him. Its blurry blue eyes opening, trying to focus on his, closing. The baby looked at him. The baby was both him and not him. It was his child and it was his grandchild and great-grandchild. The blur it saw, a mystery.

He put all his energy into shifting his hip bone off a jutting piece of rock, but could only change the pressure point by a couple of centimetres. He wanted to lie in a fetal position on his side. It would have given him such comfort in the dark to feel his own warmth against his belly, but when he went to bring his knee up, it hit rock after just a few centimetres. His heart pounded. He began the long process of calming himself down but the panic was like a wild horse he couldn't quite manage to rein in. He used the only cure he had available and willed himself back to sleep.

He dreamed eventually of a grassy savannah in Africa: yellow dry grass. Everything sunny and bright. Two lions running forward across the grass. To the left, a cluster of thirty people running and another fifteen or twenty dispersed around them. Young men jump in front of the lions and burst into a run, trying to outrun them, then break away back into the crowd. It's great fun and everyone is happy and laughing and cheering. The lions are large and with their big paws they are loping more than running, so they are playing too.

It is very likely that eventually the lions will want to catch someone and eat them, but that is not the case now.

Now is play. Play between the herd and the predators. The pleasure of the herd in running together, in the challenge of getting away. Nobody's concerned about individual loss of life. A moment in paradise.

6

April was late. Catharine slept in her infant car seat, which Carmen had lodged in the stroller. The darling little fruit of her parents' union, replete with red wool tomato hat with a little green stem on top, was still young enough that noisy restaurants did not affect her slumber.

Carmen gazed at her daughter's sleeping face, remembering what it had taken to bring her into the world. Labour had been a kind of second coming, a revelation, unexpected and remote certainly from the original act, yet strangely even more satisfying. Labour, not orgasm, had been the final consummation of Carmen's sexual desire. For her, surprisingly, God's punishment of Eve, the outrageous pain of labour, *was* the reward.

The utter extinguishment of frustration that pain had brought was strangely equivalent to the utter satisfaction of desire. Merely thinking about it re-induced the experience and sent her into a kind of trance.

All the crushes and palpitations and hopes and yearning and blushing and flutterings of young love, all the struts and ducking for cover, displaying, concealing, the drawing near and pushing away, all the Harlequin emotions—the erotic ones, and domestic ones, sublime and tragic, washing the dishes, being one with the stars—culminated in that one extended screaming, grunting moment. Delivering something from inside, alive and separate, into the world outside. Where wind could touch it and sharp teeth could bite it, where it could see its own shadow and moonlight and have its own thoughts.

April arrived at last, out of breath, lugging her newborn baby in his car seat.

"Sorry. He was hungry so I had to feed him, then all that warm milk made him have a gigantic head-to-toe shit, so then I had to change him, wash him, find a new outfit as cute as the other one and, three-quarters of an hour later, I am ready to leave again. When you're a person who's always late anyway, that extra three-quarters of an hour is a real bitch."

Carmen bent over April's sleeping newborn. It was hard to believe Catharine had been that small only four months ago.

"He's beautiful. Look at his hands folded over his tummy, like a satisfied old gentleman. Simon really suits him."

They exchanged reports on sleeping habits and lack thereof, feeding habits, glimmers of personality; Carmen described Oliver's reaction to the baby, which was mostly indifference with spurts of intense interest.

April was frustrated because it had been three weeks since she'd delivered and she still couldn't wear her old jeans. Carmen guffawed. "Three weeks? Are you nuts?"

"Listen, it's serious. I have to go to a Family Services Ball next Saturday and nothing fits. There's no point in buying anything new because it won't fit next month anyway."

"Why don't you wear that dress I have in accordion fabric? It fits whatever size you are. Get some new shoes and with the right jewellery it can be very formal."

"The black one with bands of brown, turquoise and neon green?"

"Yeah, that one. Let's look for shoes after lunch. Maybe I'll look at dresses. I want to buy something really hot now that

I'm more or less back in shape. Going out with my dad's latest wife was the last straw. I never want to be Pollyanna next to Pamela Anderson Lee again."

"Oh c'mon. I know I've seen you look sexy in jeans, with high-heeled boots or something."

They ordered lunch. Carmen looked out the window.

"How are things with Robert?" April asked.

"They're good. They're good. I believe his story about 90 percent of the time. We're pretty close these days actually. Arguing less. Just glad to be together. He and Oliver are doing a lot of things and he's happy to have a daughter.

"The other 10 percent of the time I start brooding on the contents of that letter, imagining what might have happened and fantasizing about revenge. I get in a really foul mood. I mean, whatever the case, he was testing the waters a little, seeing who he'd be with another woman, while I was pregnant and taking care of Oliver. I can work up a pretty good head of steam.

"He handles it well. His story is consistent and he keeps telling me he loves me in a way that makes me believe him. Our love life is pretty passionate."

She took a long gulp of beer. "So far so good," she laughed. "It's been liberating in a way. I don't worry about pleasing him any more. It's left me with a clearer sense of who I am. Because I was really starting to mix up what was him and what was me.

"And I've got a wolf! He and Oliver adopted one for me while I was away as an offering. My namesake, Carmen. She lives on the B.C./Yukon border. She sent me a picture of her new litter of pups. He said he felt like a wolf, that the rest of the world could fade away and all that would remain would be him and me and Oliver and Catharine and the land around us."

April smiled at Carmen. "That's really nice."

"A bit monastic perhaps, but whatever, it's a long way from my father. Carmen the wolf is like my psychic companion now. I dream about her."

"I don't think it's stupid to believe him, you know," said April. "It's not unreasonable."

"Hey, you want to go dancing tonight? My sister, Rebecca, is back from tree planting and she invited me with a couple of her friends. All girls' night."

"Not yet. I still need every wink of sleep I can get."

"I really feel like kicking loose."

Their lunch arrived and they started eating.

"What was it like, your dad having such a young wife?"

"It didn't seem like anything frankly. They looked sort of natural together. Even considering the stroke he looks pretty good for his age, I guess."

"It isn't fair."

"Fair, shmair, it's only evolution. Men don't go through menopause, that's it in a nutshell. You wait, if women start having babies in their sixties, like that woman in Italy, every-thing will change. It just takes time."

They tumbled through the glass doors of their favourite clothing store, holding the door open for each other as they manoeuvred the strollers in. Carmen had picked Oliver up at kindergarten and brought along a couple of toys he hadn't seen for a few weeks, to distract him.

Inside, two saleswomen in well-tailored suits looked at them with quickly suppressed horror, then came forward to admire the babies. Carmen prayed the attention didn't wake Catharine up because she'd be hungry and by the time Carmen nursed her, Oliver would very likely be bored with the toys.

They parked the strollers and Carmen went to work, eliminating all the clothes that weren't what she was looking for. She picked out some promising things and ducked into the change room. Simon woke up and April sat down on the expensive leather couch to nurse him. Carmen undressed quickly and wormed into something skin-tight and stretchy with spaghetti straps that looked awful over the thick straps of her nursing bra.

She'd assumed the stretchy fabric would act like a giant girdle, smoothing and tightening.

"I look like a five-pound sausage in a three-pound wrap, to quote Ralph Kramden," she said over the door.

"Let us see," April and the saleswomen clamoured.

"No way."

She began to perspire as she wriggled in and out of three more dresses. She heard Catharine start to make wake-up noises and then Oliver said he had to go to the washroom. She whipped the last dress on. She applied some fresh lipstick and asked if they had any shoes for her to try it on with. She stepped out in a pair of towering strappy black heels.

"It's unbelievable you had a baby four months ago," the saleswoman said. "You look fabulous."

In this dress, it was true.

"It's not cheap," she said to April.

"It's timeless," April said authoritatively, their code for ignoring price.

"Hmmm. I could still wear this in ten years."

"When you're sixty. Seventy. Any age."

"You can wear it through three seasons," said the saleswoman. "Even into summer here. The fabric is a very versatile weight."

"You look amazing in it so who cares. You're only middle-aged once," April laughed.

Carmen loved shopping with April. There was something about one woman encouraging another to look beautiful, sexy, powerful, that Carmen found oddly moving. Protecting a friend from looking unlovely or foolish, exerting her most discriminating aesthetic on the other's behalf. The opposite of competition: it was a female alliance, a transcendent bond of loyalty.

Catharine began to cry. Carmen felt the prickle of milk rushing toward her nipples. As she raced toward the change room to get the dress off before it got stained, the sound of an explosive bowel movement came from April's stroller. Oliver went over to a rack of Alberta Ferreti pieces and crawled underneath. "Find me, Mom."

When Carmen re-emerged from the dressing room, April was returning from the bathroom with a smelly plastic bag and one of the saleswomen was using mints from her purse to try to entice Oliver away from the thousand-dollar cashmere sweater sets.

"I'm using cloth diapers," April announced. "Better for the environment."

"Thank you so much," the friends said to the saleswomen as they levered the strollers out the door. As soon as they were out of sight, they burst into laughter.

"Oh my God, that was awful."

"But you should get that dress, Carmen. It looks amazing."

"If I wear it till I'm seventy, it'll almost be a bargain."

That night she nursed a crantini and watched Rebecca dancing with her friends. She was thinking about Robert and her father and turning forty and whether to buy that dress or not. The evening had been flat so far and she hadn't felt like dancing after all. They'd left a couple of other clubs before arriving at the Dufferin, a singularly unpretentious gay bar.

Finally AC/DC's "T.N.T." came on and she jumped out of her seat and joined Rebecca, who was dancing with a short man who sprang about like a manic wood nymph. She peeled her sweater off and tossed it on an empty chair. Rebecca and her friends laughed and they started dancing in a circle. Under the spinning lights, her hair flying wildly around her face, dancing first with masculine, then more feminine moves, she stopped thinking.

A young man dancing by himself watched her appreciatively and started mirroring her moves until they were dancing together. He seemed like a mercurially male and female cupid, like a character in a Fellini movie, boy and man yet girlish too, and she began to feel like a Hindu fertility goddess, showering rose petals around him, touching him with a maternal sexuality she'd never experienced before. It was as if she was feeling the full power of her sexuality for the first time, a power that had nothing to do with having children, but was a channel for something queenly in the universe.

Everyone she loved—Robert, Beth, Oscar, Oliver and Catharine, April, Alfred, her grandmothers, Alejandro, Rebecca who was smiling and happy across from her, even Ron and Isabel and Ivan and Daniel, everyone she'd ever cared about seemed present. *I'm a steam engine of love*, she thought. *My flesh is soft and already starting to blend back into the earth . . .*

She remembered dancing with Alfred when she was young, round and round on a polished floor, mirror ball spinning light over everything. Father and daughter the only ones dancing, everyone else sipping drinks at their tables. They'd looked at each other and laughed, surprised to have reached this charmed moment.

7

———⚬⚬⚬———

HE HEARD THE GURGLE and myriad clicks of water running over stone. It was a small river, not wide but deep. A light wooden rowboat skimmed the surface. He sensed a rower, but could see nothing in the absolute black. The malevolence that at first he'd sensed emanating from the figure was, he'd now come to understand, only indifference. Indifference to him. And that indifference gave him pleasure. He did not have to measure up. There was even warmth in that indifference, a vigorous happy freedom radiating from it. The past and future opened up in its wake and stretched as far as his eye could see.

It was true. He did not need more life. He had no need to go on repeating variations of experiences he'd already had. He could let go.

This small boat with its neutral captain was on top of the world. Alfred could see explosions, from the corner of his eye, but he wasn't interested enough to look.

And he saw space and stars and something, something with two legs, a face and eyes, brimming with love: some kind of love not motherly and not sexual, and not brotherly, or fatherly or even the love of a child. It was a unique love that he would call—if he had to bother with words any more—ancestral. Love of him and all the experiences of his life, yet a love that included all descendants and their babies, all animals and theirs. Behind this figure he glimpsed more tiny explo-sions. There was an aura of excitement combined with infinite patient curiosity.

The boatman's mouth formed the glimmer of a smile as he continued to row and Alfred understood that the indifference did not extend to the river or the boat or the job of ferrying passengers back and forth. The boatman loved those. His only pure pleasure, a pleasure that trumped conflicting urges to help others and protect oneself. The only peace. The only freedom. Moral ambrosia. Commitment to work.

Though it was amoral. Pleasure was always amoral, stolen from judgment. Momentarily he wanted to communicate this to somebody in the living world, in case it would help. But the need melted and slipped away, a shape that couldn't be examined. It didn't matter. They'll discover what they discover. It won't be my life any more.

Breathing was getting difficult. Each breath a conscious effort. Finally I'm attaining a Buddhist consciousness of breath, he thought, with an irony that was very painful because it was infinitely unshareable. He looked back at that face.

Since he first realized as a boy that eventually he must die, he'd felt hunted by death. He felt it stalking him, waiting, a predator that merely delayed the attack, but never departed. Every moment of his life had been lived with a background sensation of running, of looking over his shoulder.

Now at last he could surrender. Prey no more, nor victim, just a man melting back into the earth. Now, after all the years of running he could stop.

Stop and lie down; offer up his throat; give in, sleep. There was relief in finally not having to worry about dying. He was dying. He did not have to struggle any more.

No light, no time, no sound. Quiet, dark, warm.

Safe at last.

8

He breathed in. There was a pause. The breath came back out, warm, smelling strongly of hunger. To this last exhalation he added his ghost.

9

Two DAYS LATER the lead man of a rescue team met his boots. Established that he was no longer alive. Returned to the surface to arrange for the removal of the body. Phone the wife.

10

━━⚬⚬⚬━━

SHE DROPPED OLIVER OFF at kindergarten. She drove to the butcher shop, walked to the greengrocer's. The sun was shining and the air cool and clear. She decided to visit a nearby park and let Catharine look at trees and birds and children playing on slides and swings. She bought a large strong coffee and drove to the park.

Chose a bench in the sun, propped Catharine up in her stroller so she could watch a group of preschoolers playing on the park equipment. She had a book with her but for the moment she was content to stare at the grass and drink coffee.

She hadn't slept much the night before, not from lack of opportunity but because she'd felt so much emotion: happiness, sadness, tenderness. She and Robert had made love and while he'd fallen asleep she'd nursed Catharine in the bed. The moon was full and shone directly into their room through the unfurling leaves of a sour-cherry tree outside. She rubbed the baby's head. New thicker hair was replacing baby hair but it was still incredibly soft. Her head was also getting harder and bigger and it felt so warm, softly bristled on her bald spot, the heat of new blood circulating efficiently under the skin.

Carmen had stayed awake for hours, just rubbing Catharine's head, feeling Robert's back curved against hers, tailbone to tailbone, enjoying the warmth of the moment. It was so different from the first time.

With Oliver she'd been shocked by the constant interruptions to her sleep and the anxiety of never knowing when the next interruption would be. For months and months she'd had no libido: she'd just wanted to sleep and be left alone. And she'd been determined to get her body back into shape as fast as possible. She'd done sit-ups, drunk skim milk, eaten fruit salad, gone out walking for hours.

This time she was enjoying her slack belly. She liked the soft folds of skin, the pliableness, the intimacy, the receptivity of the flesh. Her belly was anti-fashion, not for public consumption, just for her and Robert and Oliver and the doctor. The milk, the baby, the flesh, the skin, she wanted to lie around and indulge in the luxurious abundance of it all.

Out of the corner of her eye she noticed Catharine's head move suddenly to the left. Sensed her focusing on something. She looked in the direction Catharine was looking and saw nothing special—a brown leaf on the concrete basketball court beside the grassy area of the park; a drain; an empty Slurpee cup.

Her gaze wandered back to the grass. She had a craving for tandoori chicken. She'd bought chicken breasts at the butcher, new potatoes and fresh corn at the greengrocer's. And bananas. She went to the car in the parking lot behind the playground and got a banana and a bottle of water to stoke her body for making milk. She'd read that the baby always got what it needed, but the mother's body started robbing its own bone and muscle to make milk if she didn't eat properly.

When she returned Catharine was looking up in the sky. Carmen looked up. A bat flew erratically above the field. Its radar didn't seem to be functioning. It zoomed around, up and sideways, and crashed on the grass. Carmen picked Catharine up out of the stroller and walked over to see it.

Its small face was scrunched and pug-like. It had the most beautiful soft orangey-brown fur and its wings, far from looking cold and leathery, looked warm and velvety and delicate. It had landed face down, with one wing bent and the other partly spread out. Its body pulsated with a rapid heartbeat. Carmen wanted to help it, but other than getting a box and keeping it safe until night, she didn't know what to do. It attempted to fly and after a few bumps into the ground achieved elevation again, only to crash farther afield.

It was then she heard the lawn mower. The sound had been present all along, but failed to register. A green John Deere cutting the grass in ever-widening circles. It swung round and began cutting a swath down the side where the bat was. Carmen carried Catharine over to the bat. It flopped over several times, ending up on its back. Two dark nipples were visible in the fur on its breast.

Carmen looked down the field at the lawn mower and tried to gauge whether it would cross where the bat lay. It looked to be a couple of loops away, but she worried that the bat would try to fly and crash right into it and be swept under its turning blades.

Her heart began to beat rapidly, like the bat's. She urged the bat telepathically to fly over to the trees and hang upside down under a shady branch. She worried it was dehydrated, because the sun was very hot and its beautiful moist wings spread out on the grass were taking direct sunlight. Perhaps it needed the warmth.

She prepared to stop the driver of the lawn mower, a sullen-looking man. He was wearing protective headphones so it wasn't going to be easy to get his attention. She began to walk toward him but as the noise of the lawn mower grew louder Catharine started to scream. The driver didn't notice.

The bat took flight again and veered off behind the washrooms onto some wood chips. Carmen thought: *There's nothing more I can do. It's time to take Catharine home and nurse her and put her down for her morning nap.*

She strapped Catharine into her car seat and packed the stroller into the trunk. The lawn mower was on the distant side of the field now. She walked gingerly over to where the wood chips were and looked for the bat, without success. She stood in front of the field and searched the grass for anything that looked like a bat, but saw nothing. Its fate was in its own hands now.

What did that mean, the bat's fate was in its own hands? It meant the bat's fate was in nature's hands. She was letting nature take its course. This did not mean leaving the bat to a maternal, nurturing feminine anima—Mother Nature. No, no. Would she ever consider letting nature take its course, for example, with Catharine?

It just meant she didn't care enough to intervene any more. It meant she was going to leave things in the hands of her father's randomly healing God, the uncomfortable One. Who would not intervene with the lawn-mower driver. Who would leave the bat's fate up to the chance that it might veer chaotically away from the machine's vibration, if its echolocation organs still worked well enough. Or it might not.

She drove down suburban residential streets, impressions of the bat's disorientation and beauty replaying in her mind. For the rest of her life, whenever bats came up in conversation, in books or film, she'd remember her distress. Remember never knowing what happened to this particular bat.

As she drove she was overwhelmed with not knowing the fate of so many things. The fate of almost everything, almost everyone. So much disappeared before she even looked, let alone understood. The traces melted away.

There was some relief knowing her father's fate. Yet she only knew the form of his fate. She didn't know what he'd thought before his death, what he'd felt pinned alone in utter blackness. Didn't know what death was for him. She knew the outcome but she would never know his inner fate.

There was no one left to ask. His body was there but his voice had vanished.

She pulled over in front of a rancher with a Japanese maple whose leaves were turning bright red and cried.

11

THE LEAD MAN attached a rope round both ankles and wormed backward, paying out the rope, until he arrived at a section where he could kneel. The rest of the team were waiting there. They all took hold of the rope and pulled, gently at first, testing the tension on the rope. They pulled harder. Raising the level of pressure until they worried they'd rip his feet off.

The lead man wormed back into the squeeze until his helmet light illuminated the boots again. He held in front of him a long metal rod, which he raised over Alfred's legs and used to prod the stone ceiling to find where the snag might be. Alfred's hips lay at the bend and the man could not advance past Alfred's feet to poke the rod round the bend. Before the bend he could feel no jutting rock, either on the ceiling or the sides of the tunnel.

He checked the rope again. He wanted to pull from here, nearer the body, but there was no room to exert any force. He snaked back to a point where he could raise himself partly on his elbows and called to the team to pull and he pulled. The body didn't budge. The man was definitely dead because already there was a sweetish unwashed smell. Still the lead man wormed forward again and knocked the soles of the boots and yelled. He hated to leave the poor fellow here.

12

SHE WANTED HIS BODY brought back to the surface so it could be buried. Which didn't make sense. Earth was cozier than stone? What better burial than in a cave? But the stone was hard, unforgiving, lonely. She wanted his flesh in soft ground. Also she didn't want him stuck.

The language of death was so confusing. She thought "him" for his body, but then corrected her usage to "it": *him/it/the body/my father/Alfred*, memories of an animated body, soul at home, flooded her.

She remembered arguing with him. Not this last visit, but twenty years earlier. She remembered him in his kitchen: salami, pickles, herring, pumpernickel bread spread on the table in front of them.

She was in her own kitchen at the moment, having perused the front section of the newspaper, orange peel aromatic on the table. Oliver was at kindergarten. The baby was sleeping late. She'd peeped in long enough to see the baby blanket rising and falling.

No doubt they'd been arguing about politics. His girlfriend at the time was away, a brother's wedding maybe in a town outside Buenos Aires. It had been before her twenty-first birthday party.

All she cared about now was proximity. She wanted him across the table from her, sitting there so she could reach over the table and touch him, his heart beating. She wanted to talk back and forth. So after she said something, he'd say something back. To hear the warmth and colour of his voice, the emphasis he put at unconventional points in a sentence. His gruff voice coming to her across a table, like warm breath.

Unlike the one-way conversation she had now. Telling him she loved him. She missed him. She wanted so much just to be able to dial him up and talk on the telephone. Surely there was some number in the universe she could call. He was a perfect father, she'd say. Perfect. As was. Fine. Luxury even.

He'd been someone who lived in the present. His life had tumbled out around him. He was not one to control things. Life happened to him. Fine. As was.

Her mind turned to her own body. Sitting on a wooden chair. In the kitchen. Beside the phone that she'd hung up after the man told her they couldn't get the body up. Suddenly she was freezing. Catharine woke up and she went and changed her and carried her into the bed with just her fresh diaper on and nursed her under the covers. Her small body was so warm. Her blaze seemed steady, strong, inextinguishable.

She stroked Catharine's head as she nursed. *Inextinguishable blazes.*

All his rhetoric about terrorists, *kill them like dogs*, and then his strange comment that he'd rather be a frog than a woman. He hadn't been a cruel man, nor lacking in compassion. He'd been careless, very careless of other people, but no less careless than he'd been about himself. How was it he embraced the torture and murder of people in Argentina so readily, other than that people did so all over the world, all the time?

His need to feel safe trumped compassion.

What could feel safer than being curled up in bed, feeding your baby sweet milk you made without even trying? What could be further away than the broken body of a boy by a riverbank, far from his mother's comfort?

He mistook his anger and guilt at the rape of his great aunts and the disappearance of his mother for clarity.

As she lay on her side with her knees curled up around Catharine, she wondered if his helmet light was still on or if his body lay in pure dark. Were his eyes closed? Were insects eating him?

She smiled to think what his body would do to the cave's microecology. A one-time food-chain bonanza, not to mention all the new moulds and fungi and bacteria he'd be introducing into the fragile balance of the cave ecosystem. Likely none of the new organisms would survive once his flesh was gone, but it was possible a new life form might evolve, some mutation of yeast bacteria that could survive in a light-less environment. Something new still to come from Alfred.

The image of his body alone in the narrow tunnel so far from the Earth's surface aroused a maternal tenderness that blended with what she felt for Catharine, for her plump absolute need.

What did the dead need? Well, nothing obviously. But the living, who still hoped absurdly not to disappear, needed them to be remembered.

To be remembered.

To be remembered.

She started to cry.

Her father, without whom this little rosebud mouth beside her with sweet milky air puffing out would not exist. This new brain, cooking away in its still pliable encasement, ticking and putt-putting and sparking.

In a stone tunnel were two soft and fluid pouches, fig-like, a warm traceable line from them to her. No more letters home. She was now in possession of everything she was ever going to get from him. Every look, gesture and touch.

She took a deep breath in and found she didn't want to exhale.

13

SHE AND CATHARINE DEPLANED in Vancouver. Alfred's memorial service had been an informal ceremony in a small Catholic church full of folkloric statues and paintings of Brazilian saints yet to be recognized by the Vatican. Instead of a coffin there'd been a large photograph of Alfred in caving overalls, helmet under his arm, a rakish grin on his face. All the half-siblings had been there, shyly staring at each other, picking out genetic similarities in each other, wondering how deep they ran.

Alejandro had been there with his wife and children, Alfred's friends, Dalva's family. She'd promised to keep in touch with Dalva, but it was unlikely they'd ever see each other again. All she had from her father, besides the kittel, was a pair of shoes she'd stolen from his cupboard as a keepsake.

Robert and Oliver were visiting his sister and her kids in the interior of British Columbia and wouldn't be back for three days. The house felt empty and lonely without them and Carmen decided to see if she could go to her brother-in-law's cabin on Hornby Island for a couple of days.

"The place never gets used now that the kids are in soccer and hockey," he said. "The key is under the mat."

She took a ferry to Nanaimo. From there the highway turned into a two-lane road along the coast. Carmen stopped to buy a bottle of water and a package of Cherry Nibs. She put PJ Harvey on the tape deck, turned the volume up—but not loud enough to wake Catharine, who was sleeping in her car seat. An RV and a logging truck were in front of her so it was impossible to make time. She relaxed and enjoyed the drive. She reached her brother-in-law's place by early afternoon, unpacked the car, and walked down to the beach carrying Catharine in her arms.

It wasn't a beach in the classic sense. It was shale with enormous boulders thrown down randomly and some patches of mucky dark sand. It was so shallow that when the tide was out almost half a kilometre of beach was exposed. She'd spent the summer on a beach just like it almost twenty years earlier doing fieldwork while she was at Simon Fraser University.

Carmen carried Catharine out to the waterline to introduce her to the sea. Barnacles crunched and she cringed as her gumboots stepped unavoidably on the abundance of sea anemones, clams, oysters, crabs, sea worms and sand dollars. It was like walking on a shelf of living creatures, all making sucking, popping, rustling sounds.

The smell was cloying. A sweetish fertile smell of ocean baking in the sun, dead plankton and shellfish, rotting seaweed, the scent of a food chain that included everybody right beneath her feet, food for hundreds and hundreds of species, her own among them.

A large black shape that she thought was stone arched its neck and flopped into the water on her approach—a seal ceasing to sun itself on a barely submerged rock. Another large splash resounded farther out and she looked for another seal.

Catharine started to fuss. At first Carmen thought it might be the sun, which was overpoweringly bright, reflecting off tide pools, wet sand and shale. She turned her back to the sun to put Catharine in her shadow, but Catharine's fussing didn't abate. Carmen checked her watch and realized it was an hour past feeding time. She walked back toward the shore and Catharine started to cry in earnest.

The crying made Carmen feel desperate. She stepped quickly between the slippery stones and rushed to a large log under an overhanging tree whose roots had been exposed by the ridge's erosion. She laid Catharine on a broad, flat part of the log while she unsnapped her nursing bra, then cradled her quickly into position. Milk rushed uncomfortably through the glands, the same prickling ache as when blood flooded in her legs at the beginning of a bicycle ride.

Catharine relaxed right away and closed her eyes. Milk flowed into her small stomach, and Carmen sat back and looked out at the beach. She wished she'd remembered to bring drinking water. A heron flapped overhead, its shadow passing swiftly across the shale, and landed at the water's edge. It took a few steps then tilted its head and watched for fish out of one eye.

Until now Carmen had only nursed in urban places, even with Oliver: at home, in parks, shopping malls and restaurants, airports and friends' houses. Never in the country. It was a completely different experience. Less private and personal.

Catharine seemed less the treasured all-important centre-of-the-universe baby and more like one animal among many, one who knew how to suckle when food was offered, like mice or cats. And Carmen was simply there under the blue sky, air blowing in off the water, among the sounds of other animals—a cow mooing up on the ridge behind an arbutus grove; crows cawing; the shush of a raven's wing pushing down on air; robins singing out; bees dusting pollen off the last of the wild roses; seals splashing. In the distance a rooster crowed.

Her experience of this place was so different from Catharine's, who was getting drowsy from warm milk and relaxing into her mother's arms for a sleep. Carmen, on the other hand, was very thirsty and a muscle in her back ached. Despite that she was alert to the beauty around her and took pleasure in putting Catharine in a state of blissful contentment, like a fairy godmother bequeathing a blessing at a banquet.

She would never know the full outcome of Catharine's life. Just as now Alfred would never know what happened to Carmen. Wouldn't know about Catharine or Oliver. But he'd known Catharine was born, he thought about her at least that much and those thoughts, whatever they'd been, were not retractable, even by death. They existed somewhere in the past, and they were a blessing launched, waiting to land on his granddaughter, because the past existed in some way, however attenuated.

She laughed remembering that he'd said he'd rather be reincarnated as a frog than a woman. What a thing to say. Well push had come to shove; would it still hold now the offer was on the table? He'd almost certainly been drunk when he'd said it and she knew now, from stupid things she herself had said to Oliver, that it just might not have reflected his true beliefs even at the moment, much less later on.

He was a man, however, who was very rooted in his male-ness. In fact if he'd wanted to preserve himself, "the soul Alfred," after death, it was probably true he'd be closer to his true essence as a male frog than as a human female.

The wind caressed Catharine's face, rustled through her wisps of new hair. The kind of blessing Carmen herself wanted, a blessing without anger, disappointment, hurt, guilt. Godspeed to Catharine.

Carmen stared at an almost-evaporated pool of water in the concave top of a stone: the crystallized salt along the sides made it look like a split geode, reminiscent of the salt flats in Portugal.

Her maternal grandmother, Poppy, had been a fertile and robust woman and Carmen had had her blessing. She remembered walking alone on the banks of those salt flats under a sunny blue sky, just like today's. Sensing a hand on her head, breath rustling past her ears and through her hair. Godspeed. Her grandmother's strength and resilience being bestowed on her as a wish. Bequeathing her this moment she was living right now, with her own baby daughter sitting on a log, the road ahead shortened by half since then. Seeing things through now rather than through promise. A subtle, not-subtle difference.

People were supposed to think they had their whole life ahead of them nowadays, not just at forty, but at sixty and seventy. The first day of the rest of your life. It was taboo to think otherwise. Taboo to let the young have youth, now that baby boomers were well into middle age. But the future was different after you'd hit the halfway mark. It was ungracious to pretend otherwise.

You could still change your life, but at a certain point even the most radical change would only be a change of costume. Her race was not run perhaps but the pace was certainly set.

At Oliver's end-of-year preschool picnic last summer there'd been three-legged races, and egg-and-spoon races and just plain races. Carmen, her attention usually riveted on Oliver and his powerful, energetic body, had been transfixed watching one of the girls in his class run.

She was slender, long-legged and had a fair complexion and blonde hair. A feminine demeanour. She wore yellow shorts and canvas sneakers and a white T-shirt with short puffed sleeves and she ran in a looping curve at the edge of the pack. Her long legs moved as fast as she could make them, but her face was turned up past the tops of the trees to the sky. Her thin arms moved and she was concentrating on running but she was looking at the sky too. Carmen felt breathless watching her. Caught by a poignancy. Something pure about girlhood being expressed in this girl's run, something about hope and promise. Her running wasn't social. It wasn't for an audience. It wasn't for anything, though she was trying to run her best.

When she came in fifth, it slid off her. She wasn't disappointed or elated. She simply moved on. She'd had her run. She looked around for what the afternoon would bring next.

Godspeed. A blessing that a person travel safely. May you reach your destination without the hunters catching up to you. May God make your feet fleeter than the predator's, invisible and quick.

She thought of Catharine and Oliver sitting somewhere in the future with their children thinking back to her and Robert and their grandparents. And thinking forward to their own grandchildren.

It was frightening what a hurricane time was. Everyone running alone and getting taken by gusts of wind. And race run, dying.

That night she dreamed of a madonna in a roadside chapel in the moonlight, a miracle madonna with blood, like teardrops, coming from her nipples.

And at dawn she was dreaming of a brown tree frog with long arms and legs. She holds it in her hands. Wonders if she's repelled by it. "No, I like tree frogs." She worries though about accidentally squishing part of it with the pressure of keeping her cupped hands closed. She worries about inadvertently breaking its leg or arm as it tries to escape.

She looks for a safe place to let it go. Smallish trees line the street and she goes to place it on a branch, with bark the colour of its skin. But there's a woman pruning them for the city. She's pruning them way back so there are barely any green leaves left, and therefore not enough cover for her frog. She suggests to the woman that she might be pruning too much, but the woman says, "No, it's better for the tree. This is the proper way to prune and next year the tree will be full again."

She sees a wizened old apple tree. It's too old for the pruning woman to bother with. She remembers Robert's sister, Annie, finding frogs on the other side of apples when she picked them, so even though the tree is small and sparse, she thinks it must be a good place for the frog. She sees another frog against the bark as she approaches.

She woke invigorated.

A low bank of clouds covered the sun. She walked along a trail that led first through a dark tight forest of new fir, then through more spacious older-growth trees and then through stands of red-barked arbutus and gnarly twisted Garry oak.

The path opened onto a series of breathtaking grassy bluffs above the ocean. Catharine slept in the Snugli under Robert's anorak. There was no wind. The sky was the same grey as the surface of the ocean. Mist made the shore across the strait invisible. It was a morning of uniform visual surfaces; boundaries between earth and sea and sky melted. It was possible to think of land as having depth the way the ocean did and sky as having the same gravity-induced solidity as land.

A lone duck sat on the ocean half a kilometre from shore. She looked at that duck, floating between worlds, its small warm body sitting on top of a vast, cold, dark underworld. It was migration time but the duck seemed to be pausing mid-journey. Alone for some reason.

Above it the navigable air, light by day, dark by night. Around it ephemeral phenomena, a touchable world. Something about that duck. The way it floated warmly in the middle of so much grey and cold. Way out on the surface this cloudy late fall day. Writing its name in water. Floating among worlds.

She looked down at Catharine's small face crushed against her shoulder and experienced a surge of disbelief that the child existed, at the rosy pallor and translucence of her skin.

She felt compensated.

A balance not equally weighted. The presence of a small being on one end, the weight of the death of everything including that small being on the other.

It wasn't a compensation that bore examination.

Perhaps it was just sappy baby love that would pass with the hormones.

Robert and Oliver were driving up to join them and she was glad.

EPILOGUE

CARMEN HAD STEPPED OUT into the street, painfully distracted by a mother across the street screaming at her child, "Stop your bawling or I'm going to smack you so-help-me-God."

The new models of cars were quiet, so everything else on the street was more audible. Elderly people like Carmen had trouble adjusting. She'd had several close calls in the past year because she'd failed to hear a vehicle approaching before stepping out into the road.

On this day, two days after her seventy-fifth birthday, a car had smacked into her full force. Her body had flown up in the air and come back down on asphalt, crumpled and folded wrongly. Her neck was broken. Her body had expelled one last breath and she'd died.

Carmen's funeral was held three days later at a local church and was well attended by her family, friends, colleagues, former students and neighbours.

A week after her death Robert and Oliver went driving in Oliver's vintage black pickup. They felt too restless to stay inside; they both wanted fresh air and to be in some part of the world that was not made by humans.

They picked up a cold six-pack from off-sales and drove to Jericho Beach. It was February and it was ten-thirty at night. They had the place to themselves. Oliver turned the engine off and they sat silently in the truck and watched snowflakes speed past the light of the headlights.

They cracked a beer, took a gulp. The cold brew felt good. They'd left Aunt Rebecca, Catharine, and Oliver's new wife—Madeleine—at the house sorting through Carmen's clothes. The women had found a dress Carmen had worn when she was forty, a beautiful black dress with cut-out sides. Both the young women had wanted it, but Madeleine ceded to Catharine.

The men stepped out of the truck into the cold air, hatless; snowflakes stuck to Oliver's tangled brown curls, melted on Robert's bald head. They walked to the water's edge and stood for a while staring at the darkness beyond the beam of the truck's headlights.

They heard a loud exhaling sound, four times in quick succession, sounding close and distant at the same time, then nothing. They looked at each other, then down the beach at the concession stand with its quadrant of lights, a mini-watch-tower guarding cans of pop, bags of frozen fries and tofu dogs. There was no one else.

They heard the sound again and they both thought Carmen's spirit was visiting, her love undiminished even by death.

But then, in the light of Oliver's high beams on the still water, a large glossy bewhiskered head appeared, and another one two lengths behind, accompanied by the sound—the great exhalations—and steam brushing the snow-speckled surface as below flippers and tails pushed powerfully against the water. The first body surged forward; slight caesura; surge forward. The smaller partner worked harder to keep up.

Exhale. Like a huge ship chugging down on them, the sea lions passed through the light. The two men continued to stand in front of the headlights, listening as the creatures headed for the point.

ACKNOWLEDGMENTS

For help with research: Gordon Casper, Myriam Casper, Dr. Peter Granger, Sue Hannon, Bob Hodder, Paul Lhotka, Janine Love, Dawn MacArthur, Don Miller, Michele Oberdieck, Nora Patrich, Dave Tupper and Paul Tyler. Thanks to my editor Meg Masters, my copy editor Cheryl Cohen, my agent Anne McDermid and her assistant Kelly Dignan, and my esteemed publisher Cynthia Good. For indefatigable help securing the cover: Miriam Ajovenich, Gordon Casper, Adriana Vallerga and Barbara Berson. Thanks also to James, Mary Lou Miller and Muriel Penn.

Several books were particularly instrumental in the writing of this book: *Blood Rites*, by Barbara Ehrenreich (Henry Holt, 1997); *Cloth and Human Experience*, ed. Annette B. Weiner and Jane Schneider (Smithsonian Institution Press, 1989); *God's Assassins: State Terrorism in Argentina in the 1970s*, by Patricia Marchak (McGill-Queen's University Press, 1999); *A Lexicon of Terror: Argentina and the Legacies of Torture*, by Marguerite Feitlowitz (Oxford University Press, 1998); *Mother Nature: A History of Mothers, Infants and Natural Selection*, by Sarah Blaffer Hrdy (Pantheon Books, 1999); and *Sex in Nature*, by Chris Catton and James Gray (Facts on File Publications, 1985).